I'LL BE WATCHING YOU

I'LL BE WATCHING YOU

ANDREA KANE

wm

WILLIAM MORROW

An Imprint of HarperCollinsPublishers

I'LL BE WATCHING YOU. Copyright © 2005 by Rainbow Connection Enterprises, Inc. All rights reserved. Printed in the United States of America. No part of this book may be used or reproduced in any manner whatsoever without written permission except in the case of brief quotations embodied in critical articles and reviews. For information address HarperCollins Publishers Inc., 10 East 53rd Street, New York, NY 10022.

HarperCollins books may be purchased for educational, business, or sales promotional use. For information please write: Special Markets Department, HarperCollins Publishers Inc., 10 East 53rd Street, New York, NY 10022.

FIRST EDITION

Designed by Gretchen Achilles

Printed on acid-free paper

Library of Congress Cataloging-in-Publication Data

Kane, Andrea.
    I'll be watching you / by Andrea Kane.—1st ed.
      p. cm.
    ISBN 0-06-074130-9 (alk. paper)
      1. Women psychologists—Fiction. 2. Victims of violent crimes—Fiction. 3. Radio broadcasters—Fiction. 4. Stalking victims—Fiction. I. Title.

PS3561.A463I44 2005
813'.54—dc22   2004046087

05 06 07 08 09 WBC/QF 10 9 8 7 6 5 4 3 2 1

TO BRAD,
WHO MAKES EACH "FIRST" A POSSIBILITY, A REALITY,
AND A CELEBRATION

ACKNOWLEDGMENTS

EACH NOVEL I WRITE presents new challenges to me as I strive to convey every nuance and detail as authentically as possible. *I'll Be Watching You* was no exception.

The following people were instrumental in this process. Their patience and willingness to help were surpassed only by their astounding knowledge of all the subject matter in question. I thank each and every one of them for their significant contributions. As always, any departure from reality is my responsibility—a literary license I avail myself of only when it's absolutely necessary.

Detective Mike Oliver, who brought the NYPD to life for me; who, calmly and without missing a beat, handled phone calls from me that began "Mike, suppose someone's mangled to death . . ."; who called me back in record time; and who had all the answers to my endless questions. Mike, you're a lifesaver. Murray, the cop, is a much-deserved tribute to you.

At WOR 710 AM, an amazing and dedicated radio family, I'd like to specifically thank:

Eloise Maroney, director of operations, who graciously opened the door, and the world, of radio to me, answered a deluge of questions, and pointed me in all the right directions.

Tom R. Ray III, corporate director of engineering, who deciphered the complex world of radio engineering so that even a layperson could understand.

Maurice Tunick, vice president of programming, who took me through a day in the life of a program manager, and infused in me an awed respect for the talented people in this business. Ingrained in my mind forever are his words "Radio is the theater of the mind."

And, most especially, to the amazing team that makes *The Dr. Joy Browne Show* thrive:

Bob Iorio, veteran technical engineer, who gave me a bird's-eye view of the audio control board and who demonstrated, from significant to routine, the responsibilities he handles daily.

Scott Lakefield, executive producer, a marvel himself, who has the proficiency, the maturity, and the multitasking ability of someone twice his age and with twice his experience. He managed to run an entire radio show, handle every curve thrown his way without ever losing his cool, and unfailingly answer the million questions being fired at him by the overzealous author leaning over his shoulder.

And Dr. Joy herself, who was gracious enough to let me into her inner sanctum—to sit in on her radio show, watch her in action, and listen while she expertly dealt with a wide range of psychological issues and crises. I left her studio with a feeling of admiration for and amazement at the caring, natural, and professional way she helped her callers. It's no wonder they turn to and rely on her. Thank you for helping me instill some of those qualities in Taylor.

I also want to thank:

Robert Dekoff, who graciously shared his knowledge of the Hamptons with me, explaining everything from places to marinas. In addition, his expertise as a pilot helped familiarize me with airstrips and aircraft.

Bill and Michael Stock, who gave me a crash course on yachts, engines, bilge fans, and Zodiacs, as well as an education on navigating the waters surrounding Eastern Long Island. Thanks to their precision and patience, I was able to portray *I'll Be Watching You*'s nautical settings with maximum suspense and authenticity.

Hillel Ben-Asher, M.D., whose vast knowledge of the medical field was invaluable in creating frighteningly realistic events.

Andrea Cirillo, for her unfaltering support, her input, and her ability to put me in touch with the right people at the right times. Andrea, I value your partnership more than words can express.

And my greatest blessing of all: my one-of-a-kind family—

Brad, Wendi, Mom, and Dad—who, from outset to conclusion, perpetually offer me creative input, enthusiastic support, and a reason to believe. I never take for granted how incredibly lucky I am to have you.

CHAPTER 1

IT had been a day from hell.

Four hours in Dellinger Academy's conference room. Two five-minute bathroom breaks. Three sets of hostile parents in total denial. And another one of Taylor's precious Saturdays wasted by an elite private school administration that didn't want to rock the boat.

All the parties involved were so caught up in their own agendas, they seemed to forget that at the center of this storm were three seventeen-year-old kids about to implode.

As a counselor, Taylor had tried desperately to speak for the teens. She knew their fears—fear of failure, of inadequacy, of letting down their parents.

Fear of growing up.

Didn't *anyone* remember how traumatic that transition was?

Apparently not. Because today's scenario had been as maddening and familiar as always.

After doing her tactful, psychological dance for half a day and getting nowhere fast, Taylor left the boardroom at the close of the meeting frustrated, worried, and with a splitting headache.

By the time she got home and blew through the lobby of her apartment building, she was counting her blessings that her roommate, her cousin Stephanie, was en route to the Hamptons. Taylor had the place to herself. All she wanted was a hot bath, two extra-strength Excedrin, and a long nap.

The last thing she expected, or needed, was to find Gordon Mallory in her living room, as comfortable as if he owned the place.

She stopped dead in her tracks when she saw him, wishing she wasn't already halfway to her bedroom and in full view. If she'd just realized he and Steph were still at the apartment, she would have retraced her steps, waited until they'd taken off, then returned when she could have her peace and solitude.

But it was too late. She was directly across from the living room, and from Gordon. Steph was nowhere to be found, but knowing her cousin, Taylor assumed she was in her bedroom, throwing together some last-minute surprises for her nightlong bash on Gordon's yacht—a bash she'd be enjoying with about twenty other partygoers. After all, it wasn't every day that a bunch of lucky young Turk investors made a windfall off an investment partnership like the one Gordon had orchestrated. Kudos for the fast crowd.

"Taylor." Gordon tipped his lean, dark head in her direction, raising his old-fashioned in greeting. He'd been strolling from the sideboard to the sofa, sipping his Scotch while he reorganized the contents of Steph's overnight bag. The picture of self-assurance. Right at home.

Then again, Steph had made sure he felt that way from day one. Gordon fit her boyfriend checklist to a tee and then some; rich and successful, good-looking, grand of gesture, glib of tongue. Really smooth. He knew all the right people, went to all the right clubs. On top of that, he was older, sexy, experienced, ambitious—fast-track all the way. Definitely the kind Steph fell for.

Except that this one had a dangerous edge to him that worried the hell out of Taylor. It was there in his hard brown eyes—a kind of detached ruthlessness. Taylor just didn't trust the guy.

Unfortunately, Steph did.

"Hello, Gordon." Taylor's tone was cordial but aloof.

He was dressed casually, in khakis, a golf shirt, and dock-siders, but there was nothing casual about the way he carried himself, or about his expression as he eyeballed Taylor. He was scrutinizing her, as one would assess a fine piece of art.

"What a beautiful interruption," he said. "I didn't hear you come in."

"So I gathered." Taylor was used to his I-want-you signals. It was all part of his MO. But this time he was blatant. His intensity was palpable.

And the bottle of Scotch was sitting open on the sideboard, ready for him to pour his next refill. How many drinks had he had?

Taylor tossed down her purse and folded her arms across her breasts, her eyes narrowing on his tumbler. "How many Scotches does that make?"

"Two." He set down the glass. "Don't worry. I'm chilling out. But I'm sober."

Yeah, right, she thought. *Chilling out. More like revving up.* "Good. Because you and Steph have a big weekend planned. Get drunk during the party, not before."

"Sage advice. I'll keep it in mind."

Her headache was getting worse. Taylor didn't want to spar with Gordon; she wanted him to go away. "I didn't realize you and Steph would still be here," she said pointedly. "It's almost three o'clock. Doesn't your charter leave for Montauk soon? I wouldn't want you to miss it."

Gordon's sculpted features tightened. "That's why it's called a private charter. The helicopter will wait until we get there. As for your subtle shove out the door, why the rush? Are you expecting someone?"

"Just my privacy. Look, I didn't mean to be rude. But my day was a killer. I've got a miserable headache. I was hoping for some downtime—a hot bath and a long nap."

"Poor baby." The hostility vanished. Gordon closed the gap between them and planted his hands on her shoulders, gently kneading them. "Tension has no right ruining such a perfect package. How about a back rub to ease the stress?"

His words creeped her out. His gesture wasn't friendly. It was intimate. So was his proximity. And where he'd positioned himself was like a roadblock.

Taylor's instincts took over. She took an exaggerated step backward, breaking all contact. "No, thanks." She threw a quick glance at her cousin's bedroom, wondering when Steph would emerge. Now that she considered it, the apartment seemed strangely silent. No banging of closets, no thudding of drawers, no cheerful chatter emanating from Steph's neck of the woods. That was weird. Steph was animated and exuberant; you always knew when she was around.

A frisson of apprehension crept up Taylor's spine.

"Is Steph in her room?" she asked. "I'll go give her a hand."

"She's not here."

The frisson turned into a full-fledged knot. "What do you mean, she's not here? Where is she?"

"Finishing up an audition." Gordon glanced at his watch. "She's running late. I assume she'll meet me at the heliport."

"Then how did you get in?"

A hard smile curved his lips, and he jiggled a set of keys in the air. "With these. Steph asked me to stop by and pick up some last-minute things for her. Didn't Harry tell you?"

Harry. Their doorman. Come to think of it, he hadn't been in the lobby when she dashed through. "I didn't see him."

"Oh. Right. I forgot. He left for his break."

"Really." Taylor's heart was beginning to pound. She took another backward step, gauging whether or not she'd left herself enough room to dart around Gordon and make a break for the door. "That's odd. He doesn't usually take breaks in the middle of the afternoon."

"It's hot. He was thirsty. I gave him a few bucks so he could run over to Starbucks for an iced coffee."

"How long ago was that?"

"Ten minutes. When I glanced out the window and saw you heading up the street." Gordon moved closer, effectively cutting off her escape path. "I wanted this little visit of ours to stay private." He reached out and rubbed a lock of her dark red hair between his fingers. "Now, about that stress you were complaining about . . ."

That did it. Taylor didn't know if Gordon was drunk or delusional. And she wasn't sticking around to find out. She had to get out of here.

She lunged toward the door.

Gordon grabbed her, his grip punishing. He locked one hard arm around her waist, capturing her wrists in his other hand. "Shhh," he muttered against her face, and she could smell the Scotch on his breath. "You're going to aggravate your headache." He half lifted her, carrying her toward her bedroom. "I know how to make it better."

"Let me go!" Taylor began struggling, jerking her arms around in an attempt to free them, throwing her body weight against him to slow his progress.

It wasn't working. They were already at her room.

"Stop fighting me," he commanded. "You want this as much as I do."

"No. I don't. It isn't happening. Not now. Not ever." Taylor hooked her feet on either side of the door frame, anchoring herself and giving her the leverage she need to halt Gordon. She raised her head, gazed straight at him, and strove for reason in the midst of insanity. "I don't know what made you think I wanted this. But we got our signals crossed. So just put me down and leave. We'll forget this whole ugly scene ever took place."

He looked amused, using his legs to break her tenuous hold on the doorjamb. He then carried her the remaining distance to her bed. "You're wrong on all counts. This *is* going to happen. It *won't* be ugly. And you *definitely* won't want to forget it ever took place."

White panic took over.

"No! *No!*" Taylor began fighting like a trapped animal, using every drop of strength she had. But the man had a grip of iron. And he seemed absolutely sure they were in this together. *"Let me go!"*

He pinned her to the bed, dodging the blows of her fists and the sharp jabs of her knees as she tried to kick him in the groin. He straddled her body, locking her legs in place and capturing her wrists over her head in one hand. His other hand massaged her neck as if to soothe her, his fingers threading through her hair. He crushed his mouth against hers to silence her screams. "Shhh," he whispered. "You have no idea how good this is going to be."

Taylor thought she was going to be sick.

"I know exactly what you need. I'll give it to you—all of it, and more."

"But . . . I . . . don't . . . want . . . you." She ground out each word, desperate to get through to him, to shatter whatever fantasy his mind had conjured up regarding the two of them.

"Yes, you do. I'll prove it to you. In a few minutes, you'll be begging for me. I promise." He was unbuttoning her blouse, caressing her as he did—her shoulders, her arms, her cleavage. His grasp on her wrists tightened as she flinched away from his touch. "Enough games, Taylor. No more fighting. And no more waiting. It's time."

"No, *it's not!*" She bit his lip, and he recoiled in pain. She used his moment of weakness to yank her arms free, slamming her fists against his chest with all her might. "Let me go, you crazy bastard! Get your filthy hands off me!"

The outburst would cost her. Taylor knew it the instant she saw Gordon's reaction.

A violent jolt of tension rippled through him. He went still, raising his head to stare down at her. Something scary and hard glinted in his eyes, darkening them to near black. A heartbeat later, one hand was encircling her neck, his palm pressing down on her windpipe. "Don't ever speak to me like that again. Is that understood? I won't take that from anyone."

Icy fear speared Taylor like a knife, and she rasped in air, struggling to breathe. "I . . . understand . . ."

"Do you?"

"Yes . . . I'm . . . sorry . . ."

The hard glint in his eyes ebbed. "That's better."

"You're . . . hurting me . . ."

"Am I? That's not what I had in mind." The pressure against her throat disappeared, and he bent his head, nuzzling the hollow between her breasts, tracing the path with his tongue.

Taylor's guts twisted. Think. She had to think. "Steph . . . ," she managed. "She'll be devastated. We can't do this to her."

"She won't ever find out."

"Gordon, she loves you."

He laughed, his breath hot against her skin. "Not love; passion." He was stroking her waist, fumbling with the button of her slacks. "Steph's fire," he muttered. "Exciting. Hot. Irrepressible." He slid down her zipper. "You're smoke. Elusive. Intangible. Hard to capture." His palm kneaded her abdomen, his fingers rubbing up against the top band of her thong. "The ultimate turn-on. But you knew that. You've been taunting me with it."

"No." Taylor sucked in her breath, receding from his touch. "You're wrong . . ."

"I'm right." He cut off her protest with another kiss. "I don't misread signals. Yours were crystal clear. We just had to wait for the right moment. Well, it's here. This is the perfect time to have each other. I want you frantic for what I can give you. You will be. Soon." His fingers slipped under her panties and glided down. "Stop talking. Feel. Just feel."

Like a drowning person, Taylor began struggling again, kicking and flinging her body as hard as she could.

From out in the hall, the intercom sounded.

"Gordon?" Steph's voice, tinny since it came from the lobby, drifted to their ears. "I'm back. Harry says you're still up there. Hurry down. I can't wait to see your yacht."

Freezing, Taylor watched Gordon's face, wondering if he was going to stop, wondering if Steph's voice had even registered in his passion-clouded mind.

"My cousin . . . ," she whispered. She couldn't risk setting him off again. "She's waiting for you."

A muscle worked in his jaw. "It seems that way."

"So this isn't the right time for us after all."

"Perhaps not."

Taylor felt her first real surge of hope. "You'd better go."

Her hope was dashed as his lips thinned into a grim line and his palm clamped back down on her windpipe. "I hope that's not an order."

"Not an order . . . A suggestion . . . A . . . request . . ."

"Good." He didn't release his hold. Keeping his hand locked around her throat, he groped in his pocket for something. Taylor saw him pull out a dangling silver object that glinted in the late-afternoon sunlight. Then the pressure on her windpipe intensified as he strengthened his chokehold. "We'll finish this, Taylor," he vowed. "You have my word. I'll be back. Next time, we'll have all the time we need. Be patient. Be good. Be mindful."

He squeezed down harder, until the room began to fade, black spots dancing before Taylor's eyes.

Leaning over, Gordon brushed her lips with his. "Until then," he whispered just before she lost consciousness, "I'll be watching you."

CHAPTER 2

TAYLOR came to, coughing and rasping as she brought oxygen back into her lungs.

It hadn't been a nightmare. It had happened. Her disheveled clothing was a glaring reminder, as was the pain in her throat.

Swiftly, she scanned her room. She was alone. Gordon was gone.

The beechwood pendulum wall clock said it was three twenty-five. Gordon must have met Steph downstairs. They were on their way to the heliport.

She jerked upright, only to be dragged back down, a cutting pain in her wrist. She twisted around, peering up to figure out its cause.

She was handcuffed to the brass headboard. And the night table telephone was missing. Gordon had obviously removed it, anticipating that she'd try to alert Steph, or the cops, about what had happened. He wanted to buy himself time—and he'd succeeded. Even her damned cell phone was out of reach, buried in her purse in the living room.

She was trapped.

She had no intention of staying that way.

She tried to scream. Nothing emerged but a hoarse croak.

Frantically, Taylor tugged at the handcuffs. As expected, they were locked. Okay, she'd free herself another way. She began working at the headboard, trying to loosen it, using her free hand to add leverage. The brass spindles were tubular; the weakest part of the bed. Breaking the spindle she was handcuffed to would be time-consuming but not impossible. She'd rip the damned thing out if it took all night.

She worked for nearly two hours before she felt the spindle start to crease. Redoubling her efforts, she jerked back and forth with all her might until, with a snap, the spindle broke in the middle.

She slid the handcuffs between the two severed pieces and scrambled off the bed.

At first, her legs nearly gave out. Between the physical exertion, the emotional strain, and the throbbing of her bruises—not to mention her now-blinding headache—she was a mess. She steadied herself, waiting until her legs stopped wobbling. Her gaze fell on the clock. Five-fifteen. Long enough for Gordon to sail off with her cousin.

Maybe.

Taylor made her way into the kitchen, grabbed the phone, and dialed Steph's cell number. Voice mail. Damn. That meant she was on her way and didn't want to be bothered.

Fine. Steph and Gordon were partying the night away with about twenty other people. There was safety in numbers. Gordon sure as hell wasn't going to spill his guts to Steph, no matter how drunk he got. So there was no immediate fallout.

But if Gordon thought he was getting away with this, he would soon find out otherwise. Even if he managed to pull off his overnight yachting party, Taylor planned to make sure he'd have a welcoming committee on hand when he got back.

Her next call was to the police.

She dialed 911.

"Nine-one-one. What's your emergency?"

"I want to report an assault." Taylor's voice was raspy, and her throat and neck hurt like hell. "It's 123 West Seventy-second Street, Apartment 5F."

"You're the victim?"

"Yes."

"And the perpetrator—is he still on the premises?"

"No. He's gone." The irritation in Taylor's throat won out, and she dissolved into a spasm of coughing.

"Ma'am, are you all right?" the dispatcher asked quickly. "Are you hurt?"

"I'm fine," Taylor assured her. "Just shaken." She went on to provide the necessary information, assuring the dispatcher that she hadn't been raped and that her injuries didn't require an ambulance. Gratefully, she received the confirmation that two police officers were on their way.

They arrived soon after, identifying themselves as Officers Slatter and Hillman of the Twentieth Precinct. They then perched on the edge of Taylor's living-room sofa to take her statement—after unlocking and removing the handcuffs that were still dangling from her wrist.

"This guy broke into your home?" Slatter began, once Taylor had provided him with the facts.

"No." Taylor settled back in her overstuffed wingback chair, wincing as she rubbed feeling back into her arm. "He had a key. My cousin, who's also my roommate, gave it to him."

"He's obviously not a stranger."

"His name is Gordon Mallory. He's"—an uncomfortable pause—"a friend of my cousin's."

"A friend." Slatter repeated the word skeptically. "Is he also a friend of yours?"

"Definitely not."

"Okay, we've established that there was no breaking and entering. What about a weapon—did he have one?"

"If you mean a knife or a gun, no. He just used bodily force."

"You said you weren't incapacitated by your injuries," Hillman pointed out. "So why did it take you two hours to report the crime?"

"Because of those." Taylor pointed at the handcuffs, now in Slatter's possession. "Gordon choked me unconscious and handcuffed me to the bed. He also removed the bedroom telephone so I couldn't call for help. It took me quite a while to work myself free so I could get out and call 911."

"The handcuffs—they were on your right arm. That explains why your right wrist is cut up. But you've got some impressive bruises on your left wrist, too."

"He held me down."

"Right." Hillman exchanged a quick glance with his partner. "That would explain it."

"Yes, it would," Taylor returned tightly. "And the choking would explain my hoarseness and the bruises on my throat."

"Sure would," Hillman agreed in a tone that made Taylor's teeth grit. His insinuation was coming through loud and clear.

"You said he'd been drinking," Hillman continued.

"Scotch. According to him, he'd only had two."

"Did he act drunk?"

"Not really. He acted delusional."

"Delusional. In other words, he got the wrong signals from you."

"I didn't send *any* signals."

"So the guy's an egomaniac. You said the attack was sexual. Yet there was no rape involved."

"That was pure luck on my part. My cousin buzzed from downstairs. That changed Gordon's plans. He stopped."

"He choked you—but only until you were unconscious."

"He wanted me out, not dead. He plans to finish this. He told me so."

"He threatened you? What exactly did he say?"

"That he'd be back. That we'd have all the time we needed. And that he'd be watching me." Taylor was at the end of her rope, physically and emotionally. She leaned forward, putting a halt to the unpleasant interrogation. "Look, Officer Hillman. Let's cut the double-talk. This wasn't some kinky sexual encounter that went south. It was assault. Gordon Mallory attacked me. Period. Now, are you going to arrest him or aren't you?"

Hillman stopped writing and looked up at her. "We're going to file your complaint, Ms. Halstead. A detective will follow up with you—*and* with Mr. Mallory. He'll be questioned. We'll do a background check. Whether or not he's arrested depends on what we find."

Taylor gave another painful cough. "I doubt he has a criminal record. So what you're saying is, it'll come down to his word against mine."

"I can't answer that—not until the investigation is complete." Hillman rose, and Slatter immediately followed suit. "If you're concerned for your safety, you can spend the next few nights with family or friends. You can request an order of protection, if it'll make you feel better. From what you've told us, this guy's no threat to you tonight. He's somewhere out on the Atlantic. If I were you, I'd treat those cuts and bruises, pour yourself a stiff drink, and go to bed. One of the precinct detectives will call you tomorrow, either here or on your cell phone."

"Fine." There wasn't an inch of her that didn't ache or throb, and her nerves were frayed to snapping. Officer Hillman was right. Tonight there was nothing else to be done. And she desperately needed some sleep. "Thank you, Officers." She rose, gripping the back of the chair for support. "I appreciate your coming. I'll show you out."

Thirty minutes later—after a cup of tea, two Excedrin, and a shower—Taylor wriggled into her nightshirt, double-checked the chain and the dead bolt on the front door, and crawled into bed.

She fell asleep the instant her head hit the pillow.

THE RINGING OF THE TELEPHONE awakened her. It was shrill. Persistent. Far away.

Taylor leaned over, groping around on her beveled cherry nightstand. The sharp sting in her wrist and the aching of her muscles brought back vivid memories of what she'd been through that afternoon. She also remembered that she'd never reconnected the bedroom phone.

Swearing under her breath, she staggered out to the kitchen, tripping over a stool as she fumbled for a light switch. The apartment was dark. Then again, it was obviously the dead of night. And the kitchen clock, when she finally managed to flick on the light and see it, said four-ten. Who the hell was calling at this hour?

Gordon.

Taylor's guts twisted, and adrenaline shot through her. She was instantly and totally awake.

She stared at the phone, checked the caller ID. It said "private." That told her nothing. But to assume it was Gordon? Even if he could break away from his party long enough to make a personal call, why would he call her?

Her hand trembled as she reached for the receiver. "Hello?"

"Ms. Halstead?" an official voice asked.

"Yes?"

"This is Detective Hadman of the Nineteenth Precinct. I'm sorry to call you at this hour. But there's been an accident."

"An accident?" It was the last thing Taylor had expected. Still, her insides went cold, and she gripped the phone more tightly. "What kind of accident?"

"A boat explosion. It took place off Long Island, on a yacht belonging to a Gordon Mallory. The boat was anchored about twenty miles south of Montauk. The Suffolk County Police Department notified the Nineteenth and Twentieth Precincts because most of the passengers were residents of the Upper East or West Side." A weighted pause. "One of those passengers was your cousin Stephanie Halstead."

"Yes . . . that's right." Taylor sank down to the floor, her knees up, her back propped against the wall. "Was Steph . . . was anyone . . . hurt?"

"I'm very sorry. Everyone on board was killed."

God, no. This couldn't be happening. Not to Steph.

"Are you sure?" Taylor managed. "Isn't it possible that some of the passengers were thrown clear of the explosion and—"

"I'm very sure. The accident happened around dusk. The coast guard's been combing the waters since then. They've recovered . . . partial remains and personal property. Trust me, there were no survivors."

Taylor gagged as the image of floating body parts flashed through her mind. No. Not her beautiful, vibrant cousin. So full of life—working her way up to become the Broadway star she'd always dreamed of being. Filled with hopes and dreams. With so much to live for. She couldn't be dead.

"Ms. Halstead?" the detective prompted. "Are you all right?"

"Did the coast guard recover anything that belonged to Steph?" Taylor demanded. She was grasping at straws and she knew it. "Maybe she wasn't on board. Maybe she decided at the last minute not to go. Maybe—"

"She was on board," Detective Hadman confirmed. "Witnesses saw her on deck when the yacht left the dock. They described her—tall, slender, with bright red, shoulder-length hair. Wearing a turquoise silk cocktail dress."

Taylor squeezed her eyes shut. She'd bought Steph that dress for her birthday. Steph had been saving it for a special occasion.

"Your aunt and uncle have been notified. They're out at the scene now. I agreed to call you, since they're not up for conversation. I'm terribly sorry," he added.

"Thank you," Taylor replied tonelessly. She was beyond hearing. Beyond comprehension. Beyond feeling. She was numb.

"If you're up to it, I'd like to come by and speak with you later this morning."

"What?" Taylor couldn't process Detective Hadman's words. She was struggling for rational thought. She had to call her parents, to reach her aunt and uncle, to make arrangements. No one was as close to Steph as she was. It was up to her.

"I have a few questions for you."

"Questions?" Taylor forced her dazed mind to focus. "About what?"

"Not what, who," the detective corrected. "The owner of the yacht. Gordon Mallory. He's among the deceased. I ran a victomology on him. I understand you filed a complaint against him earlier this evening."

"What difference does that make now? He's dead."

"I'm just doing my job, Ms. Halstead. You called in an assault. Officers Hillman and Slatter of the Twentieth filed a report. I'm helping them out, following up on this so the case can be closed. I'll only take a few minutes of your time."

"Fine." Taylor's control was crumbling. She had to crawl off to her bed, to be alone. "Come by early, by eight A.M. After that, I have to take care of things. For Steph. She's counting on me."

It was true. Steph always counted on her.

Only this time she'd let her down.

CHAPTER 3

THURSDAY, DECEMBER 19

4:55 P.M.

746 PARK AVENUE, NEW YORK CITY

TAYLOR Halstead. In counseling.

The whole idea still seemed so ironic to her, even after two months of weekly sessions with Dr. Phillips. As a therapist herself, she knew better than anyone just how essential these visits were, and how very much she needed them.

The holidays were approaching. It had been three months since Steph's death. And still she couldn't shake the nightmares or the feelings of guilt. If anything, both were getting worse, in frequency and intensity. As a professional, she knew the signs. She needed help.

But the truly ironic part of all this was that it was the first time in her life that she was in the position of being the dependent one, rather than the one who was depended upon. She was always the strong one, the together one, the leader. The one who dealt with her own problems—and everyone else's—without missing a beat. The one who learned since childhood to keep her vulnerabilities under wraps.

With good reason. In all ways that mattered, she'd been on her own all her life.

Financially, she'd lived like a princess. Raised in a penthouse on Central Park West, fussed over by a string of nannies. She was an only child, and while money was present in abundant supply, her parents were not. Her mother traveled madly; her father worked obsessively—which suited both of them just fine. They divorced when Taylor was eleven, after which she was shipped off to boarding school and summer camp.

End of childhood. On to adolescence—and to her tight friendship with Steph.

Her cousin's life was pretty much a carbon copy of hers. Not a surprise, since Anderson and Frederick Halstead were more like clones than brothers. Ambitious, self-absorbed clones. Steph had grown up in a palatial manor in Bronxville, New York, where her parents still lived, when they weren't abroad. They'd stayed married—probably because neither one wanted the monetary hassles of dividing up their assets.

The two families hadn't gotten together much when Taylor and Steph were kids, even though the girls were both only children and the same age, and the drive from Bronxville to Manhattan was less than an hour. Even so, they'd bonded during those sporadic get-togethers. They used to tease each other about being City Mouse and Country Mouse, except that neither of them really wanted to go home.

Their relationship was, hands down, the best thing to come out of both their childhoods. So when their parents decided to send them off to the same boarding school, they viewed it as a chance to solidify their friendship, maybe even to become surrogate sisters. Heaven knew, they both needed some constancy in their lives.

And, in Steph's case, some stability.

Emotionally fragile, Steph was starved for attention. Always looking for something to fill the void, she was impetuous, wild, besieged by more highs and lows than Taylor could keep up with—traits that seemed to intensify as the years went by. Her drop-dead beauty didn't help—it just ensured that she was continuously hooking up with the wrong crowd, getting herself into trouble. And Taylor was always there to get her out. Funny, sometimes she felt as if Steph were a kite and she the one at its strings, constantly yanking her cousin back to safety.

Steph's one healthy outlet was her acting.

She'd wanted to be an actress since playing Pippi Longstocking in her fourth-grade play. "It's not just because I'm a redhead," she'd confided to Taylor back then. "It's because I'm good. Honest, Taylor, it's like I *become* Pippi. It's kinda hard to explain. But when I'm up there, everything else goes away."

Taylor understood, better than Steph realized. The need to escape was as real as her hair color.

Motivation aside, the truth was, Steph *was* talented. Taylor saw that firsthand in boarding school, where her cousin snagged the lead in every play—and became every character she portrayed. When they graduated, she'd gone on to study at NYU's Tisch School of the Arts. She was dead set on becoming a Broadway star. She probably would have succeeded, too, if her life hadn't been snatched away.

Taylor sighed, sinking back in the armchair as she waited for Dr. Phillips. She gazed out the window of the expensively appointed office, watching the snow flurries blow by—tiny white flecks in the darkening sky—and the commuters hurrying toward Grand Central as rush hour hit its peak. She felt wistful. In the past she used to be full of that kind of energy. These days, the only energy she could muster was for her students and her radio audience. When it came to her own life, she was treading water.

"Hello, Taylor. I'm sorry to have kept you waiting." Dr. Eve Phillips strolled in, wearing a tasteful camel suit. She gave Taylor a friendly smile as she went over to her desk and flipped open Taylor's file. She was a top-notch psychiatrist with an extensive and impressive client list. No shock there. Taylor's father had selected her. And Anderson Halstead always chose the best.

Taylor hadn't planned on involving her father in the process of finding a therapist, or even telling him she intended to see one. But, as luck would have it, he'd called to discuss some aspect of Steph's estate and caught Taylor at a weak moment. Her voice had been quavery, her mind unfocused and far away. Oh, she'd held it together; breaking down to her father was unthinkable. But he was acute. He'd pressed her until she admitted that she still wasn't herself.

Her father had been all over that like tar. He'd insisted on finding Taylor the best psychiatrist in New York and paying for her sessions. Taylor hadn't had the strength to put up a fight.

So here she was.

"No apology's necessary," she assured Dr. Phillips. "I arrived early. I enjoyed the five minutes of downtime."

Dr. Phillips nodded, perching at the edge of her desk. "You look tired. Rough night?"

"That's an understatement." Taylor rose, massaging the back of her neck and walking over to the cream-and-taupe love seat, where she enjoyed sitting during these sessions. "I feel like I survived a train wreck."

"More nightmares?"

Taylor nodded.

"Anything different?" Dr. Phillips didn't mince words. She knew Taylor had a master's degree in family counseling. There was no point in implementing standard techniques that her patient would see right through.

"Not different. More intense." Taylor sighed, crossing one leg over the other. "I kept hearing Steph scream. I tried to get to her, but something was weighing me down, stopping me from going."

"Some*thing* or some*one?*"

"Either way, it was Gordon, whether symbolically or actually. He's the reason I couldn't reach Steph in time." Taylor inclined her head in the doctor's direction. "The reason it was so bad last night is that I got a copy of the final accident report. Detective Hadman faxed it to me."

"Really." Eve Phillips propped her chin on her hand. "And what did it say?"

"Just what the coast guard suspected. Their investigation suggests there was no terrorism—just a malfunction of the bilge fans. Gordon's new yacht was as flashy and live-on-the-edge as he was—a seventy-foot Hatteras, gasoline-powered for speed. Gasoline is highly combustible, much more so than diesel. The malfunction let gasoline vapors accumulate, and when they started the engine, the yacht blew to bits." Taylor's voice trembled as she spoke, but she didn't avert her gaze from the doctor's. "Now you're going to ask if seeing that report brought me some measure of closure. The answer is, not really. The 'how' was never my thing. My thing is the 'why.'"

One of Dr. Phillips's brows arched. "Actually, it never occurred to me that a piece of paper filled with engineering details would bring you closure. Your cousin's dead. You feel responsible. You also feel afraid, impotent, and angry. All those emotions tie in to one person—Gordon Mallory. Unfortunately, he's not around to vent your anger at."

"Then why do I feel like he is?" Taylor asked helplessly.

"For the same reason you feel no closure about Stephanie. Because there are no bodies. If there were, you'd be forced past denial and shock and into acceptance. And, in Gordon's case, into relief. He assaulted you, Taylor. Even without rape, he violated you. Yes, he was indirectly responsible for your cousin's death. But this isn't only about Stephanie. It's about *you*. Gordon Mallory attacked *you*. You're allowed to feel angry for yourself, not just for Stephanie."

"I know," Taylor said quietly. "And I do. I can't stop reliving what went on in my bedroom that day. He was only there for a little while, but it felt like an eternity. I hated that I had no control. I couldn't do a damned thing to stop him. He would have raped me if Steph hadn't shown up." A painful pause. "On the other hand, maybe if he'd stayed and finished, he'd have missed the boat trip and Steph would still be alive." Taylor broke off.

"More likely, he'd have left you a physical and emotional wreck, then taken the boat trip an hour later," Dr. Phillips replied calmly. "Then you'd be in worse shape than you are now and Steph would still have been killed."

Taylor squeezed her eyes shut. She knew what Dr. Phillips was saying was true. "I feel like he's a ghost that won't stop haunting me," she whispered. "That's why I did that background check. I felt like I needed something tangible. And I got nothing."

Nothing but a bio fit for the *National Enquirer*.

Gordon Mallory had grown up on a palatial estate in East Hampton, Long Island—an estate owned by millionaire investment banker Douglas Berkley. His mother, Belinda Mallory, now deceased, had been a maid at the Berkley estate, and his twin brother, Jonathan, was some hotshot international trade consultant—no surprise, given that Douglas Berkley, though not their father, had bankrolled both guys through school. An M.B.A. from Harvard for Gordon, and a B.S. from Princeton and a Ph.D. from the London School of Economics for Jonathan. The end result was that Gordon became an investment adviser and Jonathan became a specialist in international trade.

The bio made for great gossip. But Taylor wasn't looking for gossip. She was looking for . . . she didn't know what. Prior complaints filed. A history of violence. Incidents involving other women. *Anything*.

None of those things was there.

That should have brought her comfort. It didn't.

Background checks only revealed facts. They didn't delve into a person's psyche, or explore the impact of childhood events. No one understood that better than Taylor. The kids she saw in her office each day were living proof. Background checks didn't touch on emotion. They didn't describe a person's mental profile. Not unless that state of mind propelled him to act in a criminal manner. Criminal and documented.

She wanted to assemble a full and objective picture of Gordon Mallory. Maybe then she could move on.

Speaking with Gordon's colleagues revealed nothing. He was ambitious, fast-track, launching his way to the top at supersonic speed. He loved great-looking women, fast vehicles, and taking risks. Close friends? Nope. Trusted business associates? It appeared not. Just a fast crowd—one that changed from month to month.

At her wit's end, Taylor had driven out to East Hampton and tried to speak with Douglas Berkley or his wife, Adrienne, after reading about the private service they'd held for Gordon. She'd given her name to the butler, explaining that her cousin Stephanie had been one of the passengers who died in the boat explosion and that she just wanted a few minutes of the Berkleys' time. But the servant had shaken his head, saying that the Berkleys weren't seeing anyone regarding this matter. He then offered her his condolences and bid her good day.

Another dead end.

She was on the verge of going online and looking up Jonathan Mallory through his Manhattan-based consulting firm when she found an archived newspaper clipping that mentioned that he and Gordon were *identical* twins. The very thought of facing a mirror image of Gordon was more than she could bear. Besides, from all accounts the brothers traveled in completely different circles, so she wasn't even sure they stayed in touch. And, even if they did, even if she mustered up the nerve to meet Jonathan Mallory, what would she ask him: *Forgive me, but did your brother ever display any aggressive or unbalanced behavior?* That would certainly go over well. Jonathan would have her tossed out of his posh Chrysler Building offices in record time.

So where did she go from here?

She was beginning to obsess. It was unhealthy, and she knew it. She had seen it in others.

But how could she explain to Dr. Phillips—or anyone—the impact Gordon's final words had had on her? It was bad enough she could still see him, still smell the Scotch on his breath, still feel his hands on her body. But those words, the way he'd said them, the look in his menacing dark eyes when he told her he'd be watching her—they haunted her, awake and asleep. Sometimes she even found herself peering over her shoulder, as if he could still be out there—somewhere—somehow—watching her as he'd promised.

Of course that was impossible.

"Taylor." Dr. Phillips's voice cut into her thoughts. She was studying Taylor, searching her face with a knowing look. "Christmas is next week. What are your plans?"

Christmas? That seemed like an alien concept. "None in particular."

The doctor sighed. "Look, I know how committed you are to your jobs—*both* of them. But like all schools, yours will be closed until mid-January. So there'll be no kids to counsel. As for your radio talk show, I'm sure the station can do without you for a few days. Why don't you spend some time with your family?"

Her family. Taylor felt the usual bittersweet twinge at that word. Her mother didn't "do" Christmas; she spent the holiday season at the Canyon Ranch in Massachusetts, renewing herself. Her father, as per usual, was on a business trip, this time in London. Her uncle was somewhere in Japan, solidifying some big corporate merger. And her aunt, who owned an elite travel agency that catered to the Park Avenue crowd, was in Acapulco, checking out a new resort—for her clients, of course.

Nope. A family Christmas was out, even under the best of circumstances. And this year, it was the last thing she wanted.

"I appreciate the thought, Dr. Phillips," she said. "But I really need some time alone. And not just to think. To unwind. Racing from one job to another is exhausting. I'm looking forward to sleeping late, catching up on some reading, and then hanging out with the gang at the radio station before and after my show. Besides, there'll be tons of call-ins that week. You, better than anyone, know that the holidays are a source of major depression for lots of people."

"I do indeed." Dr. Phillips nodded ruefully. "I'll be seeing patients most of the week as well. I'm just taking off the twenty-fourth and the twenty-fifth." A quizzical look. "So we can have our regular Thursday-evening session if you'd like." Seeing Taylor's confirming nod, she added, "I'll bring you a piece of my famous banana-walnut loaf. In fact, I'll bring you a whole loaf—you can take it with you to the station. I'm a once-a-year baker. And that once-a-year is Christmastime. The problem is,

I tend to get overly enthusiastic. My family complains that they can't move until mid-January. So you'd be doing them a favor if you'd take the bread."

A slight smile touched Taylor's lips. "You don't have to twist my arm. I accept, with thanks. My WVNY coworkers are eating machines. They scarf down everything that isn't moving. They'll be thrilled."

"You're a pretty close-knit group, aren't you—friends as well as colleagues?"

Close-knit? The gang at WVNY had been her lifesavers these past few months. No, they hadn't been in her face, showering her with sympathy like everyone else she knew. They hadn't sent flowers, made donations, baked cakes. They'd simply squeezed her arm, or murmured their condolences, or offered to fill in for her, or just to bring her a sandwich or a cup of coffee. Little things, all of them, but offered with a wealth of sincerity. Funny, the bunch of them who worked there were all so different; they had different backgrounds, different personalities, certainly different shows—from Bill's macho *Sports Talk* to her own *Teen Talk*, a family counseling show focusing on adolescents' issues that elicited phone-ins from teens and parents alike and that aired every weeknight from eight to ten. Still, the whole staff cared about one another.

"We're pretty tight," she admitted. "Like a little radio family."

"Good. So make some extra plans with them outside the studio," Dr. Phillips advised. "Maybe even for Christmas Day. Time alone is fine. Too much time alone isn't."

"Message received, loud and clear."

And it was.

Taylor didn't have close friends, only "friendly friends." With the exception of Steph, arm's distance was her motto. It was safer. Dr. Phillips disagreed. She'd been encouraging Taylor to deepen her relationships, romantic ones included. Fine. Maybe someday—*if* the right someone came along. But so far, that someone hadn't shown up. So she counted on one person—herself.

"Taylor," Dr. Phillips prompted.

"Okay, okay. This holiday season I'll become a master mingler." Taylor tried to sound upbeat. But she knew she wouldn't take Dr. Phillips's suggestion to spend Christmas Day with anyone, and she knew the doctor knew. That day would be quiet. She'd spend it alone, working through her emotions, trying to get her life in order. She had a pile of real-estate ads to go through. That would be the first step. Time to get a different, smaller apartment. Time to stop spinning in neutral. Time to do something definitive to move on.

Christmas Day. A day of peace. Perhaps it would bring her some.

IT DIDN'T HAPPEN THAT WAY.

On Christmas morning, Taylor awakened, flipped on her computer to check the current real-estate postings, and found an e-mail greeting card waiting for her. It was a Christmas e-card, complete with falling snow, a brick chimney, and Santa Claus, cast in shadows, preparing to climb down the chimney and into the house.

As the card appeared, Taylor's speakers began to cheerfully play "Santa Claus Is Coming to Town." In sync with the tune, the lyrics to one of the song's verses appeared on her screen:

He sees you when you're sleeping
He knows when you're awake
He knows if you've been bad or good
So be good for goodness' sake.

Beneath that was a personal message. It read:

Like Santa Claus, I'll be watching you.

There was no signature.

CHAPTER 4

TAYLOR went numb.

The first thing she did was contact the greeting-card company. Or at least she tried. All she got was a recording, cheerfully wishing her a Merry Christmas and suggesting she call back tomorrow.

She did. For all the good it did her.

The customer-service manager explained that all they kept track of was the information the sender provided about himself—his name and e-mail address. And in this case, whoever had sent the e-card had provided Taylor's e-mail address in both the recipient and sender boxes. There was nothing more the company could tell her.

In short, the card was untraceable. Which meant there was no way to connect it to Gordon.

It didn't matter. Taylor knew in her gut that he'd sent it. And the very thought of it made her sick. Because it meant that the afternoon he'd forced himself on her hadn't been spur-of-the-moment lust. It meant he'd been planning it—and arranged for his calling card to follow. He'd given this whole fictitious relationship he'd conjured up in his mind far more thought than she'd realized.

Okay, fine, Taylor thought, desperately trying to get a grip on her emotions. *So Gordon had sent the card. So he'd targeted her as more than his next sexual conquest. From the things he'd said to her that day, he was clearly fixated on her. He saw her as something to capture—and to control. What dif-*

ference did it make? All that was over now. He was dead. He'd obviously inputted this card months ago, providing a December 25 delivery date.

She had to calm down.

SHE'D ALMOST CONVINCED HERSELF when New Year's Day arrived—along with another e-card. Heart pounding, Taylor clicked her mouse to open it.

As the card materialized on her monitor, she was greeted with the tinkling notes of "Winter Wonderland."

Talk about a paradox.

The graphics were anything but upbeat. Another night scene. This time a far-off cabin on a barren hill. Naked trees. A blanket of fallen snow in the forefront. Inside the cabin, a single window, dimly lit. The figure of a woman silhouetted there.

The scene conveyed an eerie sense of isolation, one that sent shivers up Taylor's spine.

The rhyme itself was inked in the snow. It was entitled "My New Year's Vow."

Like snow without footprints, the New Year unfolds
A stark new beginning, and all that it holds
Looming ahead like a snow-covered hill
Is a book of blank pages that I'll watch you fill.

No signature.

But none was necessary.

I'll be watching you . . .

There it was again. Implicit or not. Gordon's threat, thrown back in Taylor's face. And, like the previous card, her name and e-mail address had been inputted as both sender and recipient.

Taylor snapped.

At nine A.M. on January 2, she called Detective Hadman at the Nineteenth Precinct, blurting out the details of the back-to-back incidents.

"Listen to me, Ms. Halstead," he said calmly. "First of all, there's no proof Gordon Mallory sent you those cards. That having been said, yeah, given the MO and the wording, it is a little weird. So let's assume he sent them. You know the way these greeting-card Web sites work; you can instruct them to send the card up to a year after you write it. So he programmed one to show up on Christmas Day and one on New Year's."

"I realize that, Detective. I also realize that this is harassment, even if the guy who's doing it is dead. Clearly, Gordon was scoping me out for some time. God knows how many more of these cards he programmed to pop up on my computer this year."

"I see your point," Hadman replied carefully, as if weighing the best way to rein Taylor in. "My suggestion? Change your e-mail address. Then whatever else he might have sent won't ever reach you."

"But—"

"Let it go, Ms. Halstead. Gordon Mallory is dead."

"Are you sure?" she heard her own shaky voice demand. "*Absolutely* sure? Even without a body?" She was panicking, pursuing the absurd, and she knew it. But she needed the reassurance of hearing Detective Hadman's staunch verbal confirmation.

"Yes." Hadman said. "I'm sure. Mallory was identified as being aboard the yacht when it left the dock. The explosion was enormous. No one survived. The waters off Montauk are shark-infested. So, like I said, Gordon Mallory's dead. Stop torturing yourself."

Yeah, right, Taylor thought. *Easy for you to say.* "All right, Detective. I'll do my best."

"Good. And don't forget what I said about changing your e-mail address."

"I won't. I'll call my Internet provider right away. Thanks for your time."

She hung up.

JANUARY 8

8:30 P.M.

CHRYSLER BUILDING, 405 LEXINGTON AVENUE, NEW YORK CITY

Jonathan Mallory leaned back in his office chair, listening with interest to the panel discussion taking place on WVNY's *Teen Talk.*

Two renowned psychiatrists were discussing the impact of childhood trauma on the adults those kids became. Moderating the panel was the talk-show host, Taylor Halstead.

She was a bright woman. Jonathan had listened to her show for several weeks now. She had a lot to say about children and their environments, about parents and their responsibilities, about familial relationships and how to make them work.

If she wanted to hear about screwed-up childhoods, he could tell her stories that would make her head spin.

Actually, he'd fully expected to have the chance to do just that. He'd assumed she'd contact him months ago. She'd asked enough questions of Gordon's colleagues right after the explosion. Questions about Gordon and his family. She knew he existed, and that he lived and worked in Manhattan. He assumed she'd follow through by showing up on his doorstep, especially after hitting a brick wall out at the Hamptons with Douglas and Adrienne.

But she hadn't.

Too bad. It would have made keeping tabs on her much easier.

Next week's meeting would tell. Either she'd take the money and go away quietly or she'd keep poking around. The latter could mean trouble. And that would force his hand.

Rising, Jonathan walked over to his sideboard.

He paused, listening intently to Taylor's earnest tone as she posed the next question to her guests: How can a traumatized child overcome the odds and make the most of his or her future?

With a tight smile, Jonathan poured himself a Scotch.

10:03 P.M.

WVNY TALK RADIO, SEVENTH AVENUE, NEW YORK CITY
STUDIO B

The red "on the air" light went out.

Keying the mike, producer Kevin Hodges announced, "We're off."

From inside her private, softly lit recording studio, Taylor took a reviving sip of cranberry juice and eased away from the microphone and the control panel that coordinated her activities with the massive array of dials, switches, and computers sitting on the other side of the wall—the side that was her producer and audio engineer's domain.

Meeting Kevin's gaze through the long rectangular window that was her only visual connection with the outer studio, she gave him a thumbs-up. She then sat back in her chair, tugging the audio piece out of her ear and smiling across the desk at her guests. "That was great. You touched on some very important points. Especially the fact that childhood trauma doesn't have to ruin lives. It can be dealt with through counseling and emotional support. Kids need to hear that. Thanks so much for being here."

"Our pleasure." Dr. Mazer rose from one of the tufted leather guest chairs that were clustered around Taylor's kidney-shaped desk and gathered up her notes. "Let's hope we helped some people who are reluctant to call in."

Dr. Felmore shook Taylor's hand. "Your style is commendable," he praised. "A combination of compassion and clarity. You'll reach a lot of young people that way."

"I hope so. It's certainly my goal in hosting this show." Taylor glanced up as the thick door to her inner sanctum opened and her assistant, Laura Michaels, poked her head in.

"I have some things to go over with you when it's convenient."

"We have to be going anyway," Dr. Mazer assured Taylor. "Let's do this again sometime."

"I'd enjoy that."

Taylor waited until her guests had left, then turned to Laura. "So, what do we have—letters? E-mails? Phone calls?"

"All the above." Laura plopped down in a chair across from Taylor's desk and began organizing her various pieces of correspondence.

"Nice show," Kevin commented through the mike that connected the production side of the studio with Taylor's.

"Yeah, not to mention that Dr. Mazer bakes one hell of a blackout cake." Rick Shore, Taylor's audio engineer, put in his two cents, cutting another slice of cake as he popped out the minidisk containing tonight's show, then labeled it. "You know," he commented, turning to Kevin, "I think we should make bringing baked goods a prerequisite for all our guests."

"Great. Then you won't be able to reach the controls over your spare tire." Kevin continued to shut things down on his end while he spoke. "Better get out here fast, Taylor, or you won't get anything but crumbs."

Taylor smiled. "Thanks for the warning."

"By the way, Romeo called again tonight. He wanted to know if you were free for brunch on Sunday."

"And you said?"

"That you had a previous commitment, and that if he wanted advice, he should call with a question, not a request for a date."

"Straightforward enough." Taylor's lips twitched. Being in this business, she'd gotten used to all kinds of odd phone calls. It was natural that when you spoke about personal issues, people would feel a connection. Some regarded her as a personal friend, some despised her views and used her as a whipping post, and some wanted to bring her home to mother. Everyone at WVNY was a pro. They knew when a caller sounded scary. This one just wanted a date—every other day.

"Do you need us?" Rick asked, finishing the shutdown process—and his cake. "Because I've got a situation at home. If we're through, I'm going to take off."

"Go." Taylor waved them away. "I've got a few things to review with Laura, then I'll be heading out, too. I've got an early meeting at school tomorrow." She turned to Laura. "Okay, shoot."

Laura shoved a pile across the desk. "This is the take-home stuff. Read it when you have time." She pointed at another pile. "Here's what we have to go over. But before we do . . ." She pulled out a pink phone message and handed it to Taylor. "Your attorney called. He said to call back at your earliest convenience."

Taylor frowned, taking and scanning the message that read *Joseph Lehar, Esq.—call back ASAP.* "Did he mention what it was about?"

"Something about a meeting."

A meeting? That was odd. Usually, when Joseph called her, it was to discuss Steph's estate, of which she was the executor.

"I'll call him first thing tomorrow."

"He said he'd be in the office until eleven o'clock tonight, catching up on paperwork."

"Fine. Then I'll call him now."

"I'll wait outside." Laura rose, leaving the studio and shutting the door behind her.

Taylor punched in the law firm's phone number, then pressed Joseph's extension.

He picked up on the third ring, sounding fuzzy with fatigue. "Yes?"

"Hello, Joseph, it's Taylor Halstead. You wanted to speak with me?"

"Taylor, yes." Some shuffling of papers. "I got a call from Horace Randolph of Harter, Randolph and Collins. He's asked to meet with us."

Harter, Randolph & Collins? Taylor knew they were a prominent Park Avenue law firm. "What on earth does Mr. Randolph want with me? Isn't he a corporate lawyer?"

"Yes, but the firm represents some influential personal clients, too. And Horace specializes in trusts and estates."

"Trusts and estates. Does this have to do with Steph?"

"Seems so. Harter, Randolph and Collins represent the interests of Douglas and Adrienne Berkley, as well as those of Jonathan and Gordon Mallory."

Taylor felt her stomach tighten. "Did Mr. Randolph give you any details about this meeting?"

"Only that it concerns the partnership Gordon Mallory had formed with the group of investors who died in the boating accident. Horace would like us to be at his office on January thirteenth at four o'clock. Can you make it?"

She glanced at her calendar. School was over at a quarter to three. Getting over to Park by four would be no problem. "Yes, I can make it."

"Excellent. I'll meet you in the lobby at ten of four."

"I'll be there."

CHAPTER 5

THE offices of Harter, Randolph & Collins looked like a nineteenth-century English gentlemen's club—heavy wood, expensive leather, with an elite, old-world masculine feel from reception area to law library.

After a fifteen-minute wait, Taylor and Joseph were ushered into the "small" conference room—which was so big it made one wonder what the "large" conference room looked like—by a sober-faced woman of middle years.

Horace Randolph took over from there. A distinguished, gray-haired gentleman with that senior-partner air, he walked over to the threshold to greet them, to apologize for the delay, and to escort them over to the walnut table.

Two other attendees sat there—one man, one woman. The woman looked trim and efficient. Her back was ramrod straight, her hands were poised above her laptop, and she'd set up a small cassette recorder in front of her. Mr. Randolph's assistant, obviously.

The man was another matter entirely.

He was striking. He wasn't classically handsome, but he was very earthy and very male—not James Bond male, but ski-slope, camping-in-the-woods male. It was odd, given how at ease he looked in his Brooks Brothers suit. Maybe it was his features. Patrician as they were, they were still winter-tanned. He'd definitely spent time in the sun recently—golden highlights were threaded through his jet-black hair. His eyes could pin you to the wall. They were an intense midnight blue, bold and penetrating. As for his age, he was decades younger than Horace Randolph—maybe in his midthirties—but he had the same air of innate self-assurance.

He was tall, too, Taylor noted as he rose to greet her. Over six feet.

Brooks Brothers meets L.L. Bean. An interesting combo.

"Ms. Halstead, this is Reed Weston, one of our attorneys," Mr. Randolph explained. "He's going to sit in on this meeting. Joseph, you two know each other."

"Of course. Nice to see you, Reed." Joseph looked vaguely surprised, but not put out.

"You, too." Reed's gaze flickered over Taylor in instinctive male assessment, and he extended his hand. "Ms. Halstead. It's a pleasure."

"Mr. Weston," she acknowledged, meeting his handshake. She turned to Horace Randolph, her shoulders lifting in a puzzled shrug. "May I ask what this meeting's about? Specifically, I mean. Joseph tells me it concerns my cousin's estate."

"It does. Please, have a seat." Mr. Randolph gestured at the chair directly across the table from Reed Weston.

She complied. Joseph sat down beside her, stacking his file neatly in front of him.

Horace Randolph took the chair across from Joseph, interlacing his fingers on the conference table. "As you know, we represent the estate of Gordon Mallory. As you also know, Mr. Mallory's company formed a partnership with a group of investors, all of whom died in that tragic boating accident last September. Your cousin Stephanie was one of those investors. Given that she and all her co-investors are now deceased, the executor of Mr. Mallory's estate, Douglas Berkley, has determined that continuing the partnership no longer makes sense."

"I see." Taylor was intrigued. Joseph had informed her that Douglas Berkley was the executor; the will was a matter of public record, along with all the other papers filed for probate. But his decision to dissolve the partnership—now, that was interesting. "Go on."

Mr. Randolph leaned forward, his gaze steady as he studied her reaction. "In order to expedite the dissolution, Mr. Berkley is offering to purchase each investor's partnership interest, including any appreciation over and above the initial investment. If that's agreeable . . ." He beckoned to his assistant, who handed him a document. "This is a simple sales contract. It says in legalese what I've just explained. In short, our firm is authorized to give you a check for the full value of your cousin's investment. You just have to sign the contract and we can put this matter to rest." He slid the form across the table to Joseph.

Joseph looked it over, then handed it to Taylor. "It's in order."

"I'm sure it is." She met his gaze squarely. "However, I'd like some time to read it, to review it with you alone so I'm sure I fully understand it, and to discuss the matter with Stephanie's parents. As you know, I don't make any major decisions regarding her estate without consulting with them."

"Absolutely."

"Of course," Horace Randolph concurred, his expression neutral. "Whatever you're comfortable with. Joseph can get back to me in a day or two."

A day or two. Boy, wasn't he in a hurry?

Taylor turned, inclining her head at Reed Weston and trying to dig up at least one of her answers. "Are you working with Mr. Randolph on the dissolution of this partnership?"

A glimmer of amusement flickered in those midnight eyes. "Mr. Randolph doesn't require my assistance. But I do represent the Berkleys. I've known them for many years."

"I see." She wasn't sure she did.

Reed Weston pushed back his chair and rose. "If you're taking the contract with you, then you won't be needing me for questions or to witness documents. So, please excuse me."

"I'm sure Ms. Halstead has to be going, too," Mr. Randolph added smoothly, coming to his feet. "As I understand it, she has a radio show to prepare for." He turned to his secretary, addressing her for the first time. "Ms. Posner, would you print off copies of the unsigned contract for Mr. Lehar and Ms. Halstead, then escort the two of them to the reception area?"

"Certainly."

Ms. Posner was out the door like a bullet, followed closely by the rest of the group. *Talk about a New York minute*, Taylor mused, glancing at her watch after she'd gotten her papers and said her good-byes. Once they saw she wasn't signing on the spot, Gordon's lawyers ended the meeting.

She was itching to talk to her attorney alone.

That plan hit a snag when, halfway down the corridor, Joseph was waylaid by another attorney—one who wanted to catch up. Fine. Hearing Joseph's take on things was going to have to wait.

She made arrangements to call him the next day, then continued down the corridor, pausing to stop in the ladies' room before leaving.

A quick, quiet partnership dissolution, she reflected, running a brush through her hair. The whole thing sounded sketchy. Not illegal. Just off-color. Then again, everything about Gordon Mallory was sketchy. So no shock there.

She was lost in thought when she exited the bathroom, retracing her steps until she reached the reception area. Nodding at the receptionist, she reached for the doorknob on the heavy wooden door, at the exact second that the door swung open and a man strode in, nearly knocking her down.

"Excuse me," he said, reaching out to steady her on her feet. "Are you all right?"

Taylor raised her head to reply, but the words stuck in her throat as she stared into the hard brown eyes and sculpted features that had been etched in her nightmares since September. The color drained from her face, and she let out a sharp cry as she jerked away. "Let go of me!"

"What?"

"I said, *get your hands off me!*" She slapped his hands off her elbows and turned to run, feeling hysteria bubbling up inside her.

The receptionist was staring at her as if she were a lunatic. So were the half dozen other employees who had rushed out of their offices at the commotion.

Taylor stopped dead in her tracks, common sense telling her that what she was seeing was an impossibility. Simultaneously, reality descended with a crashing blow.

The twin.

A few seconds into this surreal scenario, Reed Weston materialized, making his way through to where she stood. "Ms. Halstead?" He gazed from her white face to the man standing behind her. "What's wrong?"

"I . . . I thought . . . but it's not . . ." She sucked in her breath. "It must be his brother."

"I collided with her in the doorway," the man behind her supplied. "But judging from her reaction, she wasn't prepared to see me. I apologize." He stepped around to face Taylor, but made no move to touch her. "I'm

Jonathan Mallory, Ms. Halstead. I didn't know you'd be here. I'm sorry for the shock."

"I . . ." She wet her lips with the tip of her tongue. "Right. I figured out who you were about three seconds ago." Her voice sounded high and thin. Dammit, she had to get a hold of herself. She wasn't in the habit of losing her composure. And it wasn't as if she didn't know Gordon had an identical twin. It's just that he'd caught her by surprise—a surprise she clearly wasn't ready to handle.

She had to try.

"I'm sorry, Mr. Mallory." His name tasted like chalk, and she had to force out the words while gazing at a mirror image of Gordon in a slightly more conservative suit. "I didn't know you'd be here. If I had . . ." To Taylor's dismay, she felt herself sway on her feet.

"Let's get you a chair and some water." Reed Weston took her arm, leading her away from the reception area. "Jonathan," he said over his shoulder. "I'll be with you shortly."

"Take your time."

By the time Reed Weston steered her into his office and eased her into a chair, Taylor was seeing little black specks.

"Put your head between your knees and breathe," he instructed.

Taylor obeyed.

A glass was thrust in her hand. "Drink."

She sat up and took a deep swallow. "Thanks." The cobwebs were beginning to clear. "I'm all right."

He perched at the edge of his desk, regarding her intently. "All this from running into Jonathan?"

"No. I'm not that pathetic," she murmured. "I skipped lunch. I've been running around all day. Crashing into him was just the last straw."

Without a word, Reed leaned back, pressed the intercom button on his phone. "Cathy?"

"Yes, Mr. Weston?"

"There are some muffins left from this morning's meeting. I'd appreciate your grabbing a few and bringing them to my office."

"Yes, sir."

He sat up. "Sustenance is on the way."

Taylor finished off her water and set down the glass. "That's not necessary," she said, starting to get up. "I'm fine. Just on overload."

"On overload *and* starved," he corrected, halting her progress. "I don't want you fainting on Park Avenue. It's rush hour. You'll be stampeded by the Grand Central crowd."

With a weak smile, Taylor settled back. "True enough." She glanced around, taking in her surroundings for the first time. The furnishings were as staid and traditional as the rest of the place. But the size of the office—now, *that* was interesting. It was large, much larger than the other offices she'd passed, with the exception of those belonging to the senior partners. And its location was impressive, too—a panoramically windowed, southeast corner. Nice.

Apparently, Reed Weston was held in high regard.

"So what's the verdict?"

Taylor's gaze snapped back to his, and she chose her words carefully. "That you're successful. That you're valued. And that you're probably going to be making partner at a very young age—if you aren't one already."

A corner of his mouth lifted. "I'm not. But thanks for the vote of confidence."

"I doubt you need it."

Taylor fell silent as Reed's secretary came in, carrying a plate with two blueberry muffins on it.

"Thanks, Cathy." He gestured for her to give the plate to Taylor. "Those are for Ms. Halstead." He waited while Taylor took the plate. "That'll be all for today," he added to his secretary. "Go on home. We'll finish that stack of letters first thing in the morning."

"Yes, sir." The solid, efficient-looking woman with the mousy brown hair and conservative navy suit said her good-nights and left.

Reed gestured at the muffins. "Eat."

No coercion was necessary. She took a bite of a muffin. "I'm sorry for the inconvenience, and the commotion. I'll be out of your hair in a minute."

"No problem. Take your time."

Taylor took a few more bites, then set down the plate. "I feel much better. Thanks."

"You're welcome."

He didn't seem to be in any hurry. He was still studying her.

She crossed her legs and interlaced her fingers on her lap. "Mr. Weston . . ."

"Reed."

"Fine . . . Reed. I take it Jonathan Mallory's here to see you."

"Uh-huh."

"Does that mean your representation of Douglas Berkley extends to his . . . I'm not sure how to classify Jonathan Mallory. He's too old to be a ward or a foster child."

"True." The knowing gleam in Reed's eyes told Taylor he knew she was on a fishing expedition. But it didn't seem to bother him. "I get your drift. And, yes, I represent Jonathan. We go back a long way."

"Did you meet through Douglas Berkley?"

"Nope. College. We graduated Princeton together."

"So you're friends."

"We're business associates."

He was being vague. Attorney-client privilege, no doubt. Fine. She'd go at this from another angle.

"Getting back to your promising future here, I realize you represent some major clients like Douglas Berkley. Other than that, do you specialize in any particular kind of law?"

He didn't miss a beat. "I'm pretty versatile. But, yes, I specialize in criminal defense."

Now, *that* Taylor hadn't expected. "As in representing crooked CEOs who've ripped off their investors?"

Another hint of amusement. "Sometimes. Although it's usually a lot tamer."

"Tame." Taylor waved away that assessment. "My guess is you're being overly modest. Firms like Harter, Randolph and Collins don't represent drug dealers. They represent huge corporations and affluent business moguls." *Like Douglas Berkley,* she added silently to herself. "You must be quite a brilliant defense counselor."

"I do my best." Reed arched a brow. "Is the interrogation over, or is there more?"

Easy, Taylor cautioned herself. *Don't push. Get what you can. Joseph will fill in the blanks.* "Sorry. I didn't mean to grill you."

"Sure you did. But that's fine. No harm done." Reed shifted his weight, folding his arms across his chest. "Now it's my turn. Why are you so fascinated with Douglas and Jonathan?"

His question was fair.

She went for evasive. "I'm not fascinated. I'm curious. My cousin was dating Gordon Mallory when they were both killed in that boat explosion. She and I were very close. It's natural for me to ask questions about Gordon's family and friends."

"Maybe," Reed responded. "But it's not natural for you to freak out when you come face-to-face with his twin. Or to nearly choke when you say his name."

Taylor didn't reply.

"You didn't like Gordon much, did you?"

Okay, enough was enough. "I'd better get going," she said, coming to her feet. "I have a radio show to do, and you have a client waiting."

Reed didn't push. Instead, he reached over, scooping up the napkin holding the remaining one and a half muffins and wrapped them up. "Here." He handed the makeshift doggy bag to Taylor. "Finish these on the run. Your listeners won't be happy if you collapse during the show."

"You're right about that." She smiled, taking the muffins. "Thanks again for the rescue." She turned to go.

"Taylor?" He halted her in her tracks. "It *is* Taylor, isn't it?"

"Yes." Her gaze was questioning as she watched him cross over to her.

"I think I should walk you out. It'll be easier for you." He didn't add *because Jonathan Mallory's in the reception area*. But that's what he meant.

For the second time in the past few minutes, Taylor didn't put up a fight. She wanted out. And she wanted her exit to be as fast and painless as possible.

She fell into step beside Reed Weston, heading down the corridor and toward the reception desk. She was relieved to see that the hall was quiet, with no gaping employees.

No one but Jonathan Mallory, who was sitting in the reception area, thumbing through a *Wall Street Journal*.

He rose as they approached him. "Is everything all right?"

"Fine," Reed assured him. "Taylor just needed to be fed." He reached around her, pushing open the door. "Don't forget to polish off those muffins. They'll tide you over till you have time for a decent meal."

"I will." Taylor paused, forcing herself to turn to Jonathan. "Again, I apologize. I'm tired. The resemblance startled me."

He gave her a sympathetic smile, and a shiver shot up Taylor's spine. It was Gordon's smile. "I understand. Don't worry, my ego will recover."

"I'm glad to hear that." She had to get out of there. "Well, I won't keep you gentlemen from your business. Good-bye."

FIVE MINUTES LATER, Reed shut his office door, turning around to face Jonathan. "Suppose you tell me what that was all about."

His seemingly unruffled client lowered himself into a chair. "I have no idea. Obviously, she had issues with Gordon."

"Issues? Yeah, I'd say so." Reed loosened his blue silk tie, then walked around to sit behind his desk. "Any idea what those issues were?"

"Not a clue. Gordon and I weren't exactly tight."

Reed let it drop. "What made you change your mind about showing up late?"

"I didn't. Either your meeting went a lot longer than expected or you got a hell of a late start. I arrived right on schedule."

Reed gave a tight nod. "We didn't get started until four-thirty."

"So how did it go?"

"She was cautious. She wanted to talk it over with her attorney and her cousin's parents. But she didn't refuse."

"Fine. So it'll take a few days. After that, she'll sign."

"Hopefully."

Jonathan frowned. "You don't sound too optimistic."

"I'm not. Something's bothering her. And that something concerns Gordon. Maybe she blames him for her cousin's death. Maybe it's more. Whatever it is, it might very well influence her decision. Remember, she doesn't exactly need the cash."

"She needs the closure."

"Agreed. The question is, how badly? Badly enough to appease whatever's upsetting her?"

"I see your point." Jonathan considered the possible snag, then shrugged it off. "Let's cross that bridge when we come to it. If necessary, I'll talk to Douglas. We'll figure out a way around it." He cleared his throat. "Did she ask you anything about me?"

"Oh, she went on a little fishing expedition. She wanted to know if I represented you, how we met, that kind of thing."

"Really." Jonathan sounded more intrigued than worried. "Nothing about my relationship to Douglas?"

"She made reference to Douglas being your sponsor. So if she knows anything more, she's hiding it."

"No one manages to pull that off with you, Reed. If she was hiding something, you'd know it. You'd see right through her."

"I'd probably get an inkling, yeah. I didn't."

Jonathan settled back in his chair. "She's a real head turner, isn't she? I recognized her from the photo WVNY has posted on their Web site. But she's better-looking in person. A classic beauty."

The personal, almost intimate note in Jonathan's voice took Reed by surprise. "I haven't checked out the site," he replied, keeping his tone noncommittal. "But, yeah, she's gorgeous."

"There's a certain elegance about her," Jonathan continued, looking pensive and far away. "Rumor has it her cousin was also a knockout. Dazzling red hair, perfect features—the whole nine yards. Taylor's more subtle. Her hair's that deeper, rich shade of red, and her eyes are dark, somewhere between brown and black. They're very haunting and expressive. It's hard to look away from them." His lips curved. "I should know. They were boring into me as if I were the devil himself."

This was getting more interesting by the minute. "I didn't realize you were so taken with her."

Jonathan seemed to snap out of his reverie. "I wouldn't say I'm taken with her. I don't even know her. But I have eyes. She's beautiful. I also have ears. I've listened to her radio show. She's got a shrewd head on her shoulders. How often do you find beauty, brains, and class all in one woman?"

"Good point," Reed agreed warily. "Still, I'd cut her a wide berth if I were you. Clearly she wasn't pleased to see a mirror image of Gordon."

Jonathan's gaze was steady. "Maybe. Maybe not."

CHAPTER 6

TAYLOR shut her office door and walked around to take a seat behind her desk. She could feel the surge of tension, impatience, and resentment emanating from the impeccably dressed, polished, wealthy couple sitting across from her.

Chris Young's parents. Dr. Edward Young and Dr. Olivia Young. Edward was a nationally recognized urologist. Olivia was a neurosurgeon at Mount Sinai.

This was *not* going to be pleasant.

Sure enough, Olivia Young took out her pager and placed it pointedly on the edge of Taylor's desk. "I've got a patient in recovery," she announced, leveling a cool stare at Taylor. "My time is limited."

"As is mine," her husband agreed in an authoritative voice that probably sent shivers up the spines of his medical staff. "So what's this about?"

"Chris." Taylor folded her hands in front of her. "And it's serious or I wouldn't have pulled you away from your patients."

"His grades were excellent this past term," Edward snapped. "Other than English, where he got a C. Fine. We're all aware that English is not Chris's strong suit. All his college applications are in, and between his solid average and the wide range of sports—"

"This has nothing to do with Chris's academics, or where he stands in the college process," Taylor interrupted. "It has to do with his behavior."

In situations like this, the direct approach was best. Even if it did elicit fireworks.

She leaned forward, neither blinking nor averting her gaze. "I purposely chose this time for us to meet because the entire school is at an assembly, and I'm trying to cause Chris the least amount of embarrassment."

"Embarrassment? Over what?"

"The fact that he's been making inappropriate advances toward me."

Olivia Young's jaw dropped. "Excuse me?"

"This problem didn't materialize out of the blue," Taylor continued. "To be blunt, Chris has had a crush on me since he was in eighth grade. Back then, it didn't concern me. He was coming into his own. It's not unusual for a boy who's discovering his sexuality to have a crush on a teacher or school counselor. His flirtations were harmless—a lot of guffawing with his pals when they passed me in the hall, and an occasional stare or grin. When the stares and grins got out of hand, I called Chris into my office and we had a chat. We discussed respect, and proper versus improper behavior. I made my point loud and clear. But in the end, it seemed to sink in. Plus, Chris got sidetracked by a normal, *extremely* active social life. His popularity really took off after he became captain of the hockey team. The girls started swarming around him like flies."

"Then what's the problem?"

"The problem is that this term, things took a major downward spiral."

"The college entrance process is a stressful one, Ms. Halstead," Edward reminded her icily. "I'm sure you realize that."

"I do. And I cut Chris more slack than I should have because of it. But he's gotten way out of line. Last month, he started making suggestive comments to me. If you'd like particulars, I'd be happy to supply them."

"Don't bother." Olivia held up a curtailing palm. "We get the picture."

"I thought you would. Anyway, right before winter break, I told Chris that if his behavior didn't change ASAP, I'd be calling you in. That obviously didn't deter him. Since we got back from vacation, the situation's gotten worse. He pops into my office every chance he gets and asks me out. Last week he waltzed in here after hours, draped an arm around my shoulders, and suggested that we—and I quote your son—'hook up tonight for a date—a date with benefits.' He then elaborated on what those benefits would be, and told me how adept he was at providing them. Again, I'm sure I don't need to paint a picture for you." Taylor's jaw set. "Your son is not a gawky adolescent anymore. He's a very cocky young man of nearly eighteen. He's had ample warning about his behavior, yet he's made no move to modify it. If anything, he's stepping it up to the point where it constitutes harassment. That tells me he needs help. Which is why I called you. We need to work together on this. You're his parents. You need to intervene before it's too late."

Edward Young's eyes narrowed. "Harassment," he repeated. "Are you threatening to initiate a lawsuit?"

The response was so typical, and so maddening, that Taylor had to fight to keep her tone even. "No, Dr. Young, I'm not interested in suing you. What I *am* interested in is helping your son. To do that, I need your cooperation. He's only going to be living at home a little while longer. After that, he'll be at college, on his own. He needs to be prepared for that. Right now, he's going down a very destructive path."

"A destructive path?" Now that the fear of a lawsuit had been eliminated, Edward sounded more amused than upset. "Isn't that a trifle melodramatic, Ms. Halstead? Chris might need a few lessons in self-control, and a reminder of your school's code of ethics—both of which I'll make sure he receives—but I'd hardly describe his flirtation with you as destructive. You're young. You're attractive. You're an accomplished professional. In short, you're an excellent role model. If anything, I'd say my son idolizes you."

"No, Dr. Young. Your son doesn't idolize me. He hits on me. He's got some psychological issues that need to be addressed—not just by me, but by the two of you in conjunction with a therapist who can offer him private counseling. Again, I urge you to insert yourself in this matter—*now*—before he leaves for college."

Edward opened his mouth to say God-knows-what, but his wife silenced him with a firm grip on his arm. "We appreciate your concern, Ms. Halstead." Her voice could freeze water. "We'll take it from here."

I'm sure you will, Taylor thought wryly as, a few minutes later, she shut the door behind them. *At this very moment, you're on your way to the headmaster to file a complaint against me. Instead of looking inside yourselves, you'll resolve the problem by shifting responsibility to me. No wonder Chris, like so many Dellinger students, is out of control.*

Sighing, Taylor sank back down in her chair and massaged her temples. It wasn't even eleven o'clock and she was wiped.

Then again, she'd been in perpetual motion since dawn. At nine, she'd dashed over to sign the lease on an apartment she'd gotten first dibs on, thanks to one of the teachers in her school who was a friend of the vacating tenant. The place was exactly what Taylor had been looking for. It was close to her current apartment—just two blocks over on West Seventy-fourth Street—and in great condition. It was similar in layout— a modern kitchen, a sunken living room, and a mauve marble-and-tile bathroom—but with one less bedroom, less square footage, and no horrible memories. The lease didn't start until March, which gave Taylor plenty of time to pack, to sublet her current apartment, and to work on putting this chapter of her life behind her.

Speaking of closure . . . Taylor glanced quickly at her watch, noting that it was well past eleven o'clock. Time to take care of her next priority— calling Joseph.

She picked up her phone and punched in the number.

He took her call right away. "Taylor. I'm sorry about yesterday. I didn't intend to be sidetracked for so long."

"Things happen. No apology is necessary." She pulled out her copy of the contract, glancing at it as she spoke. "Besides, it worked out for the best. I wanted to talk to you in private, and I needed to organize my thoughts first." She lowered the document to the table. "The truth is, it's not the contract that's bothering me. It's what's motivating it."

"Meaning?"

"Gordon is dead. Douglas Berkley is controlling his assets. If Gordon's company was as profitable as he led Steph to believe, why would Mr. Berkley want to dissolve this partnership? Why not step in as CEO of Gordon's company and continue operating both the company and the partnership?"

Joseph gave a grunt. "That thought occurred to me, too. All I can assume is that it's either for personal reasons or that Douglas Berkley did some projections and determined that this particular partnership wasn't as profitable as expected."

"Even if that's the case, why is Mr. Randolph rushing through the process? And why did he need a criminal attorney to monitor our meeting?"

The prolonged silence at the other end of the phone told Taylor that Joseph was surprised.

"Taylor," he said finally. "I don't know what you're getting at. But

I can tell you that Harter, Randolph and Collins is a fine, reputable firm. Douglas Berkley's reputation is equally spotless. I'm sure there's nothing unethical going on here. As for Reed Weston, I admit I was surprised to see him at the meeting. But he explained his involvement. True, he is primarily a criminal defense attorney, but he's active in other areas of the law as well. Clearly, those other areas include the legal affairs of Douglas Berkley. So I wouldn't read anything into his being there with Horace."

Everything Joseph said made sense. But that didn't placate her. The legal firm handling Gordon's estate might be on the up-and-up. But Gordon had not been.

"Would you do me a favor?" she asked Joseph. "Would you call Mr. Randolph and clarify a few particulars—such as why Mr. Berkley's opted to terminate the partnership and why he needs my answer so quickly? If you make the conversation attorney to attorney, he's more apt to be frank."

"Frank about what?" Joseph demanded. "What is it you're hoping to find out?"

Taylor blew out her breath. "I don't know."

Another pause, during which time Taylor could visualize Joseph shaking his head in frustration. He thought she was overreacting.

Maybe she was.

"All right, Taylor," he said at last. "I'll give Horace a call. I'll get back to you later today."

JANUARY 15

1:35 P.M.

EAST HAMPTON, LONG ISLAND

Jonathan took the glass Douglas handed him and sank down on the chaise longue. Outside the tempered-glass walls, a layer of snow covered the twenty-five-acre estate, but inside the domed room that housed the heated indoor pool, the air was hot, thick, and humid. Loosening his tie, Jonathan settled back to nurse his Scotch.

"You're going to sweat to death," Douglas commented, stirring his martini. "Why don't you change into trunks?"

"Not today. I don't have time. I've got to get back to the city."

Jonathan stared off toward the pool, where Adrienne was doing laps, toning her already luscious body, which looked as if it belonged to a twenty-five-year-old rather than a fifty-five-year-old. Then again, her body was her shrine. She'd pampered it and perfected it as long as Jonathan could remember.

Douglas was studying him intently. He walked over to sit down on the adjacent chaise, a towel draped around his damp shoulders. He was a distinguished-looking man in his late sixties, tall and physically fit, with steel gray eyes and a full head of salt-and-pepper hair. Mentally, he was as sharp as a tack. And he was well aware that whatever Jonathan had come here to discuss, it wasn't good.

"Fine. You need to get back. So tell me what's on your mind. Is it the business? Are you turning down my offer again?"

Jonathan gave a hard shake of his head. "It's got nothing to do with Berkley and Company. Frankly, I haven't had a minute to breathe, much less to reconsider your offer. Things at work have been crazy, and the loose ends you and I are trying to tie up aren't coming together as smoothly as we'd hoped."

Douglas twisted around so he was facing Jonathan and not his wife, who was climbing out of the pool to towel herself dry. "Gordon?" he asked, although he already knew the answer.

A nod.

"What now?"

"It's Taylor Halstead. She's back in the picture again." Jonathan sighed. "She was the only one who didn't sign the contract. On top of that, Horace called me last night to let me know that her attorney had contacted him. His client's asking questions."

"What kind of questions?"

"Why you're unwinding the partnership. Why we're in such a hurry to finalize this transaction." A frown. "That in itself wouldn't be a problem. Horace was evasive. He said he wasn't at liberty to divulge his client's reasons. But there's more. I ran smack into Taylor Halstead after her meeting. She lost it when she saw me. She yelled at me to stay away from her, darted around the reception area like a cornered rat. Reed had to take her into his office and calm her down. And, believe me, Taylor Halstead does not appear to be the hysterical type."

Swearing softly under his breath, Douglas gulped down his drink.

"Damn Gordon," he muttered. "Even dead, he's a pain in the ass. What did he do to that woman?"

"I don't know. But Reed's right. This isn't simply a matter of her associating Gordon with her cousin's death. She was terrified, not upset. And the fact that she's so suspicious—I don't know what to think."

"We have to find out." Douglas massaged his temples. "We need to terminate this investment partnership before anyone discovers it was a total fraud."

"What fraud?" Adrienne inquired, squeezing out her thick mane of auburn hair. She pulled a terry-cloth robe on over her bikini-clad body and walked over to pour herself a martini.

"Nothing for you to worry about, darling," Douglas assured her. "Just a business snag Jonathan's handling for me."

Adrienne regarded her husband over the rim of her glass. "Jonathan's an international trade consultant," she said. "He doesn't work for you, at least not yet. Which means this snag concerns Gordon."

Douglas sighed. "Like I said, it's nothing for you to worry about. Jonathan and I will deal with it."

Her pale green eyes glittered with irritation. "Please do. In the meantime, I'd put off making any announcements—business or personal—until it's taken care of. Otherwise, the scandal will eat us alive."

Jonathan stayed out of the conversation, giving his full attention to his Scotch. He'd had years of practice hiding his disdain for Adrienne. He was a pro at it. Besides, things had changed. He no longer gave a damn what she said. He had his own agenda.

"I'm off to get my massage," Adrienne announced, setting down her empty glass. She leaned over and kissed her husband lightly on the mouth. "We'll talk later." She gave Jonathan a fleeting glance as she turned away. "Good-bye, Jonathan. Have a safe trip back to the city."

He nodded, his face carefully blank as he watched her leave the room. Then he turned to Douglas. "How do you want me to handle this?"

Douglas scowled. "Clearly, you can't approach Taylor Halstead yourself."

"True. For now." He paused, sidetracked for a brief instant by his own words. Then he resumed. "I take it you still want to keep a low profile on this?"

"It's the best way. If I get involved, it'll look worse than it is."

"I agree. I was thinking of asking Reed to handle it. He's removed enough from Gordon to be nonthreatening."

"True." Douglas gave a thoughtful nod. "Not to mention he's charming as hell and incredibly good at winning over reluctant people." A quizzical look. "We still don't know how much Taylor Halstead pieced together. She's been poking around since the accident."

"And if she knows the real link between you, Gordon, and me?"

Douglas shrugged. "It's moot. If you accept my offer, the whole world will know."

"Yeah, and Adrienne will be livid. That hasn't changed. Not after thirty-five years."

"You let me handle Adrienne. You stop by and see Reed. Ask him to talk to Taylor Halstead and see if he can smooth things over. We need to clean up Gordon's mess and bury the past."

Bury the past. An interesting choice of words, Jonathan thought, polishing off his Scotch.

Some things couldn't be buried.

On the other hand, some things could.

CHAPTER 7

TAYLOR was preoccupied when she left the WVNY studios that night.

Not with *Teen Talk*.

With the legal situation.

She'd heard back from Joseph a day after she'd called him. He'd told her, in no uncertain terms, that Horace Randolph was adamant about two things: he didn't divulge his clients' confidences, and Douglas Berkley's ethics were above reproach.

Great. That told her nothing.

But the week and a half of ensuing silence did.

Mr. Randolph had wanted the contract signed and the transaction completed ASAP. Yet more than ten days had passed and he hadn't contacted her attorney to find out where things stood. Why was there suddenly no pressure being exerted by Harter, Randolph & Collins? Were they just giving her space, or were they crafting their strategy?

Taylor didn't know why she cared. Steph was gone. Her monetary investments, good or bad, were superfluous. And if Gordon had ripped her off, maybe it was best Taylor didn't know.

Making her way through the lobby, Taylor turned up her collar against the January chill and headed toward the revolving door that led to Seventh Avenue. She stepped outside and shivered. It was freezing, tiny snow flurries drifting around, trying to make up their minds whether or not to stick.

It was cold, gloomy, more desolate, and later than usual—definitely not a subway night.

She was about to hail a taxi when a black Mercedes SUV pulled up next to the curb beside her. The window on the passenger's side slid down, and the driver leaned over, calling out to her. "Need a lift?"

With a start, Taylor recognized the penetrating blue eyes and winter-tanned features of Reed Weston. "What are you doing here?" she demanded.

He pushed open the door. "Get in. I'll drive you home."

This was too bizarre for words. "Just like that."

"Just like that."

Her eyes narrowed. "Which direction are you headed?"

"Whichever one you need me to be headed in." He patted the seat beside him. "Come on. It's twenty degrees outside. And my car's a lot more comfortable than a cab."

The scenario was transparent. But it was also too intriguing to pass up.

"Fine." Taylor walked over and slid in, pulling the car door shut. "This is the part where you tell me you just happened to be in the neighborhood," she informed him, fastening her seat belt. "And what a coincidence it is that I popped up in the same place at the same time."

A corner of his mouth lifted, and he pulled out into traffic. "Sorry to disappoint you, but I knew what time your radio show ended. I was waiting for you. I've actually been around the block four times." He slanted her a sideways look. "Now, why don't you tell me where you live?"

"You mean, you haven't researched my address? I'm disappointed."

"Don't be. I'm a lawyer, not a PI. But I *am* a good guesser." He sized her up thoughtfully. "Let's see. I'd say the Upper West Side, maybe somewhere in the seventies. Close to mass transit and the park."

Taylor found herself smiling. "Not bad. It's West Seventy-second, a block from the subway station. But not near the park. Near Lincoln Center." Her smile faded. "Why don't you tell me why you're really here."

"To talk."

"Really? Did it occur to you that I might not be in the mood for conversation? I've been talking for hours. I'm beat."

"That's why I picked a Friday night. You can sleep in tomorrow."

For some reason, his rationale irked her. "And if I had a date?"

Reed didn't look the least bit put off. "Then I'd apologize and reschedule. Why? Do you?"

"No. That's not the point. If you wanted to set up an appointment, you could have used a telephone. Or were you afraid I'd turn you down?"

"Your home number's unlisted. The only way I had of reaching you was through your radio station or your attorney. I didn't want to use Joseph as a middleman, and I hardly think your listeners would appreciate my setting up a date with you on the air." Reed glanced at her as he stopped at a red light. "Am I wrong?"

Taylor gave him a tight smile. "You're right. But this isn't a date. It's a negotiation session."

He was quiet for a moment. "Maybe it's both." Before she could respond, the light changed, and Reed resumed driving. "I'm a polite and harmless guest. But if you're uncomfortable, we could grab a cup of coffee and stay in neutral territory."

The familiar tightness squeezed Taylor's chest. Reed was just being considerate. He had no idea what a raw nerve he'd hit.

"Taylor?" he pressed.

She swallowed, hard. It was time to get past this. Reed Weston had an agenda, but it didn't involve physical domination.

"My apartment is fine. There's a lot half a block down. You can park there. I'll brew some coffee."

He heard the tension in her tone, and his brows knit pensively. But he didn't question it. "Okay."

They drove in silence, and twenty minutes later, she unlocked her apartment door, showing Reed in and tossing down her keys and pocketbook—but not before plucking out her cell phone and slipping it into her pocket. Having it close at hand gave her a sense of security. "Hang your coat on the rack near the door. I'll get the coffee going."

"Sounds good." Reed complied, wandering through the hallway and stepping down into the sunken living room. "Nice place," he called out.

"Thanks. I'm moving."

"I can see that." He'd obviously spotted the boxes she'd begun packing. "Have you found another apartment already?"

"Yes." Taylor walked out, gesturing for Reed to have a seat on the sofa. "The coffee will be ready in a minute. You can start interrogating me in the meantime."

He waited for her to sit, then followed suit, keeping a cushion-wide distance between them. "I didn't plan on interrogating you. This isn't a courtroom."

"Okay, pressuring me, then. Did Jonathan Mallory ask you to come?"

"Actually, yes." Reed surprised her by stating the truth. "He and Douglas Berkley. But it didn't take much convincing. I've been thinking about you since you left my office."

Taylor blew out her breath. "I didn't intend to make a scene."

"And it wasn't Jonathan's intention to upset you. He didn't know you'd be there."

"I don't doubt that."

Reed draped an arm over the back of the sofa. "In answer to your question, Jonathan and Douglas did ask me to speak with you. Not to pressure you, just to get a handle on where you're coming from. Obviously, your reluctance to sign the contract is somehow linked to Gordon. Do you hold him responsible for your cousin's death? Is that what this is about?"

The ring of the coffeemaker saved Taylor from an immediate reply.

"Coffee's ready." She rose, walking toward the galley kitchen. "How do you take it?"

"Black." Reed followed her into the kitchen and perched on a counter stool, nodding his thanks as she handed him a steaming cup. "Are you going to answer the question?"

Taylor propped her elbows on the counter, facing him as she sipped at her coffee. "May I ask a few of my own?"

He made a sweep with his arm. "Feel free."

"What's the hurry to terminate the partnership?"

"My clients lost a loved one. So did the families of all the other people on that yacht. It's natural for those involved to want to put the past behind them. Why is that so strange?"

"It isn't. Not by itself. And not if everyone involved was as decent and honorable as you're implying."

Reed's eyes narrowed. "I'm not doing the implying. *You* are. Whose integrity are you questioning?"

"Gordon's." Taylor didn't mince words. "As for his friends and family, maybe they're protecting his memory. Which brings me to my next question. Why were you really sitting in on the meeting? You're a criminal defense attorney. Did Gordon do something illegal?"

That dark blue gaze bored into hers, but Reed's expression remained unreadable. "Why are you so sure Gordon was unscrupulous? What did he do to make you so suspicious—and so afraid?"

A humorless laugh escaped Taylor, and she shook her head. "You're good. Very good. Not only did you evade my question, you turned it back on me."

Reed set down his cup and leaned forward. "I handle more than just criminal cases. I was at that meeting because Douglas Berkley asked me to be. He's my client. So is Jonathan Mallory. Period. Now, what was up between you and Gordon? It felt personal. Were you involved with him?"

Taylor felt bile rise in her throat. "No."

"But I'm right. It was personal."

"He was an operator. He used people. Steph was just another victim. Unfortunately, she paid with her life." To Taylor's dismay, she saw that her hand was shaking. Coffee sloshed onto the counter, and she took the opportunity to grab a sponge and wipe it up.

Reed reached over, gripping her hand and halting its motion. "There's more. What is it?"

Her gaze lifted, met his. "Guilt, for starters. Steph wasn't just my cousin. She was my best friend. I feel responsible. I knew Gordon was bad news. All the signs were there. I tried to convince her. I couldn't seem to get through. Now it's too late."

"You're not responsible for—"

"Don't bother with the placating speech," Taylor interrupted. "I'm a psychologist. I know all the reasons for and ramifications of my emotions. I also know it's easier to take on someone else's ghosts than to battle your own. So let it go."

"All right, I will. But the other part of my question still stands. What did Gordon do to *you*? Not to your cousin, to *you*."

An icy calm settled over Taylor. She'd discussed the details often enough—with her therapist, with the police. The words were painless. It was the memory that haunted her. So what difference did it make if Reed Weston knew?

"You want an answer? Fine. He tried to rape me."

This time Reed reacted. His pupils dilated in shock. "When?"

"The day he died. Right here in this apartment. He was waiting for me when I got home. Supposedly, he was picking up some clothes for Steph. At least that's what he claimed. I soon found out otherwise."

Reed's lips thinned into a grim line. "You said he *tried* to rape you. What stopped him? You?"

"Unfortunately not." This was the hard part, the part that made her feel ineffectual and guilty. "Steph stopped him. She unexpectedly buzzed from downstairs. Gordon took off. He left me unconscious and hand-cuffed to the bed."

"Christ," Reed muttered under his breath. He stared at the counter.

"So now you know why I lost it when I ran into Jonathan Mallory—and why I'm a little short on faith when it comes to his dead brother."

"Yeah. And why you carry your cell phone around in your own apart-ment like a security device." Reed gave her a measured look. "Were you hurt?"

"I came through it fine. The police wrote up my assault complaint. A detective was going to follow up with me the next day. But the boat ex-plosion happened. Since there was no point in investigating a dead man, the case was closed. Whatever punishment Gordon would have received was insignificant compared to the one he got." Taylor's voice quavered. "But Steph . . . and the rest of those people . . . they didn't deserve to die with him. The injustice makes me sick."

"I can see why." Reed took a huge gulp of coffee, and Taylor got the feeling he'd prefer it was liquor. "I'm sorry. I had no idea. Neither did my clients. Now I understand why you're so on edge about signing the con-tract, and why you freaked out when you walked into Jonathan."

I doubt that, Taylor wanted to say. *There's no way you could understand the half of it.* But she bit back the words. He was trying to show some compassion. There was no point in throwing it back in his face.

"You're right," Reed replied, as if reading her mind. "I can't know what you went through, not really. But I can empathize. I have three sis-ters, two sisters-in-law, and four nieces. I taught them all self-defense. It's a scary world out there."

That personal tidbit caught Taylor by surprise. Not so much that he'd shared it. He seemed like a guy who was very comfortable with himself. And certainly not the self-defense part. That she could picture, no problem. But the big, close-knit family? That seemed incongruous somehow.

For the first time, Reed chuckled. "Don't look so shocked. Even sharks have families."

"I guess. It's just hard to imagine you as part of a big, squishy clan."

"Well, I am. There are seven of us. I've got three brothers and three sisters. All but two of us are married with kids. I've got nieces, nephews—hey, there are Westons scattered all over the country."

"Wow." The concept was unique, like something out of a storybook. "Where did you grow up?"

"In a small town in Vermont. My folks still live up there. The whole bunch of us descend on them for the holidays, and whenever else we can manage to get away."

That explained the winter tan. "That's wonderful, especially for your nieces and nephews. There's no substitute for a loving family."

"I agree." Another assessing look. "Is that a professional statement or a personal one?"

"Both."

Reed nodded. "I read your bio on the WVNY Web site. You specialize in family counseling, not only on the radio, but at the Dellinger Academy. You must have a great rapport with teens."

Taylor gave a half smile. "That depends on which ones you ask, and when. I give it my all. Working with them brings me tremendous satisfaction."

"Dellinger's a top school—and an expensive one."

"Which breeds a whole other set of pressures for the kids who attend it." Taylor rose to refill their coffee cups. "The drive to succeed is instilled in these kids from the moment they're born. Add to that too much wealth and, too often, a severe lack of emotional support to balance it out. What you end up with is a lot of lonely, spoiled, frightened teenagers with nowhere to turn and no self-esteem." Taylor settled herself back at the counter. "I'm not minimizing the challenges of kids who are financially hurting. But parental neglect can result from struggling to make ends meet and lacking time for your kids, or from jet-setting around the world and forgetting you have kids."

"I agree." Reed had been listening, sipping at his coffee. "You're very passionate about what you do."

"I can't imagine doing it otherwise."

Something flickered in his eyes—then vanished as quickly as it had come. "What about your family?" he asked. "Is it big or small?"

Nonexistent, Taylor was tempted to say. "I'm an only child," she replied instead. "Which made losing Steph that much more unbearable."

That brought the conversation full circle.

Reed cleared his throat. "Look, Taylor, I'm not going to try talking you into signing that contract. If you can't, you can't." A pause. "Just tell me which of the details you're okay with my relaying to my clients and which ones you're not."

She blinked. "You mean, about Gordon?"

"Yes."

This coming from a top-notch defense attorney? Reed Weston was certainly full of surprises.

"Your professional loyalty is to your clients." Taylor stated the obvious. "I realize that."

"So do I. But professional loyalty doesn't include invading your privacy. If you don't want them to know what happened with Gordon, I'll respect that."

Taylor was quiet for a long, thoughtful minute. "Thanks, but I have a feeling they know what Gordon was about. So tell them whatever you want."

She raised her head, met Reed's gaze. "As for the contract, I'll sign it. The more I think about it, the more I realize how meaningless it is. This whole thing is about money. It won't bring Steph back, or erase what Gordon did to me. It's better that I should sever ties. It'll help me move on, like the rest of the families you referred to." She knew as she spoke that it was true. "I'll call Joseph on Monday, make the arrangements. Tell your clients to relax. I won't stand in the way of their dissolving Gordon's partnership—even though I think their motives are suspect."

Reed didn't confirm or deny her speculation. "Are you sure?"

She nodded. "I don't need or want the money. Nor does my family. Write the check. I'll sign it over to the Theatre Development Fund in Steph's memory. She would want that."

A quizzical look. "She was in the theater?"

"Uh-huh. An actress. Actually, a budding Broadway star." Taylor's smile was sad, and she gazed into her coffee cup, not even sure why she was elaborating on this to Reed. "She was closer to realizing her dream than she knew. That last day of her life, the reason she was late getting home was because she was auditioning for a part in a new off-Broadway show. It was a major supporting role. Well, she got it. Her agent called to let me know, just out of respect to her memory. If she'd lived, she'd be opening February first."

A weighted silence hung in the air.

"She must have been very talented," Reed said at last.

"She was."

Leaning forward, Reed covered her hand with his. "Taylor—I'm really sorry."

The comfort—and the contact—felt good. Too good.

Time to call a halt to the evening.

Taylor rose. "It's getting late. I'm exhausted."

"Understood." Reed followed her lead, coming to his feet. "I didn't mean to upset you."

"You didn't. It just hurts to rehash how much Steph had to live for. But that hurt can't be changed any more than her being gone."

"It'll get easier."

"I'm sure. Time, as they say, is the best healer."

"True. On the other hand, sometimes time can use some help."

Taylor swallowed and didn't reply.

Reed shot her a questioning look. "Are you moving because of your memories of Steph, or because of your memories of Gordon?"

That one she could answer frankly. "Both. And because it makes sense to. This apartment has a lot more space than I need. I'm moving to a one-bedroom place a couple of blocks over." A hint of a smile curved her lips. "It's closer to the park."

"Ah." Reed grinned back. "So my powers of deduction are pretty good, after all."

"I guess they are." There was a moment of something—camaraderie mixed with a spark of sensual awareness—that shimmered to life, hung between them.

The attraction didn't come as a shock. Taylor had felt it brewing. But it was the last thing she was ready to handle.

Determinedly, she nipped it in the bud, taking a deliberate step around Reed. She led him into the hall and handed him his coat.

"When's the big move?" he asked, shrugging the coat on.

"My lease starts March first. So I have five or six weeks."

"Good." He paused, gazing into the living room with a discerning eye. "That gives us plenty of time. For what I have in mind, we'll need a big, uncluttered room like that one."

Taylor blinked. "Excuse me? What is it you have in mind?"

A hint of amusement flickered in his midnight eyes, but when he spoke, his tone was dead serious, and there was no mistaking the determined set of his jaw. "Making you feel less vulnerable. Ensuring that you're less on edge when you're alone with a man."

His insight surprised her. She was very good at keeping her feelings to herself. Still, he'd picked up on them. Interesting. More to the point, she was curious about where he was going with this.

"Okay, I'll bite. How do you intend to work this magic?"

He didn't miss a beat. "By giving you self-defense lessons. Pick your night. We start next week."

CHAPTER 8

REED glanced down at Taylor's signature on the contract, then put aside the document. He rose from behind his desk, walking over to stare out the office window.

She was really something, that Taylor Halstead. Beautiful, sensitive, and carrying the weight of the world on her shoulders. It didn't take a shrink to figure out that she blamed herself for her cousin's death. Or that she was still totally freaked out when she was alone in her apartment with a man.

Reed couldn't help her with the guilt, but he sure as hell could help her with the fear. He *wanted* to help. There was something about her—a soft, lonely quality beneath a poised, self-reliant, upper-crust facade—that intrigued him. Poor little rich girls weren't usually his type. But this one was different. She was complex. There was a whole lot more to Taylor Halstead than met the eye.

And, yeah, he was attracted to her. *Very* attracted. She was all Jonathan had described and more. She was principled and passionate. He could sense it.

Jonathan probably sensed it, too. Clearly, he was also captivated by her. He was going to be royally pissed when he found out about the self-defense lessons Reed had arranged to give her. Well, tough. Reed didn't owe Jonathan a damned thing. He'd given him too much already.

At college, they'd rowed crew together, taken business law the same semester, and hit a lot of the same weekend parties, where they drank warm beer and pursued hot girls. But their personalities never really meshed. So while circumstances had triggered a longer-term, more complex association than Reed had ever anticipated, that association, since graduation, had been all business.

Idly, Reed watched a few taxis zip up Park Avenue, followed by a long black limo that pulled over and stopped in front of the building. No doubt the car belonged to Douglas Berkley. He and Jonathan were due here for an update meeting. Reed would fill them in on where things stood, and show them the signed contract.

Overall, they'd be pleased with the outcome. They'd be less pleased with the reasons behind Taylor's reluctance to sign. But they'd get over it.

That was the problem. Not just with them, but with most of the clients Reed represented. They were so desensitized, so self-absorbed, that right versus wrong took second place to innocent versus guilty. And innocent didn't mean what it used to. It meant getting a verdict of not guilty, whether or not the defendant had actually committed the crime.

He'd gone into this profession hungry, young, and naive, but not stupid. He'd been the first in his family to make it beyond County College, much less to Princeton and then to Harvard Law. Meeting Jonathan Mallory had changed his life. Then again, he didn't know who Jonathan was, not at the time. Not until Jonathan was knee-deep in hot water, got drunk as a skunk, and told Reed his real relationship to Douglas Berkley. Reed was stunned, but he hadn't had time to dwell on it. He'd been too busy saving Jonathan's ass. As it turned out, he'd had to save it twice.

There'd been no strings attached. Still, Reed's actions had paid off—big. A recommendation from Douglas had placed him head and shoulders above the other equally brilliant Harvard Law grads competing for an opportunity. He'd seized his chance with both hands, walking through the doors of this prestigious firm determined to realize the future he'd busted his tail for. He could make it work, without compromising the values he'd been brought up to believe in. He was sure of it. He'd represent high-powered, influential people—and he'd do it ethically, in a way in which he could live with himself and make his family proud.

So much for that fairy-tale crap.

Ten years into the profession, he sometimes wondered if he himself could separate truth from lies, or if he was as desensitized as his clients.

The pressure to win, the pumping adrenaline that took over in the courtroom, the dangling carrot of a partnership—it had all but eclipsed the man he'd once been.

Well, no more.

Reed had had it. He wanted out.

Not out of the legal profession. Out of the win-at-all-costs callousness that defined the high-stakes world of Harter, Randolph & Collins.

He wanted to open his own practice, one that was small and selective. He'd accumulated more than enough money and contacts to do it. His goal was to represent clients he felt a connection to rather than those who were well connected. It would be a general, not a criminal defense, practice. That way, he could build relationships with his clients. And the diversity would be refreshing after so many years of specializing in criminal law. As for teaming up with other attorneys, either as partners or as counsel to the firm, he had a few names in mind, lawyers whose skills would complement his and broaden the firm's credibility and expertise. He'd pursue those people when the time was right.

But first he had to approach the powers that be at Harter, Randolph & Collins. He owed them that. Particularly Harter, his mentor, to whom he'd confided his growing ambivalence and thoughts of leaving. It wasn't going to be fun. Plus, once he opened this can of worms, there was no turning back.

A knock on the door brought Reed's thoughts back to the present, and he turned. "Come in."

"Hello, Reed." Douglas Berkley preceded Jonathan into the room, his presence as commanding as it had been a dozen years ago. He was a business giant.

"Douglas. Jonathan." Reed moved forward to shake their hands—Douglas's first, then Jonathan's. "Have a seat." He gestured at the chairs facing his desk. "Can I offer you something?"

"We're fine." Douglas was ready to get started, his elbow propped on the chair arm as he regarded Reed intently. "Jonathan tells me you handled the situation?"

Reed nodded. "Sorry I sounded so cryptic," he said to Jonathan. "But I wanted to finalize things before I got into all the specifics."

Jonathan leaned forward, gripping his knees. "I wasn't offended. I was curious. What happened?"

Lowering himself into his chair, Reed took the signed contract, slid it across the desk for them to see. "She signed."

Douglas released a sigh of relief. "Excellent. That's everyone. Now we can finally put this behind us." A quizzical look. "You wrote the check from the escrow account?"

"It's done. I messengered it over to Joseph. Taylor Halstead plans to sign it over to an organization that her cousin Stephanie supported."

"That's no surprise," Douglas said with a shrug.

"Reed." Jonathan's mind was exactly where Reed knew it would be. "Let's get back to Taylor Halstead. Obviously, you talked her into signing. Did she tell you why she was holding back, and why she lost it when she saw me?"

"Yes." Reed rolled a pen between his fingers. "To begin with, she had a pretty low opinion of Gordon—*and* a good idea that he was ripping off his investors."

Douglas's eyes narrowed. "Does she have evidence?"

"No." Reed shook his head. "She knows you're making good on the losses. And Gordon's dead. She's not interested in delving any deeper into his actions, believe me."

"Good."

"And the rest?" Jonathan pressed.

Reed tossed down the pen, stared straight at them. "It seems on that last night, Gordon stopped by the apartment Taylor shared with her cousin. Stephanie wasn't there. Taylor was. Gordon assaulted her."

"Goddammit." Douglas turned away, rubbing the back of his neck in obvious revulsion.

"He raped her?" Jonathan's expression didn't change.

"Fortunately not. Stephanie came home and buzzed from the lobby. Gordon took off with her for the heliport. He left Taylor handcuffed to the bed and unconscious."

"This gets more sickening by the minute." Douglas rose, walking over to pour himself some water. "How bad were her injuries?"

Reed eyed his client frankly. "I don't know. She wasn't eager to supply details. I do know she reported the assault, but the investigation was dropped after the boat explosion."

"So the cops know about this."

"There's a police record, yeah." Just as he'd anticipated, Reed could feel himself getting pissed off. Never mind that a woman had been assaulted. Protect the family name, and the business.

As always, he kept his personal feelings hidden. "Douglas, I wouldn't worry about it. Taylor's complaint is in a file marked 'closed' somewhere at the police precinct. There's no chance the story's going to end up in *Newsweek*."

Douglas didn't reply. He just stared into his glass.

"Did Taylor tell you that?" Jonathan asked.

"She told me she wanted to put what happened behind her. She has no grievances with either of you. So the contract is signed and you can move forward on dissolving the partnership. Problem solved."

"This time." Douglas gulped down the rest of his water, then set down his glass with a thud. "I'm sure Gordon has left other surprises for us. I gave that boy every advantage I could. It still wasn't enough."

Reed chose his words carefully. "There are other factors involved in forming character, Douglas. Some are within your control. Others aren't."

Douglas shot him a look. "You think I should have gone public right away? Why? Do you think announcing to the world that Gordon and Jonathan are my sons would have changed the outcome?"

"Sure it would have," Jonathan muttered. "Adrienne would have walked out on you years ago."

"That's not the point," Douglas countered. "Not in this case. I'm asking Reed if he thinks Gordon would have turned out differently if I'd publicly acknowledged him."

"I don't know," Reed replied truthfully. "What I meant was that sometimes people are born with character flaws that can't be blamed on their parents."

"Yeah. Biology, environment, and the luck of the draw." Jonathan's tone was flat. "In any case, let's not ask for trouble. Reed fixed things. Let's move on." He leaned back, hands folded in his lap. "How long were you with Taylor?"

Reed shrugged. "An hour or so. We had a cup of coffee."

"At Starbucks?"

"At her apartment."

"Really." A flicker of annoyance. "That must have been relaxing."

"It wasn't." Reed grabbed the bull by the horns. "Thanks to Gordon, Taylor's a nervous wreck in her own home. I'm going back to give her some self-defense lessons."

A few seconds of silence ticked by.

Then Jonathan cleared his throat. "Whose idea was that?"

"Mine. But Taylor was all for it."

"It's a good idea." Douglas jumped in, giving Reed an approving nod. "It'll build goodwill, and leave a hell of a better taste in her mouth when it comes to my family than the one Gordon left."

"I agree." Reed was looking at Douglas, but he was speaking to Jonathan. "Even though it's been a few months, her emotions are still very raw. Any reminder of Gordon is bad news."

"I can imagine." Douglas's lips thinned into a grim line. "Do whatever you have to to win her over."

This time Reed looked straight at Jonathan, his message loud, clear, and unmistakable. "I intend to."

11:50 A.M.

Reed sat quietly at his desk after Douglas and Jonathan had left. Jonathan was pissed. But it was Douglas's reaction that Reed couldn't shake. *Win her over. Make Gordon's actions a distant memory. Keep the goodwill flowing so this woman doesn't represent a potential fly in the ointment.*

Reed had had all he could stomach.

Leaning forward, he pressed his secretary's intercom button.

"Yes, Mr. Weston?" she replied.

"Cathy, find out if either Mr. Randolph or Mr. Collins are free. I need to speak with them. It's important."

"Yes, sir."

Three minutes later, she buzzed him back. "Mr. Randolph is in his office. He'll see you now. Mr. Collins is on his way back from court. He'll join you when he arrives."

"Thanks."

Reed shoved back his chair and stood up. Time to do what he'd been putting off doing for far too long.

He felt better already.

CHAPTER 9

TAYLOR parked her car in the designated area closest to the private cluster of trees that marked the Halstead family plot. She still had a healthy trek to Steph's grave. But she didn't mind. The walk would give her time to compose herself.

She hated coming here, staring at the spartan headstone that was carved with Steph's name, her all-too-brief twenty-seven-year life span, and the requisite phrase: "beloved daughter." It said so little about who Steph was, her life and her death.

But today was special. And Taylor felt compelled to commemorate it.

She gathered up the gift she'd brought, slammed her car door, and began to walk.

The sun was hovering on the horizon, a fiery ball in the western sky, as Taylor made her way across the frozen ground, the grass still covered with patches of snow from a storm earlier this week. She pulled her coat closer around her. The temperature was dropping. But Taylor had purposely chosen this time to drive up here. She wanted to be alone.

Quiet permeated the cemetery grounds as she reached her destination. As always, her heart gave a tight twist when she reached the grave. This was the hardest part. A final resting place where Steph wasn't resting. Her body had been blown to bits. Buried here was just an expensive mahogany casket purchased by Frederick and Candace Halstead, symbolically filled by Taylor. The wildly expensive, funky watch Steph had wanted for months and Taylor had bought her when she got into Tisch. The stuffed panda bear Steph had slept with at boarding school and that still sat on her bed. The frayed copy of *Pippi Longstocking* she'd kept on her bookshelf. Ticket stubs from two of her favorite Broadway shows. And the purple cashmere sweater she almost always wore to auditions—her lucky charm, as she used to call it.

Ironic. She hadn't been wearing it at that last audition, but she'd gotten the part anyway—even though she'd never known it. But lucky? No. Maybe if she'd been wearing the damned sweater, she'd have been detained at the audition for so long that Gordon's boat would have left without her and—

Taylor gazed down at the ground. Obviously, her aunt and uncle had been here recently; there was an elegant floral arrangement gracing Steph's headstone. Taylor took it all in for a long, silent moment. Then she bent down, placing the delicately wrapped bouquet of silk roses on the grave. A dozen of them in shimmering red. You'd never know they were silk. They looked as real as if they'd come off a rosebush.

But they hadn't. Real flowers died. These would last forever.

"It's opening night, Steph," she murmured. "I'm so proud of you. You busted your tail, and you got the part. You would have stolen the show. These are for you. They're for all the opening nights and all the standing ovations I know you would have basked in." A hard swallow. "I miss you, Steph."

With a long-drawn-out sigh, she sat back on her heels. This whole thing still seemed so surreal. A manicured plot. A peaceful, natural setting. An unfair, untimely, and violent death.

She didn't need this sanctified environment to feel close to her cousin. Not a day went by that Steph wasn't with her—she'd hear the song "Memory" from *Cats* on the radio, smell hot chocolate with whipped cream at Starbucks, glimpse two friends laughing together as they walked out of Pookie & Sebastian—all those things would trigger snippets of memory.

And a heavy sense of loss.

She was still tormented by the feeling that she should have done more to prevent this.

That part would never go away.

"I should have stopped you," she said aloud. "I knew Gordon was trouble. I should've shoved that down your throat. I tried—but not hard enough. I'm sorry."

There was nothing more to say.

Shivering, Taylor pulled out her leather gloves and slipped them on. "I'm going to head back to the city now." A bittersweet smile touched her lips as she imagined what her cousin's reply would be. "No, I don't have a date," she supplied. "Not tonight. Tonight I have paperwork to do. But tomorrow I have a self-defense lesson from a very complex and intriguing Park Avenue lawyer. Yes, he's great-looking. You'd say he was a hottie. For now, he's just an acquaintance. I'll let you know if that changes . . ." A shaky pause. "If I'm capable of letting it change."

Blinking back tears, Taylor started to rise.

A twig snapped behind her.

Her head jerked up. She leaped to her feet and whipped around, her senses immediately on high alert.

She scanned the area.

Nothing. Nothing but the descending shadows of dusk.

Even as she told herself that, she had the oddest feeling she was being watched. It crept through her like a dark, ugly specter. And, no matter how hard she tried, she couldn't shake it.

Her breath came faster. She was imagining things. She had to be. This was a wooded area. The noise she heard must have been a bird or a squirrel.

She'd just about convinced herself when there was a rustle from the nearby cluster of trees. Her gaze followed the sound, and she spotted a shadowy form moving among them.

A human form.

Fear gripped her. "Who's there?" she called out.

Silence.

"*I said, who's there?*" She was already starting to back away, her heart slamming against her ribs.

Footsteps thudded in the grass. Footsteps headed in her direction.

Taylor took off.

Panting, she dashed across the grounds, using the last filaments of daylight to find her way back to her car.

The footsteps drew near. Grew louder. Taylor slipped on a patch of ice. She caught herself before she fell, regaining her balance and sprinting on, cursing herself for the seconds she'd lost.

She fumbled for her car key as soon as the coupe came into view. Pulling the key out of her pocket, she aimed it at the car and pressed the button that unlocked the doors and disengaged the alarm.

A few rhythmic chirps and headlight flashes let her know she'd made contact. She was almost there. Just another ten feet or so and she'd be home free.

She reached the coupe, yanking at the door handle, half expecting someone to grab her from behind.

It was then she realized that the footsteps had ceased. The cemetery was eerily quiet.

Where was her pursuer?

She wasn't waiting to find out.

Scrambling into the driver's seat, she locked the doors, her breath coming in ragged pants as she stabbed the key into the ignition.

Abruptly, she heard the muffled sounds of someone running—not toward her, but away.

She twisted around, peering in that direction, trying to make out something tangible in the dusky sky.

A flash of movement caught her eye. A figure darting toward the gates. Obviously not another mourner.

It vanished.

Whoever he was, he was gone.

Trembling violently, she leaned back against the headrest.

Damn. She thought she'd gotten beyond this. But there it was. That sense of helplessness.

She drew in a sharp breath, trying to slow her breathing and the racing of her heart. *Stop it*, she commanded herself. *This wasn't personal. Maybe the guy had relatives here, or a thing for hanging around cemeteries. Maybe he'd seen an easy target and gone after it to try to score some quick cash.*

Maybe.

But then why hadn't he approached her while she was kneeling at the grave, rather than waiting till she saw him and then chasing after her?

Most of all, why couldn't she shake the feeling that he'd been there the whole time she was?

Watching her.

FEBRUARY 2

10:30 A.M.

WEST SEVENTY-SECOND STREET

Taylor didn't sleep a wink that night. She got up at dawn, busying herself by setting up cartons and packing up her kitchen appliances. She wasn't moving until March 1. But she needed to be busy.

She was standing on a step stool, taking down mixing bowls, when her doorman buzzed to announce Reed's arrival. She scooted off the stool and over to the intercom, advising Harry to send Reed up.

Three minutes later, he knocked.

"Hi," she said, a trifle breathless as she opened the door.

"Hi, yourself." His brows rose as he took in her disheveled state, her dark red hair pulled back in a scrunchie, her T-shirt and Lycra pants already damp. "Looks like you got started without me."

"What? Oh, no." She gave a self-conscious laugh, realizing how rumpled she must look. "I was packing."

"Already? That's pretty ambitious." Reed unzipped his parka and hung it on the hook. He was wearing black sweats, which made him look ruggedly sexy. The L.L. Bean side of him was obviously as striking as the Brooks Brothers side.

"I guess I'm just a get-it-done kind of person," Taylor replied, keeping her tone light.

Reed's gaze narrowed, and he studied her intently. "Are you okay?"

"Yes. Why? Do I look that awful?"

He wasn't sidetracked by her typically female question. In fact, his expression told her he knew it wasn't typical—not in her case. It was an attempt to dodge the question he had asked.

"I'm not taking the bait," he informed her. "This isn't about your physical attributes. It's about how exhausted you look, like you didn't shut an eye last night. And it's about the fact that I think this burst of energy stems from tension, not from a determination to get a jump-start on your packing."

Taylor's brows rose, and she folded her arms across her chest. "I'm beginning to wonder if there's as much difference between law and psychology as I thought."

A corner of his mouth lifted. "Probably not. Reading people is the foundation of both our professions. Now, do you want to tell me what's wrong, or is it none of my business?"

"Yesterday was February first," she explained simply. "It would have been Steph's opening night. I went to the cemetery to commemorate the occasion. I guess the experience was rougher on me than I expected."

Reed nodded. "I can understand that. Would you rather postpone our lesson?"

"No." Taylor wished she hadn't blurted out the refusal so quickly and adamantly. "I've already canceled on you twice," she hurried on, seeing curiosity flicker in his eyes. "Tuesday night I was held up at the radio station, and Thursday we got walloped with that snowstorm, not to mention you were in a meeting till midnight. The truth is, the weekend's really the best time for both of us. My energy level is higher in the morning, and neither of us has to be at work—do we?" she asked quizzically, realizing that Reed might very well put in Saturday and Sunday hours.

"Nope. Not today." He gestured toward the living room. "Shall we?"

Taylor followed him in. "I've got a dozen bottles of water in the fridge. We can grab them as needed."

Reed began to laugh. "Don't sound so grim. I'm not going to put you through military maneuvers. This is just basic stuff. If my nieces, who are eight, nine, eleven, and twelve, can handle it, so can you."

"Don't be too sure. Kids are a lot more elastic than adults." Taylor stopped in the center of the living room and turned to face him. "What made you learn self-defense?"

"My brother Rob's a cop. He's a stickler for safety, especially when it comes to his family."

"Are any of your nieces or nephews his?"

"Nope. He and I are the only single Westons left. I was in law school when he was getting his tactical training, and Cambridge was close enough for me to get home a lot. So I was around a lot more than the rest of the crew. Learning self-defense took the edge off studying twenty-four/seven. Rob taught me as he learned."

"And you passed that knowledge on to your other family members, particularly the female ones."

"Uh-huh." One dark brow rose. "So, do I meet the criteria? Do I get the job?"

Taylor laughed. "Sorry, I didn't mean to interrogate you. I just find this aspect of your life fascinating. Frankly, I've never had the experience of a big, close-knit family. I'd love to hear more—after I've mastered a few basic skills."

"How about we make it an incentive?" Reed sounded half teasing, half serious. "For each technique you master, I'll tell you about one of my siblings."

"And if I'm a quick study? Can we move on to your nieces and nephews?"

"Sure. But only if we order up lunch. With that much talking, I'll need sustenance."

"Fair enough." Taylor was finding the lighthearted banter a welcome relief. It seemed so . . . normal, like a balm after yesterday's creepy episode. "I'm ready."

"Good." Reed sobered, looking more like the all-business guy she'd met two weeks ago in his office. "We're going to start by helping you develop a sense of distance. We'll experiment with long, middle, and close range until you're able to maintain exactly the distance you want without thinking about it. After that, we'll move on to circling. Both those skills are essential. Once you've developed them, we'll go over some basic intercepting techniques. Later, I'll introduce some attack techniques, and an acronym to help you remember them. Okay?"

"Okay." Taylor nodded, wondering if there was anything Reed Weston wasn't proficient at. No wonder he was skyrocketing his way to the top at Harter, Randolph & Collins.

She was actually looking forward to this—both the outcome and the process.

An hour and a half later, she wasn't so sure.

She was exhausted, more mentally than physically, having spent a good portion of the time training her mind to issue instant commands and her body to simultaneously follow them. The coordination and timing were more difficult to master than the maneuvers.

"That's it." Wearily, Taylor dropped onto the overstuffed couch they'd shoved against the living-room wall to maximize the open floor space. "Between the strategizing and the circling, I'm starting to feel like a hawk. A very tired, very dizzy hawk."

Reed strolled over, grinning. Damn if the man didn't look as collected as if he'd just walked out of a meeting, with only the barest sheen of perspiration on his brow, and his breathing as even as a yoga instructor's.

"I could grow to hate you," Taylor muttered.

"Nah." His grin widened. "Because not only am I going to help you feel more empowered, I'm going to provide you with sustenance. Stay put. I'll call and order up some sandwiches. And when I return, I'll bring two cold bottles of water."

"Okay, maybe 'hate's' too strong a word. Maybe I'll just resent you." She shot a dirty look in his direction. "Couldn't you at least break a decent sweat? Or don't you do that?"

"Oh, I do that." There was no mistaking the wicked gleam in Reed's eye. "Just during more strenuous workouts than the one we just shared."

Taylor felt herself flush. She'd asked for that one. "Cute. Very cute. Getting back to the subject, I'd like a roast beef on rye with the works and a big fat sour pickle. While you order I'll start thinking of all the things I want to know about your family."

"Sounds like a plan. Be right back."

Forty minutes later, they were sitting at the kitchen counter, munching on their sandwiches and gulping down their water.

"Time to talk about your family," Taylor reminded him.

"Shoot."

"You said there were seven of you. Where do you fall in the ranking?"

"Fifth." Reed put down his turkey club. "Why don't I give you an overview? It'll save time, and answer your first round of questions."

"Okay." Taylor put down her food, too.

"Going oldest to youngest, we'll start with my sister Lisa. She's thirty-nine. She and her husband, Bill, live in Phoenix. She's a teacher; he's a high-school administrator. They've got two kids, Shari and Katie, who are twelve and nine. I'll save my bragging about them for later, when we get to the nieces-and-nephews chapter of my life; otherwise we'll never get through this list."

Taking a deep swallow of water, Reed continued. "Next is Kyle. He's thirty-eight. He's a crackerjack salesman at his wife Joy's family's car dealership in Cleveland. They've got twin sons, Jake and Scott, who are ten. Third comes Shannon. She's thirty-seven. She and her husband, Roger, are both techno-whizzes. They work in the IT department of a company out in Denver. Their daughter, April, is eight."

Another gulp of water and a breath. "Mark's thirty-six. He and his wife, Jill, are still in New England. They own a ski lodge in New Hampshire. Their kids, Kimberly and David, are eleven and seven. Then comes me. After that, there's Meredith, who's thirty-four. She's a natural-born mother. She and her husband, Derek, have two sons, Craig and Andy, and a third one on the way. They live in Dallas, since Derek works for the city. Meredith makes the most amazing cookies you've ever tasted. She's got a small baking business that she runs from home. Those lucky Texans. Last, but not least, there's Rob, who I've already told you about. He's the baby. He's thirty-two and a detective in the San Francisco police department. When he decides to settle down, hearts are going to break all over the West Coast. How's that for starters?"

Taylor's head was reeling. "Wow. That's pretty impressive. You weren't kidding when you said there were Westons scattered all over the country. What about your parents? You said they're still living in Vermont?"

"Yup. In the big, old stone farmhouse where we all grew up. They own a pottery store in town. They have for forty years. My mom loves to sculpt. She makes the pieces for the shop. They're beautiful and unusual. Not a tourist who drops in leaves empty-handed. Even the year-round residents still buy pieces. She's very talented."

Reed's pride was obvious. So were his strong ties to his family.

"I envy you," Taylor said wistfully. "It must be amazing to have so many caring people in your life."

"It is." Reed stared thoughtfully at his sandwich. "I don't think I appreciated it enough as a kid. Or maybe I just thought that's how it was supposed to be. Not anymore."

Taylor watched his expression. "Do you mind if I ask you something personal?"

"Go ahead."

"The path you took—fast-track, high-powered, lots of money, and high visibility—it seems kind of incongruous with the rest of your family. What motivated you?"

"I did." Reed propped an elbow on the counter. "I had a more high-profile plan for my future, complete with all the things you just mentioned. I had the academic ability to get scholarship money and financial aid. I took advantage of it. And here I am."

There was an edge to Reed's tone, one Taylor hadn't expected.

"You're not happy with your decision?"

He shot her a look. "Am I being analyzed?"

"No, just questioned. You don't have to answer."

"Let's just say I'm doing a little restructuring of my life, based on months of soul-searching and reconnecting with some strong, solid values I'd begun losing touch with. Going home for Christmas brought the whole thing front and center for me. It drove home some fundamental truths I'd been struggling to find, or maybe just to remember."

The way Reed said that brought a new and not very welcome thought to Taylor.

"These truths and restructuring, do they involve a woman?" she asked cautiously.

He turned to face her, his midnight gaze intensifying as he realized what she was asking and why. Slowly, he shook his head, his focus shifting to the here and now. "Nope. No woman." A meaningful pause. "At least not yet."

The tension in the room escalated, its foundation steeped in something far more immediate than Taylor had anticipated. She'd opened this door on her own. The problem was, she wasn't sure she was equipped to walk through it.

That didn't mean she didn't want to.

"I'm glad," she heard herself say, responding to both parts of the equation.

"Are you?"

"Yes."

"Good. So am I." He stood up, pulling her to her feet as he did. He tugged her closer, tipped up her chin, and kissed her.

The kiss was explicit, sexually charged, yet not overpowering. Reed took her mouth in gradual degrees, his palm massaging the back of her neck as his lips opened hers and his tongue slid inside, lightly caressing. It was as if he was intentionally holding back, determined to take only as much as she was willing, or emotionally ready, to give.

She didn't know what she was ready for. But she knew this felt better than anything had felt in a very long time.

She moved closer, gripping Reed's biceps and tilting back her head to give him better access. He took the cue, pulling her against him, nudging her arms up around his neck, then slanting his mouth across hers and kissing her senseless. It was a wildly erotic awakening, hot and slow and shivering with promise.

Maybe too much promise.

Taylor flattened her palms against his chest and pushed, her breathing uneven as she put an arm's length between them, trying to regain her equilibrium.

Reed made no move to pull her back. He just watched her, his own breathing unsteady. "Should I apologize?"

Mutely, she shook her head.

This time, he stepped closer, capturing her chin with his forefinger and bringing up her gaze to meet his. "Are you sure?"

"Yes." Taylor found her voice. "Of course I'm sure. You didn't just kiss me. I kissed you, too."

His expression remained solemn. "I know. That doesn't mean you're not regretting it now. You've got lingering memories of this kind of thing that aren't exactly pleasant."

She wasn't as much surprised by his sensitivity as she was touched. "Nothing about what just happened reminded me of Gordon. And, no, I'm not feeling regret. I'm feeling confused and off balance."

"And you like being in control."

"Not of others, but of myself, yes."

"I can relate to that." Reed picked up his bottle of water and took a swig. "So we'll go slow," he determined, setting down the bottle. "For now."

Taylor's brows rose. "For now? What does that mean?"

"It means, until we speed it up."

"And when will that be?"

"When you're ready." His knuckles brushed her cheek. "Don't worry. There won't be any miscommunications. I'll be able to tell." A corner of his mouth lifted. "And, if I'm wrong, you can always use some of the intercepting techniques I'll be teaching you on me. You'll be a pro by then."

Taylor laughed. The laughter felt almost as good as the kiss.

THE MAN STOOD OUTSIDE, across Seventy-second Street, ostensibly pausing to check his watch. He glanced up at Taylor's apartment building, a bitter glint in his eyes.

Reed Weston had been up there for hours. That was unacceptable. It wasn't part of his plan. No man was. Not Reed, not anyone. Only him. He'd have to deal with this. Before things got out of hand.

Turning up the collar on his coat, he walked away.

12:45 A.M.

Considering how exhausted she was, Taylor thought she'd fall right asleep. After zero shut-eye last night, a strenuous self-defense lesson with Reed, and the unexpected follow-up to that lesson—well, all that constituted enough physical and mental activity to make her assume she'd be dead to the world.

No such luck.

Sighing, she sat up in bed, pulling up her knees and wrapping her arms around them. Talk about emotional complications. Reed Weston was a huge one. He'd come along at a time when she was vulnerable. That was bad. And she was attracted as hell to him. That was worse. If they got involved, there was every chance it would be for all the wrong reasons.

Reed had said they'd take it slow—until they took it fast. That was as ambiguous as it was unsettling.

She just wished she knew the rules. Every relationship had them. Usually, she defined them. In this case, they seemed to be defining her.

God, this was so unlike her. In-control Taylor. Take-care-of-everything-and-everyone Taylor. Emotions-safely-under-wraps Taylor.

Unraveling-like-a-ball-of-yarn Taylor.

She pressed her fingertips to her throbbing temples, trying to massage away the pain and the insomnia.

Yeah, right.

It was no wonder she couldn't sleep. She was on emotional overload. Not only that, she couldn't stop thinking about that bizarre, frightening incident at the cemetery on Saturday. Had the guy really just been an eccentric visitor, some sleazy weirdo, or had he been there specifically for her?

This speculation was pointless. The guy was gone. The incident was over. She was blowing things way out of proportion.

THE TELEPHONE RANG. Shrilly. Insistently.

Taylor jolted awake, her entire body breaking out in a sweat. The digits on her clock radio said 3:55 A.M. The last time she'd been awakened by a middle-of-the-night phone call was when Gordon's boat exploded and Steph died.

She flipped on her lamp and stared at the telephone's LCD display. It read "private." Just like last time.

Trembling, she lifted the receiver. "Hello?"

"You're alone." A strange male voice, its pitch fluctuating unnaturally, grazed her ear. "Good girl. Keep it that way—for everyone's sake."

A click, and the line went dead.

CHAPTER 10

I T had been a crank call. It had to be.

Taylor told herself that for the hundredth time since last night. The voice had been disguised, fake. Its synthesized quality and varied pitch suggested it had been transmitted through one of those voice-changing gadgets—gadgets that were available to the general public and could be bought over the Internet for less than fifty bucks.

So maybe her caller had been a bunch of adolescent guys playing games. They could have punched in random telephone numbers, one of which happened to be hers. Then, when they heard a woman's voice, they'd decided to go for the dramatic.

Or maybe it had been Chris Young. Maybe he'd been going for payback for that talk she'd had with his parents two and a half weeks ago.

No. Impossible. Her telephone number was unlisted. Chris couldn't get it. Neither could anyone else. There wasn't any connection between the call and Saturday's incident at the cemetery. They were two unnerving, coincidental, but unrelated events.

Struggling out of her jacket, Taylor gave up the pretense. It was no use. No matter how hard she tried, how much logic she used, she couldn't calm her jitters.

She hadn't shut an eye the rest of the night. She'd lain awake, trembling, waiting to see if the caller would try again. He hadn't. But she couldn't relax. As a result, her attention span at school today had been lousy. To make matters worse, Chris Young had shot her an odd, searching look when she'd blown by him in the hall, her posture stiff, her expression glazed. Was he checking out the results of his handiwork?

God, she was a mess.

She made her way to the broadcasting booth. Passing by the operations department, she poked her head into the kitchen—where at least four staff members were gathered around a box of rapidly disappearing Krispy Kremes—long enough to offer a wave and an apologetic smile.

"Hi, guys. Sorry I'm late."

"Hey, no problem." Bill Warren, who handled *Sports Talk*, the two-hour radio spot directly preceding hers, shot her a lopsided grin. "I figured if you weren't here by seven, I'd do the show for you. I'd be a huge hit."

"Yeah, right." Jack Taft, the program manager, set down his coffee mug—which read #1 MANAGER OF THE STATION THAT TRIES HARDER—and made a snorting sound. "You'd lose half our listening audience by the time you took your first call."

"No way," Bill protested, his grin broadening. "I'm a real intuitive guy. Just ask around."

"That's not necessary," Taylor reassured him, forcing a smile. "Your reputation precedes you. You're a pussycat." She had to focus on business. She had a ton of work to cram into the hour before she went on the air. As it was, her e-mails would have to wait until afterward. That wasn't a hardship. It just meant she'd be leaving late. But, hey, she never slept anyway, so what difference did it make? As for whatever important paperwork was on tap, Laura would be in and out during radio breaks to brief her. For now, she needed to touch base with her producer. "Where's Kevin?" she asked.

"In the studio," Jack replied. "Waiting for you. He's already got a line of call-ins queued up. It's going to be a busy night."

"Good. The busier, the better. I'm not up for a monologue tonight."

The program manager shot her a sympathetic glance. "Tough weekend?"

"The toughest."

Jack respected that and dropped the subject. "Okay, enough chitchat.

Bill, break's over. You're back on in forty-five seconds. Taylor, grab a doughnut—or whatever's left of one—and head down to the booth."

Taylor gave him an appreciative look. "Is Rick around?"

"Yup. He's going over some audio details with Dennis." Dennis was a promising audio tech, a little shy, but being around this place for a while would change that. Besides, he had a few other newbies to commiserate with. Sally Carver was a perky blonde intern who was attending broadcasting school, hoping to get a jump start into the production end of the business. And James Birney was a freckled, charming guy with a degree in advertising who was working in sales, trying to help bring in new accounts.

As for Rick, he was just a great, all-around guy, who'd been having a tough time himself. His marriage was going down the tubes.

Taylor cleared her throat. "How's Rick doing? Are things any better?"

"Doesn't seem that way. He's not saying much."

"I'll go down there now." She glanced at the ravaged box of doughnuts, now a mass of crumbs and broken-off pieces, and rolled her eyes. "I'll pass on the snack." She headed off to her broadcasting booth, determined to maintain her newly established, if fragile, composure.

That resolution lasted less than a minute.

"Hi, Kev," Taylor greeted her producer as she walked through the door. "Sorry to cut things so close."

"Not to worry, at least not tonight," Kevin assured her, punching off whatever phone line he'd been talking on. "Tomorrow night, now that's another story. We've got a live guest scheduled. The author of *Bad Kids, Worse Parents*. She's a little on the schiz-y side. You'd better be here early to prep her."

"I remember. And I will. Promise."

Kevin's phone rang.

Taylor jumped as if she'd been stung.

Frowning, Kevin answered the call, scrutinizing Taylor as he dealt with the caller, asking the customary questions, getting what he needed, then queuing up the call.

"Do you want to tell me what that was about?" he demanded, swiveling his chair around to face Taylor.

She feathered a shaky hand through her hair. "What *what* was about?"

"Gimme a break. You just hit the ceiling at the sound of a ringing telephone. What's got you so freaked?"

"Life." Taylor gave a weary shrug. "I'm a basket case. 'Overreact' seems to be my middle name these days."

Before Kevin could respond, Rick walked in, followed by the new guy, Dennis, who was sorting through some disks.

He stopped behind Rick, who'd come to a halt and was scrutinizing Taylor.

"Hey." Rick's greeting was warm, but his smile didn't quite reach his eyes. He looked like hell, haggard and out of sorts. "I was getting worried about you. You're never this late."

"I know. I'm really sorry. It's been a rocky couple of days." Taylor refrained from saying more.

Dennis hesitated in the doorway, fidgeting from one sneakered foot to the other. "Rick, if you want, I'll leave these disks with you and sit in another night."

Rick inclined his head in Taylor's direction. "I told Dennis he could observe tonight's show, since it's just us and no guests."

"Absolutely." Taylor waved Dennis in. "Tonight's fine. Things are just crazy because I'm late. Grab a seat and watch Rick and Kevin work their magic. There's no one better in the business to learn from. Although if you were hoping for a doughnut, you can forget it. The last whole one disappeared into Bill's mouth a few minutes ago."

"You've got to be kidding." Rick grimaced. "That's a record, even here. That box lasted ten minutes."

"I'll pick up some more," Dennis offered. "That'll give you guys a few minutes to get started before I start bugging you with questions. Be back in ten." He ducked out of the room.

Rick eyed Taylor with concern. "The tension in here's so thick, it's like walking onto a soap-opera set. What's up?"

"We were just getting to that when you walked in," Kevin informed him. "My phone rang and Taylor flipped out."

"Why?"

Both guys stared at Taylor, waiting expectantly for an explanation.

She sighed. "Look, a few things happened over the weekend that threw me. Can we just leave it at that?"

"No." Rick didn't mince words. "What things? Did that lawyer who's teaching you self-defense try something? Did he come on to you? Is that what this is about?"

"No." The ironic part was that what had happened between her and Reed had turned out to be the highlight of her weekend. "There was just some creep hanging around the cemetery when I visited Steph's grave on Saturday. He came after me. I ran back to my car, and he took off. Probably a mugger who changed his mind. Still, the whole thing spooked me. To top that off, I got a crank call last night. Some weirdo on a voice changer who told me to keep sleeping alone. I guess the two things combined were a little too much."

"Taylor." Rick wasn't ready to let this go. "You're pretty levelheaded. Did you feel like that guy at the cemetery and the one on the phone were the same person?"

"My common sense says no. But my emotions are another story. So, yes, the whole thing got to me. As for the phone call, what made it worse is that it brought back memories of when that detective called to tell me about the boat explosion—" Taylor broke off. "Look, guys, can we not talk about this anymore? I'd rather concentrate on the show. It'll give me something tangible and normal to focus on, which will calm me down. Okay?"

"Yeah, okay." Kevin shot a quick glance at Rick, who was frowning. "Go in and get settled. Laura's on her way up. Just so you know, the first few calls I've got queued up are typical Monday nighters—we've got two rocky relationships and one Saturday-night date that went south."

Nodding, Taylor disappeared into the studio.

Rick flipped on the audio controls, speaking to Kevin without glancing his way. "I don't like the way that sounds."

"No. Me either," Kevin agreed. "So let's keep on our toes—just in case."

"Done."

Rick cut the conversation short as the door opened and Dennis walked in, a box of doughnuts in his hands.

"Pull up a chair," Rick said, waving him over. "The teenage angst is about to begin." He grimaced, his mind taking a brief detour. "Which is nothing compared to the adult angst that lies ahead for these lucky adolescents."

Taylor finished off her bottle of Poland Spring as the commercials on the half hour came to an end and the WVNY jingle sounded. Her thirst was quenched, her mouth and throat were moist, and she was ready to address the next caller.

She glanced at her computer screen, where the calls were queued up. As always, Kevin had typed in some key phrases to prepare her. The first line read: *Fred. Young guy in high school. Has it bad for a girl in one of his classes. Can't find a way to tell her. Definitely can't confide in his parents.*

A wistful smile touched Taylor's lips. Yeah, she remembered those awkward days.

She punched up the call. "Welcome back, everyone. This is Taylor Halstead, ready to take your calls. Fred, I understand there's someone special—someone you'd like to get to know better."

"I already know her," he replied in a voice Taylor instantly recognized. It was Romeo.

"In fact, I know her better than she thinks," he continued. "Like tonight, for instance. Tonight of all nights, I know she's superstressed and needs to unwind. I want to take her out for dessert. How about it, Taylor? Eleven o'clock?"

Taylor's heart began slamming against her ribs. Kevin and Rick had both gone pale, and Kevin reached over to disconnect the call.

With a hard shake of her head, Taylor stopped him. "I appreciate the invitation, Fred," she said, speaking as calmly as she could. "But I'm only available on counseling matters and, even then, only during airtime. I'm sure there's someone in your school who'd love to go out with you. Give her a call. I wish you luck."

Taylor could hear him cajoling as she hung up.

Kevin flipped to commercial. Then he keyed up the mike, his jaw tightening as he saw her bury her face in her hands. "Dammit, Taylor, I'm sorry. The son of a bitch disguised his voice. He's never tried that one before. He's also never called himself Fred. It's always been Romeo."

"Yeah, well, he picked a lousy night to get creative."

"I know. And I picked a lousy night to screw up. Regardless, it was just a coincidence. A harmless come-on. Don't let your imagination run wild." Kevin blew out a self-deprecating breath. "You can slug me after the show. I really blew it."

Slowly, Taylor raised her head. "It's not your fault," she assured him. "We all know that if someone wants to get through badly enough, they'll find a way to make it happen."

"Yeah, well, it won't be happening again."

Taylor stared blankly ahead, apprehension shimmering through her. "How did he know that I was superstressed?" she murmured. "What was it he said—that tonight, of all nights, I needed to unwind? How did he know that?"

"It's a line, Taylor." Kevin had already signaled for a prerecorded disk to be brought in, should it be needed. But he intended to calm her down. The best thing for her right now was to continue with the show.

"A line?" she repeated dubiously.

"Yeah, guys use it all the time. Romeo or Fred or whatever his name is has used it before. Every night is *the* night for him. I've told you that. He wants to go out with you. And he's dense enough to believe he can make it happen. Sure, he's a space cadet. But he's not a wacko. None of the signs are there. No psycho threats, no weird sexual references, no personal, inside knowledge about you or your life."

Taylor nodded. "True."

"I realize this is the last thing you needed to happen tonight," Kevin added in a soothing tone. "But put it in perspective. Nothing the guy said was new. It was the same old, same old. His usual come-on. So his timing sucked. Don't let it get to you."

"You're right." Taylor shot her producer a weak smile before glancing at the lineup of calls on her screen. "Are you sure *you're* not the counselor here?"

"Positive." He grinned. "I just learned from a pro. Now the commercial's ending. Grab that mike and do your stuff."

"Nice job," Rick commented once the communication line between the two rooms had been shut off.

"Yeah," Kevin muttered back. "Now let's hope everything I said is true."

Rick gave a tight nod, adjusting the audio controls. "If Romeo happens to call again—"

"I'll recognize whatever voice or name he uses," Kevin finished. "I'll grill the hell out of the guy. And if I get the slightest vibe that he's anything but a lonely, innocent nerd who's hot for Taylor, I'll call the cops and have them put a trace on the call."

"Good." Rick studied Taylor through the glass, a troubled expression on his face. "It's best not to take chances."

10:45 P.M.

Laura poked her head into the small, cluttered office one floor down from the broadcast studios that Taylor used to answer e-mails, catch up on re-search, and conduct preliminary phone interviews with upcoming guests.

"Hi." Taylor looked surprised to see her. "I thought you'd gone home."

"I wanted to check on you."

"I'm fine."

"Good." Laura cleared her throat. "Look, I know you said you didn't want me to transfer any calls through to you, but there's a guy on the phone. It's *not* Romeo," she added hastily, seeing Taylor go rigid. "His name is Reed Weston. It's the third time he's called in the past twenty minutes. I asked him what it's about, but all he'll say is that it's personal. He sounds perfectly normal. Do you want to take it, or should I blow him off?"

The relief that swept through Taylor was staggering. "I'll take the call," she told Laura. "You go on home. And thanks for being such a great guard dog." She waited until Laura had complied, then lifted the receiver and punched the flashing button. "Hi."

"Hi, yourself." There was light static accompanying his voice. He was obviously on a cell phone. "Getting through to you is like getting through to a CIA operative. On top of that, don't you *ever* go home? And here I thought *I* was a workaholic."

Taylor smiled. "My assistant is very protective. Besides, I didn't real-ize you and I had made plans."

"We didn't. I made them for us. I want to see you. I've driven around the block so many times, the cops in the neighborhood squad car are giv-ing me the fish eye. I actually considered taking my chances and double-parking long enough to come up and get you."

"Right. And your Mercedes would be towed away three minutes later."

"Exactly. So give me a break and come out."

Massaging her temples, Taylor sighed. "Seriously, Reed, I'm not up for anything heavy tonight, certainly not a self-defense lesson. I can barely see straight."

"Nothing heavy. And no lesson. I just brought you a can of pepper spray for your purse. I'll trade it for a glass of wine at your place. Deal?"

God, that sounded good. A reprieve from the tension of the past few days and, yes, a chance to see Reed. "You're a good negotiator, Counselor. Deal. Give me five minutes to wrap up. I'll meet you wherever it's easiest."

"I'll crawl down Seventh. I'll pick you up right in front of your building. Near the streetlights and the security guard," he added pointedly.

"I'll be there."

CHAPTER 11

TEN minutes later, Taylor slid in next to Reed, shut the car door, and settled back with a sigh. "Normally, I'd be furious. I don't like people making decisions for me. But in this case, I'll make an exception."

Reed pulled away from the curb. Turning right, he headed west to Tenth Avenue, then north toward Taylor's apartment. "Normally, I don't make decisions for people. But I happened to tune in and catch a chunk of your radio show tonight."

"Ah, so you heard Romeo hit on me."

"Who?"

"Romeo. The guy who wanted to take me out for dessert. He's one of my regulars. Only this time he called himself Fred and got by Kevin." Taylor explained what had happened, along with the background on her amorous caller.

"No." Reed didn't look happy. "I missed Romeo's performance. I just picked up on something in your voice—a kind of edgy quality. I thought a glass of wine might help."

"It's been one of those days. Romeo was just the straw that broke the camel's back." Taylor slanted Reed a look. "By the way, I'm also not used to being so easily read."

"That part you'd better get used to. I admit you've established one hell of a facade. Me, too. One problem. We're unusually attuned to each other—or hadn't you noticed?"

"I noticed."

They were silent for the rest of the ride, but it was a companionable silence, not a strained one.

"You look pretty exhausted yourself," Taylor commented, once they were settled on her living room sofa with two glasses of Cabernet. "In fact, as long as we're being so up-front, I got the distinct feeling that the restructuring of your life you mentioned yesterday involves something major—something that's throwing you for a loop. Care to share? I'm a good listener."

He smiled. "No arguments there. I heard your listening skills on the air tonight. Unfortunately, none of your advice would work for me. I'm not a teenager anymore."

"That's interesting, because you're acting like one," she noted. "Evading my questions and my offer to help. Typical teenage behavior. I take it you don't want to open up."

Reed's smile vanished, and he sank back against the sofa cushion. He didn't look offended; he looked weary. "It's not that I don't want to. It's that I can't. Not yet. The situation is fluid. To discuss it would be unethical."

"Ah. It involves a client you're uncomfortable representing." Taylor took a sip of wine. "I imagine you've had a fair share of those."

"Too many." He reached into his jacket pocket, pulled out a can. "Here's the pepper spray I promised. It's still one of the best deterrents out there. Burns the assailant's eyes like hell, and gives you time to run and to scream for help."

"More peace of mind." Taylor gave him a grateful smile, taking the can and tucking it into her pocketbook. "Thank you."

"Taylor." Reed set down his wineglass. "We're not playing tit for tat. I can't get into what's going on with me. When I can, I will. Your predicament is different—and a lot more dire than mine, based on what I'm seeing. Tell me what's got you so upset. You're even more strung out now than when I saw you yesterday. And you look tired enough to collapse."

Taylor wished he weren't so damned insightful. "Reed, stop." She heard the ambivalence in her voice. "I hardly know you. It's a little soon to spill my guts."

"Fair enough. So who have you been spilling your guts to—your parents? Friends? Therapist?"

She knew where he was going with this. And she was too worn-out to play dodgeball. "My parents aren't the gut-spilling type. My friends are aware of the basics. And my therapist knows my state of mind only up through Thursday of last week. Satisfied?"

"No, just proven right. The bottom line is that you've confided in no one." Reed turned to face her. "Now, why doesn't that surprise me?"

"Because you see yourself?"

"Bingo." A pause. "At least tell me the basics—the part you told your friends."

The wine and the fatigue were mingling together, swirling slowly through Taylor's consciousness. Dulling her inhibitions. Lowering her reserves.

She polished off her Cabernet and put down her glass, twisting around to face Reed. "You want honesty? You got it. When I heard your voice on the phone tonight, I saw an opportunity for two things—to numb my fears with wine and to drown them out with physical pleasure. I leaped at both chances. I've got a low tolerance for alcohol, so one glass of wine, maybe two, and the numbing's a fait accompli. As for the drowning—that kiss we shared yesterday was amazing. Thinking about it was the only thing that got me through the past twenty-four hours. So . . ." She scrambled to her knees, tilting up her chin and leaning closer so their faces were practically touching. "The wine's right on track. What about you—are you game?"

He reached out, threaded his fingers through her hair, his palm gliding beneath to caress the nape of her neck. "You do realize you just announced that you're using me?"

"Mmm." Taylor's eyes slid shut, and she moved her head against his hand. "I'm not using you. I'm losing me."

"Does that mean I get to find you?" He pulled her onto his lap, lifting her arms around his neck.

"Tonight? Yes." She'd barely breathed the word when his mouth came down on hers, absorbing the sound with his lips. He slid one arm under her back and lifted her up and into the kiss, devouring her with a hungry intensity Taylor felt to the tips of her toes. She twisted closer, her breasts flattened against his chest, her breath emerging in short, shallow pants that mixed with his. His tongue slid inside, took hers in prolonged, erotic strokes.

Taylor heard herself moan. She went with the sensations, her heart slamming against her ribs, her entire body starting a slow burn that spread and intensified at an almost frightening rate.

She had no idea how long they sat there, kissing as if they wanted to consume each other. All she knew was that it felt wonderful, that *he* felt wonderful. His hand was under her sweater, massaging the bare skin of her back, but he made no move to unhook her bra, although his fingers paused there more than once. Nor did his lips leave hers, except to move to her neck, the pulse at her throat, and, finally, to feather soft kisses across her cheeks and nose before he raised his head.

Taylor's own head was spinning. She relaxed her grip around Reed's neck, sinking back on his lap and blinking as she gazed up at him. He was as winded as she, and a fine sheen of perspiration dotted his forehead.

He watched her from beneath hooded lids. "You okay?"

She nodded, licking her swollen lips. "I'm fine. You didn't have to—"

"Yes, I did," he interrupted. "Nothing else is happening. Not tonight. I told you slow. I meant it."

She searched his face. "You're an unusual man, Reed Weston."

"Not really. I'm crazed as hell to get inside you. But I have an ulterior motive for my patience. I'm determined to make you trust me. And that's not going to happen overnight—especially not if I rush you into bed. So I'll take things in increments, physically and emotionally." His fingers slid gently up and down her arms. "Talk to me. I'll settle for the basics, as you put it. What's got you so freaked out?"

Taylor released a sharp breath. She didn't want to descend to reality. She wanted to stay where she was, floating in the removed and exquisite pleasure of the past few minutes. But, as she so often told her students and callers, escape was no solution. Your problem either followed you wherever you went, or waited to sink its claws into you when you returned.

It was time to practice what she preached.

She told Reed about the incident at the cemetery on Saturday and about the disturbing phone call in the wee hours of Monday morning.

"My common sense tells me the two incidents were unconnected, that the whole thing's just an eerie coincidence, but—" She broke off, sliding to her feet and walking over to the window, staring out into the night sky.

"But?" Reed grilled her.

"But it's thrown me. I'm a mess. Suddenly everyone seems suspect.

I start shaking when guys flirt with me on the street, when my regulars-who-hit-on-me-for-a-date call the station; you name it. This kind of paranoid behavior is so unlike me, I can't tell you."

Reed rose, came to stand behind her. His hands were tense as he planted them on her shoulders, urging her around to face him. "Taylor, do you think you're being stalked?"

The straightforward question and the harsh expression on his face sent chills up her spine. "Not stalked," she replied, opting for the least ominous interpretation. "*Watched.* At least that's what my instincts say. But I'm not sure those instincts are objective—not in this case."

"Why?"

She paused before answering. "Let's say I have a heightened sensitivity when it comes to this issue."

"A heightened sensitivity. That means it relates to Gordon's assault."

She nodded.

"Go on."

"Okay. When Gordon left that day, he promised me he'd be back. He said we'd finish what we started. He cautioned me to be patient, to be good, and to be mindful. And, at the very end, he warned me that he'd be watching me. Those words, the brutal look in his eyes—those memories just won't go away."

A muscle flexed in Reed's jaw. "I can understand why—"

"There's more." Taylor met his gaze head-on. "I was pretty messed up by what happened. But I told myself that it was one sick, spontaneous incident, exacerbated by the fact that Gordon had been drinking. Then the holidays came. With them came two e-cards."

She went on to describe the creepy e-cards to Reed, keeping her tone as impassive as possible, although she was unable to keep the tremor out of her voice. "Even though I canceled my e-mail account, I still dread every holiday, wondering if there's some ominous e-card floating around in cyberspace. The feeling of violation never seems to go away."

Reed's jaw tightened another fraction. "So between the premeditated attack and the e-cards, it's no leap to assume he was fixated on you."

Taylor lowered her gaze and gave a humorless laugh. "Yes, but these past few days I find myself making a one-eighty. Given what's been going on, I'm actually praying Gordon *did* send those cards, and that we had proof to that effect. A leftover sense of violation beats the hell out of an ongoing sense of fear and vulnerability. What if those cards weren't from Gordon? What if his sexual assault wasn't a fixation, but just a one-shot deal? What if someone else sent those e-cards—someone who's alive, and still out there watching me and stalking me? It's happened to other on-air personalities. What if this time it's me? What if whoever's doing this is the one who was at the cemetery and the one who called me last night?"

"Hey." Reed cut off her escalating outburst, pulling her against him and wrapping her in a fierce, comforting embrace. He rubbed his chin slowly across the top of her head and frowned as he felt her tremble. As he stared out the window, his thoughts took a turn in an unpalatable direction—one he'd hoped never again to revisit. But he couldn't ignore it. The pattern was there.

The fixation. The mind games. The egocentric determination. The sense of imperviousness.

He couldn't say a word to Taylor. He had to check things out on his own first. Hopefully, what he learned would put his nagging concerns to rest.

If not, he'd be screwed. Talk about being crammed between the proverbial rock and the hard place.

He turned his attention back to Taylor and the challenge of doing what he could for her. "No wonder you're at the end of your rope," he murmured. "You're coping with a hell of a lot—and you're doing it alone."

Taylor didn't reply. She squeezed her eyes shut, breathing deeply. She was half relieved that she'd blurted out the whole twisted scenario, half appalled that she'd done so with a man she'd known less than a month—a man who had a much longer, stronger relationship with those closest to Gordon Mallory than he had with her.

Well, it was too late for regrets.

"That emotional outburst I just subjected you to was far more than I planned on," she mumbled into Reed's shirt.

"Yeah, I figured as much." He drew back, framed her face between his palms, his expression dead serious. He had to buy himself time. Just a day to poke around for his answers. After that, he'd know how to proceed. In the meantime, he had to keep her safe, calm, and in control.

"You trusted me to listen," he said. "Now trust my advice. Don't let your imagination run wild—not yet. Like you said, the weirdo at the cemetery and the intimidating phone call could be two isolated incidents. As for your gut instinct that someone's watching you, I'm all for listening to gut instincts. Still, even if yours are dead-on, this person could be someone as innocuous as an overzealous fan. So, yeah, take extra precautions. Double-lock the door of your apartment. Use the inside chain. When you leave, stay among crowds. That means no solitary strolls on Seventh Avenue at eleven o'clock at night. Keep your eyes open and your pepper spray on hand. If anything else happens—another phone call, a stranger you spot hanging around your apartment, school, or radio station—anything suspicious, then you'll take action."

"What action?" Taylor demanded. "The police won't be interested without evidence. They're not big fans of gut feelings."

"Fine. Then you'll hire a PI. I'll call my brother out in San Francisco. He has a bunch of contacts in Manhattan. We'll get someone. Till then, hang tight. Go about your life. Build your confidence by improving your self-defense skills. On Saturday, we'll have our next lesson. And right now, we'll have our next glass of wine."

Taylor blinked at the change in subject. "Our wine?"

"Yup. Relaxing your mind and body, staying calm—all that's part of the process. That's where the Cabernet comes in." He gripped her hand and led her back to the sofa. "Sit. I'll refill our glasses."

She complied, sinking into the sofa as Reed took the goblets over to the sideboard and refilled them. "Not too much," she reminded him. "I told you, two's my limit. Otherwise, I'll be a headachy zombie at school tomorrow."

"Not to worry," he assured her, slowly completing his task. "I won't ruin the school counselor's reputation by letting her stagger in with a hangover. I'm only giving you half a glass—just enough to take the edge off. While you're nursing your wine, I'll give you a neck-and-shoulder massage. Then I'll send you off to bed. How does that sound?"

How did that sound? Spectacular.

Taylor felt herself smile. "You know, if you're trying to charm me by playing knight in shining armor, you're doing a damned good job."

"Glad to hear it." He winked as he walked over with their drinks. "Knights in shining armor are very trustworthy."

"So I hear."

He sat down beside her, savoring his wine for a few minutes and watching her do the same. When he saw her begin to visibly relax, he set down his goblet and turned her around so her back was facing him. "Keep sipping," he directed, settling his palms on her shoulders. "And shut your eyes."

Taylor didn't need a second invitation. She was drained from the day, from their conversation, from her own apprehension and emotional outburst. All she wanted to do was slip into mental oblivion.

She took another sip of wine and let out a soft sigh as Reed began massaging the tension from her shoulders. He found the knots in her muscles and worked them away, his fingers gliding up her neck, massaging each vertebra, then shifting back down so his thumbs could knead the tight spots in her upper back.

"Feel good?" he murmured.

"Beyond good. Unbelievable." She moved her neck from side to side, leaning into the pressure of his hands. "Do they teach this in law school?"

"Nope. At least not at Harvard. There, they you teach you to kill yourself in order to succeed. Over the summers, I signed up for a few stress management courses. One of them was in massage."

"Lucky me." Taylor's words were muffled, and she didn't resist when Reed leaned forward, took the goblet from her hand, and set it down on the coffee table.

"That was about to hit the floor," he observed, making no move to ease away from her and return to his original position. "Besides, I think you've had enough."

"Yes, Counselor." The wine was swirling through her, dulling some senses, heightening others. She shivered as Reed's breath brushed her neck. "About that decision you made for us to go slow—are you sure I can't change your mind?"

"I'm positive." He gathered up her hair, moved it aside so he could kiss the nape of her neck. "Frustrated, but positive."

She turned, angling her face up to his, her gaze open, if slightly cloudy. "You don't have to be frustrated."

Tiny sparks burned in his midnight eyes. "Yeah, I'm afraid I do."

"Why?"

"Because right now you're vulnerable." He kissed her, tasting her mouth in a way that made her heart slam against her ribs. "You're also not completely sure you can trust me—not yet." Another kiss, this one deeper than the last, his hands kneading her back simultaneously. "And you're also a little too drunk." He felt her slump against him, and he smiled, supporting her weight with his. "But, most of all, because you're asleep."

He scooped her up in his arms and headed down the hall, peeking into each of the two bedrooms. It wasn't hard to figure out which was Taylor's. Stephanie's was stark, almost bare. All that was left were a few pieces of furniture and, on the dresser, a few funky knickknacks and some Broadway-show CDs.

The adjacent bedroom was definitely Taylor's. Reed could smell her perfume as he carried her inside. The beveled cherry furniture and touches of beechwood were as classy and understated as she, and the bookcase on the far wall was filled with psychology texts. On the nightstand, a neat pile of paperwork with the Dellinger letterhead was stacked—probably for Taylor to review before going to sleep.

Gently, he stretched her out on the bed, studying her elegant features and delicately curved body, thinking that he'd never wanted a woman as much as he wanted this one. Maybe that explained the painstaking care he was taking with his timing. Either that, or he was insane for putting off something he wanted so badly he was throbbing with it.

But something told him that whatever was happening between him and Taylor was significant.

So he'd take a cold shower. Hell, he'd take as many of them as he had to. The wait would be worth it.

He leaned over and tucked the pillow beneath Taylor's head and covered her with the afghan blanket that was draped across her rocking chair, pulling it way up to her chin. He threaded his fingers through her hair, smiling at her almost inaudible murmur of pleasure at the contact. Then, with a soft sigh, she snuggled into the blanket.

Reed stood up, pausing only to set the alarm on Taylor's clock radio. She'd kill him if she was late for school. That done, he tiptoed out of the room. He stopped in the kitchen, glancing at the telephone and jotting down the unlisted number that was printed there. He'd call her tomorrow before her radio show, make sure she was all right.

Scooping up his coat, Reed left the apartment. He spent a good couple of minutes making sure the front door was securely locked. Confident that it was, he took the stairway down to the lobby. He turned up his collar, nodding at the doorman before stepping outside.

He flipped open his cell phone as he walked to the parking lot. The message had to be left. It would precipitate a very unpleasant meeting. But there wasn't any other choice.

Reed left a succinct voice mail, then snapped the phone shut.

He'd have his answers soon enough.

CHAPTER 12

FEBRUARY 4

12:30 P.M.

MONTEBELLO RESTAURANT

120 EAST FIFTY-SIXTH STREET, NEW YORK CITY

THE lunch crowd was already in full swing when Jonathan Mallory walked in. He brushed the snowflakes off his cashmere overcoat, then shrugged out of it, handing it to the coat-check girl and taking his ticket. Glancing around, he waited for the maître d' to seat him.

A minute later he was escorted to his table.

Reed was already there. He looked up from the menu when Jonathan approached. "Glad you could make it on such short notice."

"I got the distinct feeling I didn't have a choice." Jonathan settled himself in his chair, taking the menu and waiting until he and Reed were alone before continuing. "Your message sounded more like a subpoena than an invitation to lunch. You announced you needed to see me ASAP. You told me where and when, but not why. And your voice mail was left at one-ten A.M. Very ominous. So, tell me, did my dead brother put Douglas in the hot seat again?"

Reed didn't answer right away. He was studying Jonathan, checking out the subtle signs of apprehension. Jonathan's tone was flippant, and his expression was merely inquisitive, but there was a fine tension emanating from him that Reed could feel. The question was, why?

"Let's order," Reed suggested as the waiter approached the table. "Then we can talk without being interrupted."

"Okay, Reed," Jonathan said as soon as the waiter had brought over his Scotch and Reed's sparkling water, and left the table with their lunch order. "It's obvious that this time Gordon's mess is a big one. So let's get into the specifics and figure out how to make it go away."

"It's not that cut-and-dried." Reed took a deep swallow of water. "This particular mess concerns more than just Gordon. It concerns Taylor Halstead and what Gordon did to her."

"Taylor Halstead." There was a definite edge to Jonathan's tone. "That's a name I didn't expect to hear. I had no idea you'd been in touch with her again since that meeting a few weeks ago."

"Yes, you did. Remember? I told you and Douglas I was giving her self-defense lessons."

"Right. I'd forgotten."

Sure you had, Reed thought, watching the muscle work in Jonathan's jaw. "Anyway, Taylor and I are seeing each other. She's opened up to me. She shared some additional, disturbing details about Gordon's assault—and afterward. There are implications that I need to bring to your attention."

Vigorously, Jonathan ripped off a piece of bread. "Seeing each other," he repeated, his words clipped.

If that didn't speak volumes, nothing did.

As if realizing how transparent he was being, Jonathan turned his attention to buttering his bread. "Are you saying the two of you are dating?" he inquired casually, in an effort to downplay his interest in Reed's private life.

Reed wasn't buying it for a minute.

"That's what I'm saying," he confirmed. "And don't tell me it comes as a surprise. We both know otherwise."

Jonathan's chin came up, and there was a wary look in his eyes. "Why do you say that?"

Reed paused just long enough to make him squirm. "Because you got my message loud and clear that day in my office. You knew I intended to pursue Taylor."

"Right. The day you announced I was out of the running because I was physically indistinguishable from Gordon." Despite the biting quality of Jonathan's words, there was also an unmistakable flash of relief in his eyes. Had he thought Reed was referring to another, more direct reason for his knowing Reed was seeing Taylor? Like maybe because he'd watched him come or go from her apartment?

"As luck would have it, the attraction is mutual," Reed continued, purposely provoking Jonathan in the hopes of eliciting a reaction. "Actually, attraction is an understatement. It's more than that. Even though it's new, it's already pretty intense."

He knew he was pushing it. But he got the reaction he sought.

Jonathan put down his knife with a thud. "Congratulations. You're charming Taylor Halstead into bed. Terrific. Wonderful. Let's get back to the subject at hand. What did she tell you about Gordon?"

Reed leaned forward. "It bothers you that Taylor and I are involved."

"Why would it?"

"Because you have a thing for her. It was pretty obvious from the way you described her that first time in my office, the way you looked at her in the lobby, and the way you're looking at me right now."

One of Jonathan's brows rose. "How observant of you. Is that why you went after her?"

"You know me better than that." Reed didn't like what he was seeing and hearing. Or what he was feeling. "I don't play games. But I'm also not blind. You want Taylor. You're not getting her. So where does that leave you—lying in wait or moving on?"

There was a moment of dead silence.

"What exactly are you getting at?" Jonathan asked at last.

"It's a straightforward question. Are you cutting your losses, or holding out for the impossible?"

Anger tightened Jonathan's features. "Let me understand this correctly. Did you arrange this impromptu lunch so you could order me to back off of Taylor—a woman I've met exactly once? Or do we actually have some business to discuss?"

"Both." Time to slap his cards on the table. "We go back a long way, Jonathan. I know you. I know your family and your history. So I'll be blunt. Gordon was over the edge. His attack on Taylor wasn't spontaneous. It was planned, and it was twisted. What I need to figure out is, was it obsessive? You see, the harassment continued beyond that one night. But did it also go beyond one man? Gordon—or someone—was playing mind games with Taylor, scaring her. Fixating on her, keeping tabs on her, sending creepy love notes via e-mail—you know the scenario. You know because you've been there. The question is, are *you* giving a repeat performance?"

A red flush shot up Jonathan's neck. "You son of a bitch. I can't believe you're bringing this up after all these years. Did you share these sordid details with Taylor—just to make doubly sure she'll always be freaked out by me?"

"I didn't say a word. I went right to the source—you." Reed wasn't going to be deterred by Jonathan's anger. He was going to use it to his advantage. "Now answer my question. Are you, or are you not, back to your old habits of obsessing over a woman to the point of harassment?"

Slowly, Jonathan sucked in his breath. "You're talking about something that happened a dozen years ago."

"It didn't happen once. It happened twice. First in college. Again in grad school. The second time you nearly got your ass thrown in jail."

"And you rescued me with your charming intervention and your brilliant legal mind. Bravo. I've more than paid you back. Douglas's gratitude was your golden goose. He got you in the door at Harter, Randolph and Collins. You're rich. You're respected. And you're probably going to make partner any day now. Is this how you thank me?"

Reed's eyes glittered. "I don't owe you thanks. I came up with a strategy that worked. It kept both women from filing charges. As for why I did it, I did it because I truly believed you were innocent—except for an oversize ego and an arrogant belief that you could have anything, and anyone, you wanted. I never worried about those women's safety. I was well aware that your main weakness was your thinking women were in love with you when that was not the truth. Is that still the case?"

Jonathan looked furious. He swallowed, hard, and when he spoke, his voice cut like shards of ice. "I'm thirty-five. I'm smart. I'm ambitious. I'm a respected international trade consultant who makes seven figures. As my lawyer, you know I'm on the verge of assuming a senior management role at Berkley and Company. Do you honestly believe I'd jeopardize all that by stalking some woman—no matter how desirable? I'd have neither the motivation nor the time. So, no, I'm not sending love notes to your girlfriend. Does that satisfy you?"

Reed stared him down. "I suppose it'll have to."

"Yeah. It will." Jonathan tossed aside his napkin and stood up. "I'm heading back to the office. I've lost my appetite." He paused. "And, in case your passion-drugged mind suffers a temporary lapse while you and Taylor are in bed, let me remind you of your ethical responsibilities. There'll be no mention of my past misconduct. Trust me, it wouldn't do much for your professional future."

REED WATCHED JONATHAN stalk out of the restaurant, his implicit threat still hanging in the air. It hadn't come as any shock. Nor did it evoke any personal concern on Reed's part. Jonathan would never go to the senior partners at Harter, Randolph & Collins, not with this one. It would mean opening up Pandora's box and revealing his past—a past he'd worked too hard to seal.

And if he did go? Let him.

There were more important aspects of this little confrontation with Jonathan to think about.

His outrage had been a no-brainer. Guilty or innocent, it was the natural response to Reed's interrogation. As for his denial, it did have a ring of truth to it.

The problem was, there were incongruities. Jonathan's body language, for one thing. It told Reed that Jonathan was more than pissed. He was scared.

But there was more that didn't sit right.

For example, he was worried that Jonathan's romantic fascination with Taylor was irrational. The way he'd shredded his bread; his clipped comments. He still wasn't ready to let it go, no matter how much he pretended otherwise. His whole blasé attitude was a facade. He wanted her—bad. Further, his interest in what new and damaging information Reed had on Gordon was lukewarm, at best. He'd walked out of the restaurant without pumping Reed for a single detail, without demanding to know what specifics Taylor had divulged, and how those specifics might impact Douglas.

For a man who was about to become an officer in his father's company, that seemed surprisingly lax. And Jonathan was never lax.

Reed frowned, recalling the only two times he'd seen Jonathan behave in this unfocused, uncharacteristic, and self-destructive way.

Both times involved striking redheads with whom Jonathan became infatuated. Neither reciprocated.

Both times Jonathan had become obsessive and stepped over the line.

Both times Reed had intervened, earning Douglas's gratitude.

Since then, nothing.

Until now. Maybe.

Reed frowned, pushing aside his plate. Everything Jonathan had said today was true. He'd have to be out of his mind to do this again. He'd be jeopardizing his entire future—a future that was on a major upswing.

But the pattern was there. So was the profile. Taylor had the same breeding as the other two girls, the same understated beauty and class, even the same coloring. And Jonathan wanted her.

Plus, she felt like she was being watched.

Was Jonathan the one watching her? Reed still wasn't sure. Nor was he sure if today's confrontation had made things better or worse. If Jonathan was fixated on Taylor, if he was the one who had sent those e-cards and was following her around, would he now back off, or stick even closer to her, knowing that she and Reed were involved?

With a quick glance at his watch, Reed realized it was almost a quarter of two. He signaled for the check and pulled out his credit card. He'd head back to the office, check his messages, then give Taylor a call. Better yet, he'd go see her. Maybe he'd even meet her at Dellinger Academy, provide her with a personal escort home.

Fine, so he couldn't discuss his concerns about Jonathan with her.

That didn't mean he couldn't ease his mind by playing bodyguard.

CHAPTER 13

2:45 P.M.

DELLINGER ACADEMY

TAYLOR slung her tote bag over her shoulder and left her office, locking the door behind her. The school was still humming with activity as the sports teams gathered for practice and the various clubs convened for their weekly meetings.

There was something very comforting about Dellinger, she mused as she made her way through the halls. It was an atmosphere she'd always felt good in, but lately it had been like a soothing balm, given the difficulty of the past months. If she had to define its essence, she'd say it was a combination of the simplicity and hopefulness of youth mixed with the security of going through a stable, safe routine.

This afternoon, she'd probably have hung around awhile to watch the practices. But she'd barely eaten all day. She had to grab something since she'd promised Kevin she'd be in early tonight for their guest. Besides, showing up in the gym to demonstrate her support for Dellinger's athletic programs wasn't too great an idea. She'd inevitably run into Chris Young. She wasn't too keen on that prospect. The fewer chances she gave him to make a bad situation worse, the better.

She'd paused in the corridor to fish in her bag for a mint when an unwelcome voice from the blue resonated behind her.

"Hello, Taylor."

Tensing, she whirled around, coming face-to-face with Jonathan Mallory.

She didn't want to give a repeat performance of the last time. But seeing him here, in her school, on her turf . . .

"What are you doing here?" she asked sharply.

If he picked up on how alarmed she was to see him, he didn't let on. He shoved his hands in his pockets, his expression nondescript, his dark eyes veiled. "One of my clients has a daughter who's a student here. She's a member of the Young Business Leaders of America Club. They asked me to come in and speak to them about international trade. So here I am." His lips curved ever so slightly. "Why don't you join us? I'm sure you'd find it fascinating. And afterward, we could grab a cup of coffee and talk. And, by the way," he added in a low, pointed tone, "I'm nothing like my brother."

All Taylor wanted to do was run away as fast as she could. Jonathan Mallory might be nothing like his brother, but he gave her the creeps.

"I'm sure you're very much your own person," she managed, the words tasting like sawdust. "And it's very generous of you to take time out of your workday to talk to the kids in YBLA. Which student is your client's daughter?"

"Dana Coleman." He looked distinctly pleased that she was talking civilly to him. And those eyes—he looked so much like Gordon that Taylor felt her skin crawl.

"Dana, yes." If she didn't get away from him, she was going to lose it. "She's a bright girl."

"Not a surprise. Her parents are both Yale grads." Jonathan gestured toward the classroom he'd be speaking in. "So what do you say? Care to join our meeting, and then grab some coffee?"

"I can't." Taylor saw him start and realized how abrupt she'd sounded. She drew a calming breath, and took it down a notch. "The meeting sounds great. The problem is, I haven't eaten all day and, at this point, I'm feeling light-headed." *That* wasn't a lie. "I was just heading out to buy myself a sandwich."

"Even better." He gave her a slow smile—Gordon's smile. "Before the meeting gets under way, I'll send out for some pizzas. If I remember cor-rectly, teenagers and pizza are like bears and honey. The kids can chow down, and you can replenish your strength. Afterward, we can get that cup of coffee." He put his hand on her arm.

Instinctively, Taylor recoiled, tugging her arm away. "No."

She was referring to the date *and* the physical contact. She knew it, and Jonathan knew it. She could tell by his scowl.

But he wasn't going to give up. She could see it in the hard set of his jaw.

Why in the world would he want to go out with her when she acted like a skittish rabbit around him?

"No," he repeated slowly, as if the word were foreign to him. "Why not?"

"Several reasons."

"The first being that I look like Gordon."

"Yes." She wasn't going to lie.

"You can't get beyond that until you get to know me." He didn't wait for her reply. "What are the other reasons?"

"My second career." She went for the least personal, and most irrefutable, argument. "I host a talk-radio show on WVNY. It's a family counseling show. Teens call in with their problems. Parents call in about their teens." *Stop babbling, Taylor.* "I've got a guest tonight. I promised my producer I'd be there early." She glanced at her watch, unable to focus on the time and not really caring what it was. "You have no idea how much I have to shove into the next few hours. I'll be eating on the run."

"I see." He wasn't buying it, even though he couldn't dispute it. "In that case, let's make it another time."

"I can't."

"Why not?"

He was pushing her into a corner. Fine.

"That's the last reason—and maybe the most important. I'm seeing someone."

"I know. Reed Weston."

Taylor's head shot up. "He told you?"

A shrug. "He mentioned it. He also mentioned it was new. So I'm assuming it's not exclusive."

She *really* didn't like this man. "I'm not good at juggling relationships."

"Ah. A one-man woman. How refreshing."

Was he complimenting her or mocking her?

"No, I mean it," he clarified, reading her expression. "Loyalty is a rare trait these days."

"Yup, that's me. Loyal." Taylor forced a light note into her tone. "In any case, I'd better get going." She took a step toward the door. "Enjoy your time with YBLA."

"Taylor." He stopped her—verbally. He made no move to touch her again.

All she wanted was to get out of there. "Yes?"

"You can't get to know me if you keep running."

She turned around slowly. "I'm not running. I'm buying lunch, doing errands, and going to work."

"Would things be different if I weren't Gordon's identical twin?"

"As I said, I'm seeing Reed. So it's a moot point."

"Not really." He took out a business card, handed it to her. "If you change your mind, give me a call. You won't regret it."

I already do. She took the card and shoved it in her pocket. It was the only way to end this unpleasant exchange. "I really have to go."

"I understand." His expression was unreadable again. "Until next time, then."

Next time? Not likely.

TAYLOR SUCKED IN THE FRESH, cold air when she stepped out of Dellinger's front doors. So much for the comfort of her school environment. She hoped Jonathan Mallory wasn't going to make a habit of visiting.

Hurrying through the school gates, she halted, blinking when she saw Reed standing on the sidewalk.

"Hi," he greeted her. He walked over, a quizzical pucker forming between his brows as he saw her agitated state. "Are you okay?"

"Not really."

"What's wrong?"

She massaged her temples. "I'm about to pass out from starvation."

"You look white as a sheet." He hooked an arm around her waist. "Come on. I'll get you some food."

Ten minutes later, they were in a little Italian deli, munching on their roast-beef-and-provolone panini.

"Thank you." Taylor could feel her energy level returning, along with the color in her cheeks. "All I've eaten today is a Nutri-Grain bar and three spoonfuls of yogurt. The chicken breast I defrosted for dinner is pretty skimpy, and I won't have much time to eat it. I have to get to the station early. I've got a guest tonight. She's a little on the nervous side. Kevin will kill me if I'm not there to prep her."

"Then I'm glad I could rescue you."

Taylor shot him a quizzical look. "You had no way of knowing I was about to faint from hunger. So, to what do I owe this impromptu visit?"

"I came to say good night."

The quizzical look intensified. "Excuse me?"

"You fell asleep last night before I could say it. So I'm here to rectify the omission."

A glint of humor sparkled in Taylor's eyes. "I see. That's very thorough of you."

"And very gallant," he prompted.

"Yes, that, too." She took another bite of her sandwich. "Is it that easy for you to leave your office in the middle of the day?"

"It's next to impossible. I did it anyway."

Her glance turned insightful. "I appreciate the snack and the sentiment. And I'm flattered by the attention. But I have a feeling it's more than me that's pulling you away from the office these days. Am I right?"

Reed wished he could confide in her. "I suppose," he replied with a shrug. "But, believe me, you're more than enough enticement to get me away from any place, anytime."

That prompted a tiny shiver as the memories of last night flashed through her mind. "Speaking of which, I appreciate your sensitivity last night. I literally passed out. I don't remember anything after the sofa. But I realize you didn't . . . you just put me on the bed and left me in my clothes instead of . . ."

"I'm not in the habit of taking advantage of sleeping women," Reed finished for her. He brought her palm to his mouth, brushing his lips across it. "Besides, when I put you in that bed *undressed*, it won't be when I'm going home. It'll be when I'm staying. It also won't be when you're sound asleep. It'll be when you're awake—*very* awake."

Sexual tension crackled in the air, and the revived color on Taylor's cheeks deepened to a flush. "I'm glad," she replied frankly, making no attempt to play coy. It would be ludicrous to do so at this point. They both knew where this relationship was headed, at least physically. The only question was when it would get there.

"Was everything okay today?" Reed changed the subject to ask.

Taylor sighed. "Yes and no. If you're asking if anyone's been following me, no. Today's it's been just me and my pepper spray."

"But?"

"But I had an unsettling meeting."

"With the parents of one of your students?"

"No. With Jonathan Mallory."

"Jonathan?" Reed stared. "Where the hell did you see him?"

"At Dellinger. Right before I left. He was guest-speaking at a club."

Anger drew Reed's lips into a grim line. "Funny, he didn't mention that to me. I had lunch with the guy."

"Today?"

"Yup. Not three hours ago."

Taylor studied Reed's reaction curiously. "You're angry."

"Damn right I am. We discussed you. He never said a word about heading over to your school."

"You told him we were seeing each other. He admitted that."

"But he hit on you anyway."

Taylor's shoulders lifted in a shrug. "He didn't exactly hit on me. It's more like he was pleading his case, letting me know he was nothing like Gordon. Yes, he asked me out. But not in any offensive way. Not really. It's just that . . ." Her voice trailed off.

"Go on."

"The guy just makes me uncomfortable. I don't know why. I try to separate him from Gordon, but I don't like being around him. He gives me the creeps."

"That's the last thing you need right now. I'll talk to him."

Taylor felt herself smile. "Reed, you don't have to take me on as a cause. I'm very capable. I know how to take care of myself. I've been doing it for almost twenty-eight years."

"Yeah, too much so." Reed took a gulp of coffee. "It's time you learned to rely on someone else—or at least to trust someone a little."

"I already do trust you a little. It's a lot that'll take some time."

"I know." He paused, his forehead creasing as he weighed out his next words—or rather, how Taylor would receive them. "I gave my brother Rob a call this afternoon. He and his partner were heading out on some priority investigation, but he said he'd get me a few names by the end of the day. And, no, I'm not making decisions for you," he added quickly.

"What you do with the names is up to you. I'm just trying to be time efficient. So don't rip my head off."

"A few names." Taylor stopped munching on her sandwich. "You mean, of private investigators?" At Reed's nod, she pushed away her paper plate. "I'm not going to rip your head off, but I *am* confused. I thought we were giving things a day or two to play out—or at least waiting until the next time I sensed I was being watched. What's changed?"

"Nothing." The lie tasted like sand on his tongue. "I just felt better starting the process. This way there won't be a time lag—if you need to hire someone."

"Right." She folded her arms across her chest and stared him down. "Why don't you tell me what this is really about? What occurred to you between the time you left my apartment and the time you called your brother?"

Reed blew out his breath. Ethically, he couldn't tell her about Jonathan, but he sure as hell could touch on the other possibilities that had kept him up most of the night.

"A lot of things occurred to me, starting with the fact that I couldn't throw the inside bolt when I left your place, so your apartment wasn't double-locked last night. What else? How about the fact that you represent emotional sanctuary—and God knows what else—to a lot of teens, any one of whom might be unstable enough to try transforming fantasy into reality. Like the fact that you're not only a public figure, but a public figure with a rich family, which makes you a prime target for kidnappers and extortionists—potentially including professionals who have an ax to grind with your father. Is that enough? Or do you want me to go on?"

"You can stop." Taylor's tone was composed, but the intensity of her stare hadn't changed. "None of this is new territory. I've considered all of it. I'm sure you did, too, within two minutes of my relaying the situation to you. You have a sharp, analytical mind. You deliberate the possibilities at warp speed. You keep a cool, level head. All that's part of being a crackerjack defense attorney—which my sources tell me you are."

"A crackerjack attorney would inform you that that's all hearsay and supposition," he countered lightly.

"Fair enough," she returned. "Then I'll rephrase. From personal observation, I can safely conclude you're smart as a whip and not the panicky type. So try that explanation again."

Reed did just that. This time, he went for a different, equally risky kind of candor. "You're right. I'm not the panicky type. But staying cool only works in situations where I'm not personally involved—which I never am with my clients. That's not the case with you. I *am* involved. So the same rules don't apply."

He knew he had her there. She couldn't argue with him. Not when they both knew it was the truth. The question was, how would she react?

He found out soon enough. Taylor's lashes lowered, and she shifted in her seat, looking torn and unsettled. Whether she was torn by the bluntness of his admission or by her own continued doubts as to whether or not he'd been entirely honest with her—that was another story.

Either way, she let it go. "Okay, so you called your brother. Thanks— I think. In the meantime, based on your picking me up after school like a worried parent, am I to assume you've appointed yourself surrogate PI?"

Her analogy made Reed grin. "A worried parent? Hardly. More like a cautious escort. As for the title of surrogate PI, you have to admit, it would be a unique addition to my résumé."

"Not to mention a great icebreaker at parties," Taylor agreed. She studied him thoughtfully. "Your résumé, huh? Does that mean you're in the process of updating it?"

One dark brow rose.

"Reed, I'm not pushing. I'm here to talk, or just to listen. Moral support goes both ways, you know."

"Yeah, I know." He reached over to tuck a strand of hair behind her ear. "You may not believe it, but I'm looking forward to confiding in you. I have a feeling you'll give me some major perspective."

"Just not yet."

"Right. Just not yet. But soon." Mentally, he counted the days. The senior partners had asked for two weeks to review his situation and come to some sort of agreement with regard to the terms of his leaving the firm to go out on his own. He was giving them that time. One week down, one to go. But after that, he'd start the ball rolling. Soon he'd be saying his good-byes.

"By the way, Mr. Surrogate PI, you can have the night off," Taylor interrupted his thoughts to inform him. "WVNY is supplying me with a taxi home after work."

"Really. What's the occasion?"

"Jack Taft's book of rules." She smiled, going on to explain. "Jack's our program manager. He always sends me home by cab when I work past midnight. It's his way of appeasing his own guilt."

"And tonight's one of those late nights?"

"Definitely. We've got a special college-oriented show we're pre-taping. I'll be lucky if I get out of the studio by one. I'll have door-to-door service to my apartment. And my doorman will take over from there. So go home early and get some sleep. You'll do a better job of working out your dilemma with a rested, if not clear, mind."

Reed nodded. "Okay. But don't leave the building until the taxi is waiting. That way, you won't be alone. Plus, it's supposed to be freezing tonight. Subzero temperatures. So stay inside."

"Gotcha. No isolation and no frostbite."

"Right. And I'll call you tomorrow with the names Rob gives me."

Reed couldn't shake his uneasiness.

CHAPTER 14

FEBRUARY 4

6:03 P.M.

WVNY

T H E station was its usual lively self when Taylor arrived. *Sports Talk* had just launched into its second hour, and the broadcast could be heard throughout the station. Taylor smiled as she hurried down the hall, listening to Bill's heated debate with a die-hard fan about a bad call in last week's Super Bowl.

She blew into her recording studio, glancing at Kevin as she shrugged out of her coat. "Early enough?" she teased.

He looked up from the book he'd been reading—a copy of *Bad Kids, Worse Parents*—and nodded. "Yeah. Bernice Williams isn't here yet. Her publicist called, said she was on her way and would be set to go by seven-fifteen."

"Perfect." Taylor ran a brush through her windblown hair. "That gives me an hour to prep, meet with Laura, and zip through some e-mails. As for Bernice, I suggested she not arrive before then. The last thing she needs is to wait around too long before airtime. Watching us run around like chickens without heads will only stress her out. This way, I'll take her into my booth at seven-fifteen, get her centered and calm, then run through a few format questions to set the stage. Once she's in the zone, she'll be fine."

Kevin rolled his eyes, plopping the book on his desk. "That's why you're the psychologist and I'm the producer. The only zone I can relate to is the one Bill's arguing about right now—the end zone."

Taylor chuckled. "Just don't share that with Bernice."

"I won't." Kevin leaned back in his chair, fiddling with a pen as he scanned the computer screen. There was a definite furrow between his brows.

"What's wrong?" Taylor asked. "You have that look you get when something's bugging you. And you're playing with your pen—not a good sign." A hint of tension crept into her voice. "Is it Romeo? Did he call again?"

"No." Kevin shook his head. "It's Rick."

"Rick?" As soon as she realized her audio engineer was the subject of this conversation, Taylor shut the door. "Did something happen with Marilyn?"

"Oh, I'd say so. He came in a half hour ago a total mess. He'd definitely had a few drinks. He was muttering about separation agreements and lawyers' fees. Mostly, he kept talking about his kids and the what-ifs of Marilyn getting custody. He broke down, started to cry, and beat it out of here. I haven't seen him since. I don't even know if he's coming back to do the show."

"Oh, no." Taylor propped her elbows on the ledge next to Kevin's desk and covered her face with her hands. She'd prayed it wouldn't come to this. Rick and Marilyn had three great kids—an eleven-year-old daughter, a nine-year-old son, and a six-year-old son—all of whom they both adored. Especially Rick. His kids were his life. If he and Marilyn split up and the judge gave custody to Marilyn . . . well, Taylor didn't know what he'd do.

"I haven't told Jack that Rick left," Kevin continued. "But if he's not back soon, I won't have a choice."

"I know. But wait as long as you can," Taylor replied. "We both know Rick. He needs to be alone when he loses it. He could still be somewhere in the building. But even if he's not, he won't leave us high and dry, no matter how messed up he is. He's too conscientious to ditch us with no backup."

"I agree." Kevin gestured toward the door. "Go downstairs and do your stuff with Laura. I'll buzz you if either Rick or our guest shows up."

"Or if time gets too close and you have to alert Jack."

"Yeah, then, too."

———

AS IT TURNED OUT, Rick and Bernice arrived one after the other.

Taylor was back in the studio, standing at Kevin's desk as he reached for the phone to reluctantly clue Jack in to what was going on, when Rick walked in.

"Hey." His eyes were red. From drinking? Taylor wasn't sure. But his shoulders were slumped. "Sorry to cut it close. But I've got more than enough time to set things up and do a voice check on our guest."

"Don't worry about it. She's not even here yet." Taylor laid a hand on his arm. "Rick, are you okay?"

He gave her a tormented look. "No. But I can do the show, if that's what you're asking."

"I wasn't. I know you can do the show. I'm just concerned about—"

"Look, Taylor, I appreciate your concern." He cut her off, shrugging his arm free. "But there are some things even you can't fix. I don't want to talk about it. I don't want your compassion. I just want to do the fucking show and then be alone somewhere with a bottle of bourbon."

There wasn't time for her to answer. The door flew open and Jack led Bernice Williams in. "Our guest has arrived," he announced.

"Ms. Williams—welcome." Taylor extended her hand to the plump, middle-aged woman whose eyes were darting around like a frightened sparrow's. "You remember my producer, Kevin Hodges, and my audio engineer, Rick Shore?"

"Yes, of course." The author nodded, practically vibrating with anxiety as she shook everyone's hand. "And, please, call me Bernice. I'll feel calmer if we're on a first-name basis."

"Great. The same applies to all of us. We're a very informal bunch here." Taylor gave her program manager the okay signal with her eyes.

Jack took the cue. "I'm leaving you in capable hands," he assured Bernice, although he did cast a puzzled look in Rick's direction. The normally friendly engineer had said a brief hello, then gone over to his control panel. "So relax and enjoy yourself."

"I will."

Jack hesitated. "Hey, Rick, you look beat. It's going to be a long night. If you need a break, give a holler. I'll send Dennis in."

"Thanks." Rick's tone was cordial but his body language was tense. "I'm fine. Besides, I can do this job with my eyes closed by now."

"I know you can." Jack shot a quick glance at Kevin, whose slight nod said he had things under control.

"Okay, then." Jack moved toward the door. "I'll check in with you later. Have a great show."

9:45 P.M.

EAST EIGHTY-SIXTH STREET, NEW YORK CITY

Jonathan lay back on his bed, his arms folded behind his head, cushioning it as he stared at the ceiling.

The entire day had sucked.

Everything had gone wrong, from his disagreement with Douglas, to that obnoxious lunch with Reed, to being shut down by Taylor, to an afternoon of scrambling around, trying to fix things.

He'd tried getting through to Douglas since four o'clock. But he was in meetings all afternoon, after which he'd left for some business dinner where he couldn't be reached. Great. Jonathan had left a message at Douglas's Upper East Side brownstone, hoping he'd spend the night there rather than telling his driver to head all the way back to the Hamptons. In either case, Jonathan sure as hell wasn't calling the East Hampton estate. With his luck, Adrienne would answer the phone. And there was no way he was making small talk with that slut tonight.

What Douglas saw in her was beyond him. Other than the obvious, of course. The woman had a face and body to die for. But everything beneath it was trashy and shallow.

As opposed to Taylor, who had substance as well as beauty.

The comparison made Jonathan's jaw tighten. He couldn't stop thinking about Taylor—and the fact that she was falling for Reed. If he'd only had a little more time, things could have been different. But Reed had taken that time away. Plus, he was holding a loaded gun, one that could blow Jonathan's entire world apart.

He'd have to take a more aggressive stand. He'd have to move fast, accelerate his entire plan.

So be it. That's what he'd do.

He yanked his laptop toward him, dashing off a high-priority e-mail to Douglas. That should cover his last remaining base, no matter where Douglas was spending the night. The man checked his BlackBerry regularly. At the latest, he'd read it first thing in the morning. Then he'd call and Jonathan would get things on track.

Fidgeting, he glanced at the digits on his clock radio. They told him it was nine fifty-five.

Nine fifty-five?

With a muttered curse, Jonathan rolled toward the night table and clicked on the radio.

Taylor's voice filled the room immediately, responsive and intense.

"Bernice, in our final minutes together, I'd like to sum things up. Your opinion, as you express it in your latest book, *Bad Kids, Worse Parents*, is that most of the negative traits we see in adolescents are caused by their home environment. Not by their schools or their peers, but by their parents."

"Absolutely," the other women replied. "I'm not disputing that those traits are reinforced by their peers or even by the media. But, in my opinion, they originate in the home. No matter how much teenagers deny it—and many will—they ultimately are impacted most by the key adult figures in their lives; specifically, those they live with. It's a delicate balance. But, as you'll read in my book, I believe you rarely find a quote-unquote bad kid, without also finding a worse parent."

"That's a pretty sweeping statement," Taylor noted. "So just to clarify things for our listening audience, what about those parents with problem kids who try everything they can, from personal intervention to professional counseling, and still can't make things right?"

"That's a different scenario, and the statistics bear it out." Bernice paused, probably for a drink of water. "In interviewing parents such as those you describe, you'll find that, most times, they characterize their kids as troubled, difficult, or depressed—even overwhelmed by workload and social pressures. They rarely use the word 'bad.'"

"I see. So you're not lumping all problem kids together."

"Definitely not. What I'm saying is that there's a tendency for parents who are negative about their teens and who want to absolve themselves of all responsibility in helping them transition from adolescence to adulthood to describe their teenagers as bad. Frankly, it's easier to write them off than it is to admit that it's their own parenting skills that are lacking."

Taylor murmured a sound of understanding. "Well, Bernice, you've certainly given us a great deal to think about tonight. I appreciate your taking the time to talk to us, and I'm looking forward to reading the e-mails we receive from our listening audience about this complex issue. Once again, we've been chatting tonight with Bernice Williams, the author of *Bad Kids, Worse Parents*. You can pick up a copy at your local bookstore; it's fascinating, thought-provoking reading, relevant to both parents and teens. Bernice, thank you so much for being with us."

"My pleasure."

"This is *Teen Talk* with Taylor Halstead. Have a great night. Tomorrow, we resume our regular format, and I'll be back here at WVNY at eight P.M., ready to take your calls. Until then, stay warm and stay safe. Good night."

The WVNY jingle came on, and Jonathan flipped off the radio. He liked it better when Taylor did her show solo. Then he could just focus on her voice, think about the peace and pleasure it brought him.

As for the author, well, she'd only touched the tip of the iceberg with her concept of bad kids, worse parents. In fact, that phrase was the oversimplification of the century. Try "manipulated kids, depraved parents."

In the end, it didn't matter. It all came down to survival of the fittest.

CHAPTER 15

THE "on the air" light went off, and Kevin signaled Taylor that she and Bernice were free.

Then he turned to Rick. "You did a great job of holding it together. Now I want you to go home. You taught Dennis more than enough for him to manage an hour of taping. You can run through the drill with him before you take off, if it makes you feel better. But we're not starting for an hour and a half, when the college kids come alive. So go get some sleep."

Rick gave a hollow laugh. "Sleep? Where? I've been on the sofa for so many nights I lost count."

"Go home, Rick."

"I used to go home for my kids. Now who knows how long I'll have that as an incentive?" Rick rubbed his eyes, realizing he was losing it. "You're right. I'm not much good to anyone tonight. And, yeah, the new guy can handle things. He doesn't need a run-through." He glanced through the glass, saw Taylor and Bernice rising, getting ready to exit the booth. "I'm not up for chitchat with our guest."

"Don't worry about it." Kevin was already picking up the phone. "I'll have Dennis make the backup disk. And Taylor will understand. Just go."

"Yeah, thanks." Unsteadily, Rick stood, grabbing his jacket and heading for the door. "It's bourbon time," he muttered.

FEBRUARY 5

2:15 AM

WEST SEVENTY-SECOND STREET

Taylor was dead asleep.

The recording session had taken longer than usual, since it was Dennis's first time at the helm, which prompted him to be very methodical. But he was also very good, so they only lost about ten minutes. Taylor was home by one-fifteen, in her bed by one-thirty, and in dreamland five minutes later.

The shrill ringing of the phone dragged her awake, cobwebs of exhaustion clouding her mind—although not enough to prevent the knot of apprehension from forming in her gut.

God, no, not again.

She groped for the phone, crammed it under her ear. "Hello?" she managed.

"Taylor, it's me." Rick's voice was slurred, oddly strained, and Taylor sat straight up in bed.

"Rick? Where are you?"

"In your lobby. On my cell." A humorless laugh. "Your doorman won't let me up. He thinks I'm a stalker."

"Put him on."

There were some fumbling noises, and then George, the nighttime security guard, came on the line. "I'm sorry, Ms. Halstead. I didn't think—"

"It's okay, George. He's a colleague. I understand your concern. It's obvious he's been drinking. But I can handle him. So send him up."

"All right." George didn't sound happy, but an instant later the buzzer announced that he'd admitted Rick.

Taylor climbed out of bed, grabbed her fleece robe, and yanked it on, belting it at the waist. Rick sounded like he was at the breaking point. She wasn't sure if anything she said would help, but she had to try.

Running her fingers through her hair, she went to the front door and waited for the knock, checking through the peephole to make sure it was Rick before she unbolted and opened the door. "Hi."

He was leaning against the door frame, his overcoat hanging open, his eyes glassy and half shut, his face flushed. The stench of booze was so strong, Taylor nearly gagged. He reeked.

"I'm sorry about b'fore," he announced, taking an unsteady step into the foyer. "I didn't mean to tear into you. It just hurts so goddamned much."

"Come in and sit down. I'll brew some coffee."

"No coffee." Rick waved it away. "I just wanted to . . . I don't know what I wanted. For you to wave a wand and make it go away. You have that effect on people." He stared at her through tortured, bloodshot eyes. "It's over, Taylor. Everything's over. Marilyn, the kids, ev'rything."

"Rick, please." She led him inside and urged him onto a kitchen stool. "Let me make you some coffee."

"I'm not thirsty. Not unless you have Jack Daniel's."

Taylor propped her elbows on the counter and faced him. "I don't know where things stand with Marilyn. But it'll never be over with the kids. They're your children. And they're crazy about you."

"Marilyn will get full custody." Tears filled his eyes. "She said so and she's right. I've been a mess. I drink. I'm depressed. I sleep all weekend. Sometimes I'm so out of it, I can't focus on what the kids are saying. I've become a lousy father. Marilyn's lawyer will tell that to the judge. And he'll take them away from me. I can't survive that."

"You're getting way ahead of yourself. You're a fantastic father. You just happen to be going through a rough patch. Depression requires treatment. You'll see someone and get that treatment. It'll change everyone's perspective—yours, your family's, and the judge's."

"What I need is to crawl into a bottle and never come out."

"That's the last thing you need."

Rick rubbed his temples. "And the last thing *you* need is for me to dump on you like this." Abruptly, his head came up, a flicker of rational awareness crossing his face. "I'm a jerk. You must've jumped outta your skin when your phone rang at this time of night."

"It's all right," Taylor said simply. "It was you."

"Yeah, but it could have been that crank caller. Has he called back?"

"Thankfully, no."

"Good." Rick frowned, verbalizing his thoughts as they tumbled into his head. "Kevin's checking out Romeo. That lawyer you're falling for is teaching you self-defense. It's gonna be okay. You've got a lot of people looking out for you."

"So do you."

For a moment Rick didn't answer. He just stared at the floor. When he looked up, there was such futility in his eyes that Taylor wanted to call Marilyn herself, shake some sense into her. "I'm tired, Taylor," he said quietly, shoving himself to his feet. "Tired of fighting. Tired of trying to keep it together." He made an attempt to button his coat, then abandoned it. "I'm gonna get going. I need sleep."

"Yes, you do." Taylor frowned, uneasy about Rick's state of mind. "Do you want me to call Marilyn? I could tell her you're crashing on my sofa tonight."

A hollow laugh. "Right. She'd probably use that against me, too. She'd twist the story and tell her lawyer I'm screwing another woman."

"She knows better than that."

"What she knows and what she does are two different things." Rick reached over, squeezed Taylor's arm. "Thanks for listening." He headed for the door.

"Rick." She followed him, taking hold of his sleeve. "You've had too much to drink."

"Then it's good I'm not driving." He saw her concern and forced a smile. "Hey, I won't even walk. I'll catch the subway to Times Square. The number seven leaves there for Flushing every twenty minutes. I'll be home in less than an hour. See? I'm more than sober enough to get where I need to go." He patted her cheek. "Go back to bed. Things'll be better tomorrow."

3:25 A.M.

TIMES SQUARE SUBWAY STATION, NEW YORK CITY

The damned subway train was taking forever.

Rick paced around on the platform, rubbing his arms and trying to stave off the cold. The walk from Taylor's apartment to the subway entrance had left his body with a chill that wouldn't go away.

He barely remembered the ride from Seventy-second Street to Times Square, or the walk downstairs to the lower level. But here he was.

The platform was practically deserted, courtesy of the hour and the subzero temperatures. Normal people were home in their beds when it was 3 A.M. and minus seven degrees. The only other gluttons for punishment around him—not counting the poor vagrants who'd come in to avoid dying of frostbite—were four or five stoned teenagers and some guy in a hooded parka, sitting on a bench with his face buried in a book.

How anyone could have the wherewithal to read under these conditions was beyond Rick.

With a rumble, the train finally pulled into the station and stopped. Rick got on. The car he'd chosen was empty. He dropped into a seat and folded his arms across his chest to stay warm. The guy with the parka got on behind him. He made his way to the rear, stopping near the door leading to the next car, then slumped into the seat. His head was still shoved in that book.

The amount of booze Rick had consumed was getting to him. He was starting to develop a massive headache and a lurching stomach. He sat very still, staring straight out the window across from him. That worked until the train left the station. Then his stomach began pitching along with the motion of the subway car, more so as they picked up speed. Okay, watching the underground world go whizzing by was a definite no-no. He felt like he was about to puke.

He squeezed his eyes shut.

It didn't help.

Gagging, he shifted forward in his seat, fighting his body's untimely protest. He was *not* going to vomit on the subway floor.

Apparently, the guy in the parka wasn't so sure.

He jumped to his feet, shutting his book and making a beeline for the connecting door. He pulled on the handle a couple of times, then started cursing under his breath when the door wouldn't budge. He yanked again, becoming visibly agitated when it didn't give, like he was frantic to get out of there. Not that Rick could blame him. The poor jerk was alone in a subway car with a gagging drunk, whom he probably expected to barf any minute.

Rick took pity on him. Besides, a short walk might help the nausea more than a long sit. Gritting his teeth, he grabbed onto the nearest pole and pulled himself up. Then he weaved his way down to the door. The guy's hooded back was to him, and the parka was so big and bulky that it was impossible to make out anything beneath it. Still, Rick could sense the guy tense up as he approached.

"Don't worry, I'm not gonna mug you," Rick muttered. "I'm just gonna help you get away from me." He wedged himself around front, reaching for the door and giving the handle a good hard pull.

To his surprise, he met with no resistance at all. The door just slid open.

"It must've been stuck," he murmured, half to himself. He started to backtrack, maneuvering himself so the other guy could pass. "Go ahead. Problem solved."

The guy in the parka blocked his retreat. "You're right. It is."

He shoved Rick through the doorway and, with both hands, propelled him over the safety gate that linked the cars, sending him plunging to the tracks below.

Rick's scream was swallowed up by the roar of the train as it continued on its undisturbed path to Flushing.

CHAPTER 16

FEBRUARY 5

2:30 P.M.

A message from Jack. Taylor knew there was something wrong the minute she saw the pink note. He never called her at school. If there was something he wanted to speak privately with her about, he left her a voice mail at home, asking her to come in early or stay late.

The message was short and terse: come directly to WVNY when school is out.

She arrived in record time. A knot had formed in the pit of her stomach.

She took one look at Jack's ashen expression when she walked into his office, and knew the knot was only going to worsen.

"Taylor, sit down." Jack gestured toward the upholstered settee. He waited for her to perch at the edge of the cushion, then came around to stand beside her. "There's something I need to tell you. It's about Rick."

Oh, no. *No.*

"What is it?" she asked in a wooden tone, certain it was a nightmarish replay of the tragic news about Steph.

"There was an accident on the number seven train in the middle of the night. A man who'd had too much to drink lost his balance when he was walking between cars." A hard swallow. "He fell onto the tracks, and under the train. He was killed instantly. It was Rick."

Taylor's throat was working, and her hands were clasped so tightly together she could scarcely feel them. "Are they sure?"

This wasn't easy on Jack. He was trying to spare her the gory details. He looked violently ill. "Even though the body was mangled, the description, the bits and pieces of ID from his wallet, the clothing samples, and, most of all, the wedding ring—they were Rick's. They'll run a DNA test to confirm, but they're sure."

She bowed her head, everything inside her going cold and still. "Tell me everything."

"Rick never came home last night. Marilyn waited until the kids left for school, then started making calls. No one had seen him. She called here around eight. She was pretty freaked out. I told her that Rick left the station right after your show last night. Kevin was in my office when I took the call. He added that Rick had been in bad shape when he left, and was probably heading for a bar, not home. Marilyn jumped on that. She called some local bars, even a few hotels. We did the same. One bar owner remembered seeing him in there around one. Nothing after that."

"I can fill in the blanks," Taylor managed. "Rick came to my apartment a little after two. He stayed about a half hour. He'd been drinking—a lot. He was an emotional wreck. He felt as if his entire world was falling apart."

"Yeah, Marilyn told me. But, divorce or not, she still cared about the guy. She was frantic. When she got nowhere, she called the police and reported Rick missing. The precinct checked it out. Marilyn's description matched that of an accident victim they'd located around four A.M. She went down to the police station and identified the personal articles I mentioned. She called me from there. She was obviously in shock. I don't even remember what I said to her—" Jack's voice broke. "Anyway, that's all I know. What happened at your place?"

"Rick said he wanted to apologize for being so surly before the show," Taylor murmured, tears slipping down her cheeks. "What he really wanted was for me to offer him a shred of hope. I tried." She raised her head. "Has Marilyn told the kids yet?"

"I'm not sure. I haven't spoken to her since she left the police station. She was on her way down to the morgue. She had to identify the remains. Jesus, what do I say to her?"

"There aren't any right words. Believe me, I know. All you can do is be there for her and the kids in whatever ways they need." Taylor felt like she was standing outside herself, talking to Jack as a third person; an objective psychologist.

"I'll call Marilyn," she heard herself say. "I've lost someone I love through a violent death. I can listen. I can help her talk to the police. If nothing else, I can give her the name of an excellent grief counselor who deals with kids. Those poor children are going to need it."

She rose, heading toward the door. It was happening again. Another death. Another senseless, premature loss. Another funeral.

Another situation where Taylor felt responsible.

Maybe if she'd said the right words, insisted that Rick stay the night on her sofa, forced him to think about everything he had to live for . . . maybe things would have turned out differently. Maybe he'd be alive.

"Taylor?" Jack's voice stopped her. "Take the night off. I'll run one of your pretaped shows during your time slot."

She paused in the doorway, turned to face Jack. "What about Kevin? He must be a mess."

"He is. I sent him home. Sally's a great intern. She can easily handle a taped program. And Dennis can do the audio." Jack cleared his throat. "I've got the bases covered. Don't worry. Just go."

Taylor nodded. "Thanks, Jack. I'll check in with you later."

She left the building and just stood outside, oblivious to the people, to the traffic, to the cold. The chill she felt was from within, and not even frigid temperatures could compare with that. Without thinking, she pulled out her cell phone and dialed directory assistance. When the operator answered, she said, "I need the number of Harter, Randolph and Collins."

REED WAS READING a brief when his secretary buzzed him.

He punched the intercom button. "Yes, Cathy?"

"Sorry to bother you, Mr. Weston. But Taylor Halstead is on the phone. She's pretty insistent about speaking with you. She says it's important. And she sounds upset."

The brief was forgotten. "Put her through."

FIFTEEN MINUTES LATER, Cathy showed Taylor into Reed's office. He took one look at her sheet white face and trembling hands, and said to his secretary, "Cathy, that'll be all. And no interruptions. *None.*"

"Yes, Mr. Weston."

Once the door was shut and they were alone, Reed walked over, clasped Taylor's shoulders. "What is it? You sounded horrible on the phone. You look even worse. Are you hurt? Did something happen at Dellinger?"

"What?" It took a moment for the basis of Reed's concern to register. Then Taylor shook her head. "No. Nothing like that. It's not me." She could feel herself shaking, but couldn't seem to make it stop. "I'm sorry. I didn't mean to barge into your office. It was rude and unprofessional."

"You didn't barge in. I told you to come."

"I didn't think. I just called, heard your voice, and flew over. I can't go through it alone again. I don't have the emotional strength."

"Taylor, you're scaring the hell out of me. What happened? What is it you can't go through?"

She raised her face and stared at him through pained eyes. "Losing someone I care about."

Reed went very still. "Who did you lose?"

"Rick Shore. My audio engineer. We've worked together at WVNY since I started. He's like a big brother, always looking out for me, worrying when I'm stressed. When Steph died, he stuck by me like a mother hen, making sure I was holding up, taking over some of my program responsibilities. And then the other day, when I told him about that crank call I got and about the person watching me at the cemetery, he was up in arms. He was going through his own personal hell, but he still had enough caring left over for me. That was Rick. Always there for a friend. And now he's dead." Taylor's eyes were dry, but her voice was hollow.

"Was he ill?"

"No. He was killed in a horrible accident. It was early this morning. He was alive one minute and dead the next. Just like Steph. And, just like Steph, his death was violent, gruesome. He was on his way home. He took the subway. He changed cars. He fell under the train. He was mangled to death."

"My God." Reed grimaced, instinctively drawing Taylor against him, trying to shield her, knowing full well he couldn't. "I heard something on the news about an unidentified man being killed in the subway. It never occurred to me that it was someone from WVNY. I'm terribly sorry," he murmured, stroking her hair.

She nodded against his shirt.

"Come here and sit down." He drew her over to the settee under the panorama of windows. "Do you want a drink?"

"Just some water."

Reed poured her a glass and brought it over, sitting down beside her. "Were there witnesses?"

"Not from what I understand. The train was probably empty. It was three-something in the morning." Quietly, Taylor filled Reed in on the details, including Rick's late-night visit to her apartment and the reason for it.

Steepling his fingers together, Reed processed all Taylor had said. Then he asked the obvious. "Given Rick's state of mind, is there any chance this was suicide?"

Taylor had thought of that possibility. It was part of the reason she felt so guilty. Still, hearing the words spoken aloud made her wince.

"I'm not trying to upset you," Reed said quickly. "I'm just offering a viable theory. I'm doing so for two reasons. One, because the police will be asking you questions about his state of mind, and two, because—if for any reason there's merit to it—I don't want you heaping additional blame on yourself. You're already doing one hell of a job on that score." He hesitated, then went full speed ahead, blurting out a truth he wasn't sure she was ready to hear. "Look, Taylor, you're not in charge of the world. You're human. You can only do so much. You can advise people, even get in their faces to convince them to make the right choices. But you can't live their lives. That's their job. Everyone is ultimately responsible for himself or herself. That applied to Rick." Another heartbeat of a pause. "It also applied to Steph."

Without replying, Taylor took a sip of water.

"You're angry," Reed concluded flatly. "I overstepped my bounds."

Taylor inclined her head in his direction, a strained, bittersweet smile touching her lips. "I'm not angry. I appreciate your assessment. Not only is it true, it's exactly what I needed to hear. I just didn't realize it until you said it." She set down her glass. "As for your question about Rick, I've already considered the possibility of suicide. Were the signs there?

Yes, I suppose they were. Depression. Hopelessness. Exhaustion. The need to escape. Even loneliness and abandonment. But there's one thing that negates it all, and makes me absolutely sure Rick's death was an accident."

"His kids."

"Exactly. Reed, you have no idea how much he loved them. True, he was terrified of losing custody. But deep down, he knew that wouldn't happen. It rarely does these days. I just don't buy it."

Reed nodded. "I see your point."

"The fact is, he was drunk. His faculties were impaired. He was also despondent. When Rick was down, he had a tendency to pace around like a caged lion. My guess is he couldn't sit still. He must have walked— or weaved—from car to car, trying to get himself together."

"He'd certainly have no problems making his way from one end of the train to the other," Reed added. "Not at three A.M. on a weeknight. He'd be virtually alone. At most, there'd be a couple of other passengers. So if Rick started teetering around on one of the platforms between sub-way cars, or if he leaned over the gate and lost his balance, no one would be there to stop him, or even to see him."

Taylor shuddered. "I can't let myself visualize it. I just can't."

"Then don't." Reed smoothed her hair off her face. "What now?"

"I have to call Marilyn. I want to check on her and the kids, and see if there's anything I can do."

Another nod. "You're not doing your radio show tonight, are you?"

"No. Jack's substituting one of my pretaped shows and having a production intern sit in for Kevin." Taylor massaged her temples. "Thank goodness for that. I couldn't have pulled off the show, not tonight. I doubt Kevin could have either. Jack's a good man. He sent us both home."

"Home. Is that really where you want to go?"

Taylor understood Reed's question. "The truth? No. It's been hard enough living in that place since Steph died. It's filled with memories of her, and of what happened with Gordon that night . . ." Her voice trailed off. "Anyway, suffice it to say, I can't wait to move. I'm counting the days till I'm out of there. Plus, tonight—to be honest, I don't really want to be alone with my thoughts."

"Fair enough." Reed stood. "Then here's how the evening will play out. It's already almost five. I'll finish up my work. You call Marilyn. Coun-sel her for as long as you need to. When you're ready, we'll head out.

We'll stop by your apartment, pack up an overnight bag, then go to my place. We'll order in Chinese and watch a DVD. We can talk, or not talk. Whatever you want." He studied the glazed expression on Taylor's face, and clarified his intentions—just in case she felt awkward. "My guest room's made up. It has to be. With a big family like mine, there's always someone dropping in without warning. I've got to be on my toes."

Taylor understood. "I doubt I'll be able to sleep. But thank you. Your plan sounds wonderful. Another gallant Reed Weston rescue."

He took her hand and drew her to her feet, bringing her palm to his lips. "Everything will be all right, Taylor. You'll make sure of it. And so will I."

She released her breath on a weary sigh. "I hate relying on anyone."

"No kidding. You've only mentioned that a dozen times. Just like you've mentioned that you hate being easily read. Well, tough. Get used to both. Now that I think about it, there's a long list of things you'd better get used to. Tell you what. I'll draw up a list and give it to you for easy reference. But don't bother critiquing it. It's nonnegotiable."

For the first time in hours, Taylor's laugh came spontaneously. "Thanks for the warning."

11:45 P.M.

EAST SIXTY-EIGHTH STREET

Taylor lay quietly in the guest-room bed in Reed's apartment, staring at the ceiling and listening to the scream of a passing fire engine.

She was emotionally wiped out, after a wrenching, forty-five-minute conversation with Marilyn, during which they'd talked mostly about the kids and how Marilyn was going to break the news to them. The poor woman was still in shock herself, and fighting valiantly to be strong for what lay ahead. Her sister was there, staying with her, and her parents were flying in from Arizona tomorrow. Still, she'd gratefully taken the name and number of the grief counselor Taylor recommended. She'd also clung to Taylor's insistence that she not let guilt intrude on her emotional crisis. Rick's death was an accident. Period. No matter what direction the police's questions took, she was not responsible. Life dealt cruel blows. This was one of them. An impending divorce didn't negate years of caring. Marilyn had to remember that. And Taylor insisted that Marilyn pick up the phone and call Taylor to be reminded anytime she felt herself slipping.

Marilyn had thanked her profusely, then hung up to deal with a hell that no amount of counseling could erase.

Taylor had made one more call, to Kevin. She wanted to see how he was holding up and to let him know that if he needed to reach her tonight, he should do so on her cell phone, since she wouldn't be home.

He sounded numb. His girlfriend was there, making him something to eat and offering him whatever support she could. He was relieved to hear that Taylor wasn't alone either. Neither of them mentioned Rick. They weren't ready, not tonight. There'd be plenty of time for reality tomorrow.

Right after hanging up with Kevin, Taylor came to the decision that even though Jack would be issuing an official WVNY statement, she wanted to give a personal acknowledgment of Rick on her show tomorrow night. How she'd do so without breaking down, she wasn't sure. But she'd find a way. Rick had been a close member of their production family. He deserved a tribute. And she intended to give him one.

She drafted a few words while Reed was finishing up his work. She stopped when she couldn't take any more. It was too soon, and she was too drained. She'd either write it tomorrow or wing it and speak from the heart. Maybe she'd run the two options by Dr. Phillips at tomorrow's session. The psychiatrist always had valuable insights, especially when Taylor's own perspective was clouded by emotion. Besides, she needed this session. She needed to vent, to talk about what she was going through.

She'd been more than ready to head out when Reed shut down his computer and called it a day.

The rest of the evening had been just what she needed.

Reed had been incredible. He'd driven her to her apartment, waited while she packed an overnight case, then driven her here. His Upper East Side apartment was lovely and spacious, oozing warm, masculine comfort. They'd settled themselves on the cozy living-room sofa and followed Reed's plan to a tee: ordering up Chinese food, watching a DVD—a mindless comedy, which was all Taylor could handle—and talking.

They hadn't talked about Rick. They'd talked about themselves.

Reed had told her about his family get-togethers, the antics of his nieces and nephews, and the pandemonium that ensued when the entire Weston clan exploded into his parents' New England farmhouse. Thank heavens it was made of stone, he'd declared. Otherwise, it would have blown apart a long time ago.

In return, Taylor had divulged more of herself, sharing more of her life and her thoughts than she ever had in the past.

She'd spoken about her own family, which was clearly the utter antithesis of his. She'd described her stuffy, isolated, Central Park West upbringing, and the unique bond that had subsequently formed between her and Steph. She talked about boarding school, about how responsible she'd felt for Steph, and about how, beneath her cousin's spellbinding beauty and magnetic effervescence, there lay an insecure little girl, who often made the wrong decisions for the right reasons.

"And you were there for her; her constant," Reed noted. "Also, her adviser, her conscience, and her strength."

"Don't make me sound so noble. I had my own issues to deal with. I still do. Believe me, I know. I'm a psychologist. I'm well aware of how and why I wound up with my particular emotional baggage. That doesn't mean I can make it go away."

"Emotional baggage. You mean like always needing to be in control, like lack of trust, and like going it alone."

"Yup. That's the list."

"What about men?"

"What about them?"

"Where did they factor into your life up until now? Your cousin was obviously a social butterfly. What about you? Issues or not, you're a beautiful, intelligent, passionate woman. There must have been men."

"Not men. Just moments." Taylor had shrugged, answering this question as frankly as she'd answered the others. "I didn't do relationships. Those involve relinquishing control and independence. They also require trust."

"Ah. All your no-nos wrapped in one."

"Right. On the other hand, I wasn't into random hookups. I tried pushing myself in that direction when I got to college. It just didn't work for me—too empty, too demeaning. So I opted for moments."

Reed had eyed her thoughtfully. "Do you mind if I ask what a moment is?"

"It's a for-now. Not a random hookup, and not a relationship. Sometimes it's nothing more than a flirtation; sometimes it's a little more involved. It's a balancing act. But it's honest. And it eases loneliness without sacrificing pride or self-sufficiency."

"And sex? Where does that fit into a moment?" Reed's lips had twitched. "Because, in my experience, sex takes a lot longer than a moment, even when it's only mediocre."

"True. Which is why it seldom factored in, not after my experimentation stage. It didn't take me long to realize I couldn't seem to separate physical and emotional intimacy. So, for the most part, sex got shelved."

He hadn't responded. He'd just stared straight ahead, clearly pondering her words.

Not long after, they'd said their good-nights.

Now Taylor wondered if that segment of the conversation had been a mistake. Reed was already taking things slow between them. Had he inferred from her comment that she was putting on the brakes? If so, he was dead wrong. In fact, she was starting to go crazy from the sexual tension that burned between them, and which they'd barely begun to explore. She wanted to take that next step, to let the inevitable happen—even though she had a pretty good idea what was at risk.

Risk. It seemed like an absurd concept after a day like today.

A close friend was dead. Life was short, and terrifyingly unpredictable. Self-protection might be safe, but it was also lonely. And, in some cases, the trade-off just wasn't worth it.

Restlessly, Taylor rolled onto her side. She wondered if Reed was asleep and, if not, what he was thinking. Was he asking himself the same questions she was? Was he wrestling with whether the timing was wrong?

There was only one way to find out.

Flinging back the covers, Taylor got out of bed and marched out of the guest room. Reed's bedroom door was ajar, and a reading light burned inside. She headed straight for the door and, with one perfunctory knock, pushed it open and hovered on the threshold.

Reed had been lying on his back in bed—not reading, as she'd surmised—but staring at the ceiling, arms folded beneath his head, in much the same fashion as she'd been a few minutes earlier. He started when she burst in, then rolled onto his side to face her, propping himself on one elbow. "Are you okay?"

"No." Taylor walked over to the bed, stopping only when her legs bumped up against the mattress. Her heart was pounding, and she couldn't believe she was actually doing this. But she wasn't going to chicken out now. Not when she was a fraction away from where she wanted to be. Not even if she ended up an emotional basket case.

It occurred to her that all she wearing was a thin cotton nightshirt—one that was practically transparent, thanks to the light thrown off by Reed's lamp. Instinctively, she reached up to cross her arms over her chest, then realized how counterproductive that was.

She let her arms fall to her sides.

Standing absolutely still, she gave Reed an unimpeded view and loads of time to look his fill.

She wasn't disappointed with his reaction. His features tightened, and his gaze raked over every inch of her, lingering on all the right spots until Taylor's entire body grew warm.

"No," she repeated in a low, heated whisper. "I'm *not* okay. Are you?"

"No." He reached up, seizing her arm and toppling her onto the bed, on top of him, with only the down comforter separating them. He clasped the back of her neck, bringing her mouth down to his. "I'm definitely not okay. But I'm about to change that."

"Good."

They kissed, hot and hungry. Taylor could actually feel vibrations darting between them, comforter or no comforter. Her nightshirt had ridden up to her hips, and Reed's erection throbbed against her, hardening as she pressed closer, parting her thighs so she could cradle him.

A harsh groan ripped from his chest and, with a herculean effort, he dragged his mouth away, his breath coming hard and fast as he stared up at her, flames burning in his eyes. "This isn't slow."

That was the understatement of the century. "No," Taylor managed, barely able to speak. "It's not. And I don't want it to be." She moved sensuously against him.

"Taylor." He sounded like he was drowning. His fingers tangled in her hair, trembling as they tried to hold her away rather than haul her against him. "I know you want this. God knows, I want this." A shaky laugh. "Hell, I think I'll explode if I don't get inside you."

"So?"

"So are you sure you want this *now*? Because the timing—"

She pressed her fingers to his lips. "I'm sure. I want this so much I'll probably die if you lapse into the Sir Galahad routine." She sat up, tugged her nightshirt over her head, and tossed it aside. "You said you'd know, that there'd be no miscommunications. Well, know. This is exactly what I want. Here. Now."

That was all he needed.

He yanked at the comforter, and she helped him, wriggling from one knee to the other until he'd dragged the comforter out from between them. That done, he rolled her onto the sheets, on her back and under him.

He was naked. She could feel every incredible inch of him, hot and hard and desperate to get inside her. He kissed her, his mouth as hot as the rest of him, his knees wedging between her thighs, nudging them apart. He reached between their bodies, his fingers opening her, finding her slick and wet and quivering at his touch.

She heard herself cry out.

"Dammit. I can't wait." Reed's body was shaking as he crushed her into the mattress, his penis probing the entrance to her body. "Taylor . . . I'm sorry . . . I . . ."

"Don't stop." Taylor couldn't wait any more than he. She raised her hips, her knees gripping his sides to urge him inside her.

In one hard thrust, he was all the way in, and the world seemed to stop for one exquisite, unbearable moment. Reed made a harsh, inarticulate sound, gritting his teeth against the excruciating physical pleasure, and Taylor caught her breath, wrapping her arms around his back, trying to keep him where he was. There. Right there.

Impossibly, he made it better, pushing a fraction deeper, stretching and filling her beyond comprehension.

Taylor's nails dug into his back, and she could feel her orgasm already building, tightening inside her.

Reed felt it, too. He withdrew, then pushed back inside—but slowly, maddeningly, caressing her inside and out as he felt her body coiling tighter and tighter around his.

She climaxed in a rush, the sensation so powerful she couldn't breathe, much less cry out. She convulsed, again and again, her spasms radiating out from her core, growing in intensity, milking every inch of Reed's already straining erection.

His last semblance of control snapped.

Gripping Taylor's hips, he pulled out, then plunged back in, coming even as he did. He matched her contractions with his own, jetting into her and grinding out her name from between clenched teeth.

He collapsed on top of her, his face buried in her neck, and Taylor sank into the mattress, feeling as weak as if she'd run a marathon.

Real time resumed, the ticking of a clock somewhere in the apartment mingling with the rumbles and honks of traffic from the street below. Still, neither of them moved, the harsh breaths shuddering through them requiring all the energy they had left.

Reed made the first discernible sound. It was a long-drawn-out groan.

Taylor responded with a wisp of laughter, and she lifted her foot a bit, rubbed her arch against his calf.

"Are you all right?" he muttered.

"Fantastic. Spectacular." A pause. "Although, if you were counting on 'slow,' I don't think you got it."

His husky chuckle vibrated against her skin. "No, sweetheart, what I got was a lightning strike. I'm not quite sure I'm alive."

"Oh, you're alive," she assured him.

"Barely." He gave a slight shake of his head. "I've never lost control like that."

"I inspire you."

"You more than inspire me. You bring out things in me I never—" With a hard swallow, he broke off, obviously not ready to go down that particular path. "I'm too heavy. I don't want to crush you," he pronounced instead. Unsteadily, he managed to prop himself on his elbows, then made a halfhearted attempt to hoist himself off of her.

"Don't you dare." Taylor put a lid on that idea, wrapping her limbs around him. "I like you right where you are."

One dark brow rose. "Now who's making decisions for whom?"

"I am." She smiled, feeling more uninhibited than she ever had in her life. "I never said my rules were reciprocal. Besides, that lightning strike you described? It was incredible. Beyond incredible. Still, I'd like to try slow, too. Just for comparison's sake."

"Would you now?" His grin was pure seduction, and he rolled them both over so she was on top, but he was still inside her. "Me, too. I'd like to try slow . . . and a whole lot more. As soon as I have the strength."

"And when will that be?" she asked, letting her knees slide down on either side of him and shifting her hips ever so slightly.

His breath emerged in a hiss, his penis hardening inside her. "How does now sound?"

"Now sounds perfect."

THEY LAY QUIETLY TOGETHER, Reed's fingers idly threading through strands of Taylor's hair.

He was pensive. She could sense it.

She glanced up, caught him studying her from beneath hooded lids. "Okay, what? You're thinking something. What is it?"

"I'm wondering if you're really okay," he answered bluntly. "If this wasn't too soon for you, or maybe a reaction to what happened today."

"I am, and it wasn't." Taylor propped her chin on his chest. "Yes, I've been pondering life and the curves it throws. Under the circumstances, that's to be expected. But that didn't affect my desire to make love with you. That's something I've wanted for days. And it was well worth the wait." She pushed herself up so she could meet his gaze. "Reed, we both knew where this relationship was headed. To put it off until we'd resolved all my emotional baggage would be unrealistic and a stupid waste of time."

Reed's brows drew together. He didn't contradict her, but he didn't look anywhere near ready to let this go. "I still plan on getting you to trust me and to rely on me—not just in bed, but in fact."

"I know. And I hope you succeed."

"And Taylor . . ." There was an intensity about him that told her there was no room for discussion in whatever he was about to say. "Let's be clear about one thing. This *is* a relationship—*not* a moment."

"I know," Taylor replied quietly. "And, if you're asking, yes, I'm scared to death. But it's a risk I want to take."

Something tender flickered in his eyes. "Good." He drew her mouth back down to his. "Back to the subject at hand. We seem to have mastered the lightning strike. What do you say we try for something in between before we try tackling slow?"

CHAPTER 17

H E made his way to Taylor's apartment building. He'd been here earlier, but she'd been out. He hoped she was okay. She must have taken the news hard. But he'd had no choice. It had to be done.

He was glad he hadn't punished Taylor. He knew it wasn't her fault. Men kept pursuing her. But she turned them away. They never spent the night. They all tried to stay. But she made them leave. Now he'd taught one of them a lesson.

He couldn't believe how easy it had been. Following the stupid drunk to the subway station, using a Metrocard he'd bought with cash at one of those big vending machines so there'd be no chance of being traced, and riding with him to Times Square. With his head swallowed up by his parka hood and his nose buried in a book, he'd evaded identification by the video surveillance system. He'd been just another late-night rider freezing his butt off in the New York subway. Then, once he'd transferred to the Flushing line, it had been a piece of cake.

Now maybe they'd learn.

He crossed the street. Taylor's apartment was just half a block away.

He felt the usual thrill rush through him that he felt when he was near her. Only this time was better. He was back in control now, despite the earlier setback. He was on his way to realizing his dream. Soon she'd be his.

He reached his destination, excitement thrumming through him.

AN HOUR LATER, excitement had transformed to rage.

Where the hell was she?

At first, he'd thought she was asleep. But he knew she slept with a small light on. And the apartment was pitch-dark. Which meant she was still out.

Out where? With whom?

An ugly wave of suspicion began surging inside him, mingling with the fury that was already pumping through his veins.

She could be in many places—with a friend or a family member.

Or with Reed Weston.

CHAPTER 18

THE mood at the radio station was somber.

Everyone was going through the motions; going about their business in robotlike shock, talking quietly among themselves about the upcoming funeral service. Only the live-talk-show hosts—out of sheer necessity and strictly during their on-the-air time—managed to inject a modicum of enthusiasm in their tone. But the moment their two-hour stints were up, they became as solemn as the rest of the WVNY family.

Jack had gathered them together immediately after he got word from Marilyn. He'd broken the news straightforwardly, although there was a glitter of tears in his eyes as he spoke. For those who weren't present, he sent out a simple, official memo, then issued a statement of sorrow and condolence to the trade media. As for Taylor's intentions to make a more personal statement at the outset of her show, he fully supported that.

Well, that outset was just an hour away now, and the atmosphere in Taylor's studio was morose.

Taylor stood at the counter beside Kevin's desk, rereading her commemorative notes about Rick, not absorbing a single word. Kevin was queuing up phone calls on autopilot, shaking his head as Sally asked him gently, for the third time, if he'd like her to handle his desk for one more night.

"Just to give you another day to get it together," she suggested.

"No." Kevin shook his head. "Believe me, more time to think is the last thing I need." He pivoted around in his chair so he could face her. "Thanks, Sal. It's not that I don't appreciate your offer, or that I'm skeptical about your ability to handle the show. You did a great job last night. I'm sure you'd do just as great a job with Taylor on live. But I'll go crazy if I don't get back to work." A weighted pause. "Besides, I need to feel like I'm part of the tribute Taylor's about to give Rick."

"I understand."

"That's assuming I get through that tribute without falling apart," Taylor murmured, abandoning her notes and shoving them in the pocket of her blazer.

"You will," Sally assured her, squeezing Taylor's arm before gathering up her things to go. Her blond head was bowed, her usual bouncy personality tempered by sadness. "You'll find the strength—and the right words. You always do."

"Thanks." Taylor gave Sally a faint smile as she headed for the door. She wished she shared Sally's optimism. But she was feeling raw and shaky. She'd have to overcome both, not just to say what she wanted to about Rick, but, afterward, to switch gears and conduct a normal show.

Sally passed Dennis on her way out. He took one step into the room, then paused, rubbing his shaggy head and looking miserably uncomfortable. "I . . . Look, guys, I don't know what to say. Jack sent me in. But I don't feel like I should be here."

Taylor felt a wave of sympathy. Rick had been training him, and Dennis looked up to him as a mentor. Right now, he looked like he wished the ground would swallow him up.

"Dennis, please don't feel that way." Taylor gestured for him to come in. "This is exactly where you should be. It's where Rick would want you to be. Look, the circumstances may be devastating, but the fit is right. Rick believed you were a natural. The pain we feel at his loss has nothing to do with our faith in your abilities. We're grateful to have you." She extended her hand. "Welcome to our team."

Self-consciously, Dennis shook her hand. "Thanks."

"Yeah, ditto." Kevin stood, reaching across to offer his own handshake. "Good to have you on board."

"That's nice of you." Dennis stared at the ground. "I'm not much with words. But I feel . . . I mean, I just can't believe . . . I wish—"

"We know." Taylor cut him off gently. "Tell you what. We have a little time before we go on the air. Get comfortable at the control panel. I'll get us all some coffee. Then you can tell us a little bit about yourself so we can get to know you better."

He looked startled. "Are you sure you want to do that tonight?"

Taylor nodded. Under circumstances such as these, one sound psychological strategy was to inject an element of normalcy into everyone's interactions. It worked wonders toward upping the group comfort level, and toward getting some normalcy to actually sink in. "Very sure. Frankly, if I look at the notes I jotted down about Rick one more time, I'm going to lose it. I'd rather sit and talk with you guys. It'll ease all of us into pulling off a regular show."

"I agree." Kevin sounded relieved. "I'll get Dennis set up while you grab the coffee."

Ten minutes later, they sat, sipping their coffee, Kevin at his desk, Dennis at the control panel, and Taylor sitting in a chair she'd pulled up across from them.

"So, are you a long-term radio buff like everyone else here?" Taylor asked.

She could actually see Dennis relax a tad. "Big-time. I always wanted to work at a radio station. I just wasn't sure what I'd end up doing there. I've always been good with electronics and computers, and I was an audiophile in my teens. Still am. After that, I dabbled at some hole-in-the-wall stations. I learned a lot—including how much I like handling the tech aspects of the business."

"Yeah, I hear you about the dabbling." Kevin grinned. "What hole-in-the-wall towns did you hit?"

"You name it. I'm from a hick town in Nebraska. I got out of there when I was sixteen. I backpacked around the country for a couple of years, stopping here and there to do radio stints. I was everything from a gofer to an audio tech."

"What made you come east?"

"The Big Apple. It was a risk. I knew I was trying to break into the big league. But Manhattan's filled with radio stations. I just wanted to get a foot in the door at one of them. I'd do it without pay if I had to, just to learn and show them what I could do. I got lucky. Jack gave me a break."

"Jack's got a good eye for talent," Taylor said. "So it's not just luck." She switched gears, going for a lighter, more personal touch in case Dennis felt like he was in the hot seat. She wanted him to thaw, not tense up. "Since there are no secrets in this place, you might as well give us some insight into your personal life. You know, family, hobbies, interests—that kind of thing."

"Don't forget significant others," Kevin added quickly.

Dennis looked startled, but not offended. In fact, he actually started to grin. "Let's see, my family's pretty much gone. My hobby is trying to win the lottery. I buy ten tickets twice a week and keep my fingers crossed. My interests are reading computer magazines and tinkering with anything electronic. Oh, and yeah, I've got a girlfriend."

"Details," Kevin pressed. "Name? Serious?"

The grin widened, accompanied by a flush. "Her name's Ally. I guess it's serious. We'll see. She's easy to be with. And she doesn't think I'm a geek."

"How long have you been together?"

"Four or five months."

"Geez, Kev, you're like a tabloid reporter," Taylor teased. "I said we should talk, not interrogate." She turned to Dennis. "Pay no attention to him. He likes getting the lowdown on everyone else's love life." A twinkle. "Maybe for comparison's sake."

"Nope. Not necessary. I'm the champ, hands down." Kevin was grinning now, too, and looked a lot more like himself. "Oh, Taylor, speaking of love lives—"

"Forget it," she interrupted. "I'm not going there."

"Ah. So there is something going on."

"Kevin, cut it out." Taylor rose, glancing at her watch. "Just look at the time. I'd better get into my studio and get myself settled." She turned to go.

"Taylor." Kevin's voice stopped her. It was sober, not teasing, and she turned back, shooting him an inquisitive look. "Whether or not it's turning into something serious, I'm glad you weren't alone last night."

She nodded. "Yeah. Me, too. The same goes for you. I'm glad Phyllis was with you when I called." Slowly, she sucked in her breath. "I'm not us-ing the index cards," she announced. "I'm just talking from the heart."

Kevin didn't look surprised. "Wise choice. That's where your best stuff comes from."

"I hope so."

8:03 P.M.

CHRYSLER BUILDING

Jonathan listened very carefully as Taylor issued a warm, glowing tribute to her now-deceased audio engineer. It was just right, like everything she did, filled with friendship, high regard, and sorrow. Her voice quavered a few times. But, in the end, she held it together. That's who Taylor was. Still, she sounded so fragile.

He had to reach out to her.

He'd call her at a little past ten, when she was out of the limelight but not out of the building. That way, he could have her undivided at-tention—and make the most of it.

If he wanted to win Taylor over, and fast, he'd better take some pow-erful, concrete steps. He could feel Reed's presence in her life looming over him like a dark, suffocating cloud.

Speaking of Reed, he wondered if the son of a bitch had spoken to Douglas yet. Doubtful. Douglas would have mentioned it on the phone, when they'd talked to set up tomorrow night's dinner. That didn't mean Reed *wouldn't* speak to him, if he thought it over and decided to voice his suspicions to Douglas. Let's face it, Jonathan wasn't taking Reed's silence to the bank. He planned on signing those damned papers with Douglas before any monkey wrenches were tossed in the works.

On the other hand, he wasn't all that worried. Even if Reed opened his mouth before the papers were signed, it wouldn't ruin things, just slow them down.

No, Reed wouldn't be the main thorn in his side. That distinct honor belonged to the same person who'd held it for years.

Adrienne.

Well, he'd worked out a way to pluck that thorn as well.

Jonathan's mind drifted back to Taylor, and he warmed to the sound of her voice, now reassuring the mother of a teenage son that their relationship wasn't hopeless, that she was doing all the right things to let him know she cared.

He could visualize her as she spoke, all understated beauty and refinement. With her classic breeding, keen mind, and warm heart, she'd be the perfect complement to him when he stepped in as CEO of Berkley & Company. The perfect asset, the perfect wife, the perfect mother.

Idly, he wondered if she'd pass that luxurious dark red hair on to their kids.

10:15 P.M.

WVNY

Laura poked her head into Taylor's office, a worried frown knitting her brows. "Taylor, this is the third time that guy's called in the past fifteen minutes, demanding to speak with you. And all caller ID says is 'private.' Do you want me to call the police?"

Taylor folded her hands on her desk. She wasn't going to overreact. Not this time.

"He still won't give you his name?"

"No. He just keeps saying it's personal. He doesn't sound like he's drunk or high. He just sounds unreasonably urgent."

"Fine." Taylor's chin came up. "Tell him I'm on another line. Ask him to try again in five minutes. Then hang up and dial star fifty-seven."

"You want me to initiate call trace?"

"You bet. When he calls back, tell him that I'm still tied up, then do the same thing. Tell him to give me five minutes before he tries again, then hang up and do the call trace. That should do it for the police. Two phone calls are enough to substantiate harassment."

"*If* that's what he plans on doing," Laura reminded her. "He could just be some persistent fan."

"I'll risk it."

Laura nodded. "Ultimately, how do you want me to get rid of him?"

"When he calls the third time, tell him you're sorry, but you just

found out that my other call was an emergency. Tell him I just left—
escorted by security," Taylor added quickly, thinking that just in case
the guy was near her building and decided to hang around and try
getting her alone, hearing that she had an armed escort would deter
him.

"Okay. I'll also ask one of the security guys to wait for you downstairs
and put you in a taxi home."

"Thanks. You read my mind."

With a grim expression, Laura went to comply.

Taylor's heart was pounding. She forced her mind under control.
There was plenty of time for speculation. Laura had to finish the call trace,
and then the police had to take it from there. But, one way or the other,
she'd find out who tonight's caller was.

She found out sooner than expected.

Seven minutes later, Laura walked in. "The guy's not stupid. He obviously figured out what we were doing. So he caved. He just gave me his
name."

Taylor sank into her seat, weak with relief. "I guess that means you
were right. He must be harmless."

"You tell me. It's Jonathan Mallory."

CHAPTER 19

JONATHAN was ripping mad.

Taylor wouldn't talk to him. Not even after he'd supplied her assistant with his name. He'd done that to save time. Laura what's-her-name was clearly implementing a call trace on him at Taylor's request. So he saved her the trouble.

And what was his reward?

The snotty little bitch had blown him off—*also*, no doubt, at Taylor's request. He hadn't gotten through to exchange so much as one personal word. Taylor simply wouldn't pick up the phone.

Why, dammit? This couldn't be about Gordon anymore. Not after all this time. The shock must have worn off. Besides, even if she was still jittery about being face-to-face with him, that didn't explain why she wouldn't even speak to him. They'd had a perfectly civil conversation at Harter, Randolph & Collins, once she'd realized who he was, or rather *wasn't*. And, although she'd still been on edge when they ran into each other at Dellinger, she'd hadn't been unpleasant.

No, this had to be prompted by something more extensive than Gordon. Correction: not some*thing*. Some*one*.

Reed.

What the hell had he said to her? Had he found some clever way to get around attorney-client privilege? Had he dropped a hint about Jonathan's "thing" for redheaded women without divulging the ugly details of his past? If so, had he planted a seed in her mind—a seed that would destroy Jonathan's chances of getting what he wanted?

Shit.

He poured himself a Scotch, downed it in one gulp, then poured another.

There was only one way to get at the truth. He wasn't wasting time on speculation. He had to find out.

He polished off the second Scotch, got halfway through a third, then groped for the telephone receiver till he managed to pick it up and prop it under his chin. Leaning forward, he squinted at the touch-tone pad until it came into focus. Then he punched in Reed's cell number.

Reed answered on the third ring. He sounded distracted. "Hello?" In the background was a staticlike hum. Road noise. Reed was driving.

"H'llo. Where're you? En route to get your lady?"

For a moment, there was silence. Then Reed made a disgusted sound. "Jonathan? How much have you had? You sound pretty messed up."

A hard swallow of Scotch. "If I am, I owe it to you."

"I asked you a question. Are you drunk?"

"I'm getting there. Fast, I hope."

"Are you home or at the office?"

"The office. I just spent thirty fucking minutes trying to get through to Taylor."

Reed's tone changed entirely. "What are you talking about? Get through to Taylor how?"

"Jealous?"

"Jonathan, I'm warning you . . ."

"*You're* warning *me?*" Something inside Jonathan snapped. "You, who broke the cardinal bar-association rule? You told her, you son of a bitch, didn't you?"

"What the hell are you talking about? Told her what—about you? No, as much as I wanted to, I didn't. I didn't say a word."

"Then why won't she take my calls?"

"You really need to ask that?"

Jonathan swore loudly. "Don't bring up that Gordon crap again. It's old. We were twins. We looked alike. He was a screwed-up, manipulative bastard. I'm a respected businessman on his way to the top. He's dead. I'm alive. End of comparison."

Reed sucked in his breath. "Jonathan, you're raving like a lunatic. Go home. Take some aspirin, go to bed, and sleep it off."

"Speaking of sleeping, are you spending tonight at Taylor's place or yours?" The question was slurred, the bitterness and sarcasm that Jonathan normally repressed coming through loud and clear. "Y'know what? It doesn't matter. I'll just do the expedient thing—call your cell phone and ask for her. That'll work, no matter whose bed you're in. I might interrupt you midseduction. But that's a chance I'll have to take." His tone hardened. "I'm getting through to Taylor. I'm not going away. I have big plans for that woman."

That speech blasted to bits any semblance of emotional control on the other end. "Leave Taylor the hell alone, Jonathan." Shards of ice sliced Reed's warning. "Or I won't break my oath of confidentiality; I'll break your neck. Stay far away. I mean it."

"Do you? Well, I want Taylor. And I mean *that*. Don't underestimate the lengths I'll go to to get her." Somewhere in the back of Jonathan's mind, he realized he'd never heard Reed so angry. He also realized he was fueling that anger—*and* saying way too much, tipping his hand far more than he should. But he couldn't seem to stop himself.

He gulped at his drink, a little Scotch trickling down his shirt. "I'm getting through to her, Reed. Sooner, not later. And not just on the phone. Threaten me all you want to. Just get out of her bed and out of her life. As for the little secret you think you're holding over my head, forget it. Once Taylor and I are together, I'll tell her myself. She'll understand. She gets what makes people tick." A harsh laugh. "Believe me, my past is minor compared to the rest of the Berkley saga."

"Jonathan—"

"You won't win, Reed," Jonathan snapped out. "Y'know why? Because I won't lose. I planned it out too well. The whole thing's perfect. Taylor's perfect. She and I will be perfect together. So get the hell out of my way."

He smiled as he disconnected the call, silencing Reed's furious warnings for him to back off.

Taylor was lying in bed, staring at the phone and debating whether it was too late to call Reed when the buzzer sounded from the lobby.

She rose and went out to the hallway, pressing the intercom button. "Yes, George?"

"Sorry to bother you so late, Ms. Halstead. But Mr. Weston's here. He really wants to see you."

Relief swept through her. "Thank you, George. You can send him up."

She grabbed her robe, pulled it on, and went to the door. She watched through the peephole, letting Reed in before he even knocked. "I'm glad you're here. I was just debating whether to call you."

He looked drawn and troubled, and his eyes narrowed at her words. "Why? Is something wrong?"

Taylor eyed him speculatively. "You mean, besides dealing with Rick's death and getting through a tribute to him and an entire show? Yes, something's wrong. Why do I get the feeling you already know that?"

Reed blew out his breath. "Let's not do this dance, Taylor. Please— not tonight. Just tell me what happened. I'll answer you if I can."

"Fair enough. Jonathan Mallory called the radio station. Not once, but repeatedly. He insisted on speaking to me. I didn't take the calls." A pause, during which time Taylor studied Reed's unchanged expression. "I see you're not surprised."

"I'm not."

"Okay, then. Your turn."

"Jonathan told me he tried to contact you." Reed shrugged out of his coat and tossed it aside, not even bothering to hang it up. "He's determined to speak with you. He reached me about an hour ago on my cell. He wanted to find out if we'd be together tonight and, if so, at whose apartment, so he could get through to you there."

Taylor went very still. "He doesn't have my number. It's unlisted. So how could he get through to me here?"

"Unlisted numbers can be gotten. Besides, it's a moot point. He's calling my cell phone and asking for you. That way, he'll be sure to connect no matter where we are."

"Tonight?"

"Yes."

"It's twelve A.M." A prickle of apprehension darted up Taylor's spine. "This is starting to creep me out." She met and held Reed's gaze. "Whatever he wants to talk to me about, you know what it is. That's why you're here. You're worried. And it doesn't look like legal worry to me. Tell me what's going on. And it better not include the phrase 'attorney-client privilege.'"

"It won't." Reed knew he had to tread carefully. He couldn't mention Jonathan's past, including either of his borderline incidents. But he could reveal his current, insistent romantic interest in Taylor, and even his drunken state when he'd blurted it out—well, that didn't breach any rules of confidentiality. And he'd be damned if he wouldn't give Taylor enough to go on so she could protect herself—if protection from Jonathan was what was needed.

"Reed . . . ," she prompted.

"Jonathan Mallory wants you," he stated flatly. "He told me to stand aside so he can move in, now that you've had time to get over his resemblance to Gordon."

She started. "Excuse me?"

"You heard me. He's convinced that the two of you could have some kind of serious relationship."

"I don't believe this." Taylor averted her head, dragging a hand through her long hair as she tried to process what Reed had just said. "This is crazy. I met the guy twice. The first time I freaked out because I thought he was Gordon. The second time I was jumping out of my skin. He asked me out and I turned him down flat. So where would he get the idea we're en route to some kind of relationship?"

Reed frowned. "I can't answer that. All I can surmise is that between listening to your radio show and whatever karma he perceived between the two of you, he feels like you have some kind of connection, like you'd understand each other. Look, he was pretty drunk when he called me and babbled all this stuff. But that's the gist of it."

"Karma? Connection?" Taylor stared at Reed, totally thrown by the explanation, and experiencing a terrifying sense of déjà vu. "Is being delusional a genetic trait in that family? Because Jonathan Mallory sounds almost as unbalanced as—" She stopped short of saying Gordon's name. "Do you think he'd . . . do . . . anything?"

"No." That much Reed could answer honestly. "Jonathan's persistent. But he's not violent."

"Right. Neither was his brother—not until that night." Taylor was starting to shake. "Reed, I want him to go away. I'll get a restraining order if I have to. With everything that's going on, I can't handle this, too."

"I know." Reed reached out, his palms caressing her shoulders. "That's why I'm here."

Her chin lifted in a show of resolve, but her lips quivered as she spoke. "I won't take his calls. You'll have to be the intermediary. Tell him I'm not interested—not in speaking with him, dating him, or starting a relationship with him. As for his ordering you to stand aside, that's intrusive and borderline obsessive. Tell him I make my own decisions about my social life. Tell him I've had enough drama in my life to last forever. Tell him . . ." Taylor's voice faltered, and something inside her just seemed to give out. She began to cry, tears gliding down her cheeks as she covered her face with her hands. "I can't believe I'm falling apart like this," she wept. "I never fall apart. I . . ."

Reed pulled her against him, tangling his fingers in her hair and just holding her. "Maybe you need to. You've got too damned much on your plate."

"When those phone calls came into the station tonight, I almost lost it." Her voice was muffled against Reed's shirt. "He kept calling back, and he wouldn't leave his name, and . . ."

"And you were afraid it was that weirdo who called you in the middle of the night."

A nod. "Not that this is much better. I'm creeped out. And I'm scared."

"Don't be. I'll get Jonathan to go away."

"But will he listen? He's conjured up a whole scenario that's so removed from reality that—" Abruptly, Taylor stiffened in Reed's arms. "You don't think it's possible that Jonathan Mallory *is* the one who's been harassing me, do you?"

There was the barest hint of a pause before Reed answered—but it was enough to make Taylor pull back and scrutinize his expression. "Reed?"

"I don't know," he replied bluntly. "I don't think so, but I can't be sure."

"But you're not shocked by my question. Which means the possibility occurred to you, too."

"Yeah. It occurred to me."

"Based on more than random speculation."

"Taylor, don't." Reed's jaw set, but he looked more pained than emphatic. "I've already pushed my ethical boundaries to the limit. I can't say any more."

Her eyes widened. "Are you saying . . . ?"

"I'm saying I can't discuss my client. But I'm also saying I'd never stand by if I thought he was a danger to you. There's a huge difference between infatuation and physical assault. Jonathan has major issues, but he isn't Gordon. Don't let your emotional vulnerabilities drown out your reason. I'm asking you to trust me. I know you're not quite ready to. But try."

She stood there for a moment, staring up at him, her lashes damp with tears. "I'm a mess," she whispered at last. "My emotions are raw. And you're right. I can't even separate Gordon from Jonathan anymore. I feel like this is an instant replay of last September. The question is, is that irrational fear or clearheaded logic talking? I just don't know. I can't even trust my own judgment. How can I trust you?"

"Because of what's happening between us. Because you know I won't let anyone harm you. And because you know I'm in possession of all the facts, including those I can't discuss, and that I'm smart enough to know what to do with them."

Taylor's head felt as if it were going to explode. "I understand what you're saying, but . . ."

"But it's a huge leap for you. I realize that." Reed pulled her closer, tucking her head under his chin. "Make the leap. If for no other reason than because I'm more objective about this than you are. I *can* separate reason from emotion. Except when I touch you. That's the only time my objectivity goes right out the window."

That much Taylor understood only too well. "I can't even think anymore," she murmured. "I'm exhausted. Too much stimuli. Too little sleep."

"*No* sleep," Reed corrected, his lips in her hair. "Not for either of us. And talk about stimuli."

"That's not what I meant."

"I know. But it's what *I* meant. What happened between us last night was as consuming as it gets—despite the fact that the timing was even worse than I realized. The result is major emotional overload."

Taylor sighed. "I guess you're right. Ironically, I set tonight aside to recoup. I figured that if I was alone, I could sort through everything's that happened these past few days, and recharge my emotional batteries a little. It seemed like a great idea, especially since after the show, I was so drained I could barely walk. My plan was to come home, take a bath, and curl up in bed. It didn't work out that way, did it?"

Reed leaned back and tilted up her chin, searching her face with a questioning look. "Do you want me to leave?"

"No. God, no." She was suddenly wide-awake, shaking her head vehemently even as he asked the question. "Everything changed after I got those messages from Jonathan Mallory. My new wounds were still smarting, and at the same time, someone was tearing open the old ones and pouring salt in them. When you buzzed from downstairs, I was staring at the phone, debating whether it was too late to call you. I wanted to beg you to come over."

"Then I'm glad I'm here."

"Me, too. Talk about mental telepathy." Taylor fought her natural instinct for emotional self-protection, abandoning all the unanswered questions and throwing herself into the here and now. "Stay. I need you."

Tenderness flashed in Reed's eyes, and he framed her face between his palms. "I'm not going anywhere. Not till morning. I'll stay right here with you all night." He cleared his throat, clarifying what he had in mind, in case she had any doubts. "And if being held is all you want, then that's all I'll do."

"Not a chance." She dashed the tears off her cheeks, then began unbuttoning his shirt. "I want a lot more than that. I want to shut out the world and all its ugliness. I want to relive every unbelievable sensation we felt last night. I want to experience new ones we have yet to discover." A watery smile. "Besides, we're still perfecting the art of going slow, remember? It's like my self-defense lessons. Tons of practice is required to get it exactly right. Isn't that what you taught me?"

A corner of his mouth lifted, and he unbelted her robe, backing her toward the bedroom. "How could I have forgotten?"

She was naked by the time they reached the bed. Reed eased her down, then stepped back to yank off the rest of his clothes.

For the briefest instant, he paused, glancing out the window and scanning the dark street below.

Nothing.

The last thing he did before lowering himself into Taylor's waiting arms was to grope for his suit jacket, find his cell phone, and turn it off.

So much for Jonathan's call.

No upsets. No interruptions.

Nothing but Taylor.

He covered her body with his.

FRIDAY, FEBRUARY 7

4:35 A.M.

The shrill ringing of the telephone on the night table pierced the silence of the room.

Her head pillowed on Reed's chest, Taylor snapped out of her half doze instantly. "Oh, no," she whispered.

"Let me get it." Reed pushed himself to a sitting position, reaching across Taylor to snatch up the receiver.

"No." She grabbed his arm. "If it's *him*—the guy who called last time—he'll go crazy if a man answers my phone at this time of night. I'll get it."

She stared at the phone, noting the sickeningly familiar caller-ID designation of "private" on the LCD display. Steeling herself, she lifted the receiver from its cradle. "Hello?"

"Where were you last night?" It was the raspy male voice, its pitch altered this time to a low baritone. "I waited for hours."

Taylor's entire body started shaking. "Waited? Waited where? Who is this?"

"Answer my question."

She forced herself to summon up the psychologist within her. "Someone dear to me passed away. I was too upset to be alone. I stayed with friends."

"Friends." The voice was too synthesized for Taylor to figure out whether there was skepticism in his tone.

"Yes," she confirmed. "Now, who are you and why were you waiting for me?"

"I told you to sleep alone. I meant it. Don't force my hand."

Before Taylor could respond, there was a dial tone.

CHAPTER 20

DOUGLAS Berkley waved away the cup of coffee Reed offered him, not even taking the time to sit down. Instead, he stood behind one of the plush chocolate brown leather chairs, gripping its back with both hands.

"I have a nine-thirty meeting, Reed. What's so urgent that you had to see me first thing?"

Reed didn't mince words. "We have a situation," he said tersely. "It can't wait."

"Does this concern the documents? Because, regardless of the issues, those are right on track. I'm meeting Jonathan for dinner tonight. We still have a few minor points to work out. I'll be back at the brownstone Monday evening and set to sign the papers and make the necessary announcement, as scheduled, on Tuesday."

"It's not about the company. It's about Jonathan."

Douglas's eyes narrowed. "What about him?"

Reed laid out the whole series of events, from soup to nuts, sticking to the facts and none of the conjecture.

By the time he was through, Douglas's lips were drawn into a grim line. "You think Jonathan's the one harassing Taylor Halstead?"

"It depends on when you ask me. Sometimes I think it's absurd, that he'd never screw up his future that way—not now. Other times, like last night when he was ranting on my cell phone, I remember the old Jonathan, the one who convinced himself that every woman he wanted, wanted him, and that he could create a relationship simply by—"

"You don't need to remind me." Douglas walked over to the sideboard, poured himself a glass of water, and took a gulp. "She's a redhead, like the others?"

"Yes. But, unlike the others, she's already involved."

"Does Jonathan know that?"

"I told him so myself. Flat out, no holds barred."

Douglas angled his head toward Reed, hearing the underlying message loud and clear. "In other words, Taylor Halstead's involved with you."

"Right. And I was with her last night when that phone call came. She's a strong woman, Douglas. But she's about to crumple. I don't intend to let that happen."

"I see. Are you telling me there's a conflict of interest here? That you can't represent Jonathan?"

"Only if he's the one harassing Taylor. You have to find out the truth. Even if I'm out of the equation, this could get ugly. Taylor's a media personality. Her family's well connected. And Joseph Lehar is an excellent attorney. He'll be all over this in a New York minute. I don't need to tell you the scandal that would erupt, not to mention the legal ramifications. The timing couldn't be worse. You're about to launch Jonathan right into the corporate spotlight, publicly claiming him as your son and heir after all these years, and handing him the future reins to a multimillion-dollar company. I strongly suggest you get to the bottom of this potential time bomb ASAP. That way, with or without me, you can do damage control—if it's necessary."

Douglas swore softly, loosening his tie. "How much background have you supplied Taylor Halstead with?"

"You know me better than that. All I told her was that Jonathan's interested in her. But that was enough to scare her. What happened with Gordon is very fresh. And Jonathan is his twin—his identical twin."

"Not *that* identical."

"Not to you or to people who know them both well. But Taylor doesn't fall into that category."

"I understand." Douglas polished off his water and set down the glass with a thud. "It looks like Jonathan and I will be having quite a talk at dinner." He pursed his lips, a speculative expression flickering across his face. "When he called last night, he said he had one sticky matter to run by me. Maybe he plans on telling me himself."

"Maybe. But that's not exactly heartening. He ran to you both previous times as well." Reed waved away Douglas's reply. "Look, Douglas, I want him to be innocent, too. Let's leave it at that. Get back to me with whatever I should know."

"I will."

Reed cleared his throat. "Did you straighten everything out with Adrienne? Is she okay with what you've decided?"

Another frown. "As okay as she'll ever be. Look, she's not a big fan of Jonathan's. That doesn't come as a surprise, given the circumstances of his birth. And those two near disasters he got himself into in college and grad school didn't exactly endear him to her. But all that's irrelevant. Adrienne knows why I'm grooming Jonathan to take over Berkley and Company."

"He's your son."

"Yes. And Berkley and Company is my legacy. When it comes to my business, Adrienne is well aware that I have the final word. But she's also aware of Jonathan's capabilities, and of what a superb job he'll do. She likes her lifestyle, her wealth, and her social status. She won't jeopardize those, not for any reason. So whatever reservations she's harboring, she'll get over them. Especially since she knows damned well that in the event of my death, my entire estate—company and all—goes to her. Half the stock's already in her name. She watches the profits and projections like a hawk. Believe me, she'll always keep a close eye on things—including Jonathan."

"I wasn't worried about Adrienne's future," Reed returned dryly. "She's a smart woman. She'll look out for her interests. I was just hoping her relationship with Jonathan was going a little more smoothly."

"They're civil to each other. They'll never be more."

"No, I'd imagine not." Reed swallowed some of his coffee. "Will she accompany you next week for the execution of the documents?"

"The day after. My plan is to sign the papers, make the announcement, and then introduce Jonathan around on Tuesday. That night, he and I will have dinner with the company VPs. On Wednesday, my driver will bring Adrienne into Manhattan. She can shop, visit the Met, or catch a Broadway matinee, whatever she wants. After that, she and I are hosting a small, private celebration at Le Cirque in honor of Jonathan."

Douglas blew out his breath. "I was going to ask you to join us. I guess that's out. Unless, by then, you're convinced that Jonathan's not involved in this . . . this . . . mess."

"Thanks, Douglas, but it's probably a bad idea anyway. Jonathan's furious at me right now. He might have been drunk, but he meant what he said. He fully expects Taylor and me to be over. That's not going to happen. So I'll avoid a potential scene by offering him my congratulations Tuesday morning, and let that be that."

Douglas nodded, although not happily. "I suppose that's wise." He rubbed the back of his neck. "I did a great job of screwing up as a father, didn't I?" He glanced at Reed, obviously expecting some kind of answer.

Reed gave as honest a reply as he could. "First of all, I'm in no position to judge, not being a father myself. Second, it's really none of my business. And third . . ." Reed paused. "Look, Douglas, you did what you did. You gave Gordon and Jonathan every material advantage. And with their mother dying right after they left for college and Adrienne feeling the way she did . . . let's just say you had obstacles."

"Obstacles. That's a nice way of putting it. Well, I just hope those obstacles don't come back to haunt me—*again*—this time with the one decent shot I've got of carrying on my name and my company." He headed for the door. "I'll keep you posted."

2:35 P.M.

DELLINGER ACADEMY

Ten minutes till school was out. Then it would be time to go home.

Home. The last place Taylor wanted to be.

She sat at her desk, doodling on a piece of paper, her mind plagued by the same questions that had preoccupied her every spare moment of the day.

Who was harassing her—watching her, waiting for her, calling her in the middle of the night? Was it or wasn't it Jonathan Mallory? And if it was, how deep did his obsession run? Had *he*, not Gordon, sent her those creepy e-cards? Where did one twin end and the other begin? And how far would Jonathan go to get what he wanted?

She kept returning to the matter of the e-cards. At first, she'd concluded that it was highly unlikely that Jonathan had sent them. After all, at the time they'd arrived, she'd never even met the man.

But then she'd realized that *he'd* met *her*. Figuratively, at least. He'd been listening to her radio show for quite some time. And if he was truly a delusional personality, he could build all kinds of fantasies from the supposed connection he'd established with her during those listening sessions.

Then again, so could dozens of other people.

God, she was losing her grip.

She reached across her desk, starting to gather up the papers she needed to bring home tonight. It was time to pack up and call it a day.

Leaning down, she reached for her leather tote bag and placed it on the desk in front of her. Between her busy day and her unsettled state of mind, she'd never even extracted yesterday's paperwork. It was still in there, waiting to be retrieved and refiled. Annoyed at herself, she tugged out the papers, pushing back her chair as she did so.

A rectangular white gift box tumbled out of her tote bag and onto her desk. It was the kind that held jewelry—small, flat, and tied with a thin gold elastic cord.

Taylor stopped dead in her tracks. She stared at the box as if it were a foreign object.

She'd never seen it before. Not only wasn't it hers, it hadn't been in her tote bag last night, or early this morning when she'd rummaged through looking for a pen. So unless Reed had slipped it in before she left her apartment . . . No. Surprises weren't Reed's style. Especially not now, when anything out of the ordinary made her jump.

So what was it and who'd put it there?

She picked up the box, her fingers trembling as she sought the first part of her answer.

The cord slipped off, and Taylor worked the lid free.

Inside, on a bed of cotton, lay a necklace—a simple gold chain with a single gemstone dangling from it.

The stone was a bloodred ruby in the shape of a teardrop.

Nestled as it was on the snowy cotton, the contrast between crimson and white was as starkly chilling as the e-card she'd received on New Year's Day. And the symbolic impact was irrefutable. *Her* blood. *Her* tear. Wrapped around *her* throat. A gift and a threat all in one.

A card jutted up from the inside edge of the box.

A dark sense of foreboding gripped her.

She yanked out the card. It had no envelope, and the terse message on it was typed and without a signature.

A tribute to your beauty. A reminder that you're mine. Wear it for me. I'll be watching.

With a cry of distress, Taylor sank down into her chair, dropping the card and the box as if they'd burned her hands. She covered her face with her hands. "No," she whispered aloud, trembling from head to toe. "Please, please, no."

He'd put it there. In her tote bag. With her personal things. He'd been standing right next to her, possibly even touched her, somewhere between home and school. Maybe on a street corner as she waited for a traffic light to change. Or maybe when she'd stopped to pick up the morning paper. Or just outside the school. Or . . .

Stop it, Taylor. Stop it!

"Who's that from?"

Chris Young's voice permeated her panic.

Numbly, she raised her head and gazed at him. "What?"

"That necklace. Who gave it to you—the big-bucks economics guy or the hot Mr. Corporate?"

Taylor was having a hard time grasping Chris's words.

"They've both got the cash," Chris continued flatly. "Judging from how unhappy you look, I'd guess it was Econ Man who sent it. If it was Corporate Hottie, you'd be flying. You've got it bad for him."

Finally, Chris's meaning sank in. He was talking about Jonathan and Reed.

"How would you know . . . ?"

He stared her down. "I'm sizing up the competition. And, if you ask me, they don't measure up. If you know what I mean," he added crudely.

"Chris . . ." Taylor was about to snap. "When did you see—"

"I see everything, Ms. Halstead. That's what I'm best at. Watching you." He winked. "Graduation's right around the corner. After that, I'll show you what you're missing."

"Watching me?" Taylor managed.

"Like a hawk."

His choice of words was more than Taylor could take.

She flung the card and box in her tote bag, shoved by Chris, and flew out of her office.

FIVE MINUTES LATER, she stood on the school steps and glanced around—casually, the way Mitch Garvey had instructed her to. It wasn't easy to look blasé, not after what had just happened. But she'd made a quick stop at the ladies' room, where she'd thrown some cold water on her face, and regained her composure.

To her relief, he was there. Broad-shouldered and muscular, in his early thirties, and dressed in street clothes, he was standing by the sidewalk, scanning a newspaper.

He caught her eye and tipped his head slightly in her direction, then waited until she went back into the school before folding the newspaper and making his way inside the lobby and over to the private alcove where they'd arranged to meet.

"Hi, Ms. Halstead." He extended his hand. "I'm here, as requested."

This whole exchange felt surreal. Yet, here she was, turning to this guy as if he were a life preserver. Which, right now, he was.

She shook his hand. "Thanks, Mr. Garvey. I can't tell you how much I appreciate your showing up on such short notice. I thought I'd have more time before I needed . . . Actually I was hoping I'd never need the kind of protection we discussed. As it turns out, I can't tell you how relieved I am that you're here."

He scrutinized her with a practiced eye. "Something happened."

The trembling started again. "Yes, it did. I found a box in my tote bag. There was a necklace inside. With a note. They're from him."

"You're sure?"

"Yes." She yanked out both things and thrust them at him. She couldn't get rid of them fast enough. "Here."

The PI reached into his coat pocket and pulled out a Ziploc. "Drop them in here."

Fingerprints. Of course. Taylor hadn't even thought of that.

"I'll check out the necklace, the box, and the card," he assured her, pocketing the plastic bag. "Just tell me this. When did you discover them?"

"Ten minutes ago."

"And, before that, when was the last time you checked your tote?"

"This morning. Before I left my apartment."

He pursed his lips. "So the gift got there either at school, or en route to school."

"At school?" Taylor turned white. "That never occurred to me. Are you saying you think he walked in here and—"

"No." Garvey gave a hard shake of his head. "That would be too risky. I think it's more likely he mingled with the morning commuters and dropped it in your bag at some street corner."

"Unless he's one of my students," she murmured, half to herself. "Then he'd already be at Dellinger."

The PI's brows rose. "You've got someone in mind?"

"Yes. No. I don't know." She told him about Chris Young, and the history between them.

"I'll check it out," Garvey said. "Although Chris Young would have to be pretty cagey to pull something like this off. Still, it'll be easy enough to verify."

"You don't really think it's him," Taylor deduced.

"I think we should investigate every possible lead. But, no, I don't think Chris Young fits the profile."

"God, this is unbearable." Taylor feathered an unsteady hand through her hair, then shot Garvey an apologetic look. "I'm sorry."

"It's completely understandable." He spoke quietly, and with an air of authority that Taylor found very reassuring. "Let's start over. First of all, call me Mitch. It's more natural-sounding. That way, if we're ever seen to-gether, we can easily slip into the pretense of being casual friends or col-leagues. Second, don't apologize for the urgency of your timing. I'm used to jumping into the thick of things on a moment's notice. And third, Rob referred you. That gives you priority status."

Taylor managed a smile. "So you and Rob Weston worked together for a couple of years?"

"Yup. Out in San Francisco. Rob had just made detective. I was head-ing up the same path. He's a damned fine cop. So am I. He just follows rules better than I do. So he's on the force and I'm on my own." Mitch's easygoing manner faded, and he became 100 percent PI. "Let's review the rules."

"All right."

"Keep your door locked. Don't get swallowed up in crowds. But don't go anywhere deserted either. That goes double after dark. Don't change your destination without letting me know in advance. Other than that, go about your life. Don't act weird. When you're out and about, don't glance around to see if I'm there. I will be. But we don't want to clue whoever's watching you in to that fact. You have my cell number and my pager number. Any sign of trouble, use them. I'll touch base with you every day. Okay?"

"Okay." Taylor inhaled sharply. "I'll be heading home now. After that—"

"After that, you go to the radio station. I know. I did my homework." His gaze was steady and encouraging. "Try not to worry. If he comes near you again, he's toast."

CHAPTER 21

DINNER had been odd.

Jonathan couldn't put his finger on it, but something wasn't right.

He frowned, watching Douglas's face and trying to get a handle on where his head was. They'd already had a drink and eaten half their salads, and the conversation had been limited to the surprises in this week's stock market and a profitable corporate venture Berkley & Company was currently involved in.

Well, they had more important things to discuss.

"I looked over those last few word changes you made in the paperwork," he said, initiating things. "They're fine. We're all set."

Douglas's fork paused, then continued to his mouth. "You said there was a sticky situation you wanted to discuss. It's not about Berkley and Company, then?"

"Not directly. But it could certainly impact the company. It's about Gordon."

"Gordon?"

"Yes." Jonathan folded his hands in front of him, leaning forward to convey the importance of what he had to say. "After the big 'make each investor whole' fiasco we went through after the accident—which was stickier than anything we'd bailed Gordon out of in the past—I decided to find out just how deep into this dirty dealing he was. He might be dead, but whatever damage he did could come back and bite us in the ass. So I initiated some behind-the-scenes investigating."

"And?" Douglas sounded as if this answer was the last thing he wanted to hear. Which was, no doubt, the case. For years, he'd been an ostrich when it came to Gordon.

"And it isn't pretty. Gordon spent years cheating his clients out of millions by excessive trading of their investments to boost his commissions."

"Churning?"

"Right. He's made a career out of it. Oh, and whenever a client wanted to cash in his or her stock, Gordon just did a borrow-from-Peter-to-pay-Paul maneuver. He had more than enough profits to dip into. My brother amassed a small fortune, living on the edge like that." A bitter, regretful frown. "Unfortunately, he died on the edge before he could enjoy it."

Douglas's jaw was working. "Exactly why are you telling me this?"

"What do you mean? I'm telling you in case this leaks out and we have to do damage control."

"Funny that you should use that phrase. We might very well have to do damage control. But it won't be because of Gordon's dirty dealings. I cleaned those up along the way. There's nothing to leak out."

Stunned amazement surged through Jonathan. "You knew?"

"Of course I knew. Do you honestly believe I'm so stupid that I wouldn't know my son was involved in shady business dealings? I didn't get where I am by accident, Jonathan. When it comes to business, very little gets by me. Especially when it affects the future of my company. Why do you think it was *you* I was grooming to take over Berkley and Company? Gordon was brilliant. Unfortunately, brilliance isn't enough. Honest, ethical behavior—both in business and personal practices—is essential to long-term success." A pause. "You do agree, don't you?"

Jonathan was still reeling. But he didn't miss the pointed note in Douglas's tone.

A warning bell went off.

"You know I agree. That's why I brought you this information. I wish you'd told me you already knew. It would have saved me a lot of agonizing."

"In other words, you wouldn't have been so ambivalent about accepting my job offer if you'd known I'd cleaned up your brother's dirty little mess? I'm surprised at you, Jonathan. You know how good I am at making things go away."

Okay, that was two. The digs were no accident.

It was time to take the bull by the horns.

"You've spoken with Reed," Jonathan stated flatly.

"Yes. I have." Douglas waited while their entrées were being served, waving away the offer for another round of drinks. Then he continued. "Why don't you tell me what's going on?"

Jonathan kept his expression carefully nondescript. "Reed and I both want the same woman. I believe they call that friendly rivalry."

"It doesn't sound friendly to me."

"Meaning?"

Douglas pushed away his meal. "Have you been harassing Taylor Halstead?"

"Harassing . . ." Jonathan threw down his napkin. "You believe him. You think I'm stalking Taylor like some lovesick kid."

"It wouldn't be the first time. Or the second. The pattern's exactly the same, Jonathan—a beautiful redhead you've convinced yourself wants you more than she does. This time's worse. She doesn't want you at all." Douglas was visibly trying to remain calm. "According to Reed, you all but threatened him to stay away from her. Which is absurd, since he made it quite clear that they're already involved."

"Did he? Well, if that's the case, then why did he call and ask you to intercede?"

"Not to intercede. To find out the truth. He's worried, especially after last night's phone call."

"I was drunk. I said some stupid things to him. I—"

"Not that phone call. The one Taylor got at four-thirty in the morning warning her to sleep alone."

Dead silence.

"You told Reed to expect your call. You were insistent about getting through to Taylor that night."

"Like I said, I was drunk." Jonathan's voice had risen as he fought to control his anger. "That doesn't mean I'm a wacko."

"But you do want this woman." Douglas's voice had grown stronger as well.

"As a matter of fact, I do. And, yes, I think she'd want me, too—if she'd actually give it a chance. But Reed's shielding her like some kind of guard dog. He's made sure she won't even take my calls."

"It seems to me that's her decision and you should respect it."

Jonathan sucked in his breath. "I can't believe we're having this conversation. You've made up your mind."

"Convince me otherwise. Nothing would make me happier."

"What would you like? Alibis? Phone records? Letters from the senior partners in my firm telling you how stable I am and how many hours I spend at my desk?"

"Lower your voice," Douglas commanded, scanning the area and noting the curious stares aimed their way. "You're causing a scene."

Gritting his teeth, Jonathan fought his growing resentment and rage. Damn Reed Weston. If that son of a bitch had screwed up this, the most crucial part of his future, there'd be hell to pay.

"You want the truth?" he bit out. "Here it is. After the boat explosion, you and I were busy settling Gordon's latest securities fraud. Stephanie Halstead was part of that settlement. I didn't set eyes on Taylor Halstead until the day of her meeting at Harter, Randolph and Collins, when I bumped into her in the reception area. Had I heard her radio show? Yes. Did I feel a connection? Yes. Did she? Of course not. My resemblance to Gordon freaked her out. So I left her alone, gave her time to adjust. But before I could initiate anything, Reed moved in. Was I pissed? You bet. Do I think I'm a better match for her than he is? Damned straight. But am I following her around, sending her creepy e-mails, and making strange phone calls like some kind of psycho? No."

Jonathan leveled a hard stare at Douglas. "I told Reed and I'm telling you. I want Taylor Halstead. I can envision a future with her. But only if the feelings are mutual. I think they could be. So I called to ask her out. And, yeah, I got drunk and let my testosterone take over when I told Reed to back off. But none of that constitutes harassment. Just determination and interest. Convinced?"

For a long moment, Douglas said nothing. He merely sat there, his expression taut, studying Jonathan intently. Then he pulled his plate toward him and picked up his utensils. "Actually, yes. Now eat your steak. It's getting cold."

11:35 P.M.

The videotape whirred quietly, and he leaned forward, watching the same scene for the third time in the past ten minutes. Then again, it was his favorite clip. It captured everything about Taylor that meant the most.

He waited for the exact instant, then pressed pause, zooming in on her as she left the radio station. It was the night after he'd gotten rid of that drunken jerk who worked with her. Her face reflected a multitude of emotions. The fear was the most arousing, even more than the pain and resignation. Vulnerable and scared like that, she was perfect. Like a beautiful piece of clay waiting to be molded—or crushed—by him.

He swallowed the rest of his Scotch.

Soon. Soon she'd be his. The necklace was his gift to her. She'd be his gift to him.

His strategy was working like clockwork.

The dinner with Douglas had gone better than expected. He'd accomplished all he'd intended and more.

Which left Adrienne.

He sat back in his chair, envisioning how that would go. When she realized what was happening, she'd be blown away. He could visualize her face in his mind's eye. First there'd be shock, then fear, and last, sheer terror.

He'd waited a long time for this.

Just a few more days to go.

CHAPTER 22

REED scanned the documents one last time. Then he buzzed Cathy and had her make copies and take them to the conference room. His clients would be arriving any minute.

He hoped Douglas knew what he was doing.

Sighing, Reed rose, pacing around his office. Douglas was convinced that Jonathan was innocent. According to Douglas, everything Jonathan had said at dinner rang true.

Reed still had doubts.

But he'd advised Douglas to the best of his ability. Ultimately, the decision to bring Jonathan into his company, acknowledge him as his son, and give him a spot at the helm was Douglas's decision. Just as the ramifications, if Douglas had misjudged the situation, would also be his.

Reed's conscience was clear. He'd done his job. And, the truth was, the future of Berkley & Company wasn't his main concern.

Taylor was.

There'd been no more gifts. Not since that damned ruby pendant four days ago. Mitch had left no stone unturned in his efforts to figure out where that necklace had come from. He'd checked out swanky jewelry stores like Tiffany's, Cartier, and Harry Winston, where rich guys like Jonathan shopped. None of them recognized the merchandise. He'd pounded the pavement from one end of the jewelry exchange on Forty-seventh Street to the other. No luck. No luck in the fingerprint department either. Taylor's prints were the only ones on the necklace, the box, and the note.

Chris Young was definitely out. Mitch's investigation had revealed the kid to be exactly as he'd pegged him: a spoiled, rich teenager who'd never bought anything without using the credit card Mommy and Daddy had given him—*and* whose statements went straight to his parents.

With no follow-up gifts, no fingerprints, and no viable suspects, the whole necklace lead was a total dead end.

As for phone calls, there'd also been none of those since Friday. Then again, Taylor had spent every night alone, with either Mitch or his partner, Jake, outside, watching her apartment like a hawk.

Reed missed her like hell. They talked on the phone every night for hours, like two teenagers. And Sunday, she'd spent all afternoon at his place, in his bed. When she got up to put on her clothes and go home, he'd wanted to choke the bastard who was harassing her. If it hadn't been a matter of her safety, he'd have locked the damned door and convinced her to stay.

Everything between them was amazing, and not only in bed. The more they got to know each other, the stronger the connection between them grew. Even the trust that Taylor found so difficult was starting to come.

As long as Jonathan's name didn't crop up. If it did, the tension grew so thick you could cut it with a knife.

Taylor understood the facts. Jonathan was Reed's client—a client who'd denied ever having called her except that night at the radio station. Reed had to take him at his word. Taylor said she respected that. On a cerebral level, Reed was sure she did. But on an emotional level? That was another matter entirely. The fact was, until they found out who *was* harassing her—and that someone turned out *not* to be Jonathan—the gap between them couldn't be bridged.

Mitch had better get to the bottom of this—and soon.

Reed paused to stare out the window. Ironic, how things were all coming to a head at once. His relationship with Taylor, her personal crisis, and his professional one.

The senior partners had scheduled a meeting with him for Thursday afternoon. It could be anything from cordial to downright unpleasant. Time would tell.

A knock on the door interrupted Reed's thoughts, and he turned as Cathy poked her head into the office. "Excuse me, Mr. Weston. You said to let you know when Mr. Berkley and Mr. Mallory arrived. They're here. I just showed them into the conference room. Mr. Randolph is already there."

"So it's showtime." Reed buttoned his jacket, tucked his pen in his pocket, and headed for the door. "Thanks, Cathy. I'm on my way."

6:15 P.M.

Another phase of the plan was complete.

He finished washing up in the men's room, thinking about what a hectic day it had been.

The signing of the papers. The faxing of the announcements. The mass distribution of the e-mails. The notification of the press. And now, in forty-five minutes, the dinner with the company VPs.

The business end of things was right on target.

The personal end had to be dealt with. *Now.*

Taylor had slept with Reed Weston again. Not at her place, at his. That infuriated him even more. She was mocking his intelligence *and* disobeying his orders. An egregious error on her part. She thought she'd gotten away with it, too. Then again, he'd let her think that. It was why he'd purposely avoided calling her Sunday night. Let her think she was safe. Let her be lulled into a false sense of security. He wanted to catch her off guard. And he would. Then her fear would be stronger, more palpable, and far more enjoyable.

That would keep Taylor in line.

The next step was Adrienne. She arrived tomorrow.

What a surprise she would get.

FEBRUARY 12

3:40 A.M.

WEST SEVENTY-SECOND STREET

Taylor was awake when the phone rang.

It was almost as if she'd expected it. Maybe she had. Things had been too quiet, conveying an eerie sense of security, like hovering in the eye of a hurricane. But, as she knew, that eye always passed, as did the false sense of calm it brought, and the hurricane tore through, wreaking its damage.

She glanced at the caller ID. It was a perfunctory gesture, just so she could report to Mitch. She knew it would say "private." And it did.

She lifted the receiver. "Hello?"

"Making house calls now?" the male voice rasped.

House calls?

Taylor's heart rate accelerated as she prayed she'd misread his insinuation. Calm. She had to stay calm.

"I don't understand," she managed. "What does that mean?"

"It means I'm smarter than you. It means I know everything you do, and everyone you do it with. It means your Sunday-afternoon romp made me angry. *Very* angry. Especially after that stunning necklace I gave you. You're mine. *Only* mine. Remember that. You *don't* want to make me angry."

She hadn't misread anything. He knew. God in heaven, he knew.

White panic surged through her, and she racked her brain for the right answer to give someone so close to the edge.

She went for something safe. "You're right. I don't want to make you angry. Maybe if you tell me—"

"You also don't want to patronize me," he interrupted to warn.

"Fine." Something inside Taylor snapped, and raw emotion took over. "What I want is for you to go away," she blurted. "Stop calling me. Stop giving me gifts. Just leave me alone." She was shaking all over. *"Leave me alone!"*

She slammed down the phone, lifting it only long enough to press *57, the way Mitch had drilled into her to remember to do. Then she pushed herself upright, sitting back against the headboard and taking slow, deep breaths to bring herself under control.

With control came reason, and Taylor wanted to kick herself for succumbing to such a stupid outburst. She'd no doubt made things worse.

Sure enough, the phone began ringing again, sharply, insistently.

He wasn't giving up.

She lifted the receiver, brought it to her ear.

At first there was an unbearable silence, punctuated only by shallow, angry breathing. Then came the response, every bit as ugly as she'd expected.

"You bitch." Fury vibrated in his voice, something no voice changer could disguise. "That was your biggest mistake yet. No one speaks to me that way. *No one.* And no one hangs up on me."

"I apologize," she replied quickly. "I didn't mean to be rude or nasty. I'm just so . . . so—"

"Scared? Good. You should be. Especially now."

"Please tell me who you are, and what it is you want from me."

"You'll know when I'm ready. Just pray I calm down before then."

Or what? she wanted to cry out. *What is it you're planning to do to me?*

"I make the rules. You live by them. No other men. I'm it. Address me with respect. Never hang up on me. And don't try to outsmart me. You'll lose—and you'll pay. So don't ever defy or insult me again."

Click.

4:25 A.M.

EAST SIXTY-EIGHTH STREET

Reed lunged up and grabbed the phone on the second ring. There was only one person it could be. "Taylor?"

"He called again." Her voice was trembling. "Twice. I hung up on him. He called back."

"Did you let Mitch know?"

"Right away. He said there was no one hanging around my apartment. So whoever it is, he called from somewhere else."

"Or somewhere where he couldn't be seen." Reed couldn't stand it. He wanted to hold her, to comfort her. "Taylor, let me come get you. I'll drive around to the service entrance and bring you back here. I don't want you to be alone—"

"*No!*" She practically shouted the word, and he could tell she was crying. "He knows when I'm with you. That's why he called."

"What do you mean? What did he say?"

Taylor relayed the conversations to him.

"Shit." Reed dragged a hand over his jaw. "So he isn't just harassing you. He's threatening you. He's also watching you, just as you suspected—not only outside your apartment, but everywhere you go."

"Yeah." Taylor forced herself to laugh, desperately struggling to fight off hysteria. "Lucky me. I have a bona fide stalker."

"Did you press star fifty-seven?"

"Both times."

"Then listen to me. Mitch will be all over this. He'll go to the police. They've got to take this seriously at this point. They'll follow up on the call trace. They'll track this guy down. And they'll send over a detective."

"I suppose so. But damn." Taylor drew a shaky breath, tears choking her voice again. "Why did I let myself lose it like that? What was I thinking? I'm a trained psychologist. My stalker is unbalanced. So what did I do? I fed right into his control issues. Before, I had a shot at keeping his fixation channeled into adoration, rather than hostility. Not anymore. He wanted to keep me on a pedestal. That meant being submissive and chaste. I blew both things by sleeping with you. And now I've challenged his authority. That was the last straw, at least to him. How could I have been so stupid?"

"Cut it out." Reed's fingers tightened on the receiver. "Stop blaming yourself. You're human. You're scared. Listen, it's almost dawn. We'll talk for a while. Maybe you'll doze. Either way, I'll stay on the line. I won't hang up until you get ready for work."

Taylor couldn't remember ever feeling so touched by a gesture. "You're amazing. Thank you. And, yes, I'm pretty shaken. So, for tonight, I'll take you up on your offer. But it's not a permanent solution, Reed. You can't spend the entire night, every night, on the phone with me."

"Wanna bet?"

She had to laugh. "Will those be billable hours?"

"Don't worry about that. My client base and my legal focus might be undergoing some changes soon anyway."

"What does that mean?"

"We'll talk about it over the weekend. By then, I can fill you in on everything. We'll have lots of time to talk—about that and a few other fundamental issues I have on my mind."

"I see. So we're going to become phone pals."

"Not a chance. We're going to get away. Together. Alone. We're getting out of Manhattan and going somewhere, just the two of us. Not only to put some distance between you and this insanity, but to be alone together. If we're not, *I'm* the one who'll be going insane. Besides, Friday's Valentine's Day. It's the perfect weekend for a lovers' mini break."

"A mini break?" Taylor repeated, smiling through her tears. "You're starting to sound like a romantic."

"Sure seems that way." He paused. "We're going, Taylor. I need to be with you."

"What if *he* figures it out?"

"He won't. We'll talk to Mitch and the cops. We'll figure out some way to evade him."

Taylor felt her first tinge of hope since that creep had called. Maybe there was a chance she and Reed could enjoy a shred of normalcy. "Where are we going?"

"Leave that to me. You just have a bag packed on Friday. After your radio show, we're out of here."

CHAPTER 23

ADRIENNE let herself into the brownstone, slipping off her fur coat and hanging it in a closet.

The exhibit at the Met had been exquisite. One hundred and twenty of Leonardo da Vinci's extraordinary drawings, on special display this month. She'd wandered through the museum for hours. It had been just the diversion she needed to keep her mind off tonight.

With a disgusted sigh, she glanced at her watch. She still had several hours to enjoy before she played hostess at that farcical dinner for Jonathan. She'd use the time to unwind. Step one, a pitcher of martinis. Step two, she'd sip at one while relaxing and soaking in the upstairs Jacuzzi. That would sufficiently mellow her out. She'd be composed and ready when Douglas arrived home—undoubtedly brimming with enthusiasm over the past few days' events and the appointment of his precious son. She'd listen, smile, then get dressed and get made up for Le Cirque.

The whole thing made her sick.

But she'd handle it. As she always did.

She ran her fingers through her thick auburn hair, which was damp with snowflakes. She'd wear it up in a chignon tonight, and she'd wear her black silk Armani with the low-cut back. She might feel like hell, but she'd look fabulous. Even at her age, she'd have the eye of every man in the room.

Her mood slightly uplifted, she walked into the living room, heading directly for the sideboard.

"Adrienne. Right on schedule."

She jerked around, staring at Jonathan, who was seated on the sofa, nursing a Scotch. "What the . . ."

"The martinis are made." He gestured toward the end table. "Nice and dry. Just the way you like them. Shall I pour?"

Her shock was fading into wariness. "By all means." She gestured for him to do so, folding her arms across her breasts. "To what do I owe this surprise visit?"

Jonathan filled a martini glass and handed it to her. "What, no congratulations? No kind words of welcome? I'm crushed."

"I doubt that." She lowered herself into a plush chair, crossing one slim leg over the other and sipping at her drink. "You finally have everything you've always wanted. You must be elated." Her brows drew together. "How did you manage to get away from the office for this little drop-in?"

"I left early to get ready for tonight's big bash. Actually, I expected you sooner. Then I remembered the da Vinci exhibit. I assume that's where you were?"

Adrienne's eyes glittered. "I doubt you're assuming. You never assume, Jonathan. You know."

"You're right. I do. I make it my business to know everything that affects me." He polished off his Scotch. "Which brings me to why I'm here. I thought we should have a little chat."

"About what?"

"Gordon."

"Really." She took another sip of her drink. "What about him?"

Jonathan leaned forward. "I'll cut to the chase. I know everything. The whole sick arrangement, right down to how you planned on implicating my mother. What's more, I have proof. Concrete proof. Gordon was screwed up, but he was smart. Smart enough to know he should have something on you. It took a while, but he managed to find the right occasion. It was during one of your less congenial tête-à-têtes. He taped your conversation. I have the tape. And I'll use it—if I have to."

All the color had drained from Adrienne's face. "I don't believe you."

"I didn't expect you to." He flourished a mini–cassette recorder and pressed the Play button. Two voices emerged, Adrienne's and Gordon's. Their words were angry, but clearly distinguishable. They were having an argument about a threat made years ago—a threat that had changed lives. "This is a copy, by the way," Jonathan commented, pressing Stop and watching Adrienne's expression. "I have the original."

"What do you want?" she snapped.

"That's the beauty of it. Nothing. I want absolutely nothing." Jonathan's mouth thinned into a tight, grim line. "Except for you to stay the hell out of my way. Berkley and Company is *my* baby. My future. Not yours. Go ahead and keep on being Douglas's trophy wife. Enjoy your cash cow. I don't give a damn. But don't interfere in the business, or in any other financial or personal decisions my *father* makes in my favor. Just smile, give me your support, and take the dividend checks I hand you. Otherwise, I'll be forced to go to Douglas and play him this nasty little tape. You don't want that, do you?"

Deadly silence.

"Just think," Jonathan taunted. "You can start tonight, by being the perfect hostess, welcoming me into the family and the business with open arms."

"You miserable bastard." Adrienne's glare was lethal.

"Bastard, yes. Miserable? That depends on who you ask. Now, what's your answer? Can I count on your cooperation?"

She finished her martini and rose, setting down the glass. "For now, yes. After that, we'll see."

"What does that mean?"

"It means, I want to see how you manage your new role. Also, I want to make sure you continue to be the good boy you've been since you finally grew up. You *have* been a good boy, haven't you?"

Jonathan's eyes narrowed. "Where is that question coming from?"

"You're not the only one who keeps on top of situations."

"I have no idea what you think you know. But whatever it is, it's bullshit. Which means you don't have a shred of proof."

"Are you willing to take that risk?" Adrienne gave him a tight smile. "Two can play the blackmail game, Jonathan. I give as good as I get. So let's just call it a draw. I admit, your trump card may be more interesting than mine. On the other hand, I wield a lot more power with Douglas than you do. I don't think I need to elaborate on how."

"Spare me the details of your sex life."

"Fine. So, to answer your question, yes, I'll go along with your ultimatum. For now. Douglas thinks you've got what it takes to make his company thrive. So I'm willing to cut you some slack. But know that I'm keeping a close eye on you. After all, you've got Douglas's company, and my future, in your hands." Adrienne shot him an icy look. "I'm going upstairs to take a bath. You go home and get dressed. My supportive-stepmother act begins at seven-thirty."

6:15 P.M

WVNY

Taylor sat alone in her recording studio. Kevin and Dennis were both outside at the controls, but she didn't feel like socializing. She was lost in thought.

She'd always been a take-charge personality. Now she felt like a victim.

She'd pored over every one of the current professional journals that touched on elements of abnormal psychology. After that, she'd checked out several Web sites that outlined, in detail, the psyches, character traits, and behavior of stalkers. She had a pretty good handle on this guy. He suffered from, at the very least, a delusional disorder, if not a more severe psychiatric disorder like schizophrenia. He was obsessive. Resentful. Predatory. Unlike more benign stalkers, this one was *not* interested in keeping his identity a secret, not forever. Right now, he was enjoying the power and control that his anonymity provided. It enabled him to terrorize her, with no fear of repercussions. But he fully intended to show himself. Taylor was convinced of that. He had a plan of attack—one that would make his taunting prelude look like a joyride.

That's *what* he was. But *who* was he? *Who?*

She'd contacted the police. Her call had been transferred to Detective Hadman of the Nineteenth Precinct, the same guy who'd notified her about Steph's death. He'd met with her, not at the precinct, lest Mr. Stalker was following her, but at the Krispy Kreme & Coffee on West Seventy-second. Mitch had joined them. It had looked like a business meeting to anyone who happened to glance in the window. Hadman had taken a list of all the names Taylor could come up with of potential stalk-

ers. He'd also agreed to check out the call trace and get back to them
with the results.

And in the meantime, there was one name that haunted her, day and
night.

Jonathan Mallory.

She tried not to fixate on him, but she couldn't help it. There was
something about him that unsettled her. She kept telling herself it was
because he was a carbon copy of Gordon—at least physically. But some
inner voice kept niggling at her, maintaining that it was more.

She should have spoken to him when he called the radio station that
night. If she'd heard his voice, maybe she could have ruled it out as the
synthesized one that kept calling her at home—if not by the pitch, then
by the tone or choice of words. Maybe if she'd listened to him, she could
have assessed his state of mind, and put her own at ease. Maybe she
should even have met with him.

No, that was foolish. To encourage him, put her safety and her emotional well-being at risk—no, it was out of the question. If only there was
another way.

Her head came up.

Of course. Why hadn't she thought of it before?

She snatched up today's newspaper, skimming the business section
until she found what she was looking for.

There. Just as she remembered reading this morning over coffee.

She rose, walking over and yanking open the door. "Kev? Dennis?"
She caught their attention. "Any chance of your subbing in a generic
tape for tonight?"

Kevin's eyes narrowed, and he gave her a guarded look. "If we need
to, sure. Why?"

"Because Reed and I are going to a party."

7:45 P.M.

LE CIRQUE

455 MADISON AVENUE, NEW YORK CITY

Several dozen guests were already milling about the Library—one of Le
Cirque's elegant reception rooms—sipping fine wine and helping them-

selves to hot and cold canapés, when Reed guided Taylor through the door.

"Quite a party," Taylor noted, glancing around. "My father would approve. It looks like something he'd throw."

Reed didn't smile. He knew that Taylor's attempt at light sarcasm was all a facade. She was as tight as a drum. He could actually feel her vibrating.

He must have been crazy to agree to this.

"Thanks for bringing me," Taylor said quickly. "I know you have reservations. But I need to see Jonathan Mallory—not alone, where I might be putting myself in danger, but in a nonthreatening, group environment. I need to talk to him, to observe him while he interacts. I've got a trained eye. Maybe I can put my fears to rest."

"Or maybe you can become even more anxious, and be pushed one step closer to your limit."

"I'm willing to take that risk."

Sucking in his breath, Reed took the tension down a notch. "You look gorgeous," he murmured, smoothing his palm down the sleeve of her chocolate brown knit cocktail dress. It was straight-lined and simple, finely detailed with gold and tonal beading along the edges of the sleeves and neckline, and formfitting, emphasizing her slender figure and making her vivid coloring stand out even more. It was Taylor—classy all the way.

"Thanks." She forced a smile. "You look pretty incredible yourself. Italian suit, silk tie—I'm impressed."

He caught her hand in his. "You can still change your mind. No one's seen us yet. We can leave."

"Not a chance," Taylor returned flippantly. "I spent too much time on my makeup."

She continued to assess the room.

Despite the festive atmosphere, this was one big-time power scene. Influential, well-dressed men and women were making the rounds, chatting politely while straining to hear all the other conversations taking place around them. Uniformed servers were weaving their way around, offering the guests hors d'oeuvres and fluted glasses of champagne to complement the drinks being served at the bar.

One server spotted Taylor and Reed and hurried over, flourishing his silver tray. "Would you care for mousse of foie gras on a brioche?" he inquired.

"Thank you, not just yet." Reed had just spotted the guest of honor, who was standing across the room beside Adrienne and Douglas. Guests were flocking up to them, offering their congratulations with practiced smiles and perfected grace.

"Ah, there he is," Taylor commented. "The newly acknowledged Berkley."

Reed edged a quick look in her direction, gauging her reaction. She'd paled a bit, but other than that, she looked composed.

"I assume that's Douglas and Adrienne Berkley standing with him," she clarified.

"Yup."

"Adrienne's quite stunning."

"She should be. She works at it twenty-four/seven," Reed retorted under his breath.

"Well, good for her. That shows tenacity and self-respect."

"Self-love is more like it."

Startled, Taylor twisted around to gaze up at him. "You don't much care for her, do you?"

"Gee, what gave you that idea?"

This time, Taylor's smile was genuine. "Just a lucky guess." She pursed her lips. "This can't be easy on her. Press coverage in both the business and society pages. A stepson she has to lovingly acknowledge—at least in public. I shudder to think what *that* relationship's really like."

"You don't want to know. As for the shock, it's nonexistent. This is no news to her."

"Not to you, either. No wonder this whole legal representation of the Berkleys has been so complex." Taylor drew a slow, deep breath, then hooked her fingers through Reed's arm. "Anyway, back to what we're here for. Let's not put this off. Right now, we've got the element of surprise going for us. Come on."

They crossed the room, weaving their way through the growing crowd of guests.

Douglas saw them first. His brows rose, but he looked pleased, maybe even relieved. Adrienne followed his stare, spotting the two of them and giving Taylor a typical female-to-female once-over. Then her gaze settled on Reed's arm, now wrapped possessively around Taylor's waist, and her lips curved in some kind of private amusement.

"Reed." Douglas shook his hand. "I'm so glad you could make it after all. And this must be Ms. Halstead. I've heard so much about you. It's a pleasure to meet you at last. I'm Douglas Berkley. This is my wife, Adrienne. And I believe you and Jonathan have already met."

"Mr. Berkley. Mrs. Berkley." Taylor shook their hands, all the while keeping Jonathan in her peripheral vision. He looked positively stunned, and a hard glitter of anger flashed in his eyes as he got his first glimpse of her and Reed as a couple.

Taylor refused to let that anger intimidate her. "Hello again, Mr. Mallory." She turned and extended her hand to him. "Congratulations. This must be an exciting evening for you."

"It is," he replied in a clipped tone. His handshake was as stiff as his demeanor.

"I didn't realize you'd be coming," he declared to Reed. "Or that you'd be bringing Ms. Halstead with you. I thought you were otherwise engaged."

Reed didn't miss a beat. "I was. I managed to move things around. I wanted to be here to offer you my best wishes."

"How thoughtful. And Ms. Halstead?" Jonathan inclined his head at Taylor, openly assessing her reaction. "Your radio show airs from eight to ten. Isn't it live?"

Taylor kept her response impersonal. The less of herself she revealed, the more he'd probe and, hopefully, the more he'd give away. "You're right. It is. Except when I'm ill, on vacation, or attending a special event like this one. Then my producer runs a pretaped show."

"You consider tonight special. I'm honored."

Honored, yeah. Maybe that was why he was still clasping her hand.

"I'm glad to be here," Taylor assured him. "I can only imagine how gratified you must feel. Personal and professional recognition from someone you respect and care for. I can't think of anything more rewarding."

She didn't know if it was her approach that did the trick, or Jonathan's own thought process. But it was like someone flicked a switch.

Abruptly, he became a different person, warm and charming. His tension vanished, and he smiled, a one-on-one personal smile, covering their joined fingers with his other hand. "You're right. It *is* rewarding. And I'm delighted you're here to share it. As you know, I've been trying to reach you. This will give us a chance to talk."

The next move was hers. And she'd better execute it carefully. As much as she wanted to get a handle on Jonathan Mallory, she had no desire to give him the wrong impression. Even if he was totally innocent of harassment, he was definitely much too fixated on her. And his mood swings were unsettling, at best.

Graciously, she smiled back, but was careful to keep that smile impersonal rather than friendly. "Assuming you can break away, that would be nice."

Douglas cleared his throat. "Ms. Halstead, now that you're here, I want to offer my condolences on the loss of your cousin—and to apologize for not meeting with you when you came by my home. Frankly, I wasn't myself. I was in shock. Gordon was also my son, as you now realize. My pain was . . . well, I don't need to explain it to you. You experienced the same pain yourself. In any case, I wasn't up for visitors. Even well-meaning ones like yourself. So please, forgive me."

"No apology is necessary." Taylor actually perceived an element of sincerity behind his words. "It was a terrible time. I'm sorry for your loss as well."

"We appreciate your sensitivity." Adrienne Berkley spoke up for the first time, a saccharine-sweet smile on her face. "Jonathan." She turned to her stepson, darting a quick, pointed glance at Taylor's hand, still clasped between Jonathan's. "Why don't you give Reed and Ms. Halstead a chance to enjoy the food?" She resumed addressing Taylor. "There's a tray of lobster with avocado on its way over. You simply must try it."

"I'd love to."

"Of course." Jonathan released Taylor's hand and signaled the server, but Taylor could see a vein throbbing in his forehead. And his jaw was clenched so tight, she was afraid it might snap.

Reed's implication had been an understatement. There was a tidal wave of tension surging between Jonathan and his stepmother, one big enough to capsize a naval fleet.

Taylor helped herself to a lobster medallion, using the time she was nibbling at it to step aside so other guests could move in and congratulate Jonathan.

Reed joined her, reaching over to take two flutes of champagne off a tray and handing her one. "You okay?"

"So far, so good."

"That depends on your perspective." He gave her a relaxed, partylike smile—a smile that belied his next words, muttered under his breath. "If that bastard keeps looking at you like you're a piece of Godiva, I'm going to knock his teeth out."

Taylor's lips twitched. "What an uplifting thought. But I'm not sure I'm ready for the caveman routine."

"Me either. But when it comes to you . . . everything I feel is a constant surprise."

Something about his tone made Taylor look up, her champagne glass poised halfway to her lips. She studied the intense expression on his face, and her heart did a quick flip-flop in her chest.

"By the way, our weekend is all set," Reed said huskily, holding her gaze. "I booked a private cabin at a very small, very exclusive ski lodge in Vermont. We'll leave Friday night. We can return as late as Monday—if you want to play hooky from school. You must have some unused personal days."

"I do." Taylor swallowed. "And it sounds wonderful. The problem is, I don't ski. I guess I never mentioned that."

"Oh, you mentioned it. That's why I chose this place."

One sexually charged moment ticked by.

Then Reed covered Taylor's fingers—still wrapped around her champagne flute—with his, and eased the glass the rest of the way to her lips. "Drink. It'll fortify you for our weekend."

"I don't need fortifying." A hint of a twinkle. "But *you* might, after three days alone with me in that cabin."

Laughter rumbled from Reed's chest. "I'll take my chances."

SEVERAL FEET AWAY, Adrienne was watching Taylor and Reed's exchange with great interest. While she couldn't hear their actual words, the chemistry between them was impossible to miss.

She stepped behind Douglas, who was chatting with a colleague, and leaned toward Jonathan.

"Whatever fantasies you might be harboring about Taylor Halstead, you can forget them," she murmured. "The woman is head over heels in love with Reed Weston. And the feeling is mutual. *Very* mutual. See for yourself." She gestured with her eyes.

Jonathan glanced in that direction, then continued drinking his Scotch. "Shut up, Adrienne," he muttered. "Just shut the hell up."

"It wouldn't have worked out anyway," she said in a low, taunting voice. "She's the kind of woman who wants a man with innate strength and power—not one who inherits it from Daddy or wears it like a practiced veneer."

"Dammit, Adrienne, I'm warning you . . ."

Douglas freed himself up at that moment, wrapping a firm arm around Adrienne's shoulders and angling his head toward Jonathan. "Cut it out," he hissed. "Can't you control yourself for one night?"

"Talk to your wife."

"I'm talking to you. This party is in your honor. Now act like it."

"You're right. Time for another celebratory drink." Jonathan strode off toward the bar.

"Adrienne," Douglas said quietly to his wife. "Don't antagonize him, please. He's edgy enough."

She shrugged her slim shoulders. "He's not edgy; he's obsessed. Again. And the woman he's obsessed with doesn't know he's alive. Again. Correction: she knows he's alive. She'd prefer to ignore that fact."

"He'll get over it."

"If you say so, darling." She reached up to caress his jaw, just as the next guests strolled over.

Taylor was studying Jonathan's progress over the rim of her glass. "I think the happy trio just had words," she informed Reed.

"It wouldn't surprise me."

"Jonathan's at the bar. I think I'll wander over there for a glass of Merlot." She placed her champagne flute on a passing tray. "I won't be long."

Reed caught her arm. "I'll go with you."

"If you do that, nothing will get accomplished except ruffling Jonathan's feathers even more. You go talk to Douglas and Adrienne. I'll be right across the room."

"And if he comes on to you?"

"Then I'll signal you for help."

With great reluctance, Reed nodded. "Okay. You've got five minutes."

"Ten."

"Fine, ten. Unless I don't like what I'm seeing. Then I'm coming over there."

"Just promise you won't make a scene."

"No scene," Reed assured her. "I'll just drag you out of here."

TAYLOR APPROACHED THE BAR, feathering her fingers through her hair as if she were deep in thought.

"What can I get you, ma'am?" the bartender inquired.

"Hmm? Oh, a glass of Merlot, please." She fiddled with a cocktail napkin, absently taking the goblet when it was handed to her.

"Drinking alone?" Jonathan asked from beside her.

She pivoted around, feigning surprise at seeing him. "Oh . . . I didn't realize you were here. I was thinking."

"Obviously." He took another healthy swallow of Scotch. "You don't look too happy. Is there trouble in paradise?"

"I assume you're talking about Reed and me. No, no trouble. I'm just going through a rough time now. It happens to the best of us."

"I can't argue that one." Jonathan paused only long enough to get a refill. He swallowed down some Scotch, then inclined his head to eye her speculatively. "If I ask you a question, will you answer it honestly?"

Taylor's chest tightened, but she remained outwardly calm. "If I can."

"Oh, you *can*. It's more a question of if you *will*."

"I won't know until you ask."

"Fair enough." He met and held her gaze. "Are you still afraid of me?"

She weighed her reply carefully. "Afraid of you? In what way?"

"Let me rephrase," he amended. "Do you still see Gordon when you look at me?"

"For fleeting instances here and there, yes." This was a case when honesty would be her best course of action. "It's hard not to when your appearances are . . . *were* . . . identical. But, if you're asking if I confuse the two of you in my mind, the answer is no."

Jonathan stared into his half-filled glass. "What my brother did to you was despicable. I'm sorry you had to go through it."

Was that remorse or manipulation talking?

"It's over," Taylor replied. "Besides, I was lucky. It could have been worse."

"So I heard. I'm grateful Gordon was interrupted." He gazed at her again, an odd, probing look in his eyes—probing, but glazed. Taylor suspected he was half drunk. "What is it you're afraid of, then?"

He was fishing. But for what?

"You know the answer to that," she stated bluntly, watching to see if she was inciting him. "You invented an emotional connection between the two of us that doesn't exist. You ordered Reed to back off so you could pursue me. In my book, that counts as domineering and delusional."

Not even a flicker of an eyelash. "You certainly tell it like it is, don't you?"

"I try to, yes."

"And you see me as irrational and controlling."

"Am I wrong?"

Jonathan polished off his Scotch. "Life is a chess game, Taylor. I'm a cunning and competitive player. I like to win. I manipulate and capitalize on circumstances so I can achieve that outcome. Does that make me controlling? I suppose that depends on one's perspective. But irrational? No. Quite the opposite. I'm very systematic. Nothing less will yield the desired results. Does that answer your question?"

Taylor responded from her gut. "Not really. What it does is make me feel unhappy and uneasy. Or is that your goal?"

This time he arched a brow. "Now why would that be my goal?"

"Because winning might mean more to you than simply acquiring. It might mean gaining power through intimidation. Does it?"

There was that flash of anger again. "Is that Reed's theory, or yours?"

"Mine. Reed's not being stalked. I am."

"And you think I'm your stalker."

"Are you?"

"If I said no, would you believe me?"

"I don't know."

"Then we're at an impasse, aren't we?"

Taylor couldn't argue that one. "Yes, I guess we are."

"For the sake of argument, if you knew for a fact I *wasn't* your stalker, would you give us a chance?"

"There is no 'us.' There never will be."

His jaw was working. "Why? Because I look like Gordon? Or because I'm not Reed?"

"Because I don't feel that way about you."

Jonathan set down his glass. "Time will tell, won't it?"

"No, time *won't* tell," Taylor shot back. Her frustration was mounting. Maybe he wasn't delusional. Maybe he was just a businessman unwilling to accept defeat.

But something told her otherwise.

She stared him down, trying desperately to get inside that unfocused and unreadable gaze, to get a handle on his thoughts. Then she put the icing on the cake—or the nail in her coffin, depending on which way things turned out.

"Listen to me, Jonathan. This is never going to happen. Not now. Not ever. Clear?"

A flicker of something. Resentment? Determination? Taylor wasn't sure.

"Clearer than you realize. Then again, I possess all the facts. You don't—not yet. But that'll change. In time, so will your feelings. I know you, Taylor. I know what you're about." Jonathan's fingers brushed hers, the contact as brief as it was unnerving. "Now, if you'll excuse me, I'll rejoin my guests."

He walked off into the crowd, leaving Taylor chilled.

CHAPTER 24

TAYLOR jerked awake, drenched in sweat.

Clutching the blankets, she peered around the pitch-dark bedroom, her heart slamming against her ribs.

It was all right. There was no one there. A nightmare. It had only been a nightmare.

She reached for the alarm clock, glancing at the digits and shuddering as she realized that dawn was still two hours away.

She'd slept less than forty minutes. She'd been in bed since midnight. The rest of the time she'd spent staring at the phone, steeling herself for it to ring.

It had remained silent.

Her eyes burned from exhaustion. She squeezed them shut, willing herself to rest, if not sleep. She had a full day ahead of her, including a session with Dr. Phillips. Also, with a modicum of luck, Detective Hadman would have some information for her regarding the telephone number he'd traced. Maybe it would give them some answers, or at least point them in the right direction. And she'd find out if that direction included Jonathan Mallory.

Abandoning the idea of resting, Taylor clicked on her lamp, opened the psychology text that was propped on her night table, and reread the section on psychopathic personality traits.

SHE MUST HAVE DOZED. There was a hint of weak sunlight trickling into her room when she snapped awake the next time. It was morning. Her clock told her it was six-fifteen, almost time for the alarm to go off.

The son of a bitch hadn't called. He was taunting her, keeping her fearful and uncertain about when the ax would fall.

Her head throbbed from lack of sleep. She climbed out of bed and went into the kitchen to brew herself some coffee. God, she was in desperate need of caffeine. It was the only thing that was going to get her through the day.

She was sipping her second cup of the strong black liquid when the phone rang. Caller ID told her it was Reed.

She lifted the receiver. "Hi," she said, tucking it in the crook of her shoulder. "I hope you got more sleep than I did."

"I didn't." Reed sounded like hell. "I want to find this nut job and get him out of your life."

"You're not alone. I had horrible nightmares every time I shut my eyes. Whoever this guy is, he's still out there. That makes my skin crawl. On top of that, I can't shake this feeling that something terrible's about to happen. I've felt that way ever since my conversation with Jonathan."

Reed grunted. "Yeah, well, it sounded like a pretty weird conversation. I don't know if it was because he'd had too much to drink, or if he's really delusional. But you can be damned sure I intend to find out." A weighted pause. "I've got a heavy-duty meeting at the office this afternoon. I have no idea how long it'll run. But I'll call you when it's over, either before you leave for your counseling session or later, on your cell phone."

Taylor didn't miss the sober note in Reed's tone. "This is *the* meeting, isn't it? The one that's going to change the course of things for you?"

"Yup, this is it."

She searched for the right words to say, wanting to offer him the same kind of emotional support he'd been offering her. "Reed, I know we haven't been able to get into this issue too deeply. But I know it's a biggie. I also have a pretty good idea what it's about, or at least what the crux of it is. I hope it turns out the way you want it to. Just know that I'll be thinking of you. And that I'm here whenever you want to talk."

He was quiet for a moment. Then he cleared his throat. "Thank you." He sounded more moved than she'd expected. "I mean it. Your being there for me—it means a great deal."

Taylor smiled. "Even a knight in shining armor needs a lady fair. Who else would cheer him on?"

"True. Just be aware that this particular knight needs this particular lady to do the cheering. No one else will do."

"I won't forget."

"I'll call you later." Reed paused. "And Taylor . . . be careful."

Her smile vanished. "I will."

9:30 A.M.

HARTER, RANDOLPH & COLLINS

Reed was reviewing a deposition when his intercom buzzer sounded.

Absently, he pressed the button. "Yes, Cathy?"

"Mr. Harter just came in," she announced in a hushed, strained tone. "Mr. Randolph and Mr. Collins are with him. They buzzed me and said for you to meet them in the conference room ASAP."

Brows raised, Reed put down his papers. "Mr. Harter's here?"

"Yes, sir. And he wants you to drop whatever you're doing."

"I'm on my way." Reed punched off the intercom and rose. This was weird. Richard Harter rarely came in. Reed had hoped he'd be there this afternoon when he had his meeting with the other founding partners, but that was six hours from now. And Reed wasn't self-centered enough to believe that something defined as "urgent" was about him and his future.

He yanked on his suit jacket and headed down the hall.

THE MOOD IN THE CONFERENCE ROOM was somber. The three men who'd hired Reed were huddled together, talking in tense whispers. The door was ajar. Reed gave a perfunctory knock and poked his head in.

"Reed." Richard Harter spoke up first. "Come in and shut the door."

Reed complied, getting more uneasy by the minute. "What's this about?"

"A double homicide." Horace Randolph didn't waste words or time.

"Last night. The two bodies were discovered over an hour ago." His solemn gaze met Reed's. "The victims were Douglas and Adrienne Berkley."

"*What?*" Reed's jaw dropped. "Did I hear you right?"

"You did," Harter confirmed. "Douglas never showed up for a breakfast meeting. That's unprecedented. His colleagues contacted his office. His secretary tried his home phone and his cell. No answer. She caught a cab to East Eighty-second, to check out his brownstone. She got no response there either. Finally, she called the police. Two officers came by to check out the place. Apparently, the murders occurred sometime between one and six A.M. Douglas's neck was snapped. Adrienne was raped and choked."

"Christ." Reed sank down into a chair. "Was it a break-in? Do the police have any leads as to who the killer or killers were?"

"No and yes. It wasn't a break-in. The lock wasn't forced, the alarm wasn't tripped, and nothing was taken. And, yes, it seems the police have a suspect, although no arrest warrant has been issued. They want to speak with Jonathan Mallory. He's on his way to our office, after which he's been asked to stop by the Nineteenth Precinct."

Everything inside Reed went still. "They think Jonathan killed Douglas and Adrienne?"

"As Richard said, there's been no arrest—yet," Albert Collins said. "But the detectives did question Jonathan at the crime scene. They want to question him again. He called here a few minutes ago to fill us in and say he was on his way."

"He must be a wreck."

"He is. The detectives notified him of the murders as soon as the bodies were discovered. He was at his office. He rushed right over." An uncomfortable cough. "The circumstantial evidence is mounting. No forced entry, no sign of a struggle—and right on the heels of the very publicized media announcements of Jonathan's appointment at Berkley and Company and Douglas's acknowledgment that he was his son. Let's just say the NYPD has questions."

"I'm sure they do." Reed's mind was racing as the defense attorney in him took over. "You said Adrienne was raped. Was there any semen found?"

A nod. "The detectives asked Jonathan for a DNA sample. He agreed, but said he wanted his lawyers present, for that and any other questioning."

"Good."

Richard Harter flattened his palms on the table and leaned forward. "Bottom line—when Jonathan gets here, we want you to talk to him alone."

Reed's eyes narrowed. "Why?"

"Because we don't want to be privy to what he says."

The reality was slowly sinking in. "Richard, with all due respect, cut to the chase. What exactly are you telling me?"

"Just what you think I am. Look, Reed, this whole situation is a hornet's nest. Our firm represents the interests of Douglas and Adrienne Berkley. If for any reason, Jonathan *is* found guilty of these crimes, we've got a major conflict of interest on our hands." Harter paused. "I'll be blunt. We all know you want out. You want to set up your own practice. And you want to do it with our blessings, and probably with a few of our clients who'd prefer to stay with you. Well, here's the deal. We'll make your leaving as smooth as possible. We'll help you get started, including sending you referrals and passing along our overflow. And we won't stand in the way of any of your clients who choose to follow you to your new firm. It'll be a clean, amicable parting. In return, we want to determine your first client."

"Jonathan Mallory."

"Right."

Reed pursed his lips. "That's an interesting offer. Let me ask you something. What if the DNA sample taken at the crime scene and the one Jonathan supplies don't match?"

"Then your case will be that much easier. And you'll have the undying gratitude of an extremely wealthy, well-connected young man. Either way, your fledgling law firm will make an outstanding debut, and reflect well on our firm."

"Translated, innocent or guilty, you want no part of representing Jonathan."

Collins sighed. "This story is going to be all over every newspaper in New York. It's already on the local TV news as we speak. Jonathan's name will be linked to the case whether or not he's ultimately found guilty. We don't want that kind of press. Plus, we still have Douglas and Adrienne's trusts and estates to handle."

"Jonathan's the successor-executor of both estates," Reed realized aloud. "And, with both Douglas and Adrienne gone, he's also the sole beneficiary." He blew out his breath. "Talk about incriminating."

"So you see our position."

"Clear as glass."

"And?"

A few seconds ticked by.

Then Reed made his counteroffer. "I'll meet with Jonathan when he gets here—alone, as you asked. I'll apprise him of the situation and the terms of his representation—that it'll be Reed Weston, Esquire, and not Harter, Randolph and Collins who'll be his counsel. If he chooses to accept those terms, fine. I'll hear what he has to say, then accompany him over to the Nineteenth Precinct as his attorney of record. However, if he refuses, I don't expect you to rescind your offer. I want your assurance that you'll give my new firm your full cooperation, including all the perks you just described, regardless of the outcome of my talk with Jonathan. I give you my word that I'll do all I can to convince him to retain me. But I can't force him. So, if he chooses to seek out different representation, I still expect you to live up to your agreement. Is it a deal?"

The partners exchanged glances. Then Harter nodded. "It's a deal."

REED WALKED INTO HIS OFFICE and clicked on the Sony LCD WEGA flat-panel TV he kept on the corner table, turning to the local news. Sure enough, there was the breaking story.

"The double homicide occurred at the Berkley brownstone, located on the Upper East Side just off Fifth Avenue, near the Metropolitan Museum of Art," a news correspondent was saying. "The police aren't releasing much information at this time. All we know is that Douglas and Adrienne Berkley were murdered sometime between one and six A.M. There was no evidence that this was a burglary—"

Reed pressed the Off button on the remote control.

Then he sank down in his desk chair, trying to process everything that had just happened and the colossal hurdle that now faced him.

He was taking a huge risk, one that was even bigger than the senior partners realized. There was a lot more to Jonathan Mallory than they knew, and a lot more circumstantial evidence stacked up against him.

There was the antagonism between him and Adrienne, the resulting tension between him and Douglas, and his own precarious state of mind these days. Add that to the skeletons in his closet, and you had a prosecutorial field day.

As for Jonathan's state of mind, that opened up another ugly can of worms.

Taylor.

Was Jonathan the one stalking her? Reed hadn't thought so, but in light of this horrifying double homicide, he didn't know what to believe. Just the conversation Jonathan had initiated with Taylor last night had been strange enough to raise eyebrows. Once the cops got wind of it—and they would, since they'd undoubtedly interview everyone who attended the gala at Le Cirque—they'd be all over it. Taylor would have to divulge all her suspicions relating to Jonathan. And his client would be screwed.

That was a professional take. But there was also a personal one. If it turned out Jonathan was arrested and tried, Taylor would be called as a witness for the prosecution. Reed's job would be to tear her to pieces.

Reed massaged his temples. He couldn't go there, not yet. First, he had to meet with Jonathan. He had to hear him out, to study him while he talked. Body language spoke volumes, especially under traumatic circumstances such as these. As for their discussion, it wasn't going to be pretty. It was going to be blunt. No bullshit. Cards on the table. Not only would Reed get a more accurate assessment that way, he'd get a better handle on Jonathan's state of mind. No more diplomatic talks, no more placating tactics. He had to know if Jonathan was guilty or innocent—not only of the homicides, but of stalking Taylor.

He prayed his instincts were right. That Jonathan had a ton of psychological baggage, but wasn't a criminal. Because, like it or not, Reed was in this now. He'd given his word to the senior partners. So if his instincts turned out to be wrong, he was screwed, both professionally and personally.

Taylor would never accept this situation, much less cope with it.

Enough. Reed pushed away from his desk and rose, walking over to pour himself a glass of water. Facts first. Speculation later.

He glanced restlessly at his watch.

Jonathan would be here any minute.

Taylor couldn't stand the wait anymore.

She went into her office and called Detective Hadman.

There was a commotion in the background when he answered. "Hadman," he said briskly.

"Hello, Detective, this is Taylor Halstead. I was wondering if you'd had a chance to trace that telephone number."

"The telephone numb—oh, yeah." He was big-time distracted. "I was going to call you this morning, but it's been wild here since I got in. Yes, I traced the number. But, like I figured, it got me nowhere. The number belongs to a prepaid cell phone."

"Well, can't you find out who bought it?"

"Not a chance. These phones are purchased in convenience stores, airports, you name it. If we're lucky, we could trace it to a specific location. But even that wouldn't do us much good. The perp probably paid cash, and no ID is required to buy one of these things. Anonymous cell phone purchases escaped the Patriot Act. No way we could connect it to your phone pal."

"I see. So we're no closer to finding him than we were before." Taylor fought her mounting frustration. "Is there anything else we can do to—"

"Listen, Ms. Halstead, I don't mean to cut you off, but this double homicide just landed in our laps. Your stalker's going to have to go on the back burner."

That explained the commotion.

Despite her personal anxiety, Taylor felt a tinge of guilt. "I'm sorry, Detective. I had no idea. I'll leave you to your—"

"It's all over the news," he interrupted. "I'm surprised you haven't heard."

"I've been at school since early this morning."

"The murdered couple was Adrienne and Douglas Berkley."

"*Adrienne and Douglas Berkley?*" Taylor's hands began shaking. "They were *murdered?* But I just saw them last night. How did it happen? Do you know who did it?"

"I'm not at liberty to discuss the details of the case with you. However, now that I know you were with them last night, we'll need to talk to you. Yeah?" he called out to someone in the precinct. "Ms. Halstead, I've gotta go."

Click.

Taylor replaced the receiver in its cradle, staring at it as her mind raced. Then she punched up the cbsnewyork.com Web page on her computer and scrolled down to the breaking story on the double homicide.

The Berkleys . . . dead. Murdered in their own home.

The article said nothing about a break-in. Had the killer been someone they knew? Someone who had other motives for getting rid of them?

An icy chill shot up her spine as a creepy thought took hold.

Someone else. Someone who stood to acquire great wealth and power from their deaths, not to mention great satisfaction from executing them with his own hands.

Bile rose in Taylor's throat as the logical name insinuated itself in her mind. No. It couldn't be.

But it would explain why she'd had that edgy feeling all night, the feeling that something was drastically wrong—even though she'd never received a phone call from her stalker.

She'd assumed he was toying with her.

What if that wasn't the case? What if he hadn't called because he'd been preoccupied with something far more heinous?

Taylor shuddered.

No media reports would answer questions like these. She had to talk to Reed. He'd know about the homicides by now. The Berkleys were his clients. He'd have more details.

She grabbed the phone and punched in his office number.

"Harter, Randolph and Collins."

"Reed Weston, please."

"Just a moment."

The call rang through, and Reed's secretary picked up. "Mr. Weston's office."

"Yes, Cathy, this is Taylor Halstead. May I speak with Mr. Weston, please?"

"I'm sorry, Ms. Halstead, he's with a client."

"I understand. But this is very urgent. Mr. Weston knows I wouldn't interrupt otherwise. If you tell him it's me, I'm sure he'll take the call. I promise to make it brief."

Cathy cleared her throat, discernibly ill at ease. "Normally, I'd do as you ask. But, in this case, my instructions were no interruptions whatsoever. And no exceptions. I apologize, Ms. Halstead, but I can't put you through."

A weighted pause.

Then Taylor let the poor girl off the hook. "All right, Cathy, I understand. Please leave Mr. Weston a message to call me as soon as possible."

"I will."

With a growing sense of unease, Taylor hung up.

Reed with a client. No interruptions whatsoever.

She propped her elbows on the desk, dragging both hands through her hair.

God help her, but she had a sinking feeling she knew exactly who Reed's client was.

CHAPTER 25

JONATHAN stared at Reed as if he'd seen a ghost.

"You're telling me this firm doesn't want to represent me anymore? In other words, they think I'm guilty. Without even hearing a word I have to say."

"No." Reed folded his hands on his desk. "They think there's a conflict of interest since they represent Douglas and Adrienne's estates. They know I'm going out on my own, and that I'm a damned good trial attorney. So they're giving me the case. Unless you don't want my representation—which would be pretty stupid, considering how much I know about you, your background, and your relationships with Douglas and Adrienne. But that choice is yours. Make it."

"Great." Jonathan eyed Reed darkly. "You're hardly biased in my favor."

"That's irrelevant. I don't need to like you. I don't even need to believe you're innocent. I need to represent you. And I need you to give me the facts so I can protect your interests. This is business, Jonathan, not personal. You could be in a lot of trouble. You need a good criminal attorney. So either you trust my legal abilities or you don't."

"You arrogant bastard, you know you're the best." Jonathan rose, rubbing the back of his neck and pacing around. Emotionally, he looked like he was hanging on by a thread. "I still can't believe they're dead," he muttered.

Reed watched him carefully. He was definitely in shock. But was it from finding out about the murders or committing them?

"Jonathan, before you say another word, I need your answer. Am I representing you or not?"

"Yeah. You're representing me."

"Fine. Then sit down." Reed pointed to the chair. At the same time, he rose, walked over, and poured Jonathan a glass of water, which he shoved in his hand. "Drink this. And try to relax. We're due over at the Nineteenth Precinct shortly. We don't have the luxury of time. So let's start with the basics. How do you want to plead?"

"Not guilty." Jonathan shot him a scathing look. "Which happens to be the truth. I did *not* kill Douglas and Adrienne."

"Can anyone vouch for your whereabouts between one and six A.M.?"

"Unfortunately not. I was home, in bed, the way most people are in the middle of the night."

"Did anyone see you arrive at your apartment—the doorman, a neighbor, anyone?"

A slow exhale. "The doorman. We said a few words before I went upstairs."

"What kind of words?"

"I asked him to keep the media away. There were a couple of obnoxious reporters who'd followed me home."

"Good. Then you have several people to attest to your whereabouts at . . ." A questioning look. "What time did you get home?"

"Around midnight. And I stayed there, all night," he added emphatically.

"What about Douglas and Adrienne—did they leave Le Cirque the same time as you did?"

"No. They were still there, saying good night to the last guests."

"Right." Reed jotted something down, his expression unchanged. "And they sent you home early because you were drunk, pissing them off, and starting to become noticeably embarrassing."

Jonathan's jaw tightened, but he didn't deny it. "Something like that, yes."

Reed put down his pen, met Jonathan's gaze head-on. "I don't have the official police report yet. So tell me what you know. I don't want any surprises. I know how they were killed. Douglas's neck was snapped and

Adrienne was choked and raped. Evidently, there was semen present. What else should I know?"

A hard swallow. "When I got there, the crime-scene investigators were dusting for fingerprints, looking for clothing fibers, footprints, all that forensics stuff. I wasn't allowed in. When they carried out the body bags, they unzipped them just long enough for me to identify Douglas and Adrienne. Then they took the bodies to the medical examiner's office. The cops said they won't have any more details until autopsies are performed."

"What kinds of questions did the detectives ask you?"

Jonathan took a gulp of water. "When was the last time I saw Douglas and Adrienne alive, did I know of anyone who'd want them dead, and what were my whereabouts between one and six A.M. They asked about the party at Le Cirque, and about the added benefits and responsibilities that would fall in my lap with both Douglas and Adrienne gone."

"To which you said?"

"Nothing coherent. I was in shock. But when they asked if I'd be willing to provide a routine DNA sample, it suddenly clicked in my head that I was a suspect. So I agreed to the DNA test, but said I wanted my attorney present."

"Anything else I should know about the crime scene?"

Grimly, Jonathan nodded. "One of the things I saw them bag was an empty old-fashioned they found on the coffee table. If it's the glass I think it is, the prints on it will turn out to be mine."

"And why is that?"

"Because I was at the brownstone yesterday prior to the party."

"To visit Douglas?"

"No—Adrienne."

"Adrienne? Why in God's name would you go see her?"

"She's my father's wife."

"Cut the crap, Jonathan. You hated Adrienne's guts. She hated you, too."

"She was handling it."

"Yeah, right. Adrienne didn't just *handle* anything—except Douglas. He would have acknowledged you and Gordon years ago if it hadn't been for her pressuring him not to. That pissed the hell out of you."

"Not enough to kill her. And you know how much I respected Douglas. He was my father, for God's sake. Okay, so he didn't make that public until now. But he still provided for me—a home, a top-notch education, important business contacts. He gave me everything."

"True. But you'll have a whole lot more with him and his wife out of the way."

Jonathan slammed down his glass. "Goddammit, Reed, I didn't kill them."

Reed pursed his lips. "Okay, let's say for the moment I believe you. We'll bypass the circumstantial evidence, the motive, everything. Be aware that the police won't be so generous."

"I'm sure not."

"Let's move on. Let's talk about your state of mind. You're one screwed-up guy these days. And you're a suspect in more than just last night's tragedies."

Jonathan tensed. "You're talking about the situation with Taylor."

"Yes. And we *are* going to talk about her. Not with emotion or threats, but with facts and truth. I need to know just how irrational you are. It could sway the police."

"You're going to tell them that Taylor thinks I'm stalking her?" Jonathan asked incredulously.

"Of course not. But she was at the party last night. They're bound to question all the guests. And when they get to her . . ."

"Jesus Christ." Jonathan dropped his head in his hands. "This is an endless, fucking nightmare. I'm not only going to be painted as a greedy, violent, homicidal maniac, but a psychotic stalker, too. They might as well shove me in a cell and throw away the key."

"Don't let your mind go down that road," Reed advised, scrutinizing every last detail of Jonathan's reaction. More and more, he was sure the guy was innocent. "I don't want you losing it on me. No matter what, you've got to keep it together. Remember, if you didn't commit last night's crimes, the DNA will prove it. Lots of people hate their families. Some even come into a lot of money when their families die. But very few people snap their father's neck or rape and choke their stepmother just to come into their own." Reed's eyes narrowed. "We have two major unanswered questions to explore before we leave this office. One—why did you go to see Adrienne? And, two—what's your agenda with regard to Taylor?"

"You know my agenda," Jonathan replied, addressing the second question first. "I was very up-front with you about it. I think Taylor's the right woman for me. I plan to win her over."

"You've got a strange way of showing it. That was one weird conversation you had with her last night."

"She told you what I said?" Jonathan blew out his breath. "Of course she did. I must have sounded like a drunken lunatic. Maybe I am a lunatic. God knows, I have reason to be. That's what I wanted to share with her and what I meant about her not having all the facts. I would have told her there and then, but it wasn't the time or the place. But, yeah, I believe that once she knew everything, it would have made all the difference. Taylor's an emotional healer. She would have understood who I am, and why. And she'd have helped me find the peace I've been searching for."

Reed's forehead creased. "I'm not following."

"How could you?" Jonathan rose again, crossing over to the sideboard. He ignored the water and poured himself a Scotch.

"Easy," Reed cautioned. "You want to be sober when we talk to the police."

"I will be." Jonathan took a healthy swallow. "Believe me, it'll take more than one Scotch to dull my mental faculties. And a hell of a lot more to erase my demons."

He turned, his expression stony, almost removed, as he spoke. "You asked why I went to see Adrienne. I went to let her know that I have some ugly evidence against her—evidence that would have knocked Douglas's socks off if I'd shared it with him."

"So you blackmailed her?"

A shrug. "It depends on what you call blackmail. I told her to stop interfering with my relationship with Douglas and my career at Berkley and Company. That's it. I told her she could have all the money, prestige, and notoriety she wanted. Just so long as she let me do my thing. I would make Douglas an even bigger fortune than he already had. I guess Adrienne knew it, because she didn't fight me on it. She said that if I did as I promised, she wouldn't throw any obstacles in my path."

Reed leaned forward. "What was this evidence?"

"A tape. Gordon made it years ago. I guess he figured it might come in handy someday."

"Gordon?" That was the last name Reed had expected to hear. "The two of you were in this together?"

Something about Reed's choice of words seemed to strike Jonathan as ironic, because he gave a humorless laugh. "No, Reed. What Gordon was *in*, he was in by himself. He was just smart enough to include me in the proof, just in case."

"What was on this tape?"

Another bitter smile, and Jonathan downed the rest of his drink. "An argument. One that revealed a facet of our stepmother's perverted, sadistic mind."

Reed was starting to put together some very ugly pieces. "You'd better explain."

"I'll make it brief so neither of us pukes. You know that my mother, Belinda Mallory, was a maid at Douglas's estate. That's how they met and how Gordon and I were conceived."

"Yeah, you told me."

"What you don't know is how deep Adrienne's hatred ran. It festered over the years, especially when she never managed to give Douglas a child of her own. She was obsessed with Gordon and me. Especially Gordon. He was the bad boy of the two of us, the wild one, the challenge. When he was a kid, those traits pissed her off. When he was a teenager, they turned her on."

Reed went very still. "Are you telling me there was a sexual relationship?"

"Hey, haven't you ever seen *The Graduate?* The difference was, Gordon was only fifteen. And, much as he wanted to get laid, he didn't want it from Adrienne. He turned her down. She gave him an incentive to change his mind. That's what I have on tape."

"What incentive?"

"She threatened to plant something valuable in our mother's room— like one of the numerous extravagant pieces of jewelry Douglas bought her—then accuse our mother of theft. She'd fire her and have her arrested. If the accusation became a conviction—great—our mother would rot in jail. If not, Adrienne promised to make sure she never worked for another well-to-do family again. End of income. End of everything. As for us, who knows? Adrienne would have used all her wiles to convince Douglas to toss us out in the streets. She might very well have succeeded. After all, he hadn't acknowledged us. We had no official place in his life. Our mother was really all we had. We were just kids. So, Gordon became Adrienne's unwilling sex slave."

Reed grimaced. "You knew?"

"Not then, I didn't. Not for a couple of years. I found out by accident. One night I needed some air. I jumped in the car and drove out to Douglas's yacht club. I strolled down to the dock where he kept his yacht. I overheard Gordon and Adrienne, going at it like rabid animals. I threw up. Then I went back to the house. When Gordon came home, I confronted him. He told me what the situation was. Frankly, I didn't believe him. He wasn't exactly the helpless-victim type, or a decent, devoted son. True, he was trying to save his own ass as well as our mother's, but I still figured he was getting a real charge out of screwing his father's wife. That would be right in character. But when he gave me that tape, I knew he wasn't lying." Jonathan's lips curled in a bitter smile. "I'll make you a copy. You can hear for yourself."

Reed blew out his breath. "The woman was more dangerous than I realized, and a sexual predator to boot. Did your mother ever know?"

"Thank heavens, no. She died blissfully ignorant of the whole sordid arrangement, while we were in college."

"Yeah. Cancer. That much I remember." Reed ran a palm over his jaw. "The problem is, these facts don't help your case. They hurt it. They'll explain why your empty Scotch glass was at the brownstone. But they'll also give the authorities an additional motive to use against you. What Adrienne did to your mother, your brother—they'll say you wanted to get even, to hurt and humiliate her, and finally to kill her. You see my point."

Somberly, Jonathan nodded. "Yeah, I see. But why would I kill Douglas?"

"For ignoring the obvious. For standing by his wife and turning his back on his kids, and on their mother, when they needed his protection. For expecting you to show respect for a woman you considered to be a twisted bitch and a whore. Believe me, the prosecution will have a field day."

"I didn't do it, Reed. Not the rape. Not the murders."

"Okay, I've heard enough to know where we stand." Reed rose. "Let's go over to the police precinct. Give them their mouth swab for a DNA sample. We'll offer to help in any way we can. But, during the questioning, let me take the lead. Don't lose your cool. Don't answer anything unless I tell you to, and then be as brief as possible. No details. Just be a shocked, grief-stricken son who's horrified by what's happened."

"Which I am," Jonathan said pointedly.

A nod. "Which you are."

CATHY LOOKED UP from her desk when Reed and Jonathan emerged.

"I'm going out with Mr. Mallory for a while, Cathy," Reed informed her. "I'll be reachable on my cell. Any calls?"

She leaned forward, handing him two pink slips of paper. "These two messages are urgent. Everything else can wait."

Reed glanced down. The top message was from Richard Harter. It asked Reed to stop by his office ASAP and let him know the outcome of the meeting with Jonathan. Fine. He'd go do that now. That way the partners could heave a collective sigh of relief, and start making the necessary provisions to disassociate Reed from the firm and pave the way for his new practice.

The second message was from Taylor.

Frowning, Reed looked up. "Cathy, call the Nineteenth Precinct and tell them Mr. Mallory and I are on our way over. Jonathan, have a seat in the reception area. I have to pay someone a quick visit before we take off."

Jonathan shot Reed a derisive, knowing look. "I'm sure you do. Tell the good ol' boys to curtail their enthusiasm. They're off the hook."

Reed headed down the hall and around the bend. He paused at the desk of Richard Harter's secretary. "He's expecting me," he announced.

She nodded, picking up the phone and pressing the intercom button. "Mr. Weston's here to see you, sir. Go right in," she told Reed.

"Thanks." He walked over and gave a perfunctory knock.

"Come on in, Reed."

Stepping inside, Reed shut the door behind him. "Everything's on track," he said, cutting to the chase. "But I can't stay. I'm on my way to the Nineteenth Precinct with Jonathan."

The message got through loud and clear.

Crossing over to where Reed stood, Harter cleared his throat. "I realize this will be a rocky start for you. I also realize the irony of the situation. In order to launch the practice you've been pushing so hard for, you have to begin with the very kind of case you're determined to get away from. But you're a damned good attorney. Jonathan Mallory's lucky to have you on his team. My advice? Keep your eye on the prize."

"You're right. I'll do that." Reed paused, studying the man who'd been his mentor. "Richard, I appreciate everything you've done for me. I know you're in a lousy position yourself. But, remember, it's not the practice of criminal law that offends me. It's defending animals who I *know* are guilty of vile, unspeakable crimes, but who are rich and powerful enough to pay me to get them off scot-free."

"Vile, unspeakable crimes," Harter repeated quietly. "I think rape and murder qualify as those."

"So do I."

"Then this might turn out to be one of those cases."

"Maybe. But I don't think so. I honestly believe Jonathan's innocent. I doubt the cops will even come up with enough for an arrest. But if I'm wrong, at least I won't have to take a shower each time I walk out of court."

Harter chuckled. "You've got balls, Reed. You're going to do just fine. As for believing in your client, to most attorneys, that's a bonus. To you, it's a necessity. So I feel a little less guilty and a lot more pleased." He clapped Reed on the shoulder, then stuck out his hand. "I wish you the very best of luck."

"Thanks." Reed met his handshake. "I'm looking forward to the challenge."

"Keep me posted."

"I will."

Reed whipped out his cell phone the minute he left Harter's office, punching up the number of the Dellinger Academy as he retraced his steps to the reception area.

The switchboard operator answered and connected him to Taylor's office.

She picked up on the first ring. "Taylor Halstead."

"It's me. Everything okay?"

"Okay?" she asked incredulously. "Two of your clients were murdered last night. How could everything be okay?"

"I was referring to you."

She ignored the question. "Reed, I've been glued to the Internet, reading the news updates. They tell me nothing but bare-bones facts. I need you to fill me in."

"I can't."

A weighted pause.

"You can't," she repeated. "Why not?"

"Because I don't have a whole lot more details than you do."

"Are the police close to making an arrest?"

"I doubt it. The investigation's just getting under way."

"How heavily does Jonathan Mallory factor into that investigation?"

Another silence, this one more strained than the last.

Reed could actually feel the rift between them forming.

He blew out his breath. "I can't talk now, Taylor. I'm in the middle of a client meeting. The only reason I'm calling is because your message sounded urgent, and I wanted to make sure nothing was wrong."

"You're with Jonathan Mallory, aren't you?"

He didn't reply.

"Oh, God, he *is* a suspect." Taylor's voice quavered.

"I can't discuss this with you. You know that. I've got to go. Like I said, I just wanted to make sure you hadn't gotten any more threatening phone calls."

"Nope. Not a one. Then again, that's no surprise. The stalker I'm more and more convinced has been making those phone calls is in a client meeting with you."

Reed was nearing the reception area. He could see Jonathan pacing around, waiting for him.

"We can't have this conversation now," he said into the phone. "I'll call you later."

"I'm not sure I'm composed enough *or* objective enough to listen."

"There's only one way to find out." Reed paused, waiting for her reply.

It took a moment for her to give it.

"All right, Reed," she responded, her tone distinctly cool. "I'll wait for your call. In the meantime, I won't bother packing that bag. Something tells me our weekend at the ski lodge is off."

A quiet click told Reed she'd hung up.

6:45 P.M.

WVNY

Jack was sitting with Kevin, Dennis, and Laura when Taylor walked into her recording studio that night.

Her brows rose slightly. "Hi. The program manager himself, here to greet me along with my entire staff. To what do I owe this honor?"

"We're worried about you." Jack didn't mince any words.

"Why?"

Kevin snorted. "Don't try the clueless approach, Taylor. You cut out of here early last night to go to that bash for Jonathan Mallory at Le Cirque. Several hours later, the host and hostess were murdered in their own home. We're a radio station. We do have news sources here. We know the police questioned Jonathan Mallory. Was it routine questioning, or do they think he did it?"

Taylor shrugged out of her coat. "I don't know. You've read the wires— you know as much as I do."

"What about that guy you're seeing?" Jack demanded. "Isn't he Mallory's lawyer?"

"Geez." Taylor blinked. "I didn't realize my life was such an open book."

"If your relationship with Reed Weston is private, you'd better mention it to him," Laura interjected. "He's called your private line four times in the past twenty minutes." She waved the messages in the air. "He wants to talk to you before you go on the air."

"I see."

"He's not the only one who called." Dennis shifted in his chair, scratching his shaggy head and looking very ill at ease. "The police called, too. Laura wasn't at her desk, and the call was forwarded up here, so I answered. Detective"—he glanced at the message he'd jotted down—"Hadman wants to meet with you sometime tomorrow."

Kevin leaned forward. "Why is Hadman calling? He already checked out Romeo, and that was a dead end. So was that kid at Dellinger, Chris Young. Did Hadman trace the calls to someone else?"

"Nope. The number he got from the phone company turned out to be a dead end."

"Then why is Hadman calling you?" Kevin demanded.

"Because all the party guests will be questioned. As for my stalker, he's a low priority now."

"Nothing was said about Jonathan Mallory?"

"No. Nothing." Taylor adjusted the sleeves of her sweater. "Honestly, guys, I appreciate your worrying, but it's not necessary. I'll be fine."

"Yeah, well, there's fine and there's fine," Jack retorted. "You've taken a few too many hits these past months. First your cousin. Then Rick. Next a stalker—one who still hasn't been found. And now this." He folded his arms across his chest, his stance purposeful. "I'll take you over to the Nineteenth Precinct tomorrow. Just let me know what time."

"Same here," Kevin chimed in. "I'll break away whenever you need me to."

"I've got an early class at NYU tomorrow." It was Laura's turn to offer. "I can skip it. Just say the word."

"I have fewer responsibilities here than anyone." This time when Dennis spoke up, it was without shyness or hesitation. It was with loyalty. "So if this Detective Hadman needs to play your meeting by ear, and it ends up being a spur-of-the-moment thing, I'll take you."

Taylor felt a surge of warmth. "Thanks. All of you. I mean it. But it won't be necessary. Mitch, my PI, goes everywhere with me. He'll run me over to the police precinct either first thing in the morning or right after school. I'll be okay."

"The last part's a matter of opinion." Jack's tone of voice said he was getting to what he'd really come in here to say. "We all think you need a vacation. Two weeks, starting right away. You need to get out of Manhattan, away from painful memories and ongoing crises. You'll be back in time to move into your new apartment. And who knows? Maybe there'll be some resolution to all this by then."

"Jack, I can't." Taylor was shaking her head.

"Why not? Because of Dellinger? Isn't next week midwinter break?"

Taylor stared.

"Yeah. Go ahead, call your boyfriend and ask him to join you."

That suggestion hung heavily in the air.

"Sorry," Jack muttered. "I guess that's a sore spot."

"More like a moot point," Taylor replied, a definite edge to her tone. "I doubt Reed will be free."

There was another brief, uncomfortable silence.

"Maybe you should check," Laura proposed tentatively. "Or at least just call him back. He seemed pretty frantic."

"I'm sure he is. He probably wants to explain why he'll go to the wall for Jonathan Mallory." Taylor gave a brusque shrug. "I'll call Reed now and find out. No need to press your ears to the door. I'll come out and tell you what's going on the minute I hang up." She took a step toward her inner studio, then turned to face them. "Thanks again. You're the best."

She went inside.

For a moment, she stared at the phone. Maybe Kevin was right. Maybe circumstances had changed since she'd spoken to Reed this morning.

But she doubted it.

She picked up the receiver and punched in Reed's cell.

Obviously, he saw her number come up on caller ID, because he answered right away. "Finally," he greeted her. "I was beginning to wonder if you'd planned on returning my calls."

"I said I'd listen. I will."

"Good." Reed's tone was intense. "A lot's happened. A lot we need to talk about. So I made some arrangements. Mitch will head over to your place tonight. He's got the key you gave him. He'll let himself in, put on the right lights, and make it look like someone's there."

"Until when?"

"Until tomorrow. He'll spend the night."

"Really. And where will I be?"

"At my place. With me. Jake's picking you up outside the radio station. He'll drive you over to my apartment." A heavy pause. "Don't say no, Taylor. We need to talk."

Taylor felt torn, confused, and, in some unfathomable way, betrayed. Which was absurd, considering she still had no idea what Reed had or hadn't done, and where the investigation—not to mention things between the two of them—stood.

She owed it to herself and to Reed to find out.

"Okay, I'll come," she said at last. "But just to talk. Or, in this case, listen. I'm not planning to stay. Not unless I'm overwhelmed by what I hear."

Reed blew out his breath. "I won't pressure you. You set the rules. All I ask is that you come over to my apartment, sit down across from me face-to-face, and hear me out—with an open mind."

"The coming-over, sitting-down, and hearing-you-out parts I can manage. It's the open mind that's the rub. I'll try, Reed. That's the best I can do. As I said, I'm not objective when it comes to Jonathan Mallory."

"I realize that." He sounded so tired that Taylor couldn't help but feel pangs of compassion. Whatever she'd been through today, he'd been through the wringer as well.

"You sound beat," she said gently. "Maybe we should do this another night."

"No. This conversation can't wait." He paused. "But I appreciate your concern, and your caring."

"Yeah, well, both those things extend only to you," she warned. "*Not* your client."

"Fine. I understand where you're coming from. I'm not blaming you. What I *am* doing, is counting on you."

"For what? My presence? My undivided attention? You've got both. Anything more . . ." Taylor sighed. "Let's just say I wouldn't hold my breath."

CHAPTER 26

REED took Taylor's coat and shut the door behind her. "Jake got you here okay?"

"Like clockwork." She glanced around the apartment, wondering how a place that had felt so warm and homey a few days ago could feel so cold and foreign now.

"Make yourself comfortable." Reed gestured toward the rich bourbon-colored leather sofa in his living room. "I'll pour us some wine." As he headed toward the sideboard, he caught her guarded expression, and came to a rigid halt. "I'm trying to relax you, not lower your reserve. I think you know from firsthand experience that I don't seduce intoxicated women."

Taylor felt a twinge of shame. "You're right. You didn't deserve that. It's just been an unbearable day."

"I rest my case." He continued on his path, pouring two glasses of Merlot and carrying them over to the sofa as Taylor got settled.

She nudged off her low-heeled slingbacks and tucked her feet beneath her, noticing that he'd started a fire. The flames crackled cheerfully in the fireplace, sending a warm glow throughout the room. It took away some of the chill—but only the part that was externally generated.

The internal part would take a lot more to warm away.

"Bad news first," Reed began, sitting down beside her. "You were right about the weekend. I had to cancel. I'm sorrier than you can imagine. But there's too much happening for me to get away."

"I'm sure," Taylor acknowledged, sipping at her Merlot. "I, on the other hand, am on an enforced vacation. Jack ordered me to take two weeks off, starting immediately. I guess he's right. I need it."

Reed's frown had deepened with each word. "You're going away?" he demanded.

The severity of his tone startled her. And a niggling, unpleasant thought intruded. "Is that a legal question or a personal one?"

He slammed down his goblet. "Goddammit, Taylor, is it really going to come to this? Are you going to interpret every question I ask you, every word I say, as a fishing expedition meant to enhance my legal position?"

"I don't want to. But I'm not sure I can help it."

"Then let me give you a reason to try." He seized her glass and set it down on the coffee table, gripping her shoulders tightly. "I asked you what I did because I don't want you going away. Not without me, and certainly not alone. I'll worry about you and, more important, I'll miss you. Why? Because I'm in love with you. Believe me, I didn't plan to be. But I am. And it couldn't have happened at a worse time. And I wanted you to know that before we got into everything else we have to discuss."

His grasp eased as he felt a tremor run through her, and he searched her face for a reaction. "Say something."

A tight knot of emotion clogged Taylor's throat, and she swallowed hard to get past it. "I don't know what to say," she managed.

"At least tell me you believe me."

"I believe you."

"That's a good start. Now tell me you feel the same way."

Her chin came up, and she gave a hard shake of her head. "I don't want to. I want to stand up and walk out of here when you announce that you're representing Jonathan Mallory, which I know you're about to do. I want to stick to the resolution I made that I'd never become a stupid fool who let herself hope that love could conquer all. I want to. But I can't. Because I'm in love with you, too. Happy?"

"Yeah." He brushed his lips across her cheekbones—first one, then the other—before covering her mouth in a slow, tender kiss. "Very happy."

"Good," Taylor muttered, tugging her mouth away. "Because I don't see how this is going to work."

"Why? Because we don't agree about the identity of your stalker?"

There it was.

Taylor wriggled a few inches away and picked up her goblet—as much a physical, if symbolic, barrier between them as an emotional balm for the conversation ahead. "After all that's happened, how can you think Jonathan Mallory is innocent?"

"I can't explain. I'm not asking you to agree. I'm just asking you to trust in the fact that I'd never let anyone hurt you."

"I trust that you'd never *willingly* let anyone hurt me. Does that count?"

Reed sighed, sank back against the cushions. "I guess it'll have to. For now."

"It's not your loyalty I'm questioning. It's your judgment. I'm the psychologist, not you. And I don't think Jonathan Mallory is rational."

"Maybe he's not. But he's not dangerous either." Reed made an impatient gesture. "Let's shelve this part of the talk, for now. I have something important to tell you. Something I can finally share with you, since, as of today, it's a fait accompli." He leaned toward her again, delivering the news with pleasure and pride. "I'm leaving Harter, Randolph and Collins and starting up my own firm."

She blinked. His big meeting. She'd assumed it had been postponed.

"Your meeting—it happened?"

"Sure did."

Once that sank in, Taylor leaned forward and gave him a big hug. "I thought this might be where you were headed." She drew back, studied his expression. "You feel good about this."

"Very. It's been a long time in coming. I can't go this route anymore. It's time for a change. I want long-standing clients, not just high-profile cases. I want to build relationships with people I believe in. I guess I've gotten idealistic in my old age."

"Old age?" Taylor grinned. "You're thirty-five."

"Okay, maybe not old. But definitely cynical. You'd be surprised what happens to your idealism after ten years of practicing in the big leagues."

"I can imagine." Taylor's forehead creased in concern. "And you're right that Harter, Randolph and Collins is not known for its idealism. Still, you were a strong asset. I shudder to think of the partners' reaction when you made your announcement. I assume they were opposed to your leaving?"

"Let's say they were less than thrilled."

"Which is why you were wrestling with the logistic and ethical repercussions of your decision. You were trying to find a mutually acceptable way to part ways."

"Exactly. That's what these two weeks were about. Finding a solution we could all live with."

"Which you obviously did."

An odd expression crossed Reed's face. "I believe so, yes. When I walked out today, we were all on the same page. They've agreed to support my decision. They're also helping in any way they can—with referrals, references, whatever I need."

"Just like that?" Something about that scenario seemed very strange. The break was just too clean, too abrupt. "I don't get it. The timing sounds bizarre. Not to mention, you can't represent Jonathan Mallory if you're not part of the firm. So who will they get to . . ." Taylor's voice trailed off as the truth struck home.

The timing wasn't bizarre. The timing was intentional.

Her insides gave a twist. "Oh, Reed, please don't tell me you cut a deal with the senior partners. Don't tell me you agreed to take Jonathan Mallory on as your first client in exchange for Harter, Randolph and Collins's blessing to start your own firm and their help in making it happen."

A muscle flexed in his jaw. "It's not that simple."

"God." Taylor put down her wine. "I don't believe this. Your giant career step—the one meant to help you sleep at night and like yourself better—is all falling nicely into place as a result of the Berkley homicides."

"Taylor, stop it." Reed caught her arms. "I'm not a patsy, or an idiot. And I'm certainly not a hypocrite. Yes, I'm striking out on my own so I can expand my professional horizons. But I never said I planned on abandoning criminal law altogether. I'm not. I'm just becoming more selective about who I represent. So don't make this sound like I was bought off in some dirty deal worked out to get what I want. I was leaving the firm either way. It makes me sick that Douglas and Adrienne were murdered. Do I think Harter, Randolph and Collins used the situation to their advantage? Of course I do. But Jonathan is entitled to representation—assuming he needs it. Remember, he hasn't been charged with anything, nor do I think he will be. I talked to him. I happen to believe he's innocent."

"Innocent." Taylor said the word as if it were foreign. "Is that a fact-based assessment or wishful thinking?"

"It's instinct." Reed's eyes glittered. "I've got ten years' experience to back it up. Don't question my ability or my integrity. It's an insult to me and far beneath you."

That barb struck home, and Taylor flushed. "You're right. I'm just having a hard time accepting all this."

"I assumed you would. And I'm sorry you have to be in the middle of it. Ideally, the case will come to a speedy resolution and we can put it behind us. The same goes for whoever's stalking you." He paused, and Taylor could see he was struggling to get out his next words. "For the record, I don't capitalize on people's murders. In case you need to hear me say it, I'd much prefer to have fought this fight the hard way, if it meant Adrienne and Douglas would still be alive. Unfortunately, I don't have that option."

Taylor felt a massive wave of guilt. Reed was not only the man she loved, he was a good man. "Reed, stop." She reached out, took his hand, and interlaced her fingers with his. "You don't need to say any of this. I know who you are. And you're right. If I didn't have such strong, negative personal feelings about Jonathan, I'd be applauding the way you handled this." She frowned. "I have so many questions. But I can't ask any of them, can I?"

Reed brought her fingers to his mouth. "By the end of the weekend, Jonathan should no longer be a suspect."

"In the murders, maybe. But what about with regard to me?"

A hard sigh. "Those suspicions can't be erased until we find the stalker."

"You really don't think it's Jonathan, do you?"

"No. I don't. And if it's any consolation to you, he knows how bizarre he sounded when he talked to you last night. But there were reasons for it, reasons I can't get into. The good news is, I think he's starting to believe that you and he aren't going to happen. Give me time. Doing my job could result in putting an end to his fixation with you. I have a couple of ideas. Like I said, give me time."

"Okay." Taylor bit back the slew of questions she was dying to ask. There was no point. Reed couldn't tell her any more than he already had, at least not yet.

But there was something she had to tell him.

"Detective Hadman wants me to come to the precinct tomorrow and talk to him, since I was a guest at the reception. I hope you realize I have to be honest. If he asks me about Jonathan Mallory's behavior that night, or if I perceived any tension between him and his father and stepmother, I plan on telling him the truth."

"I expect you to." Reed didn't miss a beat. "Answer all his questions openly and honestly. Hedging can only hurt the investigation and make my client look even more suspicious. On the other hand, I'd ask that you try to be as objective as you can, under the circumstances."

"In other words, stick to the facts." Taylor nodded. "That's more than fair." A shrug. "Besides, Hadman already knows I'm uneasy about Jonathan, since he was on my list of potential stalkers. He might touch on the subject as it goes to character, but I doubt it'll hold much weight when it comes to investigating a double homicide. I just wanted to make sure you and I were on the same page."

"We are." Reed's brows were drawn, and there was clearly something else on his mind. "Did you talk to Hadman about the call trace? Did he have anything for you?"

"No." Taylor filled him in on what Detective Hadman had learned about the prepaid cell phone.

"The cops won't take this any further," Reed said. "It's too much of a needle in a haystack. Mitch, however, is another story. Let's see if Hadman can be persuaded to turn the telephone number over to him. If so, he can track down the store where the phone was bought and send one of his guys to talk to the clerks. Maybe someone will remember something."

"Maybe. But it's a long shot. Just finding the place could take weeks. And then, trying to get several-months-old information out of a store clerk who was probably yakking with a coworker when he or she sold the cell phone? I think we're talking next to impossible." Taylor stared off into space, pervaded by a hollow sense of hopelessness.

"What about the Berkleys?" she went on. "According to the sketchy news reports I read there was no break-in." A shudder. "Which suggests it was someone they knew. God. And here I am, obsessing over a stalker. It sounds pretty minor in comparison, doesn't it?"

"It sounds normal. Crazies come in all forms. One of them is fixated on you. That's not minor." Reed paused, studying their joined hands. "You never did answer my question. Are you leaving town?"

"Honestly? I haven't had time to think about it. But maybe it's a good idea if I do. I'll get a mental break from all this insanity. I'll also get away from that memory-ridden apartment. By the time I get back, it'll be almost moving day. I'll go someplace warm. Palm Beach. My father has a place there. Mitch or Jake can come with me and guard me the same way they do here. I'll lie on the beach and just veg. Who knows? Maybe Jack's right. Maybe all these crises will have been resolved by the time I get back."

Reed nodded. "Maybe." He drew her closer. "I meant what I said. I'll worry. And I'll miss you."

"I know. I'll miss you, too." Taylor gave him a wistful smile. "I was really looking forward to that weekend in the ski lodge. It sounded wonderful."

"We'll reschedule."

"Promise?"

"Promise."

Silence, punctuated only by the crackle of the fire.

"Stay with me tonight." Reed's request was uttered in a low, urgent tone, his hand unsteady as he raised her chin to meet his gaze. "You'll catch a flight to Palm Beach tomorrow. I'll put you and either Mitch or Jake on the plane myself. But for one night, let's forget the whole damned world. Let's just have us. We deserve that, don't we?"

"Yes. We do." Taylor didn't have to ponder that one. She threw herself into it, as eager as he to block out the world. Reaching up, she began unbuttoning his shirt.

They made love on the rug by the fire, after which Reed carried Taylor to his bed, where they lost themselves in each other again. Their lovemaking was different tonight, not in its fervor, but in its emotional intensity. There was something deep and powerful underlying the motions of their bodies, a poignant quality that scared the hell out of Taylor.

Reed was right. This feeling wasn't going away.

She cried out his name when she climaxed, everything inside her shattering at once. She heard herself gasp out that she loved him, and she felt the reaction to her declaration jolt through his whole body. He lost it entirely, his grip becoming almost bruising as he jetted into her in hard, racking spasms. He shuddered, his hips jerking convulsively, pounding him into her, the force of his orgasm shoving them both up on the bed until they collided with the headboard, which, in turn, collided with the wall.

When the wildness finally subsided, and awareness returned, they were in a half-sitting position. The pillow that Reed had shoved beneath Taylor's hips had inched its way up her back—which turned out to be a major source of salvation, since it served as a buffer between her and the heavy mahogany headboard. Her throbbing body was more than grateful.

Reed wasn't so fortunate. His head was pressed against the wall, and his shoulders were crunched into the headboard.

He let out a pained groan, and Taylor began to laugh.

"I'm glad you think it's funny," he muttered, shifting to his knees so he could wriggle them both down to a prone position. Another groan, this time with a heavy dose of male satisfaction. "I think I broke something."

"Nothing important," Taylor assured him, arching her hips just enough to keep him inside her.

A husky chuckle brushed her ear. "It's good to know you've got your priorities in order."

"Mmm." Taylor trailed her fingers along his spine, wishing she could freeze this moment, wishing she was as sure of everything as she was of the magic their bodies made together.

Reed must have felt the change in her mood, because he raised up on his elbows and gazed intently down at her. "I know you're scared. Don't be. This is about as right as it gets." He lowered his head, brushed his lips across hers. "We're going to make it, Taylor. You'll see." A slow, sexy grin. "Although I can't promise we won't injure a few body parts along the way."

She smiled back. "I'll bear that in mind."

"I love you," he said quietly. "Bear *that* in mind."

A shaky nod. "I will."

Out in the hall, the grandfather clock chimed two. Reed stroked Taylor's hair off her face, then kissed her again. "Happy Valentine's Day."

Her arms tightened around his back. "Happy Valentine's Day."

FRIDAY, FEBRUARY 14

4:45 P.M.

LAGUARDIA AIRPORT, NEW YORK CITY

Reed watched Taylor's flight take off, pissed as hell that he couldn't be with her, relieved that Mitch was. She'd met with Hadman today, who'd asked the usual string of questions pertaining to the party at Le Cirque. Whatever Taylor's answers had been couldn't have helped Jonathan, but that was life. He'd deal with the fallout as he had to.

He left the airport and was halfway back to Manhattan when his cell phone rang.

"Hello?"

"Reed, it's me." Jonathan sounded rattled. "Thank God I reached you."

"Why? What's going on?"

"I'm at my office. The cops are here. They're arresting me for the murders of Douglas and Adrienne."

Shock was eclipsed by training. "Okay, Jonathan, listen to me. Don't make a scene. Just go with them. Don't say a single word. I'm on my way. I'll meet you at the precinct in forty minutes."

CHAPTER 27

FOOTSTEPS approached the holding cell, and Jonathan's head came up as the cop fit the key in the lock and swung open the barred door with a clang.

"Finally," he muttered, jumping up from the chair as Reed stepped inside. "I've been rotting in this cell for an hour."

"Sorry. I hit traffic." Reed shrugged out of his overcoat and draped it over his arm.

Jonathan's eyes were frantic, his face flushed and sweaty. "They handcuffed me right there in my office. They read me my rights in the middle of the fucking Chrysler Building. I was hauled in, fingerprinted, and shoved in this dark little hole over an hour ago. I'm losing my mind."

"That's the idea." Reed spoke in a steady, reassuring tone. "They start with the shock effect of the arrest. Then they dump you in here while they're filling out reports and conferring with the assistant district attorney. They're joined by a detective from the Manhattan North Homicide Squad—he or she will assist the precinct detectives on the case. In short, they're hoping you'll freak out enough to confess. They would have taken you to the interrogation room, but I nixed that. I called the precinct and let them know I was on my way and that there was to be no communication with you until I arrived."

"Great. So this is *good* treatment." Jonathan yanked off his basket-weave silk tie, which was already hanging askew, and unbuttoned the top few buttons of his rumpled shirt. "What in God's name could they have on me?"

"You tell me."

"How the hell should I know?" Jonathan slammed a fist against the wall, then began pacing around, plainly as freaked out as the police had hoped to make him. "Maybe it's the fingerprints on the old-fashioned glass. They probably figured out they were mine."

Reed gave a hard shake of his head. "I don't buy it. You told Hadman you were at the brownstone the afternoon of the murder, and that you had a Scotch."

"Then I don't know what evidence they concocted."

"The police don't concoct evidence, Jonathan. They find it and piece it together." Reed scowled. "In this case, whatever they found convinced the district attorney's office that they had grounds for an arrest." He gripped the back of the chair and stared Jonathan down. "Before we talk to Hadman, you're sure there's nothing you haven't told me. Nothing at all?"

"I'm sure," Jonathan snapped.

"Then let's not speculate. Let's find out." Reed paused. "Remember two things. Hold it together at all times. And let me do the talking."

"Yeah. Right." Jonathan rubbed the back of his neck. "Let's get this over with."

"Okay." Reed walked over and called out to the cop, "Tell Detective Hadman we're ready to speak with him."

The cop gave them a tight nod as he unlocked the cell door. "Come with me."

They were ushered into the interrogation room, which was small, windowless, and starkly furnished, then left alone.

"Nice accommodations," Jonathan muttered, glancing at the metal table and hard chairs. "Right out of *Architectural Digest*."

"It's meant to make people break down, not move in," Reed replied. "Just relax. It's all a game. They'll make us sweat for a while longer while they all huddle together. Then they'll come in, ask questions, and take copious notes. Don't let it get to you."

Ten minutes passed. Fifteen. Twenty.

After half an hour, Jonathan pushed back his chair. "Where the hell are they already?"

As if on cue, the door swung open and Detective Hadman strode into the interrogation room, joined by another man—his partner, Detective Murray Olin. Olin looked like a nice, average joe. But Reed had dealt with him in the past, and he was well aware that beneath the easygoing, chatty manner, the guy was sharp as a tack and had earned a reputation as an outstanding detective. That wasn't his only rep. According to the grapevine, Olin's poker game was as good as his poker face, which told Reed that the guy was taking home a healthy pot of his fellow officers' cash every week.

Hadman pushed the door shut behind him. "Hello, Counselor."

"Hadman. Olin," Reed acknowledged. "Let's hear what you've got. It had better be pretty good. You humiliated my client at his place of business."

"He'll get over it. It was after five on Valentine's Day. So only a handful of people were there to witness his humiliation. Besides, why should your client care after Wednesday's big announcement?" Hadman shot Reed a penetrating look. "He's moving out, and up, on his way to run Berkley and Company. So what difference does it make what the old crowd at the Chrysler Building thinks?"

"Detective, cut the sarcasm and—"

Hadman waved away Reed's protest. "I'll get right to it. The circumstantial evidence is damning enough. We've got no forced entry and no burglary." A quick look at Jonathan. "You did tell me you have a key to the house."

"Douglas gave one to each of his sons when they were teenagers so they could use the place when they stayed in the city," Reed answered for him. "Sounds normal to me. Not to mention that the housekeeper has a key, too. Anyone could have 'borrowed' it."

"Right. Then there's that empty Scotch glass. No surprise that the fingerprints we lifted belonged to your client. He told us he was at the brownstone that afternoon, and that he had a drink." Another glance at Jonathan. "Scotch is your drink, isn't it? It's what you were guzzling Wednesday night at Le Cirque. Then again, you were celebrating. Or were you fortifying yourself for knocking off your father and stepmother later that night?"

"Don't even dignify that with an answer, Jonathan," Reed instructed.

"On the other hand, your client had lots of other reasons to drink that night," Olin pointed out. "Talk about stress. From what we've heard from the guests and the staff of Le Cirque, he was bickering with Adrienne Berkley, arguing with Douglas Berkley, and trying to pick up Taylor Halstead, all in one night."

"True." Hadman eyed Jonathan, who had begun to sweat. "Ms. Halstead doesn't like you much, by the way. In fact, I think she's afraid of you. But then, that's no surprise either. As for Adrienne Berkley, you two never much got along. So face-offs with her were status quo."

"Where are you going with this, Hadman? So far, all you've done is badger my client."

Hadman turned to Reed. "You want information? Fine. It seems your client had lunch with his father last Friday. According to the maître d' at the Oak Room, as well as two of the waiters, the conversation at Mallory's table escalated into an argument. Douglas Berkley was upset about something. Care to tell us what?"

"I'll answer that," Jonathan replied before Reed could intercede. "We were talking about Gordon. I'd uncovered some unethical dealings he was involved in before he died. I passed the information on to Douglas. He had a right to know, in case it affected the company. He was very upset."

"Sorry, that doesn't wash." Hadman pulled out a chair, propping one of his legs on it. "Although I don't doubt you touched on the subject of your brother's dirty dealings. But that's not what your argument was about. According to the e-mails you and Berkley exchanged the weekend *after* that dinner, it's clear he already knew about the securities fraud Gordon was conducting when you broke the news to him. I'm sure you were very disappointed. Hot information like that might have bought you an even sweeter deal at Berkley and Company."

"What's the source of these e-mails?" Reed demanded, making sure to hide the fact that he hadn't a clue what the hell Hadman was talking about. What securities fraud had Gordon been involved in that Jonathan uncovered?

Obviously, his client had *forgotten* to mention something to him. And he'd screwed it up further by opening his mouth and lying to Hadman.

More damage control for Reed to effect.

"We found the e-mails on Mallory's computer," Olin supplied. "Your client kindly allowed us access to his apartment, and to his laptop. We retrieved some messages between him and Douglas Berkley. There are specific references to the major bombshell Jonathan had assumed he was dropping on his father, but that, as it turned out, came as yesterday's news to Berkley."

Hadman's features hardened. "But that's not what the fight at the Oak Room was about, was it? It was about Taylor Halstead, and your father's concern over your obsession with her. In fact, you were overheard defending yourself, swearing that you weren't the one harassing her."

Jonathan's jaw was working.

"What happened, Mallory? Couldn't you convince Douglas you were innocent?"

"Cut it out, Hadman," Reed said. "The only one who's doing any harassing is you. If Douglas doubted Jonathan on any level, he wouldn't have appointed him to a high-level position at Berkley and Company, and set things up so he'd be running the company one day."

"Maybe. Maybe not. We've still got lots of time to dig, and to find out if your client was blackmailing or threatening Berkley. Trust me, the prosecution will have everything they need by the time this goes to trial."

"Trial? This won't even get past arraignment." Reed shoved back his chair and rose. He knew in his gut that Hadman and Olin were playing cat and mouse. Which meant that they had some ace in the hole. It was time to push them to reveal it. "Everything you've said is either circumstantial or speculative. Douglas was a powerful man. Like every powerful man, he had enemies. Including enemies he assumed were friends and would therefore welcome into his home. So much for needing a key to gain free access to the intended victims. As for Jonathan's relationship with his father—"

"Save it for the jury, Weston," Hadman interrupted, cutting to the chase in one punch-in-the-gut announcement. "We've got a positive DNA match. The semen taken from Adrienne Berkley's body belonged to your client."

Dead silence.

Then Jonathan reacted, lurching to his feet. "That's impossible!"

"It's not impossible. It's fact."

"Run the damn test again! I'm telling you, it's wrong!"

"Try again, Mallory. DNA testing is damned close to a hundred percent accurate. And in this case, when you add motive and circumstantial evidence . . ." Hadman eyed first Jonathan, then Reed. "Care to change your story?"

Reed jumped in before Jonathan could start raving again. "I want to talk to my client alone."

Hadman made a grand sweep with his arm. "By all means. Maybe you can talk some sense into him. It'll be easier on everyone."

"Good idea." Olin glanced at his partner, then jerked his head toward the door. "Come on, Roy. I could use another cup of mud with half-and-half anyway."

"You're on." The two of them headed out. "You've got ten minutes," Hadman called over his shoulder.

REED DIDN'T WASTE a single one of them.

The instant the door shut behind Hadman and Olin, Reed pulled his chair over to Jonathan, gesturing for his client to put his butt in his own. "Sit."

Jonathan complied, his breath coming in shallow pants. "This can't be happening."

"It is." Reed leaned forward until he was in Jonathan's face. "Look at me."

Again, Jonathan complied.

"Tell me what happened that night."

"I already told you everything."

"You were drunk. Maybe you forgot something."

Shock was eclipsed by anger, and Jonathan jolted upright in his seat, his eyes flashing. "Forgot something? You mean like raping Adrienne and killing her and Douglas? No, Reed. That's not something I'd forget. I didn't do it." He gazed wildly about, like a drowning man clutching at straws. "The DNA test was fixed. It had to be."

"The medical examiner's office doesn't fix DNA test results."

"Then how else do you explain it?"

"I can't," Reed answered quietly.

The skepticism in his tone must have come through, because Jonathan turned sheet white, the reality of the situation sinking in. "You don't believe me. You think I'm guilty. Hell, even *I'd* think I was guilty if I didn't know I wasn't. I'm screwed, Reed. Totally, utterly screwed." All the fight seemed to drain out of him, and he dropped his head in his hands. "I've got no alibi. I'm up to my ass in motives. And they've got irrefutable evidence.

I'll either rot in jail for the rest of my life or be executed for something I didn't do."

Reed's mind was racing a mile a minute. Only one of three possibilities was true. A: Jonathan was guilty and one hell of an actor. B: Jonathan was guilty but delusional, and didn't remember committing the crimes. Or C: Jonathan was as innocent as he claimed, and there was some other, bizarre explanation.

But what?

"Jonathan, let me ask you something. Would you agree to take a polygraph?"

"What good would that do? From what I understand, they're not always accurate. They're not admissible in court. And they won't hold a candle to DNA evidence."

"All that's true. But we've got nothing to lose. If you pass, it'll be something in our favor to share with the police and the DA. It'll put a chink in their ironclad resolve that this is a done deal. If you fail, you'll be no worse off than you are now."

"Which is pretty bad." Jonathan blew out his breath. "Okay, fine, yeah, I'll take the polygraph. I've got to pass. I'm innocent. Now tell me, what happens next? I'm not exactly familiar with criminal proceedings."

"The arraignment's next. It'll be set for tomorrow."

"That's a bail hearing, isn't it?"

Reed nodded.

"What if the judge refuses to release me on bail? We're talking two counts of murder one here."

Reed didn't avert his gaze. "I won't lie to you. He might refuse bail. You're not a flight risk, but the state will argue that you're a threat to society. I think I can convince the court otherwise. But I can't make any promises. With a modicum of luck, you'll be able to walk out of here until the grand-jury hearing—once you've forfeited your passport and paid a ton of money. And Jonathan, I do mean a *ton* of money. Bail will probably be set at a million dollars or more, a tenth of which has to be put up in cash."

"Whatever it is, I'll come up with it. If I hit a snag and run short—" Jonathan's voice quavered, and he broke off, looking like he was going to puke. "I was about to say that Douglas would help me out. He always has. Only now he can't."

"No, he can't. What's more, you can't touch a single dime of his assets. Whatever you come up with has to be on your own. You have the resources, don't you?"

"Yeah. I'll liquidate whatever I have to. I'll do anything to avoid jail." Abruptly, Jonathan turned to Reed. "I'm spending the night here."

Another nod. "Yes, and I'm spending it poring over the facts and starting to build our case."

A weighted pause. "Reed, I need to clear something up."

"I'm listening."

"I realize I'm repeating myself. But in this case, it's necessary. You think I'm delusional. Maybe I am—in some cases."

"Cases like Taylor."

A nod. "If I'm to be brutally honest with myself, I'm aware that I need help. Extricate me from this nightmare, and I'll get it. You have my word. But, in return . . ." Jonathan cleared his throat. "You said it's not necessary for you to believe I'm innocent in order to represent me. I understand that's true—legally. But *I* need you to believe me. I *am* innocent. I'm not a stalker, and I'm sure as hell not a rapist and a murderer. I did *not* commit those crimes. Please believe me. And for God's sake, help me."

Reed rose. "I'll do what I can."

CHAPTER 28

ʀᴇᴇᴅ stared at the phone on his night table for a long time.

Then he unfolded the slip of paper Taylor had given him and punched in the Florida number.

"Hello?" Her voice was weary and edgy as hell.

"Hi, it's me."

"Hi." Her relief was a tangible entity he could feel. Even now, more than a thousand miles away, she was still apprehensive each time she picked up the phone. "I'm glad it's you."

"Did your flight get in okay?"

"Right on schedule. I grabbed a sandwich, took a cab to the house, and soaked in a hot tub. Tomorrow I'll hit the beach. It's right on the other side of the row of palm trees outside my window. The weather's supposed to be eighty degrees and gorgeous."

Lighthearted words. Taut tone.

"Where's Mitch?" Reed asked.

"In one of the four downstairs guest rooms." A half laugh. "Don't worry about Mitch's comfort level. My father doesn't do anything half measure. This place is a lavish Spanish-style palace. Between the Olympic-size pool, the high-tech exercise room, the ocean at our feet, and a choice of opulent bedrooms, each one with a private bathroom that's bigger than his entire Manhattan apartment, Mitch won't want for anything."

"I wasn't worried—at least not about Mitch." Reed gripped the phone more tightly. "I needed to hear your voice."

"Miss me already?"

"More than you know." He paused. "Taylor, there's another reason I'm calling."

A heartbeat of silence as she absorbed his words and his tone. "Reed, what's wrong?"

He blew out his breath. "I hate laying this on you. Especially now. Jonathan's been arrested for Adrienne and Douglas's murders."

She gasped. "Arrested—when?"

"He called me right after your plane took off. I went straight to the Nineteenth Precinct from the airport. I arrived home a little while ago. The file is spread out all over my bed. It's going to be a long night."

"That doesn't sound too promising." Taylor was shaken. "I know you can't discuss it with me."

"No, I can't."

She let out a frustrated sigh. "Reed, you sound like a wreck. Is there anything I can do?"

"Just have faith in me. No matter what spin the press puts on this, believe that I know what I'm doing."

"That's not an issue. It's a given." Taylor paused again. "Do you want me to come home?"

"Definitely not. Stay put. Relax and enjoy the sun. I feel better knowing you're safe. Mitch is with you. And the only people who know you're in Palm Beach are the gang at WVNY and me. So there'll be no creepy phone calls for you to contend with."

"There might not be any more of those anyway," she answered quietly. "Not if my stalker's in jail."

"*If*," Reed replied. "Which I don't think he is."

That was the truth. Still, Reed felt like a bastard. Taylor was assuming that Jonathan would be incarcerated for the long haul—until his trial. But if Reed's efforts were successful, Jonathan would be back on the streets tomorrow.

He had to tell her.

"The arraignment's tomorrow. Jonathan's willing to post any amount of bail."

Another silence.

"Are you telling me the state releases murder suspects on bail?"

"If the defense attorney makes a convincing-enough case that his client's not a flight risk or a threat to society, yes."

"Which you intend to do—don't answer that," she interrupted herself. "Of course that's what you intend to do. It's your job."

"Yes, it is." He was beginning to wish he'd told her to come home after all. "Taylor, listen to me—"

"You don't need to explain. I understand. And I appreciate your honesty. Now, I'll give you the same. I don't blame you for doing what you have to. But don't blame me for hoping you fail. I'd feel a lot better if Jonathan Mallory stayed behind bars."

"I know." Reed rubbed a palm over his jaw. There was nothing else he could say, no way to bridge this gap. Not unless he proved Jonathan's innocence—on all counts.

"You'd better go," Taylor said, as if reading his mind. "You've got a lot of work ahead of you."

"Yeah. I do." He drew a slow breath. "Just one more thing before we hang up. I love you. Don't forget that."

"I didn't plan to."

"Good."

She must have sensed the underlying tension in his voice. "Reed, are you sure you're okay?"

"Okay" was a relative term.

"I'm fine," he assured her. "This is the world of a defense attorney. I've lived it for ten years. I'm a pro at it. I love the challenge. Now go to sleep. I didn't let you get much of that last night."

A soft laugh. "No, you didn't. But I'm not complaining." Her laughter faded. "I love you, too, by the way. And if you need me, I'm here."

SATURDAY, FEBRUARY 15

1:35 A.M.

Sleep wouldn't be coming tonight.

Then again, he hadn't expected it to. Not under the circumstances.

Still, he had to rest. Tomorrow was an important day.

He stared at the ceiling, not noticing the ugly cracks in the plaster.

Instead, he saw Taylor. She was always his last mental image at night. He'd visualize her in bed, her dark red hair spread out across the pillow, her body his for the taking.

And oh, how he planned to take it.

He shifted uncomfortably, his erection nearly painful in its magnitude. Soon. Not yet. But soon.

Usually, he settled for calling her. But tonight, that was an impossibility. Although he'd love to hear the shock in her voice if he did. She thought she was safe.

She wasn't. She'd find that out soon enough.

But not tonight. Tonight, he'd have to sweat it out.

She was alone. That in itself was comforting. Reed wasn't leaving New York, not until the double homicide was resolved.

By then it wouldn't matter.

Taylor would be his.

10:15 A.M.

CRIMINAL COURT

100 CENTRE STREET, NEW YORK CITY

"We're talking about murder one," Judge Martin proclaimed from the bench. "Ordinarily, I would remand the defendant without bail. However, the arguments of defense counsel are compelling. The defendant has no prior record and has cooperated fully with the authorities. In addition, I was impressed by the eloquent character reference provided by defense counsel, who is highly respected by this court and who has a long-standing association with the defendant. Taking all those facts into account, it is the opinion of this court that the defendant is not a flight risk or a threat to society. That having been said, due to the serious and violent nature of the crimes he's being charged with, I'm setting bail at one million dollars, cash or bond. Defendant will also surrender his passport to the court."

The sound of the gavel echoed through the room.

Beside Reed, Jonathan heaved a huge sigh of relief. "Thank God," he muttered. He turned to Reed. "And thank you."

"We're a long way from the thank-yous. That was just the beginning." Reed snapped his briefcase shut. "I've made preliminary arrangements with the bail bondsman. I'll give him a call, tell him the dollar figure. He'll head over and post the million bucks. It'll cost you a hundred grand, but you don't have much choice if you don't want to spend another night in jail. It's Saturday. There's no way you'd have access to the sizable number of assets you'll have to liquidate."

"Fine. Anything. Just get me out of here."

"Hang tight," Reed advised as Jonathan was escorted back to the holding cell. "I'll make the call and take care of the paperwork. You'll be out in a couple of hours. Oh, and we're stopping at the DA's office. I've arranged for you to take a polygraph before we go home. Hadman's agreed to meet us there. That way, he, the ADA, and I will all be firsthand witnesses."

Jonathan nodded, but his eyes were glazed, as if Reed's words were barely registering in his mind. He kept walking, docilely allowing himself to be led out of the courtroom.

Reed frowned. He wasn't thrilled about having put his reputation on the line for Jonathan. But Judge Martin wasn't the most liberal of judges, and Reed had known instinctively that a personal push would be necessary to make this fly.

Still, Reed was relieved they'd gotten this far. It was necessary to keep Jonathan out of jail, not only to retain the guy's sanity, but to have sufficient time and opportunity to build their case. The grand jury would convene later this week, and there was no doubt they'd get their indictment. So everything hinged on what Reed could uncover between now and the trial. And he needed Jonathan ready, willing, and accessible at all times.

Striding out of the courtroom, Reed turned on his cell phone and contacted the bail-bond company. After that, he called Paul Mills, who had been alerted to the situation and was expecting his call.

Paul was the attorney who'd been Reed's first choice to come on as his associate since he'd made the decision to start his own firm. Paul was young, only two years out of Columbia Law. He'd been working as a junior associate at a top Park Avenue firm, and Reed had seen him in action, both in court and in civil matters. And, young or not, the guy was shrewd, articulate, and already earning a reputation as an outstanding litigator and all-around top-notch attorney. But he wasn't happy at the big, prestigious Park Avenue law-firm scene, and he'd jumped at the chance to work with Reed when Reed had approached him.

They'd spoken twice over the past two weeks, and on Thursday Reed had made him a firm offer, which he'd accepted.

Now the question was, would Paul's current practice waive the traditional two-weeks' notice? Because Reed sure as hell needed his assistance, and *now*.

Paul answered his home phone right away. "Hello?"

"It's Reed."

"How did the arraignment go?"

"Jonathan was released on a million dollars' bail. How did your conversation with the partners go?"

A chuckle. "Congratulations are in order for both you *and* me. You for accomplishing the impossible and me for moving a mountain. I'm a free agent as of now. I guess I was too junior to miss. So I'm all yours."

"Excellent." Reed felt a huge wave of relief. Normally, it wouldn't have been a problem for Paul to come on board in two weeks. Reed had a lot of initial setup to attend to, from having stationery and business cards printed up to having an interior decorator work some magic on his recently vacated office space. It was pure luck that the previous tenants had moved out early. Then again, he'd expected to ease into this new practice gradually, first settling in himself, then hiring additional staff. But Jonathan's arrest had nixed that idea and sent the whole process into overdrive.

"Do you need me today?" Paul asked.

"Yeah, if you're free. I know it's Saturday, so if that's a problem . . ."

"Nope. No problem."

"Good. How about if I meet you at the office around three? I can bring you up to speed on the case and my preliminary strategy."

"Works for me. Just one question."

"Shoot."

"Where's the office? You mentioned to me that we'd be in a brownstone in midtown, but you never gave me the address."

Reed gave a derisive laugh, shaking his head in self-censure. "That would be helpful, wouldn't it?" He rubbed his forehead. "Sorry. My mind's just racing a mile a minute. It's on East Fifty-fifth, between Third and

Lex." He gave Paul the exact address. "The heat's on, the water's running, and the phones are in. I'll give you a key when we meet up there."

"Which floor are our offices on?"

"Take your pick. I own the building. I bought it a few years back as an investment. We're going to be doing some pretty quick renovating, but you've got first dibs on where you want your office space to be. Whoever comes on board next will get second dibs."

"Squatter's rights. Sounds good," Paul replied amenably. "Okay, you wrap things up at your end, and I'll meet you at the office at three. And Reed? Thanks again. It's an honor and a privilege."

"You're welcome. I appreciate your kicking into high gear on a dime. You're going to be a real asset to the firm. And I doubt you'll be thanking me by the time we wrap up this case. You probably won't see sunlight for days." A pause. "Maybe weeks."

"I'll live."

"Yeah, let's hope Jonathan will, too."

11:15 P.M.

WESTON & ASSOCIATES, ATTORNEYS AT LAW

EAST FIFTY-FIFTH STREET, NEW YORK CITY

His first late night at the office.

Reed leaned back in the leather chair that was the sole piece of furniture in the big, empty room. Actually, it was the sole piece of furniture in the entire brownstone, not counting the cheap computer station, telephone, and coffee machine.

He rubbed his eyes, reviewing the events of the day.

Jonathan had passed the polygraph. And, since polygraphs were between 90 and 95 percent accurate, the defense had its first ray of hope.

Reed had met Paul in the office, and together they'd studied Reed's case notes. They were in solid agreement. There was no way to eliminate Jonathan as a suspect. The only way to go about winning this case was to create reasonable doubt by implicating others as potential suspects.

That was easy enough to accomplish with regard to the circumstantial evidence. Paul was already on it, digging into friends, personal acquaintances, and business associates who might have motive, opportunity, and a relationship with the Berkleys that would explain the lack of breaking and entering.

But DNA evidence was another story entirely.

Reed picked up the stack of printouts he'd gotten off the Internet. A seventy-five-page accumulation of the most recent studies on genetics and DNA. There had to be something in here. Some logical explanation that would give him the loophole he sought.

He was flipping through the pages when his cell phone rang.

"Hello?"

"Hi." Taylor's voice drifted through the line. "It's me. Bad time?"

Reed put down his work. "Actually, I don't even know *what* time it is."

"Eleven-thirty." A pause. "I saw the news on TV. It occurred to me that you weren't calling me because you were afraid I'd flip out. I won't. You must be one hell of an attorney, though. According to both CNN and Fox News, bail in murder-one cases happens next to never. Congratulations."

Again, he rubbed his eyes, realizing he'd been totally disconnected from the outside world. He should have realized that word of Jonathan's release would be on the evening news, and that Taylor might see it.

"Reed?" she prompted.

"I'm sorry." He forced his mind into the here and now. "I should have called you. But you're wrong about the reason I didn't. I wasn't ducking your reaction. I'm lost in space. I've been closeted in either a courtroom or an office since early this morning. I don't know whether I'm coming or going." His brows knit. "Did the media make a big deal over it?"

A soft laugh. "The media sensationalizes stuff like this, especially when it involves a well-known family. I don't pay attention to the fluff, just the basics. Jonathan's out on bail. He pled not guilty. There'll be a grand-jury hearing sometime this week. Oh, and there was a pretty good shot of you and Jonathan leaving the courthouse. You look intense, like a warrior marching into battle. Very formidable."

"Yeah, that's me. Formidable." Reed sighed. "Are you okay with this? Not happy, but okay?"

"I'll have to be," Taylor stated frankly. "In the meantime, you'll be glad to know that Mitch pitched in for you. He gave me two self-defense lessons today. It was a very eclectic day. I spent a few relaxing hours tanning on the beach, flanked by a blood-pumping morning and afternoon workout. You should see my finger rake and ear slap. They're amazing."

"Wow." Reed's lips curved. "I'm impressed. I'm also jealous. It sounds like I've been replaced as your martial-arts instructor."

"Nah," she quipped. "I like the outcome of getting sweaty with you much better."

Reed blew out his breath. "God, I miss you."

"You don't have time to miss me. Where are you, by the way? I tried your home number first."

"I'm in my new office." Reed ran through the explanation for her, telling her about Paul at the same time.

It was Taylor's turn to exhale sharply. "Geez. Like I said, you don't have time to miss me. A new office, a new associate, and a murder case all at once. I'm breathless just listening to you."

Reed had just opened his mouth to reply when his call waiting beeped in. "Taylor, hang on a second." He punched the send button. "Hello?"

"Reed, it's me." Jonathan sounded strung out. "I ate. I showered. I slept. And now I'm up again, going nuts. I keep thinking about being locked in a cell forever, or being stuck with a lethal injection. My life might be over. And I can't do a damned thing about it."

"You're wrong. There's a lot you can do about it. Stay there a minute." Reed punched back to Taylor. "Taylor?"

"I'm here."

"I've got to take this call. Are you turning in right now, or can I call you back in a while?"

"I'll be awake. Call when you can."

"Thanks." Reed punched off. "Okay, Jonathan, I'm back."

"You were about to give me a pep talk."

"No, I was about to tell you that you're at the core of our entire defense. You know you didn't do this. Which means you can't fall apart. Instead of going nuts, start making lists. Think of anyone Douglas or Adrienne had problems with, from domestic help to the gang at the country club. Concentrate on Adrienne. She was a sick woman. Maybe Gordon wasn't her only victim. Jealousy is a prime motivator. So is rejection, if she shot the guy down."

"What about the DNA? How do we counter that?"

"I'm working on it. I've got a stack of papers to read through. Maybe there's a way the semen was planted. Have you ever donated a sperm specimen?"

"Huh? No."

"Fine. Let's go conventional. Think about the last woman you were with. How long ago was it? Did you use a condom? If so, where did you toss it out? Who would have access to it? If you had sex in your apartment, does your cleaning woman wash your linen? Take out your garbage? Could someone have paid her off to get their hands on either of those? I know I'm reaching, but that semen got inside Adrienne somehow—and by someone. So stop freaking out and start thinking."

Jonathan sucked in his breath. "I never considered that. Jesus, planting my semen. That means someone's framing me."

"Bingo. So who'd do that? Who'd have reason and access? More thoughts for you to ponder."

"You're right." Jonathan sounded stronger, more in control. "Reed, do me a favor. Throw some more questions out at me. It'll get my mental juices flowing. Then, whenever I freak out or can't sleep, I'll work on compiling those lists."

Reed glanced at his watch. He'd told Taylor he'd call her back soon. On the other hand, this session with Jonathan might be crucial to their case.

His call to Taylor would have to wait.

"Okay. Let's do it."

11:50 P.M.

PALM BEACH

Taylor was curled up in bed, reading a James Patterson novel, when her telephone rang.

She smiled, reaching over and lifting the receiver. "Hi. Business done for tonight?"

"On the contrary. Business is just beginning."

It was *him*.

Everything inside Taylor went cold at the sound of that synthetic voice. *No.* This couldn't be happening. Not here. Not when she'd run all this way to be safe.

"How did you get this number?" she demanded.

A muffled laugh. "I'm resourceful. You can't escape me, Taylor. I always know where you are. And I can reach you, even at a private Palm Beach estate. I would have called sooner. But I've been tied up since yesterday. Not to worry. I'm back." Another dark, muffled laugh. "Miss me?"

She fought the nausea rising in her throat. "I don't miss anyone. I needed a vacation. I came here to get away."

"From the world? Or just from me?"

She didn't reply.

"Who were you expecting to be at the other end of the phone just now—Reed Weston?"

Again, no reply.

"Bad girl. My instructions were *no* men. But I suppose talking on the phone isn't breaking the rules. The important thing is, you're alone in that bed. Poor baby. You're going to be alone a lot. Your friend Mr. Weston's tied up in Manhattan for the long haul. You won't be seeing him for months. And by that time, it won't matter."

Another underlying threat. "Why won't it matter?"

"Because you'll be mine. And Reed Weston will be busy with his new practice."

That she jumped on. "How do you know about Reed's new practice?"

"How do you think I know?"

It was Jonathan. It had to be. And he was taunting her.

"My poor, beautiful Taylor," he continued. "How lonely you must be. Be patient. This is the last vacation you'll take solo."

A cold chill shot up her back.

"I'll be with you soon," he rasped. "In my mind, I'm with you now. Watching you. Having you. You're tan. But the luscious parts of you that are reserved just for me are still creamy white."

Taylor couldn't help herself. She slammed down the phone, then ran to the bathroom and threw up.

Afterward, she rinsed out her mouth and sank to the floor, leaning her head against the cool tile. She was a prisoner. And he was closing in on her like a wolf on its prey.

She couldn't take it. She was going to snap.

Standing, she marched back into the bedroom. She didn't even buzz Mitch. She scooped up the phone and punched in Reed's cell number.

"Yes?" he answered, sounding distracted.

"Your client just called me." Her voice was high, thin, and bordering on hysteria.

"What?"

"Your client. My stalker. He just called. He knew where I was. He had the phone number. He said he was tied up yesterday, which is why I didn't hear from him. We all know why—no cell phones in jail. He asked if I was lonely. He said he'd take care of that soon. He told me to forget about you, that you'd be stuck in Manhattan for the long haul. He knew about your new practice. He made sure I was aware of that. Then he went on to provide some sick details of his fantasies about me." She stopped her frantic outburst just long enough to gasp in some air. "Reed, I can't take this anymore. You've got to get Jonathan Mallory thrown back in jail. I'm—"

"When?" Reed fired at her. "When did this bastard call?"

"Ten minutes ago." She still couldn't breathe right. She was dizzy and her breath was coming in short, shallow pants. "I thought it was you. But it was him and—"

"Taylor, it wasn't Jonathan."

She gave a wild shake of her head. "Stop! I can't listen to you defend a man who—"

"Taylor!" This time Reed cut her off forcefully. "Sweetheart, listen to me. I'm not defending him. I'm stating a fact. It wasn't Jonathan who called you. Remember that phone call I got while you and I were talking? That was Jonathan. He and I have been on the phone ever since. We still are. I asked him to hold when you beeped in."

Dead silence.

"Oh, my God," she whispered, sinking down on the bed, lowering her head between her knees to make the black spots swimming before her eyes go away. "Oh, my God."

"Stay put," Reed ordered. "I'll be right back." There was a click, and he disappeared for a few seconds. Then he was back. "Talk to me." A pause. "Dammit, Taylor, say something!"

"I'm here," she murmured absently, lifting her head and squirming into a sitting position with her back against the headboard.

"Thank God. I thought you'd fainted, the way you were hyperventilating."

She stared blankly across the room. "Just now, when you asked me to hold—was Jonathan still on the line?"

"Yes. I told him I had a personal emergency. We hung up."

"And the two of you have been talking this entire time?"

"Without a single interruption. We were hammering out some details about his case." Reed didn't sound relieved. He sounded crazed with worry. Then again, he'd never believed Jonathan was her stalker. So to him, nothing had changed. Whoever was hounding her was still out there. Only now he'd found her.

Which meant he was even more cunning than they'd realized.

"He called your father's unlisted number?" Reed demanded. "He knew you were staying there?"

"Yes."

"Tell me exactly what he said."

She heard herself relay the entire conversation, almost verbatim, although it sounded like someone else's voice speaking the words.

Reed swore under his breath. "Where's Mitch?"

Taylor was so panic-stricken, she could barely hear past the roaring in her head. This was even worse than before. She hadn't realized the odd but tangible comfort it had brought her to be able to mentally assign an identity to her stalker. Suddenly this monster who was after her had truly become faceless, nameless.

"Taylor!" Reed dragged her back to the present.

"What?"

"Where's Mitch?"

"Mitch. Oh. Downstairs. He doesn't know."

"Change that—*now*. Put on a robe. Buzz him. Tell him to come upstairs."

"Okay." She did as he asked, operating on autopilot.

Mitch was there three minutes later, wearing a T-shirt and jeans. "What happened?"

She didn't have the strength or presence of mind to repeat the whole story again.

Wordlessly, she handed Mitch the phone. "Talk to Reed."

"Reed, yeah, I'm here." Mitch listened intently, nodding periodically, his jaw tightening as he absorbed the explanation. "No," he said finally. "I don't. But that doesn't make it any easier. I already have one of my guys digging around for information on the cell phone. Yeah, I understand. Let me talk to her and get the details. Don't worry on that score. The alarm system in this house is like Fort Knox. Sure. Here." He handed the phone back to Taylor. "Reed wants to talk to you."

She put the receiver to her ear. "Hi," she managed.

"Have a glass of wine," he instructed, not mincing words. "Then sit down and tell Mitch everything. He doesn't think the guy's in Palm Beach; he thinks he's still here in Manhattan."

"I was so sure it was Jonathan," she whispered, her eyes filling with tears. "The things he knew. The timing of the calls."

"Yeah, well, I doubt that was an accident." Reed's voice had hardened. "In fact, the more I think about it, the more sense it makes."

"What does?"

"Whoever your stalker is, he knows you. He knows you suspected Jonathan. He's reinforcing that suspicion carefully and methodically. Only this time he screwed up. And we're going to bring the son of a bitch down."

CHAPTER 29

SUNDAY, FEBRUARY 16

8:55 P.M.

TAYLOR and Mitch caught the last flight out from Palm Beach to New York that night.

It took Mitch the whole day to work things out to his satisfaction. But Taylor was so relieved, she didn't care. She was eager to get out of that house, that city. Maybe she was being irrational, since she was flying right back to where her stalker was based. But she didn't care. Even here in Florida, he knew where she was. He knew how to reach her. So she felt just as exposed, just as vulnerable. Alone. She needed to be home.

When the plane touched down, they didn't drive to her apartment. They drove to Reed's.

MONDAY, FEBRUARY 17

12:30 A.M.

EAST SIXTY-EIGHTH STREET

Reed was waiting.

He peeked around the curtain and saw Jake's car pull up and let them out. But, as planned, he stayed inside, having advised the doorman to escort his "guests" into the building. He paced around his foyer, yanking open the door as soon as he heard them approach. He didn't say anything, waiting until they were both safely inside, the door shut behind them, before reacting.

Then he heaved a huge sigh of relief, tugging off Taylor's sunglasses and pressing her against him, holding her the way he'd been aching to do since last night when he'd heard the wild fear in her voice.

"Hi," she mumbled into his shirt.

"Hi back." Reed regarded Mitch soberly over the top of Taylor's head. "Thanks. I owe you big."

A corner of Mitch's mouth lifted. "I'll take it out of Rob's hide. Then you can owe him."

"Deal." Reed eased Taylor away, searching her face and scrutinizing the look in her eyes. She was still a little freaked out, and very, very tired. "You holding up okay?"

"I'm holding up. I don't know about okay." She tugged off her hat, masses of dark red hair tumbling out from under it. She shook them out, then ran her fingers through them—a gesture of nervousness rather than vanity. "I feel like I'm walking around in some sort of dream. Correction— nightmare. This is the same way I felt after the boat explosion. It's shock and post-traumatic stress. I'll survive."

"You'll do better than survive," Reed stated flatly. "The bastard finally made a mistake."

"I already contacted Hadman," Mitch supplied. I told him what happened. He got my points loud and clear—one, he can't ignore my investigation, since this guy is dangerous, resourceful, and apparently plugged in to Taylor's life in more than a casual way; and two, he can take Jonathan Mallory off the suspect list."

"I'm sure he was thrilled about both," Reed replied, his tone laced with sarcasm.

Mitch shrugged. "Actually, he was fine. The NYPD will follow up on any concrete leads I give them. But the proactive stuff is still going to have to come from us. Without this stalker performing some type of physical act—an attempted assault on Taylor, breaking and entering her apartment, anything—there's not much more the cops can do."

Taylor didn't flinch. "Is that why you wanted my apartment to stay empty—to see if he tries to break in?"

"That would be a plus, but no. I wanted you in a safe place. No one but my office, the cops, and Reed know you're back in town. I want to keep it that way."

Her brows drew together in puzzlement. "Why would he break in if he knows . . . or *thinks* . . . I'm not there?"

A flicker of reluctance crossed Mitch's face, but he candidly told Taylor what she needed to know. "Sometimes, these perverts get a charge out of actually being in their obsession's bedroom—lying in her bed or going through intimate articles of clothing—"

"Okay, I get the picture," she interrupted with a shudder. "Just the idea makes me sick."

"Don't let it. Jake and I have twenty-four-hour surveillance on your place. If the perp puts a foot in the door, we'll nail him." Mitch's forehead creased in concentration. "In the meantime, I'm going to WVNY tomorrow, and Dellinger Academy next week when it reopens. I want to talk to all your colleagues and a few of your students."

"Why?"

"Because you work with them on a daily basis. And because your coworkers are the only people who knew you were on vacation, and where. We need to start with the obvious to figure out how this guy found you." Mitch turned to Reed. "I also want to talk to your former secretary. I want to know how public the news of your leaving Harter, Randolph and Collins was, and how many people were aware that you were starting up your own firm."

"Not many," Reed answered quietly. "The timing wasn't exactly right for fanfare. Later on, I'll send out announcements, place a notice in the *New York Law Journal* and on law.com. But for now, very few people know. Present company excluded, it's only the senior partners, my secretary, and Paul Mills, my new associate."

"*And* Jonathan Mallory," Mitch reminded him. "Which is the whole point. Whoever called Taylor in Palm Beach knew that Jonathan knew. It's the only way the attempt to cast suspicion on him would work."

Mitch's words triggered a flash of thought in Reed's mind. But before it had time to take shape, Taylor teetered on her feet, swaying toward him. And the fragmented idea vanished.

"You're exhausted," Reed pronounced. "It's bedtime."

Mitch took his cue, reaching for the doorknob. "Jake's camped outside.

I'm heading home to get a few hours of rest, then it's off to WVNY. I'll check in with you late tomorrow afternoon." He pointed at Taylor. "You, stay in here and out of sight. Anything you need, one of us will get. Your apartment is off-limits."

She managed a faint smile. "Yes, sir."

"Good night."

"Mitch?" Taylor called quietly after him. "Thank you so much."

A wink. "Wait till you get my bill."

TAYLOR INSISTED ON TAKING a shower to relax her muscles. Afterward, she didn't even bother blow-drying her hair. She just toweled out the excess moisture, then padded into Reed's bedroom, where she wriggled into one of his shirts and climbed into his bed.

By the time he came in with the cup of chamomile tea she'd requested, she was fast asleep.

He set down the cup, watching her for a few minutes and marveling at how deeply he'd come to care for her in such a short time.

With a tired sigh, Reed yanked off his clothes and chucked them aside. Between Jonathan's case and Taylor's crisis, he hadn't slept more than six hours in the past three days. He was wiped. And now that she was safe beside him, he could actually get a decent night's rest.

He slid into bed beside Taylor, taking great care not to disturb her. She murmured something in her sleep, then snuggled against him, curling up in his arms as if she belonged there.

The fact was, she did.

Reed turned off the light, tucked the blankets around them, and shut his eyes.

The scent of Taylor's shampoo was the last thing he remembered before drifting off.

6:35 A.M.

Reed had assumed he'd leave Taylor a note, check in with Jake to make sure he was still outside, and then leave for work.

It didn't happen that way.

He opened his eyes to find Taylor propped on her elbow, gazing down at him.

"Good morning," she murmured.

"Good morning." He frowned, blinking away the final vestiges of sleep. "What are you doing up? Did my alarm wake you?"

"Nope. It hasn't even gone off yet. Nor will it. I turned it off about ten minutes ago."

"Now, *that* sounds intriguing." Reed was instantly and totally awake. "Any particular reason why?"

Taylor laughed at the hopeful gleam in his eyes. "The truth? I wanted some time for us to talk. But I'm adaptable. I'm also an excellent compromiser. So, as long as you promise me coffee and conversation before you dash out the door, I'd be delighted to send you off to work with a smile on your face."

"I promise." He tucked her hair behind her ear and began unbuttoning her borrowed shirt. "Coffee and conversation." He made quick work of the shirt, tossing it to the floor. "Can I have dessert first?"

Her lips twitched. "Only if you share."

"Oh, I'm a great sharer," he assured her, rolling her onto her back and covering her mouth, and her body, with his. "A *really* great sharer."

IT WAS WELL after 8 A.M. when they finally sat down for that coffee and conversation.

"You were right," Taylor said, filling two mugs to the brim and setting them on the kitchen counter. "You *are* a great sharer." She gave him a tender, intimate look as she settled herself on the stool beside him. "You're also an amazing lover."

"I'm glad you feel that way." His expression was intense, his midnight eyes delving deep inside her. "Because you're going to have years and years to discover just *how* amazing."

Taylor didn't pretend to misunderstand. "That's why I came back," she heard herself say. "I needed to be with you. I didn't realize how much until now. I kept asking myself why I was flying home. I'm uncomfortable in my own apartment; it feels weird and scary. I'm a nervous wreck when I walk around, knowing there's some psychopath out there who's obsessed with me. Steph's gone. My life's in turmoil. I'm on hiatus from work. So why was I running home? Why was I even still thinking of it as home? The answer is you."

Reed brought her hand to his lips, then interlaced their fingers. "This nightmare you're living will soon be behind us. Then we'll get on with our lives. I want you to drive up to Vermont with me for Easter. The whole family will be there. You can thank Rob in person."

Taylor blanched. "The whole family? You mean . . ." She took a mental count. "Fourteen adults, nine kids, and one baby-in-waiting?"

"Nice counting." Reed chuckled. "But it's fifteen, including you. Actually, maybe sixteen, if Rob's latest girlfriend comes with him. Oh, plus two chocolate Labs, one beagle, an orange tabby with a new litter, and God knows how many other animals I have yet to be introduced to."

"Wow." Taylor swallowed a large gulp of coffee. "Are you sure it's not too soon? Maybe they'll feel like I'm intruding."

"They'll love you. And you won't be intruding." A profound pause. "You'll be joining the family."

Emotion clogged Taylor's throat. "Will they be upset that I don't ski?" she asked faintly.

"They'll be thrilled that we're crazy about each other. Any more questions?"

"I'm sure there will be. For now, I'm just overwhelmed. Good overwhelmed," she clarified. "Happy overwhelmed." A sigh. "God, that feels good for a change." Decisively, she put down her mug. "It also makes me twice as eager to defuse the bombs we're each sitting on. *Your* bomb is what I wanted to talk about this morning."

His brows drew together. "You lost me."

"Jonathan Mallory. The mountain you have to climb to win this case. Look, Reed, I'm not a lawyer, but I'm smart enough to know I'll probably be called as a witness for the prosecution. My testimony won't have as much punch as it would have if I still believed Jonathan was my stalker. But I'm sure the ADA will figure I can contribute to the ugly picture of your client he plans to paint. I can describe my encounters with him, say how unnerved he made me, how suggestive and delusional he seemed about having a relationship with me—the works. I'm sure you've thought of all this."

"That's my job. So, yes, I've thought of it." Reed looked a bit surprised—and perplexed. "Although I must admit I hadn't expected *you* to be thinking about it."

"Well, I am. And what I want to know is, is there anything I can do to offset the impact of my testimony?" A flicker of dry amusement. "*Before* you tear me apart on cross-examination, that is."

Reed's mug struck the counter with a thud. "Are you saying you want to *help* me? Even though it's Jonathan I'm representing?"

Taylor blew out her breath. "I'm saying I have a great deal of faith in your instincts. I don't want your client punished for crimes he didn't commit."

"You're amazing," Reed said, cupping her face and leaning forward to give her a deep, heartfelt kiss. "You're willing to do this, despite all your misgivings about Jonathan?"

"Yes." A flicker of realization crossed her face, and she voiced that realization aloud. "You wanted my trust. Well, it seems you've got it."

This time his kiss was tender, his thumbs gentle as they brushed her cheekbones. "I'll take wonderful care of it. I promise."

"I know you will." She captured his fingers in hers. "Now tell me, what can I do to help?"

Reed's wheels were already spinning at supersonic speed. Taylor could see it.

"You have something in mind," she deduced.

"Yeah, I do. But it's not the something you're expecting." Reed hunched forward, concentration furrowing his brow. "You mentioned your qualms about Jonathan. If you agree to what I'm about to propose, I think it'll put some of those qualms to rest. It'll also serve a couple of very important purposes—some emotional, some legal."

"Now *you've* lost *me*."

A pause. "Let's just say that Jonathan needs to get a few things off his chest. They relate to you, and yet they don't. They clarify who he is and why. You're a family counselor. You could listen and understand. It would help Jonathan, and I think it would give you some peace of mind. That's the emotional part. The legal part's a little dicier." Reed took another absent sip of coffee. "The way I see it, the only conceivable way Jonathan is guilty of committing these crimes is if he blocked it all out. He took a polygraph. The results concurred with my instincts: he's not guilty. Which means that at the very worst, Jonathan's guilty but *believes* he's innocent. For that to be true, he'd have to have been a hell of a lot more than just drunk or pumped up with some vague delusions of self-importance. He'd have to be severely psychologically ill. Wouldn't you agree?"

Taylor nodded.

"I'm still determined to go for a not-guilty verdict, because I believe that's what Jonathan is. However, I need a backup plan. Mental incompetence or insanity or long-range scars from emotional abuse. Something. Believe me, his history warrants it. You'll understand once you've spoken to him. The problem is, I'd need expert testimony corroborating his precarious mental state from someone trained to formulate that opinion."

His meaning sank in, and Taylor's eyes widened. "Me?"

"You've got the degree and the experience."

"Not really. I'm a family counselor, not a criminal psychiatrist. My training and expertise—"

"—enable you to deal with a lot of screwed-up teens and their reasons for becoming that way," Reed interrupted. "In this case, that's a perfect fit. It goes without saying that it would be incredibly beneficial for Jonathan—on many levels."

Taylor digested all that, then nodded. "All right. I'll think about it."

THURSDAY, FEBRUARY 20

11:17 P.M.

The telephone in Palm Beach just rang and rang.

Still no answer. And no voice mail.

On top of that, her cell phone was turned off. It had been for days. Goddammit.

He threw his own cell phone onto the bed, then picked up a lamp and hurled it across the room, not even noticing as it crashed against the wall and shattered into pieces.

How dare she pretend he didn't exist?

His fingers interlocked, clenched together, tightening until he could actually feel her neck between his hands, his thumbs pressing down on her windpipe, squeezing the life out of her.

She wasn't different.

She was just like the rest. Snotty. Manipulative.

He'd planned to make the sex good for her. It would have been a final explosion of sheer, perfect pleasure before eternal oblivion.

No more.

Now the bitch would pay in full.

CHAPTER 30

THURSDAY, FEBRUARY 27

7:15 P.M.

WESTON & ASSOCIATES, ATTORNEYS-AT-LAW

THE murmur of voices drifted out from behind the closed doors of the firm's new law library and into the reception area, where Reed was pacing.

The words were indistinguishable. The tone was not.

It was a taut, emotional session. Then again, it was a taut, emotional subject. Several times in the past few minutes, Reed had considered breaking his promise to Taylor and charging inside. But he had to respect her professional ethics just as she did his. Client privilege was client privilege. Besides, she'd laid down the law in no uncertain terms.

"Alone," she'd stated flatly. "I said I'd talk to Jonathan, and I will. But it has to be alone."

Like Reed had much choice.

He was desperate. He'd come up with nothing but dead ends. No one with a vendetta against the Berkleys, personal or professional. No acquaintances of theirs with a history of violence. And no one but Jonathan to benefit from their will. He was their only living relative, except Douglas's niece, who hadn't seen the Berkleys since she was a child and would therefore have no idea she was last in line to inherit.

Things were looking grim for Jonathan.

Time was short.

Suspects were scarce.

Paul wandered down the stairs and glanced from the shut door to Reed. "They've been in there for over an hour," he noted.

"An hour and six minutes. I know. I haven't done a stitch of work since the session started."

A strained smile. "What kind of outcome are you expecting?"

"The truth?" Reed met Paul's gaze. "I think Taylor's going to agree with us. I think the strategy of pleading either diminished capacity or temporary insanity is a long shot. I think Jonathan's innocent."

"Yeah." Paul sat down on the bottom step. "I assumed you'd feel that way." A weary sigh. "And, as we both know, it's going to make our job that much harder."

"Tell me something I don't know." Reed paused, then shook his head. "Too much here doesn't fit. Jonathan's smart. He'd never leave his semen at the crime scene only to cooperate fully with the authorities by providing a DNA sample. And he'd know he'd never inherit Douglas's fortune if he was found guilty of murder.

"Then there's the polygraph. Even Willard, the ADA, was bothered by the results. He was also bothered when his evidentiary trap yielded nothing. He went to great lengths to divulge the details of the murders, purposely describing the bite marks on Adrienne as being on her *right* breast. It was her *left*."

"Obviously, Jonathan didn't take the bait," Paul clarified.

"Take the bait? He didn't bat a lash. He wasn't evasive; he was clueless. The only time he reacted was when Willard described the strangulation. And then, he gagged, remembering how red Adrienne's face had been when he'd identified her body. Not exactly the reaction of a killer. In my book, that makes way too many inconsistencies, with no explanations to go along with them." Reed frowned. "Willard's tough, but he's honest. He sees the same incongruities we do. And they're bugging him."

At that moment, the door to the law library opened, and Taylor stepped out. "We're finished."

Reed's head snapped up, and he scrutinized Taylor's face, trying to read her. She looked pensive, and very solemn. But that was all.

Paul facilitated things. "I want to speak with Jonathan about tomorrow's arraignment," he announced, coming to his feet and heading toward the library. "We'll be with you shortly."

Taylor gazed after him, and a corner of her mouth lifted in wry amusement as the door shut behind him. "Now *that* was subtle."

"We're not going for subtle. We're going for answers." Reed tipped up her chin. "First of all, are you okay? No adverse affects?"

"None. *I'm* fine. Your client's another story." Taylor gestured toward the coffee room Reed had set up across the hall. "Let's go talk."

They poured two cups of coffee and sank down into chairs.

"Okay, shoot," Reed prompted.

"To begin with, I understand why you wanted this session to happen, for my sake as well as Jonathan's. It's amazing what a difference having the full picture makes. I also see why it was so easy for you to convince Jonathan to talk to me."

"No convincing was necessary. He jumped at the chance."

"He *wanted* to confide in me. He figured if I was aware of everything he'd been through, it would elicit my compassion. He hoped those feelings would spark a relationship between us and that, eventually, I'd come to care for him."

"I know."

"It worked. Not the relationship part, but the understanding and compassion. I now have a strong idea of what makes Jonathan Mallory tick, and what motivates him—personally and professionally." Taylor took a sip of coffee. "We're pressed for time. So let's get to my assessment. For starters, I don't believe for one minute that Jonathan is delusional enough to have committed the heinous crimes he's being accused of and blocked it out. In my opinion, he's not only nonviolent, he's in mourning and in shock—both very normal reactions. Oh, he's got lots of baggage, thanks to not being formally acknowledged by his father, to his strained relationship with his brother, to feelings of inadequacy, and most of all, to his predator of a stepmother. Adrienne Berkley definitely screwed up his relationships with women."

"No question," Reed muttered.

"Yes, but the result is that he's become insecure, not unfeeling. True, he hated Adrienne's guts. Rightly so, if you ask me. She used his father and his brother, threatened his mother, and spit in his face every chance she got. But Jonathan's agenda isn't about revenge. It's about proving himself. That applies to his relationships with women, too. Which explains the two incidents in college and grad school." A pause. "And his fixation on me. The last thing he wants to contend with is more rejection."

"Yeah." Reed looked grim. "I'm sorry I couldn't tell you about those two harassment incidents, but I'm glad he did. I think he views you as some kind of savior."

"Exactly." Taylor sighed. "What he really craves is normalcy, a real and stable relationship, a woman who cares about him as much as he cares about her. His behavior is a little over the edge. But, under the circumstances, that's understandable. So there's my assessment. And if you need me to serve as your expert witness, I will."

Reed squeezed her hand. "Thanks."

"I really feel sorry for the guy," Taylor mused aloud. "But if you want to know the truth—and God help me, I never thought I'd say this—the person I *really* feel sorry for is Gordon. He's the one who went through the trauma of being blackmailed into bed with his stepmother. Who knows what kind of power trip she pulled on him? He was already a prime candidate. Cold. Egocentric. A use-and-abuse personality in the making. Adrienne just clinched things in a big way. No wonder he turned into such a heartless, devious bastard."

Taylor stared broodingly into her coffee cup. "The ironic thing is that if anyone had the psychological composite and the motive to do what Jonathan's being accused of, it was Gordon. If he were alive, I'd bet money on his guilt. As it is, he's probably getting a real charge out of all this—even if he is in hell."

There it was again. That flicker of an idea. Only this time, Reed saw the idea through to completion.

An impossibility.

Or was it?

"Talk to me about Gordon's personality type." Reed barked out the order like a drill sergeant.

His harsh tone caught Taylor off guard, as did the command itself. "There's nothing new to say," she replied. "Gordon was arrogant, manipulative, violent, and perverse."

"He was also calculating, self-obsessed, filled with delusions of grandeur, and totally without conscience or remorse. The psychologists I've heard testify in court cite traits like those when they're describing a megalomaniac and a psychopath."

A cold shiver ran up Taylor's spine. "Reed, why are you doing this?" she managed, pushing aside her coffee. "I don't want to discuss—"

"I know," Reed interrupted in a slightly gentler tone. "And I don't want you to have to discuss him. But Jonathan thinks he's being framed for murder. Mitch thinks Jonathan's being framed as your stalker. Maybe he's being framed for both. And I can only think of one person with the means and the motive to do it."

Realization struck—hard.

"*Gordon?*" Taylor whispered.

"You yourself just said he had the psychological makeup for it."

"Except that he's dead."

"Yeah, he is, isn't he?" Reed's wheels were spinning wildly. "But let's pretend, for the moment, that he's alive. Wouldn't he see it as divine justice to rape and kill Adrienne and get away with it?" That triggered a burst of insight and, abruptly, Reed bolted to his feet. "Jesus Christ." He stalked out of the room, taking the stairs two at a time as he headed for his office. Reaching his desk, he began rummaging through the files and papers. There. He grabbed the pile of DNA material he'd printed, tearing through pages until he found the section he was looking for.

He'd just zeroed in on what he needed when Taylor walked in.

"Reed, what is it? What's going on?"

He shoved the page at her, pointing at a specific section. "Read this."

Taylor complied, scanning the paragraph and reading it aloud. "'Identical twins come from one fertilized egg that splits in two. This separation can occur up to the twelfth day of conception, around the time the egg is implanting in the uterus. The fertilized egg, and its single complete set of DNA, splits to form twin embryos, each with its own set of DNA that is identical to the other. As a result, identical twins share the same sex and a hundred percent of their DNA.'" Taylor lowered the page, a guarded expression on her face. "Where are you going with this?"

"Toward a not-guilty verdict."

"Oh God." Taylor's hands shook as Reed's words sank in. "Identical twins have identical DNA." She dropped the page onto Reed's desk. "If what you're suggesting is true, then Gordon Mallory is *alive.*"

Reed looked as shaken as Taylor. "I realize how crazy this sounds. But it would certainly explain a lot. The DNA match. The fact that a homicidal rapist—one who was both proficient and meticulous—was careless enough to leave semen behind. The brutal way Adrienne was raped."

"*And* the way she was killed," Taylor found herself adding. "She was choked, Reed. So was I—by Gordon. He knew just when to stop so I'd live." Taylor's breath was coming in shallow pants. "Jonathan mentioned that you were troubled by his propensity for redheads, and how that might relate to me. Well, look at Gordon. Steph was a redhead. *I'm* a redhead. And, obviously, Adrienne was a redhead. Two of the three of us are dead. I'm being stalked."

"Okay, okay." Reed's training held him in check. "Let's not get ahead of ourselves. There's a lot of ground to cover here. First of all, for all this supposition to be fact, Gordon would have to have planned everything in advance, starting with rigging his own bogus death. How did he manage that? His boat blew up. We know that for a fact. So how did he escape? Where did he go? I've got to find that out ASAP."

"He'd known he was coming back." Taylor's mind was taking a panic-stricken detour. "Reed, that would explain why he said he'd be watching me." She raked both trembling hands through her hair, remembering the encounter she'd tried so hard to forget. "He promised me he'd finish what he started that night."

"That fits with how he's played things since then. Sending you e-cards. Calling you. Harassing you. Threatening you."

"Closing in on me," Taylor added softly.

Reed's lips thinned into a tight, angry line. "If it is Gordon who's after you, we're on to him. We know what he wants. And it's not going to happen."

"But where is he? Unless we can prove Gordon's alive, we're spinning in neutral. So how do we do that?"

"First, you need to clear up some gray areas for me. Psychological areas. I need to have a clear picture before I go charging into the fray."

"Fine. Ask away."

"Why would Gordon kill Douglas? Why not just Adrienne? Or am I barking up the wrong tree? Is it just something basic like Douglas caught Gordon attacking Adrienne and tried to defend her, forcing Gordon to kill him, too?"

"I don't think so." Taylor's evaluating skills kicked in. "Gordon's sharp as a tack. There's no way he'd go into that brownstone without knowing exactly who'd be there."

"Then my question stands. Why Douglas?"

"My guess? Since Gordon was a twisted teenager and an even more twisted adult, his mind was working in twisted ways. He might blame the whole thing on Douglas. Maybe he thought Douglas knew what was going on and chose to sacrifice Gordon to protect his wife. Or maybe he thought Douglas was in denial—that he didn't know simply because he didn't *want* to know. There are a lot of possibilities here, all of which could make Gordon hate his father enough to kill him."

"Okay. I'll buy that. Now, what about framing Jonathan? He's Gordon's brother. They weren't close, but they weren't enemies. There was no justification for a hatred strong enough to provoke such cruelty."

"None necessary. It was expedient. Remember what you said? Psychopaths have no sense of conscience or remorse. That's true. So, if Gordon is behind this, his only focus is his revenge. Jonathan is an expendable pawn."

Reed averted his head, a muscle working furiously in his jaw. "I'm not sure which would make me sicker, if we turned out to be right or if we turned out to be wrong. But let's say this whole far-fetched theory is true. The million-dollar question is, where's Gordon now? Where's he hiding?" A self-derisive laugh. "Who am I kidding? He doesn't have to hide. He's dead. Or, at least everyone thinks he is."

"If he's my stalker, we know he's in Manhattan."

"Great. So are hundreds of thousands of other people. He could commute in every night to keep an eye on you, then take off for parts unknown." That prompted Reed's jaw to tighten another fraction. "This theory would tie up another loophole—the fact that there was no break-in at the Berkley brownstone. Gordon could have let himself in with his key, or knocked and pretended to be Jonathan. By the time Douglas and Adrienne realized the truth—and recovered from the shock—it would be too late."

Taylor wet her lips. "What do we do now?"

Reed studied her grimly. "We don't discuss this with anyone. Not even Jonathan. Right now, it's pure speculation. We need something to go on before we light this fuse and watch it explode."

"Like what?"

"I'm going to call Hadman first thing tomorrow, see if he'll agree to contact the Suffolk County Police and convince them to give me a copy of the file and police report on last September's boat explosion. It's a closed case, so I doubt they'll care. If they give me a hard time, I'll subpoena the damned file. I want to pore over that material word for word. Maybe, knowing what we know—or at least what we suspect—it'll tell us something."

"My assault complaint is also in the closed files, right here in Manhattan's Twentieth Precinct," Taylor reminded him. "Subpoena that as well. I told the police about Gordon's near rape, including everything he said, pretty much word for word. Maybe there's something in their report that'll pop out at you."

"I will." Reed stared at her, his thoughts clearly turning to the danger she was in if Gordon had masterminded all this. "I'm amending what I just said about not discussing this with anyone. We are telling one person. Mitch. I want him to be on the lookout, in case Gordon gets cocky enough to show himself. He just might, figuring everyone will assume he's Jonathan. And my guess is he's probably getting desperate by now, not to mention livid. Remember, he hasn't been able to reach you in over a week. That might prompt him to start taking chances."

"Sounds terrific." Taylor strove for a touch of levity, which instead emerged as fear and strain. "Maybe I should put Mitch permanently on my payroll. At this rate, he'll be working for me forever."

"No, he won't," Reed said vehemently. "We *will* resolve this. We need answers. And we need them yesterday. But I promise you this. If Gordon Mallory's alive, he'll wish he weren't."

CHAPTER 31

TAYLOR couldn't stand it anymore—the imprisonment, the waiting, the inactivity. She had to do something or she'd lose her mind.

She called Jack and told him she was back in town. She also reminded him that she was moving to her new apartment the following week. So it made sense for her to come in tonight, not only to do a live show—which she was eager to do—but to record a few extra shows, just in case circumstances prevented her from coming in next week.

They both knew what "circumstances" meant.

"Everybody knows," Jack had informed her. "You're going to get a deluge of questions."

"I'll handle it."

"Taylor." Jack's tone had been subdued but tense. "Are you sure you want to do this? Maybe you should have stayed in Florida for another week or two."

"I'm sure," she'd replied firmly. "I need to get back to work. Mitch is the best. He sticks to me like flypaper. No one will get near me."

An uneasy pause. "If you say so." Jack cleared his throat. "Where are you staying?"

"For the time being, at Reed's. At least until moving day. My current apartment's a zoo. All half-packed boxes and papers waiting to be shredded. Besides, I'm a little on edge these days. At Reed's place I'm not alone."

"Yeah. You shouldn't be." Another pause. "We'll see you tonight."
She'd wished he sounded a touch less grim.

6:15 P.M.
WVNY

Walking through the double doors with the initials WVNY etched on them, Taylor realized why Jack had been so reticent. She felt like an alien at her own place of business.

A hush settled over the reception area when she stepped in. Tonya, the receptionist, saw her first, and went white, shushing the secretary and two interns she'd been chatting with. They greeted Taylor in taut unison, then stared after her as she headed toward the recording studios.

It wasn't much better down there. There was a chorus of "welcome backs" as Taylor passed by, but they were strained, and the expressions on everyone's face ranged from pity to curiosity to nervousness—probably fear that whatever danger Taylor was in would invade the station and affect their own safety.

She pasted a smile on her face, greeting everyone in return, and trying her damnedest to act as normal as possible.

Jack's office was empty. So was Bill's and a few of the other regulars'. Strangest of all, the coffee room was deserted. Now *that* was a first.

Maybe half the place had evacuated when they heard she was coming.

On that thought, Taylor pushed open the door to her own studio door. She was grateful to hear the murmur of voices from inside.

"Hey," she began. "I'm glad you guys are here. I was beginning to feel like a pariah—" She stopped dead in her tracks, her mouth falling open as she was greeted by almost the entire WVNY staff, all arranged in a horseshoe with a big blackout cake sitting on the counter in front of them. The cake read: WELCOME HOME, TAYLOR.

"Surprise!" they bellowed.

She blinked, tears welling up in her eyes before she could suppress them. "Wow," she managed. "I don't know what to say."

"Say hi," Kevin suggested, walking over and giving her a huge hug.

"Yeah," Bill called out. "And then cut the cake. We've been inhaling the chocolate for half an hour. I was about to do a swan dive into the damn thing."

Laughter rippled through the room, and suddenly Taylor really did feel like maybe, just maybe, it would be okay.

She sniffed back her tears. "Thanks, guys. I really missed you." She hugged Kevin back. "Hi," she dutifully replied. "I'll bet I know whose idea this was." Breaking away, she dried her eyes and winked in Bill's direction. "Now where's the cake knife?"

The ice broken, they all gathered around, eating cake and chatting.

Laura weaved her way through the crowd, putting down her cake plate to kiss Taylor's cheek. "Welcome back. We all missed you like crazy. Did you have fun?"

The question was so incongruous with reality that Taylor almost laughed aloud. "The weather was gorgeous," she answered truthfully. "But I spent most of the time indoors, unwinding."

"Good. You needed it."

Dennis came forward, then pumped her hand warmly. "It's really good to have you back."

"Yeah, and not only because we missed you," Kevin called out. "Dennis has some hot news of his own he's been dying to share."

Taylor turned to Dennis, her brows knitting quizzically. "That sounds important."

"It is," Kevin assured her.

An unwelcome prospect dawned on Taylor, and she gave Dennis a pleading look. "Please don't tell me you're leaving, that you found some high-paying job at another station."

"Would I be smiling if that was the case?" Kevin asked with a grunt. "I'm already too overworked as it is."

"That's true," Taylor conceded. "Okay, so don't keep me in suspense. What's your news?"

Her engineer grinned shyly. "Ally and I got married the other day."

"Married?" Taylor's eyes widened. "Oh, Dennis, that's wonderful. Congratulations." She gave him an enthusiastic hug. "The other day?" she repeated as that part sank in. "Then what are you doing at work? You're a newlywed."

"I gave Dennis the rest of the week off," Jack assured her. "He hasn't been in since Wednesday. But he wanted to be here for your welcome back party. So he popped in an hour ago, and then he's popping out till Monday."

Taylor felt a rush of gratitude. "Thank you. That means a lot to me. Please tell Ally I'm sorry I pulled you away from her, even for a couple of hours."

"Coming in tonight wasn't exactly a hardship," Dennis replied. "Blackout cake's my favorite. And Jack said I could bring a piece home for Ally."

"Of course." Taylor's eyes twinkled mischievously. "Although you're not getting off the hook that easily. Because we want to meet Ally."

Dennis grinned back, this time more easily. He looked happy, even giddy, like a newlywed should be.

"Thank you, everyone," Taylor called after the staff as Jack shooed them back to work. "This was an amazing surprise."

Jack achieved his objective, pausing in the doorway when only Kevin, Dennis, and Laura remained in the studio with Taylor. "You're sure you're up for this?"

"Positive," she assured him.

"Because if you're not ready, you can put this off."

"I realize that. But I am ready. And I don't want to put it off."

"Is your PI outside the building?"

"Right there, with his beeper and cell phone on."

A tight nod. "Well, stay only as long as you're up to it. Don't overdo." He looked like he wanted to say more, then changed his mind. "Have a good show. And welcome back."

Taylor shot Kevin a questioning look as the door shut behind Jack. "What was that all about?"

No reply.

"Yoo-hoo." She glanced from one of them to the other. "I asked a question."

Dennis gave in first. "Jack was kind of freaked out by your PI," he offered hesitantly.

"Freaked out?" Taylor frowned. Mitch was one of the most decent, straightforward guys she'd ever met—certainly not the type to intimidate people. "Why? Was he rude to him?"

"No, nothing like that," Kevin supplied, shaking his head. "But you know how protective Jack is of WVNY. When word spread that your PI was here and that some of us were being questioned, a couple of staff members got nervous. Mitch explained—loud and clear—that no one here was in danger or was a suspect, that he was only trying to determine if anyone might have, inadvertently, mentioned your whereabouts."

Taylor's spirits sagged again. "Maybe I should take a sabbatical."

Dennis's black brows shot up. "You just got back."

"I know. But I don't want to cause any trouble, not for you guys, and not for Jack. You've been my lifeline through all this."

"Jack will settle down," Kevin said. "Give him time."

Time.

The word tasted bitter on Taylor's tongue. Everything was moving in slow motion. Yet, she had the eerie sensation the sand in her hourglass was running out.

11:30 P.M.

She was back.

She'd gone to the radio station. She'd just left.

He watched her walk toward the waiting car.

Damn, she was sexy. He'd forgotten how hot he got just looking at her. The anger that had been building inside him just made him hotter. Rage and sex. It didn't get any better than that. Not for what he had in mind.

He was tempted to follow her. But he couldn't. It wasn't time yet.

CHAPTER 32

REED was scribbling down notes at the kitchen counter when Mitch and Taylor arrived.

He strode over and pulled open the door, feeling the now-familiar sense of relief that swept through him when Taylor showed up at his place safe and sound. "Hey. How'd it feel to be back?"

"Mixed reviews. Good and bad. And a little like the main attraction at a freak show. But, hey, at least they threw me a party." Taylor shrugged off her coat and turned to Mitch. "Thanks, as always."

"You're welcome, as always," he replied. "Get some rest. I'm going home to do some catch-up reading on Gordon Mallory. Jake's been doing an extensive search: old articles, announcements, that kind of stuff. Maybe it'll give us a hint about where Mallory's laying low—if he's alive."

"I'm reading similar literature, only mine's about a boat explosion and a physical assault," Reed said wearily.

"You got your hands on the files?" Taylor jumped on that.

"Yup." Reed jerked his thumb in the direction of the kitchen. "Both are right in there. Hadman was very cooperative, especially after Mitch spoke with him. He and Olin insisted on knowing why we wanted the files, so we had to fill them in. No hardship there. They'll keep it quiet. They think we're grasping at straws. But they're good detectives."

"Sure are," Mitch concurred. "Anyway, happy reading. We'll compare notes tomorrow, see whose stuff was more interesting." He shot a wave in their direction. " 'Night."

Reed closed and locked the door behind him, then turned to Taylor. "I tuned in to part of your show tonight. You sound as cool and composed—"

"—as you do when you're in court," Taylor finished for him. "That's my job. My callers depend on me. I've got to keep it together when I'm on the air. That doesn't mean—" She broke off, sinking down on the sofa and pressing the heels of her palms against her eyes. "Reed, I'm sorry. I'm tired and strung out. I didn't mean to snap at you."

"No apology necessary." He sat down beside her, massaging the tension from her shoulders.

"How did the arraignment at supreme court go?"

A shrug. "As expected. The judge didn't revoke bail. That's all Jonathan was afraid of. I, on the other hand, was half hoping he would."

Taylor twisted around and shot Reed a startled look. "Why?"

"Purely selfish reasons. If Jonathan's locked up, Gordon can't masquerade as him—not without getting caught."

"Oh." She blew out a tired breath. "I see your point. But something tells me Gordon's too smart to get caught. If Jonathan were locked up, Gordon would somehow find out about it, and crawl back into the sewer like the rat that he is." A humorless laugh. "And, like that same cunning rat, he'd emerge only when he knew it was safe."

"He's never going to be safe," Reed returned in a hard, determined tone. "Not with me gunning for him."

Taylor gave him a weak, grateful smile. "Have you read through the police reports yet? Anything new?"

"Nothing that jumped out at me. Except for the fact that none of the partial human remains found at the scene of the boat explosion were Gordon's. Just his monogrammed life preserver."

"He could have tossed that overboard to make it look convincing."

"Exactly. On the other hand, it could have been propelled by the force of the explosion, and his whole body could have been blown to bits. So let's just say that the lack of physical remains raises a red flag—for us. For the police and the prosecution—well, under the circumstances, our red flag is weak. And it's certainly not enough to build a credible case that Gordon's alive."

"He's out there, Reed. I know it. I don't need proof. He's circling me like a hawk. Who knows when he'll swoop down? I don't have the luxury of time that you do. Any day, any minute, he could—" Taylor broke off, hopeless and frustrated, and terribly ashamed of what she was implying. "I'm sorry," she whispered. "That was completely uncalled for."

Reed pressed her head against his chest. "Taylor, listen to me. I know you feel like you're coming apart at the seams. And I know you're scared. But we both knew that getting our hands on Gordon wasn't going to be a cakewalk. He's smart. He's meticulous. And his intentions are *not* to be caught. That's not the way it's going to go down. We *will* catch him. I promise you that. In the meantime, never doubt my priorities. You and I have the exact same timetable. Jonathan is my client. You're . . ." He swallowed. "I love you. Your life and your safety are the most important things to me. I'm working on this Gordon angle round-the-clock. I've got Mitch doing the same. That's for you, not Jonathan."

"I know." She leaned into him. "I just want this whole thing to be over."

"Amen."

"Anything new on the DNA front?" Taylor asked. "That was pretty fascinating stuff you showed me last night."

"I did some more reading on the DNA profiles of identical twins," Reed answered reluctantly. "Without getting into too much scientific detail, there are two genetic terms involved here: phenotype and genotype. Genotype is the makeup of our genes—in other words, our DNA. Phenotype is the external stuff—our physical characteristics, which result from the interaction of our genes with the developmental environment inside the uterus. The last part's the relevant part. Since each fetus interacts differently with its environment, identical twins have identical genotypes but different phenotypes."

"What physical traits does that affect?"

"The operative ones in a criminal case are fingerprints and teeth marks. Both those characteristics differ slightly in identical twins. Unfortunately, the killer was smart enough *not* to leave any fingerprints. But Adrienne did have teeth marks on her left breast. I read a precedent case where the defense attorney elicited the expert testimony of a dentist who displayed dental casts, Styrofoam impressions, and CAT scans of the casts of the defendant's teeth, which the court overlaid on the actual wounds to compare them. They were different. If necessary, I can try that tactic in court. It's not foolproof, but it might create reasonable doubt."

He massaged his temples. "What makes me crazy is that it's sure as hell not enough to get Hadman and Olin's cooperation on your stalker case."

"Nothing's going to do that, short of Gordon showing himself," Taylor said quietly. A long pause as she contemplated her own words. "Reed, maybe we should use that fact to our advantage."

"Meaning?"

"Let's get Gordon to show himself."

"And how do you propose we do that?"

Reed wasn't going to like this. Taylor herself didn't like it. But it might be their quickest solution. Maybe even their *only* solution.

"My new lease starts tomorrow," she explained. "I'm sure Gordon knows that. I'm sure he also knows where I'm moving. He seems to know everything about me. So why don't I oblige him and move? Without anyone's assistance but the moving company. Once they're gone, it'll just be me. That should give Gordon a clean shot."

"Forget it." Reed's entire body had gone rigid. "You're talking about making yourself a target."

"If it'll ferret Gordon out, I'm willing to risk it."

"Well, I'm not. The idea's crazy. You'd be leaving yourself wide open to a psychopath. The subject's closed. We'll find Gordon through less radical means."

"Whatever those are." She blew out her breath. "It just occurred to me that sometime between yesterday and today we both stopped saying 'if' when we refer to Gordon as my stalker. We're now both sure, hard evidence or not."

"Yeah," Reed concurred. "We are."

MARCH 1

1:15 A.M.

D-day.

Her new lease had started seventy-five minutes ago.

He eyed the apartment that would soon be hers, wondering when she'd be moving in. Her old place was in chaos, and had been for days, as moving preparations were under way.

The boxes would be sent over on schedule. Her old place would be vacated. But as for when she joined them, that was still iffy.

She was staying with Reed Weston. She had been since she returned from Florida.

A few weeks ago, that would have been enough to make him wild with rage. Picturing her with another guy. Knowing she was in his bed. He'd been furious enough when he realized she was turning off her cell phone every night so he couldn't contact her. Stupid bitch. Didn't she know that if he wanted to reach her, he could?

Anyway, none of it mattered now. His plan had entered its final stage.

She was getting antsy. He could see it in her movements, the restlessness in her step and in her eyes. She hated living like a prisoner. Pretty soon, she'd shake herself free, if only for a little while.

A little while was enough. He'd be waiting.

Her time was running out. So let her screw Reed Weston to her heart's content. When she died, *he'd* be the one inside her, not Weston.

First he'd tell her everything. That was a given. He had to tell someone. His plan was too ingenious to keep to himself.

Pity he couldn't share it with the rest of the jackasses involved. Especially the cops. The looks on their faces would be priceless.

Unfortunately, it wasn't meant to be. He needed to move on, to begin his new life.

And, oh, what a life it would be.

CHAPTER 33

MARCH 3

3:30 P.M.

DELLINGER ACADEMY

TAYLOR left school late.

She didn't have to glance across the street to know Mitch was there. She was acutely aware of his presence. Posting himself outside whatever building she was in was becoming second nature to the guy.

She turned up the collar of her coat and started walking.

All the stable components that made up her life were being yanked away, one by one.

Her first day back at school. It had been a carbon copy of her first day back at the radio station. Anxious glances from the faculty. Silence when she entered the teachers' lounge. An optimistic but uneasy pep talk from the headmaster. And odd looks, accompanied by whispered conversations, from the students.

It had been like rubbing salt in wounds that were already so raw they were bleeding. She shouldn't have been surprised. Dellinger was small and tight-knit. When something juicy went on, news traveled like wildfire, no matter how hard people tried to keep it quiet. Still, she'd pinned hope against hope that somehow the powers that be would have been able to sit on it, that she'd escape the fallout.

She hadn't.

It wasn't Mitch's fault that he'd lit the fuse by talking to the administration and a couple of faculty members. He'd just been doing his job.

But once he'd stepped through that first hallowed doorway, ears had gone up everywhere. And the rest had been a fait accompli.

Quickening her step, Taylor headed toward Starbucks. She desperately needed a few minutes alone.

Alone. That was a laugh. Mitch would be right behind her. He'd wait five minutes, then stroll in and order himself a grande Coffee of the Day to go. After that, he'd post himself outside, skimming the newspaper and drinking his coffee.

Talk about the ultimate chaperone.

Taylor opened the door and stepped inside. The place was warm, and smelled of coffee and scones. It felt good.

She went up to the counter, ordered a grande decaf Americano. No caffeine for her. She was already twitching.

After she'd sat down at the counter near the window, her thoughts returned to the semi–pep, semi–prep talk she'd received from her headmaster. He'd been very kind. But he was worried, and she knew it. He had good reason to be. Dellinger was an exclusive private school—one of the most selective in Manhattan. Once a majority of the parents were tipped off as to what was going on, they'd band together and put a ton of pressure on the board of directors. Taylor would become an "undesirable"—a danger to their precious offspring. Offspring that many of them barely noticed except at times like these, Taylor thought bitterly. Still, financial pressure was financial pressure, especially when it was exerted by powerful people. Unless Taylor's stalker was caught, and pronto, she might be out of a job by the end of the school year.

She slammed down her empty cup. She was suffocating. She needed some air.

And by God, she was going to get it.

3:45 P.M.

STARBUCKS

LEXINGTON AVENUE AT SEVENTY-EIGHTH STREET, NEW YORK CITY

"Mitch, look. I don't want to argue with you." Having pulled Mitch aside as soon as he'd bought his coffee, Taylor was delivering her announcement with unyielding intensity. "I'm not asking to go jogging alone in Central Park. Actually, I'm not asking at all. I'm telling. And, not to be rude, I can do that. I'm paying your salary."

She paused to suck in a breath. "I'm stopping by my new apartment. I'm riding up in the elevator, letting myself in like a normal person, and checking out the place that one day soon, I'm going to call home. I'm seeing where the movers stacked my boxes, if they put my bed on the far wall of the bedroom near the window like I asked, if they were careful with my plants or dumped them all over the kitchen floor. Dammit, Mitch, I need to be regular person, a normal new tenant, if only for a half hour."

"Fine," he returned flatly. "I'll go up with you."

"No, you won't." She fought to keep her voice down. "Don't you understand? I met my new doorman once. His name's Ed. I want to meet Ed again, without a PI hovering around me."

"He'll think I'm your boyfriend."

"I don't *want* him to think you're my boyfriend. I don't want him to think you're my anything. I don't want to provide some fabricated explanation. I just want to be myself. Please, Mitch, don't give me a hard time. I'm at the end of my rope. I need a flicker of reprieve, a concrete glimpse of something real in my future. Thirty minutes. That's all it'll take. You can watch the building from across the street. No one's more of a pro at that than you."

Mitch shrugged. "Fine. Like you said, you're the boss. For the record, I'm not happy. I doubt Reed would be either."

"Duly noted. I'll call you the minute I set foot in the apartment and see that the coast is clear. If you don't hear from me five minutes after I go upstairs, you can summon the entire NYPD."

"Very cute. Let's just go and get this over with."

4:12 P.M.

WEST SEVENTY-FOURTH STREET, NEW YORK CITY

Finally. Taylor Halstead, in the flesh.

He straightened, watching her approach the building.

Once again, he'd been right. He'd been dead sure she'd come by. So sure that he'd showed up a dozen times over the last three days. He'd really been pushing it. He couldn't be seen. And he couldn't answer questions about his absence.

But most important, he couldn't miss her. He had to seize his chance when it came.

Well, here it was. His tenacity had paid off, as always.

She stopped right in front of the building. So did her trusty PI, he noted with a smirk. A regular Kevin Costner. Well, Mr. Bodyguard was about to have a chance to prove how good he was.

Flipping open his cell phone, he prepped his digital voice recorder containing the sound clip he'd spliced together of her previous conversations.

Here goes, he thought. He punched in Jonathan's number.

4:14 P.M.

EAST EIGHTY-SIXTH STREET

Jonathan reached for his ringing cell phone. "Hello?"

"It's Taylor." Her voice was dulled by cell phone static. "I'm with Reed. We've got to see you immediately. Come to my new apartment. One twenty-three West Seventy-fourth Street. Hurry. This could be it."

Click.

4:16 P.M.

WEST SEVENTY-FOURTH STREET

Taylor turned the key and let herself into her new apartment.

The paint smell was strong, but it was in better shape than she'd expected. Oh, the parquet floors were piled high with boxes. But the furniture was in place, right down to her computer desk and PC, positioned in the living-room niche, as requested. The only item of significance still missing was a telephone. She'd remedy that soon enough.

She poked her head into the kitchen, the bedroom, and the bathroom. All devoid of intruders. She flipped on her cell phone and called Mitch. "Everything's fine," she reported. "I'm just getting acquainted with the place. I'll be down soon."

"Twenty-seven minutes," he reminded her.

"Yes, sir." She punched off the phone.

The rooms were spacious and bright, just as she remembered. The bed was set up against the long wall by the window, precisely as she'd asked. The plants were intact, lined up on the windowsills for her to arrange as she pleased.

She smiled, strolling back into the living room and plopping down on the sofa. Strange surroundings mixed with familiar possessions. It already felt more comfortable than her old place.

Her gaze returned to the computer. It was dark and silent, since it wasn't plugged in. She kept a steady gaze on it, feeling somehow empowered by doing so. She'd celebrate her move by getting a new e-mail address. It was way past time. A different user name. A different Internet provider. But Gordon would *not* intimidate her, not any more than he already had.

She considered plugging in the computer and flipping on the power—a sort of symbolic gesture. No, she decided. She'd wait until she could unpack her surge protector.

Was she stalling? Maybe a little.

She wouldn't lie to herself. That computer still gave her the heebie-jeebies. She hadn't used it since New Year's Day, when the last e-card had come. Instead, she'd relied on her laptop. And, since she'd cut off her personal e-mail address, the only e-mail she received was what she accessed from Dellinger or WVNY.

That situation was going to change. Now that she knew Gordon was alive, she also knew her fears were irrational. If he wanted to terrorize her by e-mail, he would have rerouted his e-cards to one of her other electronic addresses.

Except that he was playing dead.

Taylor pressed her lips together. It didn't matter. She wasn't going to fear a machine, or anything it sent her. Fine, so she'd probably be checking her in-box constantly as she unpacked, praying there'd be no new e-cards waiting for her.

There couldn't be. Not unless Gordon wanted to expose his hand, let everyone know he was alive.

So whatever else he'd sent was floating in cyberspace, never to reach her.

Not that he cared. He planned to reach her in person.

4:20 P.M.

WESTON & ASSOCIATES, ATTORNEYS-AT-LAW

Reed paced around his office, mentally reviewing all the files, reports, and snippets of information he'd read through over the weekend. Mitch had given him copies of the articles he and Jake had dug up. Announcements of Gordon's successes. Significant investments he'd made on behalf of his clients—all of which paid off huge. Big splashy parties he'd attended, always with a redhead on his arm. The guy loved the limelight almost as much as he loved the high life.

Goddammit, it didn't make sense. Gordon wanted revenge. Okay, fine, so he'd killed Adrienne and Douglas and gotten it. Whatever horrible thing he had planned for Taylor was still a question mark, but after that—then what? He'd want to start over, and not as a termite in the woodwork. His ego wouldn't allow it. So he obviously planned to flee the country. And live on what? He'd been on his own for half a year now. He must have blown most of his savings, no matter how much he'd stocked up from the churning he'd been involved in.

The guy was a hedonist and a megalomaniac. He'd plotted and carried out a whole elaborate scheme. There was no way that revenge was all he had in mind for himself. His ego was too huge, his lifestyle too extravagant. Something was missing.

Douglas's estate.

No matter how Reed cut it, he kept getting back to that. If Gordon could somehow get Jonathan convicted of homicide and get his hands on their father's assets . . . But how? It was a catch-22 for the bastard, any way Reed cut it. To claim his inheritance, Gordon would have to come forward and announce he was alive. At which point, he'd be arrested for a list of crimes so damning he'd never see the light of day again. Jonathan would become the sole beneficiary, and Gordon would fry.

So what was his angle?

Time to check out another long shot, Reed decided, walking over to his desk. He picked up the phone and punched in his old work number.

"Harter, Randolph and Collins," the receptionist answered.

"Mr. Randolph, please."

"Just a moment." The call was transferred.

Horace's secretary picked up. "Mr. Randolph's office."

"Hello, Ms. Posner. This is Reed Weston. Is Mr. Randolph available? It's important."

"Good afternoon, Mr. Weston. Let me check." She put Reed on hold, returning a moment later. "I'm transferring your call."

"Thanks."

Two rings later Horace Randolph picked up. "Reed. What can I do for you?"

Reed launched right in. "Horace, I know this entire situation is awkward. But I need confirmation of something concerning the Berkley estates, as it pertains to Jonathan's case. I won't impose upon your integrity any more than I have to. All I'm asking is for a slight clarification of what we've already discussed. I wouldn't ask at all if I hadn't been affiliated with the firm when Douglas's will was drawn up." A weighted pause. "And if I didn't feel the information might be crucial."

"Very well." Horace cleared his throat. "I'll do what I can. What is it you need to know?"

"Douglas's sister, the one who passed away—it's her daughter who'd be next, and last, in line to inherit if Jonathan is found guilty."

"That's correct."

"I realize Douglas hadn't seen or spoken to his niece since she was a child, which is why she'd have no idea she stands to inherit. But she is his only living relative." *Maybe,* he amended to himself. "So I was wondering if you'd object if I spoke to her."

Silence. "That depends," Horace replied cautiously. "On what you plan to say."

"Nothing about the terms of the will. Nothing about Douglas or Adrienne. I only want to ask her questions that pertain to my client." *Or his twin brother.* "It's possible she was in touch with Jonathan over the years. If she can shed any light on his character, his relationships within the family, it might help. I'm reaching. But reaching is all I've got right now to prove my case."

"If that's what you're contacting her about, you don't need my permission. There's no overlap. Your questions are relevant only to Jonathan Mallory's defense, not the Berkley estates."

"I agree. I wasn't calling for permission—although I did intend to give you the courtesy of a heads-up. I was calling to ask you for her name and address. Her telephone number, too, if you have it."

"Why not just ask Jonathan?"

"Because he's in pretty bad shape. I don't want to give him false hope. But if you don't feel comfortable sharing the information with me, I will go to him."

"Not necessary. I don't see a conflict here. The will's a matter of public record." Horace shuffled through some files and plucked the one he was looking for. "Here it is." He flipped through the will. "Douglas's sister's married name was Roberta Elmond. Her daughter's name is Alison. There's no record of her having married, so I assume she goes by the name of Alison Elmond. She lives on West Houston Street in Greenwich Village. I don't have her telephone number handy."

"I'll get it," Reed quickly replied. "Thanks, Horace. I owe you one."

A pause. "You really think Jonathan's innocent, don't you?"

"Yeah. I do."

"If you're right, and you can prove it, that little firm of yours is going to burst at the seams in a month. You won't even need our referrals."

Reed didn't respond. Sure, the comment rankled him. But it didn't come as any great surprise. Horace would never understand that freeing an innocent man was his goal, not making a splashy name for himself and, as a result, attracting more high-profile clients. Then again, that emphasis on billable hours above all else was why Reed had wanted out of Harter, Randolph & Collins to begin with.

"I'll keep you posted," he assured his former boss.

Disconnecting the call, he punched in 411 for information.

Two minutes later, he had Alison Elmond's phone number and had placed the call.

The line rang. Voice mail picked up, generically stating, "You have reached 212-555-8664. Please leave a message after the beep."

He kept it terse, hoping that, by doing so, he'd elicit enough anxiety to prompt an immediate return call. "Ms. Elmond, this is Reed Weston. I'm a defense attorney. I have a few questions to ask you with regard to the Berkley homicides. I'd appreciate your calling me back ASAP. I won't take up much of your time. Thank you." He provided his cell number and hung up.

Time to wait—again.

Jonathan jumped out of the cab and rushed toward the apartment build-ing. He couldn't imagine what Reed and Taylor had found. But he prayed it would be the key to his freedom.

He'd barely reached the first outside step when a stocky guy grabbed him from behind and dragged him away.

"What the hell are you doing?" Jonathan demanded.

"Stopping you." The guy shoved him against the side of the build-ing, clutching his shirt in two ironclad fists. "Who're you going to visit, Mr. Mallory?"

"That's none of your damned business. And how do you know who I am?"

"I've been on the lookout for you. What a coincidence that you showed up."

"What are you talking about? I was asked to come. And, I repeat, who are you?"

"I think you know. But, fine, I'll confirm. My name's Mitch Garvey. I'm a private investigator, hired to protect Ms. Halstead."

Jonathan shook his head in baffled confusion. "Then why are you grabbing me? You know I'm not her stalker."

"Do I?"

"Yeah. She must have told you she's helping me."

Mitch arched a brow. "Is she?"

"Yes." Jonathan started to struggle again. "I've got to get upstairs."

"And why is that?"

"Because I need to see her. Because . . ." Jonathan tried to shove Mitch away. "I don't have to explain myself to you!"

"Excuse me." Ed, the doorman, had walked outside. He was a broad-shouldered, imposing man himself, and he didn't look the least bit in-timidated by the scuffle going on. He looked angry. "Whatever the problem here is, take it elsewhere. Otherwise, I'll have to call the po-lice."

BINGO. The doorman had heard the escalating commotion. And, like a good safeguarder of a prestigious building, he was interceding. Just as planned. Excellent.

He inched his way toward the apartment entrance. It was too early in the day for the corporate gang to head home. So the building was quiet. But that's the way he wanted it. All he needed was one tenant . . . just one . . .

There.

A middle-aged woman exited the building. He watched her descend the steps and pass by without even seeing him. His gaze shifted quickly to the inside glass door, now slowly swinging shut.

He didn't wait. He seized his chance.

He darted into the building, wedging his foot in the sliver of space still provided by the closing door. Pulling it open, he slipped inside.

Forty-five seconds. Record time.

He took the stairs instead of the elevator.

"THE POLICE MIGHT not be a bad idea," Mitch had just finished informing Ed. "But this isn't a problem. It's a potential crime." Leaning his weight against Jonathan to keep him pinned in place, Mitch reached into his pocket and pulled out his PI license, flashing it at the doorman. "I was hired by Ms. Halstead. This man was on his way up to her apartment. I believe he's a threat to her life."

"I'm no threat!" Jonathan began wrestling for his freedom again. "Taylor called me. She said she found something, and that she and Reed needed to see me right away. She gave me this address."

Mitch's eyes narrowed. He wasn't impressed by the excuse. It was lame and easily discredited. So why would Mallory use it? He was too shrewd for that. And what about his feeble attempts to free himself? They were pathetic. If this guy had sophisticated enough martial arts skills to snap someone's neck, then he was the Dalai Lama.

Something was wrong.

"Show me your driver's license," he commanded.

Jonathan stopped struggling. "Why? You know who I am."

"I said, show me your license."

With a peeved look, Jonathan fished in his pocket and pulled out his wallet. "Here." He stuck it in Mitch's face. "Happy?"

An uneasy expression crossed Mitch's face. "Actually, no." He patted Jonathan down and then, convinced he was unarmed, released his hold on him. "What's your social security number—off the top of your head," he grilled, continuing to block Jonathan's path.

"Are you crazy?"

"Answer me."

"Fine." Jonathan ticked off the nine-digit number.

With a disgusted grunt, Mitch turned toward the doorman. "It's okay. Mistaken identity. I apologize."

Ed glared at them. "If there's another commotion, I'm calling the cops."

"Feel free," Mitch replied.

The doorman returned to his post.

Mitch clamped a restraining hand on Jonathan's forearm as he took a step toward the building. "Wait."

Jonathan stared. "You're *still* not letting me go? Look, Garvey, I don't know what your game is—"

"No game." Mitch waved away his protests. "But you're not going up there. Taylor didn't call you. Reed's not with her. So tell me about that phone call you allegedly got."

TAYLOR FINISHED WATERING her favorite pothos, then placed it on the windowsill where it would get the proper amount of sunlight.

Stepping back, she glanced at her watch. Five minutes to go. She'd better not press her luck, or Mitch would be furious.

With a final glance around, she scooped up her purse, tucked her cell phone inside, and headed out the front door. She was just about to lock it behind her when she sensed a presence.

She whirled around, letting out a soft cry of surprise and dropping her keys.

He bent over, scooped them up, and handed them to her. "Hello, Taylor," he said with a smile.

CHAPTER 34

"SHIT." Mitch punched End on his cell phone. "She's not answering. I'm going up."

He blew past Ed, his hand already reaching for his weapon. "Buzz me up. Now." He yanked out his pistol.

"I'll have to notify the—"

"Call Detective Hadman at the Nineteenth Precinct," Mitch instructed. "Tell him what's going on. Now open that goddamned door."

The doorman complied.

Mitch raced up the four flights of stairs, holding his pistol in front of him as he reached Taylor's apartment and saw that the door was ajar.

He shoved it open.

"Taylor!" he shouted, his voice echoing through the empty apartment. Pistol raised, he continued calling her name, checking out every room as he did.

All empty.

"Shit," he muttered again. "That son of a bitch."

"Who?" Jonathan demanded, having followed him. "What the hell's going on?"

Mitch wasn't wasting time on explanations. He pushed past Jonathan and out into the hall, squatting down just outside the doorway and peering around to see if his sense of smell had deceived him. He found what he was looking for, rubbing his fingers over a damp spot on the carpet, then bringing his fingers up to his nose. He inhaled the familiar fruity scent.

"Dammit," he rasped, furious at himself for being taken. "Chloroform." He grabbed his cell phone and called the Nineteenth Precinct, reiterating the message Ed had just called in. Thankfully, Hadman had acted. He and Olin were on their way.

Next, he punched in Reed's cell number.

4:53 P.M.

WESTON & ASSOCIATES, ATTORNEYS-AT-LAW

Reed grabbed the phone when it rang. Hopefully, it would be Alison Elmond, returning his call. "Hello?"

"It's Mitch."

The somber tone of the PI's voice registered right away. "What's wrong?"

"Taylor's gone. I think he's got her."

"*What?*" Reed shot to his feet. "How the hell could that happen?"

"Get over to her new apartment. I'll explain when you get here. Hadman and Olin are already on their way." A pause. "Jonathan Mallory's with me."

"I'm there." He was out the door even as he spoke.

5:25 P.M.

Reed literally ran the whole way, shoving commuters and other pedestrians out of his way. No car, taxi, or subway could get him there faster.

Panting heavily, he arrived at the same time as Hadman and Olin. Their sedan roared up to the curb. They parked in the no-parking zone, jumping out and following a half step behind Reed.

They all burst onto the scene at the same time. Olin stayed in the lobby to question Ed. Hadman and Reed took the elevator up to Taylor's apartment.

"Start talking," Reed ordered Mitch the second he exploded through the door.

The PI ran through the preliminaries quickly, ending with Jonathan's arrival.

"Mallory." Hadman turned to him. "How do you fit into all this?"

"Tell them about the phone call," Mitch instructed him.

Jonathan complied, although he looked stunned and shaky.

"You're sure it was Taylor's voice?" Reed demanded.

"Definitely."

"But she obviously didn't place the call," Mitch said. "Which means that someone went to the trouble of taping her voice and splicing the right phrases together."

"Whoever's framing me." Jonathan rubbed the back of his neck. "He wanted it to look like I was coming here to hurt her."

"That's not all he wanted," Mitch muttered. "He wanted a diversion. And he got it. While the doorman and I were arguing with you, he slipped into the building and upstairs to Taylor. Her front door was ajar. I smelled chloroform in the hall. After I called Reed, I went around to the side of the building and checked the delivery entrance. Since it rained earlier this afternoon, there were puddles all around. I was hoping to find some telltale marks, like tire tracks or footprints. I found both. There were tire tracks running down the ramp to the side door. A vehicle was driven down there recently. There was also a set of footprints leading from the door to the tire tracks. One set. My guess would be that Taylor was unconscious and being carried to the car."

"Christ." Reed felt bile rise in his throat. "Gordon has her. He's planning a repeat performance. First Adrienne. Now Taylor."

"Gordon?" The shocked outburst came from Jonathan. "As in, my brother?"

"Yeah." Mitch answered for Reed, who was in no shape to explain. "That's who we mean."

Olin strode in. "I've got a couple of witnesses who saw a silver minivan speed away about thirty minutes ago. No make or model. And no license-plate number. Apparently, the vehicle came close to causing two accidents at two separate intersections as it headed south toward midtown. Driver's probably in a hurry to get out of Manhattan. Silver minivans aren't exactly rare, which I'm sure is why our perp chose it. We've alerted the other boroughs. They'll get word to their patrol cars."

"Let's hope someone gets us a lead." Hadman turned to Mitch. "Time to cut to the chase. I gave those files to Weston. I know what you two were looking for. So, tell me, do you have actual proof that Gordon Mallory's alive?"

"We will when we find Taylor."

"That's not an answer."

"It's the only answer we've got right now, Hadman." Reed countered grimly. "And it'll have to be enough. *I'm* convinced Gordon's alive. But even if I'm wrong, our psycho-stalker's got Taylor."

With that, he whipped around to his client, who'd sunk down into a chair, white-faced. "Jonathan." He grabbed his arms. "I know you're reeling. But you've got to think. Where would Gordon take Taylor?"

Jonathan gazed up at Reed with a vague expression in his eyes. "Why didn't you tell me?"

"We planned to, as soon as we had conclusive evidence. We're close. But now everything's changed."

" 'We,' " Jonathan repeated. "Taylor knows?"

"Yes. She was doing a forensic profile on Gordon, based on his personality and what he endured as a teen."

"God. He hated Adrienne's guts." Jonathan swallowed. "So he didn't die in the boat explosion?"

"We don't think so. Now answer my question. Where would he take Taylor?"

It was no use. That vague look was still there as Jonathan fought to process the enormity of what he was learning. "Do he and I have identical DNA?"

Reed wanted to shake him until he talked. But he had to snap him out of his shock first. "Yes. And he's got motive, means, and access. Jonathan, listen to me. I'll explain everything later. But we're fighting the clock. Taylor was trying to help you. Now it's your turn to help her. Please."

That did the trick.

Jonathan raised his head, and Reed could see the fog in his eyes clear. "Okay. Okay." He wiped beads of perspiration off his brow. "I don't know much more about Gordon's habits than you do. I do know that most of the places he hung out were very chichi, very visible. No way he'd take her there. His apartment's been sold, so that's out." A quizzical look. "Where's he been living all this time?"

"Good question," Reed muttered.

"If no one knows, then maybe that's where he's taking Taylor."

"Excuse me for interrupting," Hadman inserted. "But this whole theory doesn't fly. Not in my mind. First off, I don't buy that anyone survived that boat explosion, much less planned it. But even if I'm wrong, Gordon Mallory was a flashy, extravagant guy. No way he's living in some slum just so he can bump off the Berkleys, stalk Taylor Halstead, and frame his brother."

"You don't know how much Gordon hated Adrienne, or how screwed up he was," Jonathan countered bitterly.

"Fine. I'm sure he was a nutcase and a scumbag. But he was also smart. He'd think through his plan. He'd know we'd fry his ass if we found him. He'd have two choices. Live underground or get a fake ID and passport and flee the country. What would he plan to subsidize his lifestyle with— love? No way. Like I said, he liked the good life too much." Hadman's brows rose. "Unless you know something we don't—like the existence of some Swiss bank account?"

Reed shrugged. "I'm sure he had secret accounts. But even if he set himself up financially, it was a short-term thing. The amount he cheated his clients out of wasn't enough to set him up for life, not by a long shot. You want my opinion? I think Gordon plans on getting his hands on Douglas's estate. That's why he's framing Jonathan. As for how he'd claim his inheritance when he's supposedly dead, there's got to be an angle we're just not seeing—"

The ringing of Reed's cell phone interrupted him.

"Maybe it's Taylor. Maybe she found a way to call." Reed punched on the phone. "Hello?"

There was a long pause. "Mr. Weston?"

"Yes? Who is this?"

"It's Alison Elmond. You left me a message. Something to do with my uncle's murder?"

Speaking of the unexplored angle.

"Oh, yes—Ms. Elmond. Thank you for returning my call." Reed massaged his temples, trying to reassemble the questions he'd mentally prepared to secure information on Gordon. Only now those questions had to be slanted toward a more urgent and immediate goal. Finding Taylor.

His prolonged silence must have made his caller nervous because she gave an uneasy laugh, then began talking to fill it. "Actually, it's not Ms. Elmond anymore. Not since last week. I got married."

"Congratulations," Reed replied on autopilot. "My mistake, Mrs. . . . ?"

"Kincaid," she supplied with the obvious pride of a newlywed. "Mrs. Dennis Kincaid."

Everything inside Reed went still. "Dennis Kincaid? I know a Dennis Kincaid who's the audio engineer at WVNY. Is he your new husband?"

"Why, yes."

"I'm dating Taylor Halstead."

"Oh, what a small world." Another awkward laugh. "Dennis talks about Ms. Halstead all the time. He thinks the world of her. He was thrilled to work with her. Even though he was devastated by what happened to poor Rick Shore. What a horrible tragedy. Dennis took it hard."

"I'm sure he did." Reed had to keep her on this subject. This coincidence was far too bizarre to be a fluke. "Rick's death was a shock to everyone at WVNY. They're a close-knit group."

"I know. And Dennis felt a particular bond with Rick. He taught him so much. I can't tell you how grateful Dennis was. And not only to Rick. To Jack Taft, the program manager. Mr. Taft is the one who gave Dennis the opportunity to do audio for Ms. Halstead's show."

"So I heard. Although, as I understand it, Dennis is great at his job."

"Did Ms. Halstead say that?" Alison asked eagerly.

Reed went with his gut. "She says it all the time. She feels very lucky to have such a competent crew."

"It's Dennis who feels lucky. He constantly mentions how smart Kevin Hodges is. But, most of all, he talks about Ms. Halstead. He says how amazing she is, how fascinated he is by her abilities with people. He says he learns something new from her every day. When she's on the air and he's working the control panel, he just watches her through the glass partition. He says that by watching her, he can soak up some of her energy. He's her biggest fan."

He just watches her through the glass partition . . . watches her . . . watches her . . .

The phrase struck Reed like a ton of bricks.

What was it Mitch had said about the call Jonathan just received? He'd said that someone had made a sound clip of Taylor's voice. The caller had taped her voice, then spliced together the right phrases.

Well, he wouldn't have to work too hard to make that sound clip if he were right there in the studio. In fact, he'd have immediate access to copies of all her shows. And splicing together just the right phrases would be a snap—*if* the caller were a trained audio tech.

Taylor's audio tech.

Reed's insides lurched. God. Was it possible?

"Mr. Weston?" Alison prompted. "Are you still there?"

"Yes, I'm sorry." Reed pulled himself together. He had to ferret out the rest. "Mrs. Kincaid, if you don't mind my asking, how long were you and Dennis engaged?"

"We didn't do the engagement thing. We just got married. It was very spontaneous. Dennis just came over one night last week all pumped up, and said, 'Let's get married.' And we did."

Pumped up? More like frustrated—and in a hurry to tie a crucial legal knot.

Another piece fell into place.

"That sounds very romantic." Reed had to fight to keep his voice even. "Is Dennis usually that spontaneous? I mean, you must have known each other for quite a while now."

"Not really. We met around Thanksgiving. We just happened to click right from the start. I have a pottery shop in the Village. Dennis came in to buy a gift. The rest, as they say, is history." Alison paused, as if it suddenly occurred to her that Reed's questions had taken an odd turn. "I think we got sidetracked. You wanted to talk to me about my uncle and his wife's murders. I felt ill when I saw the news on TV. But I'm not sure how much help I can be. I haven't seen Uncle Douglas since I was a child. My mother was an artist, kind of the black sheep of the family—a bohemian, in the minds of the Berkleys. So we weren't in touch."

"Were you in touch with either Gordon or Jonathan Mallory?"

"No. I'm sorry."

"That's okay. I'm just covering all my bases." Reed's jaw was working. He had to get back to the subject of Dennis. He knew she'd become wary of his personal questions. He didn't care. He had to try one last time. He couldn't force her to talk, not without a warrant. And a warrant required evidence, which he didn't have. Nor did he have time to gather it. Not with Taylor's life on the line.

He'd tread carefully.

"Before we hang up, is Dennis at WVNY tonight?"

As Reed had expected, she was instantly alert. "Why?"

"Because I'd like to send a congratulatory bottle in honor of your marriage," Reed replied smoothly. "What does Dennis drink?"

Her relief was tangible. "That's lovely of you. He drinks Scotch. But he won't be in tonight. He'd planned to be, since our honeymoon is now officially over. But at the last minute, he asked Mr. Taft for one more night off. He told me it involved something personal and important." A shy giggle. "He was very mysterious. All he'd tell me was not to wait up, because he had no idea how late he'd be home. He said he was planning a surprise that would secure our future." It was pathetic how eager she sounded.

Reflecting on the "surprise" Dennis was really planning, Reed nearly threw up.

"Maybe he's looking at a cottage upstate, like in Dutchess County," she added wistfully.

Reed jumped all over that. "Why? Is that where you two want to move?"

"*I* do. Not Dennis. He'd prefer to look closer to the city. But houses in the suburbs cost a fortune. We can't afford them. And we want a place of our own. Especially Dennis, who's been living in dumps, as he described them, since he moved to the city. They were so bad, he never even let me visit him. We're living in my place now, but it's cramped. So a nice cottage upstate would be a start. Maybe he's considering it for my sake." Alison's voice took on an anxious note. "I realize it's far. But tell Ms. Halstead not to worry. Dennis will commute by train, no matter how many hours it takes."

It won't be necessary, Reed thought grimly. *Not after what he has in mind.*

"I'm sure he will," he said aloud, pursuing the transportation angle in the hopes of hearing the magic words: "silver minivan." "But since you work in the Village, maybe you two could drive in together, rather than taking the train."

"That would be great if we had a car. But we don't. Not yet. We're saving up for one."

Okay, so the minivan was a rental. Not a surprise. As for saving up for anything, Alison had a rude awakening ahead of her. *She* might be saving. But *Dennis* had his whole pension lined up.

"Truthfully, Mr. Weston, I think Dennis is putting off buying the car. He's a little gun-shy about getting behind the wheel after his accident."

Now, *that* came out of left field.

Reed went after it like a lion to meat. "I didn't realize Dennis had been in an accident."

"He doesn't like to talk about it much. But he was in a head-on collision right before he moved to New York. The whole trauma left him pretty shaky."

"When did this happen?"

"Mid-September, I think."

Bingo. Pay dirt.

Reed's knuckles were white as they gripped the cell phone. "Was he badly hurt?"

"The impact sent him right through the windshield. His face was completely torn up by the glass. Other than that, he was lucky. A few broken bones, lots of cuts and bruises, and some horrible memories."

That shot holes in Reed's theory. The injuries Alison was describing were inconsistent with those suffered in a boat explosion. Still, the timing was too similar to ignore.

"That sounds serious," he tried. "Wow, an accident of that magnitude and there were no extensive body injuries?"

"Thankfully, no. Not on either side. The woman who hit him suffered only from whiplash and a totaled car. Dennis's car was wrecked, too. But his face . . ." Her voice trembled a bit. "It breaks my heart what he went through."

"I can imagine. He must have some nasty scars."

"Fortunately not. He underwent extensive reconstructive surgery. The poor man's cheekbones had to be rebuilt, his nose reset . . . plus some skin grafting and a lot of other surgical procedures I try to block out, they sound so gruesome. I'm not the medical type. I'm just grateful that Dennis is alive and well."

"Of course."

Dennis is alive and well.

There it was. The reality. The reason why Gordon had no bodily injuries. He hadn't been on his yacht when it exploded. He'd gotten off beforehand. And there'd been no accident—not for him. The shrewd SOB had simply gotten a new face.

Enter Dennis Kincaid.

Reed had to hang up. He'd gotten as much as he could out of Alison Kincaid, at least for his purposes. The cops would have tons of questions for her later. But that was their thing. Right now, all that mattered to him was Taylor. Alison obviously had no clue where her husband was headed.

Time for the police to take over.

"Well, Mrs. Kincaid." He wrapped up the call in as few words as possible. "I won't keep you any longer. Congratulations again. I wish you the best."

He punched off the phone, staring at it for a moment before raising his head to gaze at Hadman. "I have answers. Call your men and tell them to change the description of the man driving that minivan."

"It's not Gordon Mallory?"

"Oh, it's Mallory all right. He's just made some alterations."

CHAPTER 35

6:47 P.M.

THE bouncing motion of the car penetrated her consciousness.

With a Herculean effort, Taylor cracked open her eyes. Her head was throbbing. She felt achy and groggy. Like she had the flu. Like she should be in bed. Why was she in a car?

She was half slumped over on the seat. Her arms were cramped, twisted behind her. She tried to free them and push herself into a sitting position, but they wouldn't budge. It was like something was holding them down. Same with her feet, which were stuck together like glue, making any leg motion impossible.

What the hell was going on?

She blinked, forced herself fully awake. Headlights reflected in the passenger's sideview mirror. It was evening.

"I see you're awake. Good. I could use the company."

Taylor's head snapped around, and she stared blankly at the man who was driving. Dennis. Why was she in a car with Dennis?

"You picked the worst time of day to visit your new place," he continued. "Rush hour sucked. We sat in the Midtown Tunnel for thirty minutes."

Her new place?

Memory flooded back in a rush.

She'd been leaving her new apartment. She'd walked smack into Dennis in the hall outside her door. He'd pressed something over her nose and mouth. A handkerchief. It smelled like citrus-scented Formula 409 household cleaner. That's all she remembered.

Instinctively, she started to struggle, trying to free her hands and feet. Gazing down, she realized why she couldn't. Her ankles were bound together with thick cord. So were her wrists. Between that and her seat belt, she was effectively imprisoned in the car.

"Dennis?" It *was* him. Yet he seemed like a different person, someone she didn't recognize. "Where are we?"

"The Long Island Expressway. We've got another hour to go, now that traffic's finally letting up."

"Where is it we're going?"

A tight smile. "To your ultimate destination. And your final resting place."

His message was clear as glass. Taylor shuddered, fear eclipsing the last vestiges of haze from her mind. Fear and, to a lesser extent, confusion. None of this made sense. Dennis? Why Dennis?

She continued staring at him, trying to resolve the inconsistency. She licked her lips, forcing out the one-word question. "Why?"

He gave a humorless laugh. "Where do I begin?" He glanced to the right, then flipped on his directional signal and eased over, first to the right lane, then off the highway and onto the shoulder. Breaking to a stop, he put the car in park and turned to face her.

"Why are we stopping?" Taylor asked, a shiver of apprehension shooting up her spine.

"Two reasons. One, you're dehydrated. Drink this." He uncapped a bottle of water and held it to her lips. "Trust me. You'll need your strength for later."

She hesitated, then realized how absurd she was being. His plan was to kill her. But poisoning her water wasn't what he had in mind.

She began gulping down the much-needed liquid.

"Take it slow or you won't hold it down," he warned. "You've been out longer than I planned. I had to reapply the chloroform a couple of times. I didn't count on all that traffic. And I couldn't risk your coming to when we were at a standstill and yelling for help. That's it. Nice and easy." He waited till she was finished, then recapped the bottle and put it in the holder.

"What's the second reason we're stopping?" she asked, leaning her head back against the seat and fighting the cobwebs of dizziness.

"So I can answer your question. I'll have to make it brief so we can get back on the road. I'll happily fill in all the blanks for you while we drive. But for the pièce de résistance, the moment I've dreamed of, re-envisioned over and over—for that, I have to see your face. And, since we're about to lose the benefit of twilight, that moment is now."

Flipping on the dome light for emphasis, he leaned toward her, and Taylor scrutinized his face. He wore an expression she'd never seen on him before, or maybe she'd just never looked closely enough. It was an expression of cruel, detached resolve.

"You've been stalking me," she deduced quietly. "It's been you all along."

"Right from the beginning," he confirmed. "But that still doesn't answer your question, does it? I believe you asked why. Well, here's your answer."

He bowed his head, his chin close to his chest. Reaching up, he pulled down first one eyelid, then the other. Taylor realized he was popping out contact lenses. That done, he sat up, shoved the mop of hair off his forehead, and leaned all the way forward, until Taylor could feel his breath on her face. He opened his dark eyes wide, his hard, icy gaze boring into her.

"Because I gave you my word that I would," he said in a voice that no longer belonged to Dennis, but to a nightmare from her past. "I told you I'd be back. That we'd have all the time we needed to finish what we started. And, I told you I'd be watching you. Well, I was."

Taylor let out a soft cry. She wanted to scream, but it wouldn't come. Not that it mattered. No one would hear her if it did. Not over the roar of cars whizzing by on the LIE. "Oh, my God," she gasped, trembling violently as the inconsistencies gelled into truth. "It's you." She broke off, gagging as the water she'd drunk came back up, along with the rest of what she'd eaten that day.

Dennis obliged her by pressing the power button and lowering her window. She leaned out, vomiting until there was nothing left inside her. Even then, she continued to retch helplessly for a moment or two, before sinking back weakly in her seat.

He watched her as he raised the window back up, a brittle smile curving his lips. "That reaction was worth all the waiting." Calmly, he popped his lenses back in, resettled himself in the driver's seat, and flipped on his left blinker.

He pulled out onto the highway.

"I don't understand," Taylor heard herself stammer.

"Of course you don't." He didn't bother reverting to Dennis's voice anymore. That facade was no longer necessary. The monster sitting beside her was unquestionably Gordon. "My plan was too intricate. It was also too brilliant to keep to myself. Unfortunately, after today, that's what I'm going to have to do. So I left ample time to tell you everything. Where would you like me to start?"

"Douglas and Adrienne Berkley. You killed them."

"Of course. Shall I tell you why?"

Taylor's mind was starting to work again, the initial paralysis that had gripped it ebbing. "I know why. Adrienne sexually abused you for years. And Douglas did nothing to stop it."

A flicker of surprise crossed Gordon's face. "You did your homework. I'm impressed. It pays to sleep with the lawyer of the accused."

She ignored that barb. "Speaking of the accused, you did a superb job of framing Jonathan."

He acknowledged the compliment with a nod. "It wasn't hard. I hacked his computer password. It's 'Berkley,' of all things. The man has no imagination whatsoever. Anyway, I monitored all his e-mails to and from Douglas. I even tapped his phones, office and home. I knew where he was going, what he was thinking, the works. Everything I did was choreographed around his whereabouts. As for the windfall genetics handed me—the fact that identical twins have identical DNA—that I owe to nature. I just took advantage of it."

Gordon's tone and demeanor took on an aura of violent hatred. "Leaving my reproductive calling card inside that bitch while I choked her to death was sheer pleasure. Watching her face, knowing she understood what was happening to her and why, prolonging the suffering—nothing will ever match that feeling." A quick glance at Taylor. "Well, almost nothing."

Taylor was glad her stomach was empty. Otherwise, she might just vomit again. "And Douglas?"

"He went fast and with only the pain of knowing who was responsible and why." A pensive frown. "I thought of keeping him alive long enough to make him watch me screw Adrienne, after which I'd kill them both. But I decided against it. Douglas was weak, useless—and blind to the truth about Adrienne. I saw the expression on his face when I told him, the revulsion in his eyes when he looked at her. The stupid old man had no clue what a perverted whore he was married to. So I put him out of his misery and spent the rest of the time torturing her. The experience was revitalizing."

Okay, enough deranged, heinous details. Taylor couldn't take any more.

"How did you become Dennis Kincaid?" she asked. "More important, *why* did you become Dennis Kincaid? To escape when all this was over?"

He gave a disgusted snort. "That would be a lot of work for nothing. No, my dear Taylor, I became Dennis Kincaid for several reasons. One, to accomplish all I needed to while staying invisible. Two, to watch you as closely as I promised I would. And three, to get everything that's coming to me when Jonathan is convicted of double homicide."

He rubbed a hand over his face. "The 'how' should be obvious. At least from an aesthetic perspective. Cosmetic surgery is a remarkable thing. The surgeons in Thailand were astounding. They raised my eyebrows, added fat to my cheeks, removed a few bags under my eyes to erase several years, remade my nose and mouth, even darkened my skin a few shades to go with my new look. And all with only a few weeks' recovery. The hair took longer to grow into this unruly mop. Oh, and I put lifts in my shoes. They added two inches to my height; actually, two inches on the left side and two and a half on the right. That took care of changing my walk. Tinted contacts altered my eye color. So, you see, I'm a whole new person. Not as handsome, but with a far rosier future.

"As for the mundane part of 'how,' the real Dennis Kincaid was a nobody. He was born and died in a little town in Nebraska. I did a little digging, found what I needed. He had no family, no one to catch me at my little game of pretend. I created a whole new Dennis Kincaid, with a little help from my newfound friends who specialize in creative passports and the like. Then again, that's how I got out of the country in the first place."

"To go to Thailand for your plastic surgery?"

"Uh-huh. I flew there right after the boat explosion. During my recovery, I honed my technical skills. I've always had the aptitude, so it wasn't much of a challenge. An Internet course or two, and I was all set. Then I spent another month on an advanced martial-arts class, and I was on my way. I had my fake passport doctored with my new photo and flew back to the U.S. I volunteered at a couple of small-town radio jobs to get references and experience. The rest was easy."

Taylor had to force out the next question. But it was one she had to ask. It had haunted her since she realized Gordon might be alive. "The boat explosion—you orchestrated the whole thing?"

"Of course. I orchestrated *everything*." He gave her a mocking smile. "For example, do you really think your friend Rick just tripped onto those railroad tracks that night?"

All the color drained from Taylor's face. "You . . . you pushed him?"

"I needed to be on the other side of that glass when you did your nightly radio show. It was just a matter of finding the right time to get rid of Rick so I could fill his seat. He made it easy. Rick was so drunk, he never knew what hit him. Or who. Ever since then, I've been there. Night after night. For hours on end. Up close and personal. Watching you, just as I planned. And you didn't have a clue. Talk about the ultimate power trip. You were like a wriggling insect under a microscope. My microscope."

This horror show was getting more grotesque by the minute.

"Ah, you wanted to know about the boat explosion. Allow me to explain. I planned it down to the tiniest detail. On Friday, the day before the bash on my yacht, I drove out to Douglas's East Hampton estate. He and Adrienne were vacationing in Greece, so I knew no one would see me. I swapped my magnificent Mercedes CLK320 for the beat-up old Chevy truck I used as a teenager. I took my boat trailer and Zodiac with me."

"Zodiac?" Taylor asked numbly.

"A lightweight, heavy-duty inflatable boat." Memory flashed in his eyes, and Taylor could see the madness there. "Mine's been in use for years. Adrienne christened it. It was her favorite playpen, and I was her favorite plaything. We'd go out on Douglas's yacht. From there, she'd order me to accompany her in the Zodiac and steer into any one of a dozen secluded coves. I satisfied her physical needs du jour, after which she'd supervise me scrubbing down the Zodiac and the yacht. She loved to watch me sweat my ass off like a common laborer. It turned her on."

He shrugged. "On the other hand, the experience had its perks. I learned how to be a proficient and creative lover at a time when all my peers were still virgins. And I learned the best places to take women for a very private, very good time. Those coves came in handy over the years. I used them with lots of women, right up through your cousin Stephanie."

Just hearing him say Steph's name made Taylor's blood boil. At that moment, she didn't feel a shred of compassion for the abuse he'd endured. All she felt was rage. He'd cold-bloodedly murdered her cousin. And Rick. And a yachtful of people.

Her fingernails dug into her palms as she fought for control. She couldn't lose it. Not yet.

"What did you do with the Zodiac that Friday night?" she asked, wishing she could stop pursuing a subject that would only cause her pain. But she had to know everything she could about Steph's death. And this bastard was the only one who could provide her with answers.

"I collapsed it, drove out to the Montauk boatyard, and stashed it on my yacht with the outboard motor and gas tank. Then I drove the truck to Napeague Harbor and left it, and the trailer, in the parking lot near the boat ramp. I jogged the three miles back to Douglas's estate, picked up my Benz, and drove back to Manhattan by nightfall. According to my Rolex, I was forty minutes ahead of schedule. Pretty impressive, even for me."

Taylor wanted to scream: *Shut up! I don't give a damn about your depraved plan or how brilliantly it was executed. I just want to know what you did to my cousin. Did she suffer? How long did it take her to die? Did she die in the explosion or on your filthy Zodiac?*

Her nails dug deeper into her palms, the pain somehow grounding her in reality. "On Saturday you and Steph flew out to Montauk," she prompted.

"After you and I were interrupted, you mean?" An icy smirk. "Yes. We left Montauk Harbor late afternoon with the party in full swing, and headed south for about an hour and a half. We passed lots of vessels coming in for the day, so we were pretty much alone by the time we reached our destination. I dropped anchor. The party raged on. Around five-thirty, I got some of the guys to help me inflate the Zodiac and attach the outboard. Steph and I hopped in and zoomed off for some private time."

He shot Taylor a cruel, sideways glance, twisting the verbal knife in deeper. "That was business as usual with Steph. She liked life wild and dangerous. And she loved our hot little sexual encounters on the Zodiac. The thrill of being out in the open, maybe being caught—that turned her on. No need to search for a cove. We just maneuvered the Zodiac about three or four hundred yards away from the yacht, and went at it. I made sure to keep one hand on the remote control I'd hidden in my slacks. When the timing was right, I pressed the yellow button. That activated a solenoid spliced into each gas line, which poured gasoline into the bilge. Steph had no clue what was going on. Her mind was on other things."

Taylor gagged again.

Her reaction seemed to please Gordon, and he continued with his story. "Right before Steph climaxed, I pressed the red button. There was a deafening explosion. I knew that meant I'd succeeded. Bye-bye yacht. Which left only Steph. She was still in the throes of orgasm. I placed my thumbs over her windpipe and choked her to death. After that, I took a full minute to stare off and admire my handiwork—a million-dollar yacht that was nothing more than a flaming ball of garbage, sinking into the ocean. I knew the physical remains would be slim to none, since that area is shark-infested. Oh, speaking of sharks, back to Steph. I cut her arms before I slid her over the side of the Zodiac, and let her go. That way, her blood would attract the sharks, which would eliminate the chance of her body—or pieces of it—ever being found. I tossed the knife and remote overboard. Then I just whipped out my handheld GPS, fired up the engine, and sped back toward shore."

"You sick, demented bastard," Taylor choked out, wrestling with her bonds until her wrists and ankles were raw. "*You* deserve to die that way! No, even being strangled or blown to bits is too good for you. You deserve to feel every drop of pain you inflicted on everyone you murdered. And Steph. My God. Steph never did a thing to you. She loved you. And you killed her in cold blood, then fed her to the sharks like bait." Taylor sagged against the seat, totally spent from her struggles and her outburst. Tears streamed down her cheeks as she visualized Steph's body sinking downward, the trail of blood signaling to the waiting sharks.

"Taylor, Taylor." Gordon made a tsk-tsk sound with his tongue. "Haven't you learned to show me the proper respect? You know how I react when you're abrupt or nasty."

"I don't give a damn," she snapped. "You're going to kill me anyway. So why should I appease you?"

"Good point," he acknowledged. "You *are* going to die. But not right away. We have some unfinished business to attend to first. Something I've spent six months dreaming about. In the meantime, let me finish my story."

He went on, as if he were relaying a fascinating and well-written epic.

"My timing and execution were impeccable. Just before dusk, I passed the Montauk lighthouse, and navigated around the South Fork of Long Island, hugging the shoreline. When I reached Napeague Harbor, I headed for the secluded boat ramp. I beached the Zodiac and walked to the parking lot where my Chevy pickup and boat trailer were waiting. I drove down the boat ramp, pulled the Zodiac onto the ramp, and headed toward Montauk Highway. I arrived at Douglas's estate, and returned the boat and trailer to the boathouse. After that, I grabbed my knapsack, which was packed with everything I needed. Clothing. Fake passport. Laptop computer. Airline ticket to Bangkok. And account numbers for the bank accounts I'd set up in the Cayman Islands. Knapsack in tow, I walked to the East Hampton train station. I took the last train, the eight thirty-eight, to New York. Just to be on the safe side, I exited the LIRR in Jamaica—that was about ten forty-five—and took a cab to Kennedy Airport. My flight left for Bangkok around two A.M. Ingenious, wasn't it? I truly thought of everything."

"I'd applaud, but my hands are tied," Taylor retorted, her eyes closed as she tried to shut everything out.

She could feel him bristle. "Don't push me, Taylor," he warned in that on-the-edge tone. "There are many ways to die. The more pissed off I am, the more pain you'll endure. Bear that in mind."

With that, he flicked on his turn signal and started slowing down, simultaneously easing off to the right.

Taylor's eyes flew open and she gazed around. Exit 70.

"Can you tell me where we're going?"

"If you ask nicely."

She licked her dry lips. "Please, Gordon, where are we going?"

"See how easy that was?" He pulled off the highway and made a right turn off the ramp. "We're going up to Sag Harbor. To the yacht club. It's a beautiful night. You'll love the view."

Taylor turned away. She didn't reply. But she understood.

Gordon was taking her to his father's yacht. There, she'd be a stand-in for Adrienne. His rage would come full circle.

She'd be raped. And then she'd die.

CHAPTER 36

T H E past hour and a half had been hell.

Reed had paced around Hadman's desk, gulping black coffee and feeling unbearably helpless. Hadman and Olin had put out a ton of feelers. In the meantime, they kept firing ideas back and forth, then making phone calls to see if any of those ideas had merit.

Nothing.

Mitch was in a separate cubicle, talking on and off with Jake as they tapped into their own resources. Jonathan was slumped in a chair, head in hands. Reed had asked him to accompany them to the police precinct in case they turned up anything.

The whole ordeal seemed like forever, but in slow motion. The clock was ticking. Gordon had Taylor. Where would he take her? It had to be somewhere no one would find them until he was through with her, and her body was disposed of.

How many times had Reed run through this scenario in a professional capacity? But this time he couldn't muster a shred of professionalism. The very thought of Gordon touching Taylor, much less raping or killing her, was more than he could contemplate, much less calmly discuss.

Still, the reality kept crawling into his brain like some odious insect.

It had been more than two hours since Taylor had been taken. God only knew what Gordon might have done to her by now.

No. He couldn't think that way. He had to believe that Gordon was still driving, that he was taking her to some out-of-the-way location. Taylor was terrified, but unharmed.

She *had* to be.

Hadman had called Alison Kincaid in for questioning after all. He'd kept his request nice and calm, just asking for her cooperation in the police investigation of the Berkley homicides, and offering to send a patrol car over to pick her up. She'd been flustered, but amenable. Now she was in the waiting room, sipping coffee and waiting to be interviewed.

Reed understood Hadman's concerns. If he hadn't been so emotionally involved, he would have thought of them himself. Alison was as naive as a babe in the woods. But that very naïveté might just bite them in the ass. Left to her own devices, she could inadvertently tip Gordon off. If he called her from the road, just to keep things with his new bride nice and copacetic, and she mentioned Reed's phone call, they were screwed. The last thing they wanted was for Gordon to realize they were onto him. Right now, he felt omnipotent, safe, and free of suspicion. That false sense of security would lower his guard, make him behave in ways he wouldn't if he had the slightest idea that the cops knew he and Dennis Kincaid were one and the same person. Security would fuel his megalomania. He'd be in no major hurry to finish things off. He'd want to boast to Taylor about his accomplishments, and savor his ultimate sexual gratification. It would give him the sense of power and domination he craved.

That would buy Taylor time. Terrorized time, but time nonetheless.

The question was, *where* were they going? Where had Gordon staged this final encounter?

It could be anywhere. Anywhere remote, where he could ensure himself privacy and freedom from interruptions.

Douglas's East Hampton estate? No. Too risky. The place was padlocked and well patrolled by local police. Gordon was too smart to walk into such an obvious trap.

Upstate was a possibility. The drive was long and vacant land was plentiful. On the other hand, wherever Gordon had been living these past months was another possibility.

Then again, those places were not necessarily mutually exclusive. Alison didn't have a clue where her husband had lived prior to their marriage. That line he'd given her about skipping from dump to dump was a pile of crap. No way in hell would Gordon live in a dump. He just didn't want to give her his address.

He'd given a fake one at his place of business.

Reed had insisted on being the one to contact WVNY. Police business or not, the radio-station employees weren't just Taylor's coworkers, they were her friends. They'd do everything they could to help—including supplying any personal information they had on Dennis Kincaid.

"Forget the call," Hadman had advised him. "I'll just send over a couple of detectives to talk to the staff and search Kincaid's workstation."

"Send whoever you want," Reed had returned, already punching in Taylor's private number at WVNY. "But while you're getting your warrant and dispatching cops, I'm talking to Taylor's producer and program manager. They know who I am. They'll talk to me. And they might know something, or have a better idea about where to look than anyone else at the station."

He'd scarcely heard Hadman's mutter of agreement.

Laura had answered Taylor's line. She put Reed through to Kevin the minute he said the word "emergency."

Kevin picked up two seconds later. "What's wrong?"

As briefly and unemotionally as possible, Reed filled him in.

"Shit." Kevin croaked out the word. "All this time, he's been sitting right next to me and . . ." With a hard swallow, Taylor's producer brought himself under control. "What can I do to help?"

Reed told him.

A minute later, Kevin was ripping Dennis's work area apart, inch by inch, searching for any leads that could help. On the list of things for him to search for were notations of any kind on Dennis's calendar, especially for the month of March. Also, Post-its, or notes-to-self, with any writing on them, even indistinguishable. The cops would decipher whatever Kevin couldn't. As for personal items, Reed instructed Kevin to search for brochures on homes in upstate New York, real-estate ads for country cottages, even printouts of routes or driving directions. *Anything.*

While he ransacked the place, Kevin transferred Reed through to Jack, who, upon hearing the story, went to human resources and dissected Dennis's job application line by line. The address: False. He'd given his cell number as his home phone. As for his emergency-contact information, it had been left blank—again, up through last week. After that, he'd updated the information with Alison's home address and phone number. He'd listed her name as Ally Kincaid, and her relationship to him as wife.

Wife. The woman didn't know a damned thing about him. Not where he lived. Not how he thought. Not who he was.

Christ. It was one dead end after another.

Reed was about to go insane, when Olin's phone rang. He grabbed it, barked some questions into the receiver, then, two minutes later, slammed it down and rose. "We've got a solid lead. An off-duty cop from Queens just spotted a silver minivan—a newer-model Dodge Grand Caravan Sport— with two occupants, a man and a woman. The occupants match the descriptions of Taylor and Dennis. The cop who called in the lead was on his way home. He lives in Ronkonkoma. He was just pulling off the LIE at Exit Sixty when the minivan zoomed by him on the highway, headed east."

"East Hampton," Jonathan concluded, his head coming up. "Gordon must be taking her to Douglas's estate after all."

"I don't buy it." Having come in to hear what the lead was about, Mitch shook his head. "You're talking about a secured piece of property. It's regularly patrolled by the East Hampton police. If some strange guy and a panic-stricken woman showed up there for no ostensible reason, they'd be grabbed in a minute. Gordon's just too damned smart to take that kind of risk." A frown. "On the other hand, he's obviously headed toward the Hamptons. Which means he's picked out a different, equally precise, location. Somewhere secluded and familiar. Any ideas?"

Secluded. Familiar. Precise.

Reed's wheels were turning, reviewing all the things Taylor had explained to him over the past week. Gordon was a sick man, fighting demons too deeply ingrained to eliminate. He was obsessed with the need for revenge, for resolution. Adrienne had left indelible scars on his life. In some sick way, he'd purged himself by murdering her. He saw her in every redhead he pursued, including Taylor. Possessing them. Killing them. All out of the need to obliterate Adrienne.

Full circle. That's what he sought.

And there was only one place he could find it.

"The yacht," Reed exclaimed, leaping to his feet. "He's taking her to Douglas's yacht. He wants to finish this where it began."

"Yes," Mitch agreed definitively. "Now *that* makes sense. Especially because this time the roles will be reversed. Gordon will be the domina-tor, not the dominated."

"Where is it?" Reed demanded, grabbing Jonathan's shoulders. "Where's Douglas's yacht docked?"

Not a heartbeat of hesitation. "At the Sag Harbor Yacht Club."

"Bingo. It's winter. The yacht club will be deserted." Hadman reached for the phone. "I'll contact the Suffolk County Police Department in Yaphank. They'll call the unit in Sag Harbor. The local guys can have men on the scene in minutes."

"You want them to close in on Mallory?" Olin asked, sounding du-bious.

His partner's answer was the one he'd expected. "No."

"Why the hell not?" Reed demanded.

"To begin with, they might show up on the scene before Gordon. If he pulls into the parking lot and sees a bunch of police cars and detec-tives waiting for him, he'll blow out of there like a bat out of hell."

"So tell them to wait. They can jump him after he gets out of the car. And if he beats them there, they'll spot the silver minivan in the parking lot. They can sneak in and storm the yacht."

"Yeah, they could." Hadman frowned. "But the idea doesn't thrill me. Gordon's homicidal and psychotic, and if he knows he's been cornered, he'll become desperate. Not a good combo, considering he doesn't have a goddamned thing to lose. Olin and I are familiar with him, and with this case. The locals aren't. I'd rather be the ones who make the arrest."

Reed did a fine job of reading between the lines. "In other words, the cops out there don't handle too many complicated cases. You're worried that if they screw up, Taylor will pay the price. Gordon will give up the idea of a slow kill, and go for the quick fix, like snapping her neck, the way he did Douglas's."

Hadman stared at the phone, avoiding Reed's gaze. "Look, Weston. The Sag Harbor Police Department is competent. But, yeah, the NYPD deals with more violent crimes. And, like I said, this is our case. So—"

"Just answer me," Reed interrupted.

"Yes. That's what I'm worried about. But if we run out of options, I'll tell them to go for it." Hadman punched in the number of the Suffolk County Police Department. "Hang tough," he told Reed. "We'll meet them there." He signaled Olin with a circular, whirring motion of his hand, his forefinger extended in the air.

Olin responded with a quick nod of his head, then picked up his phone.

"How the hell can we make it in time?" Reed asked, bile rising in his throat.

"It'll be tight," Olin replied. "But Gordon's got some distance to go. Remember, he was fighting rush-hour traffic when he left. It was just before five when he grabbed Taylor. And when he gets off the LIE, he's got local roads to navigate. That means speed limits and traffic lights. The entire trip's bound to take him over three hours. That leaves around forty-five minutes." He, too, punched in a phone number.

"Who are you calling?"

"The NYPD Aviation Unit. They're at Floyd Bennett Field in Brooklyn. They'll dispatch a police helicopter and put it down in Yankee Stadium in under ten minutes. Which is exactly how long it'll take us to drive to the stadium with our siren blaring. The flight to Sag Harbor is about forty-five minutes." Olin shot a quizzical glance at Jonathan. "How big's the yacht-club parking lot?"

"Big," Jonathan confirmed. "The club's one of the largest in the Hamptons. Oceangoing pleasure craft dock there, not just smaller boats and sailboats."

"Good. We'll arrange to put the helicopter down right in the lot. We'll be there an hour from now. Yeah, it's Olin. Nineteenth Precinct," he said into the phone. "We've got a potential rape and homicide we need to intercept." While he was talking he tossed Jonathan a pencil and pad. "Draw me a diagram of where your father's yacht is docked," he hissed. "Also write a description of the boat—size, color, name, anything you can think of."

Rising from behind his desk, Hadman hung up, having alerted the Suffolk County Police Department to the situation. "All set." His gaze shifted to Reed, noting his drawn expression. "Mallory might beat us there by fifteen minutes tops," he said in a gruffly reassuring tone. "After that, he's got to park the minivan and get Taylor onto the yacht. She's a smart woman, Weston. She'll buy herself time."

"Yeah," Reed said grimly. "I hope to God you're right."

Gordon pulled through the main entrance slowly, glancing around as he edged forward. He didn't expect anyone except maybe a few adventurous guys who'd taken their yachts out to go fishing.

The parking lot was practically deserted. Excellent. Just the way he'd planned.

He pulled over to the clubhouse, which was farther away from Bay Street, and closer to the private basin where Douglas's seventy-five-foot yacht was docked.

Flipping off the ignition, he turned toward Taylor, who was staring ahead, glassy-eyed.

"Party time," he announced. He got out of the minivan, walked around to the passenger side, and unbuckled Taylor's seat belt.

She snapped out of her reverie, flinching away from him as he lifted her out of the car and slammed the door. "I can walk," she said.

"Not with your ankles tied you can't."

"Then untie them."

"Nice try. If I do that, you can not only walk, you can run." Carrying her, he headed toward the boat, which was bobbing gracefully on the water. "I'll untie them soon enough—when I need to. In the meantime, I'm doing this for your own good. If you ran, I'd be forced to punish you. You don't want that."

"I don't want *you*," she shot back. "Then again, I've told you that repeatedly."

"I don't believe you. Then again, it doesn't matter. Because *I* want *you*. Last time I wanted you willing. This time, go right ahead and fight. It'll only increase my pleasure and your pain."

God, this couldn't be happening.

She opened her mouth to scream and was stopped with a hard, brutal kiss that made her gag.

"You want to play ugly?" Gordon taunted, icy chips glinting in his eyes. "Fine." He reached into his pocket, pulled out a handkerchief, and stuffed it in her mouth. "Another sound and I'll use the chloroform. Understood?"

She nodded, trying to curb her escalating panic. She scrutinized the area, half praying she'd see someone lurking in the parking lot. But the club was deserted. As for intervention by law enforcement, that was a desperate hope. Even with Reed's prodding, the cops would be searching for Gordon Mallory, not Dennis Kincaid. There was no way they'd make the connection in time.

Douglas's regal yacht loomed just ahead. It was illuminated by the first rays of moonlight, and Taylor winced as she saw the name *Fair Adrienne* printed across its bow.

"My sentiments exactly," Gordon muttered.

He reached the edge of the dock and, doing a careful balancing act, swung Taylor onto the yacht, placing her in a half-sitting position on the main deck. Then he followed, stepping aboard himself.

He squatted down, stared into her eyes. "I'm going to untie you so you can turn around and back down the ladder to the berth deck. I'll be right behind you. Don't try anything stupid."

She nodded. Whatever she planned to try, now was not the time. Nor was the rebellion she'd been displaying the right approach. She had to get past her panic, use her brain. She knew what made Gordon tick. She had to press the right buttons, not those that would make him retaliate, view her even more as Adrienne.

She had to bide her time—and thereby gain some.

She sat very still, leaning forward as Gordon unbound her wrists, then sitting back as he unbound her ankles. She rubbed them vigorously, nearly weeping with relief as pinpoints of pain signaled the return of her blood flow. She shook out her hands, then pointed mutely to her mouth with a questioning look.

"Good girl." Gordon seemed genuinely pleased. "You asked. Yes, you can remove the gag."

Taylor pulled out the handkerchief. Her mouth felt like cardboard. She licked her lips, then began to cough.

"There's water down below. You can have some if you continue to behave."

"Thank you," she managed.

"Time to get moving," Gordon instructed.

It took Taylor three attempts to stand. She succeeded only when Gordon yanked her to her feet.

"Regain your balance," he commanded.

"I will." She wobbled around for a minute or two. More than that would be pressing her luck. "I'm okay now."

"Good." He gestured toward the ladder.

Without argument, Taylor descended, going as slowly as she dared without arousing his suspicions. She reminded herself that she was dealing with a very clever man. Any hint that she was manipulating him and she'd be brutalized.

The berth deck was luxurious, with a kitchen, a sitting area, and Lord knew how many bedrooms.

She found out soon enough.

"The master suite's in the stern," Gordon informed her, stepping off the bottom rung onto the deck. "There are two other bedrooms up front, but they're smaller and not as lavish. I've chosen the master for you."

Taylor fought back her shudder. "May I have that water now?" she asked.

"To put off the inevitable?"

"No. To get the taste of dry linen out of my mouth."

"Fair enough." His eyes narrowed assessingly, and he pointed to the bench in the kitchen. "Sit down over there where I can see you."

"All right." She did as he asked. "I'm not an idiot, Gordon." Her gaze was unwavering as it met his. "I realize who I'm dealing with. It would be pretty stupid on my part to make a dash for the ladder while you're pulling out a bottle of water. I wouldn't make it to the third rung before you grabbed me."

"True." One brow rose. "I'd forgotten what a challenge you are. Intelligent. Subtle. An exciting blend of fineness, sensuality, and psychological manipulation. You're right. I don't think you'd make a break for it now. You'd wait for a better time, one where your chances of success were high. Too bad that time won't come." He walked over and got her the water. "Here."

"I appreciate it." She drank, rested, then drank again. "May I use the bathroom?"

He waved his arm in that direction. "Feel free. There are no portholes in there. Oh, and don't bother looking for your cell phone. It's gone, as is your purse."

No surprise there. She'd hardly expected him to provide her with a link to the outside world.

She used the toilet, then washed her hands and face. Staring at her reflection in the mirror, she barely recognized herself. Her eyes were huge and frightened, with dark circles beneath them. Her face was sheet white, and her hair was a tousled mess. She gazed around the bathroom, willing there to be some hidden vent she could crawl through, some panel in the ceiling she could hoist herself out of in order to reach safety.

She squeezed her eyes shut. Her mind was running wild. She was grasping at absurd straws, and she knew it. But she was alone with a killer. And she was terrified.

Hands balling into fists, she faced the cold, hard facts.

This wasn't a question of buying time. No one knew where she was. This was a question of saving her own life. Because she was the only one who could do it.

Quietly, she opened the medicine cabinet and rummaged through it. No razor. No scissors. Not even a pair of tweezers she could arm herself with. Discouraged, she shut the cabinet door and leaned her elbows against the sink, resting her head in her hands. She couldn't give up. She'd leave the bathroom, return to the kitchen, and check out the rest of the berth deck as unobtrusively as she could, keeping Gordon talking all the while. And, God help her, if it came down to it and he forced her back there, she'd scrutinize the master bedroom. There had to be something, somewhere, she could use as a weapon.

Mentally, she reviewed the self-defense techniques Reed and Mitch had taught her. The whole circling thing wasn't going to work—not in such close quarters. And running? Forget it. Especially once she was backed into the master suite. Escape would be an impossibility. She'd never get past Gordon. Not unless he was physically incapacitated.

Swallowing hard, Taylor accepted the inevitable. The victim was going to have to become the assailant. It was the only way she'd get away. And given Gordon's cunning mind, superior strength, and more advanced martial-arts skills, there was only one interval during which she'd have the upper hand to the point where she could pull it off.

When he got her onto that bed.

He'd be distracted. His physical capabilities and mental focus would be compromised.

That's when she'd act. With or without a weapon. She wait for Gordon to put his filthy hands on her. Then she'd strike like a coiled cobra.

Bile rose in Taylor's throat, and a wave of panic seized her again. How could she do this? How could she survive him touching her? And how could she pull off this whole Superwoman thing? She'd had only a handful of self-defense lessons, and an equal number of practice sessions.

How in God's name could she translate informal workouts into the real thing—saving her own life?

The answer was simple. She had to. Because the alternative was unthinkable.

8:12 P.M.

Reed stared out the window of the NYPD's Bell 206 Jet Ranger, watching the lights of the town below, as if by doing so, he could make them grow closer, make the damned helicopter fly faster.

As it was, the bunch of them were already operating at lightning speed.

The Sag Harbor police had called in a report five minutes ago. They were surrounding the yacht club, waiting for Hadman's instructions. Gordon had just arrived and carried Taylor onto the yacht. Her wrists and ankles were bound, but she seemed alert.

That was then. Reed couldn't bear to think what was going on now.

He slammed a fist against his leg. He felt so goddamned helpless. But he had to have faith in the detectives. Hadman's instincts were good. As for Olin, his time frame had been dead-on from the get-go.

It had taken them eight minutes to get to Yankee Stadium. The pilot had just put down the helicopter when Reed, Mitch, Hadman, and Olin ran across the field to climb in. They'd left Jonathan behind—and not just because the helicopter had seating for only four passengers. The guy was an emotional wreck. He'd be a detriment, not an asset. Even he'd admitted he wasn't sure he could control himself when he first saw Gordon, masquerading as Dennis or not. After everything his brother had put him through, he might just lunge for his throat.

For Taylor's sake, for everyone's sake, Jonathan had gone back to his apartment, where he was glued to his cell phone. When there was news to tell, he'd hear it.

According to the pilot's last announcement—which had come

a minute and a half ago—they'd be landing in nine minutes flat. Olin had been right-on again. The Sag Harbor cops were poised and waiting. So far, Hadman had them on hold.

Reed prayed that was the right decision.

"This is interesting," Olin commented, glancing at the report that had been handed to him as he ran out the precinct door.

"What is?" Reed asked numbly.

"Our background check on Dennis Kincaid. The real Dennis Kincaid died fifteen years ago in a little town in Nebraska. No family. No ties. Gordon picked a winner. He must have dug up Kincaid's information from old copies of local newspaper obituaries. Small towns tend to put lots of personal data in their obits. You know, the deceased's survivors— or lack thereof—his age, date of birth, cause of death, parents' names— the works. Once he dug up Kincaid's mother's maiden name, he'd have everything he needed to request a duplicate birth certificate, money order enclosed. He probably got himself a hot social-security card and photo ID. With those, he could go to the passport office and get himself a passport. And, voilà, a whole new Dennis Kincaid. All he had to do was have some new photos taken after his surgery, and he'd be good to go. Or return, in this case."

"Great," Reed muttered. He was only half listening.

"After he got back to the U.S. from Thailand—which was in November, incidentally, not September—our friend Dennis Kincaid hit the Midwest, where he did a few monthlong radio stints to build his résumé. And guess what? No record of any head-on auto collision in either of the towns he worked in. Not in September, October, *or* November. In fact, there was no accident at all involving a Dennis Kincaid. The funny thing is, he doesn't even have a driver's license. No roots, no credit cards, no friends. Gee, it's like he wasn't planning on staying in the country."

"Surprise, surprise," Hadman replied in disgust. "Gordon planned on waiting for Jonathan to be convicted, for the Berkley estates to make their way through probate, and for Alison to inherit the whole kit and caboodle. Then I bet they'd be leaving the country ASAP."

"*They?*" Olin arched a dubious brow. "More likely, *he*. At that point, *Ally* would become expendable."

"True. But, hey, let's give the guy the benefit of the doubt. Maybe he planned on giving his wife a belated honeymoon before he bumped her off somewhere halfway around the world. You know—a great international tour as a final send-off."

"It touches the heart."

Reed wasn't amused by the banter. In fact, he was about to jump out of his skin, when he felt the helicopter start to descend. "We're landing." He was already unbuckling his seat belt.

"Get ready to jump when the chopper touches down," Hadman instructed. "The pilot's been told to get outta here ASAP so if Mallory hears the whirring sound, he'll figure it's a passing aircraft on its way to the airport."

"I doubt he'll be listening," Reed responded grimly, watching the docks come into view. "His mind's on other things—like killing Taylor."

CHAPTER 37

8:31 P.M.

FAIR ADRIENNE

SAG HARBOR YACHT CLUB

THE moment of truth had arrived.

Taylor saw it in Gordon's eyes as they walked back into the kitchen area, having returned from a minitour of Douglas's yacht.

The tour had been a mistake. Taylor knew it the moment Gordon announced he was conducting it. And if it hadn't been essential for her to check out the boat for something to arm herself with, she would have stopped his walk down memory lane before it began. She knew what it would do to his state of mind, coming face-to-face with his past, reliving specific moments when Adrienne had degraded and exploited him.

And she'd been right. He was now angrier, more hostile—in a worse place psychologically than he had been before.

This wasn't going to play out well.

Gordon grabbed a bottle of Scotch from the liquor cabinet and poured himself a double.

He downed it in a few deep swallows, then slammed the old-fashioned glass on the counter.

"I'm not drunk," he informed Taylor, his stare hard, filled with rage. "I'm in top form, mentally and physically. My reflexes are well trained and fast. So don't get your hopes up."

"I'm not. I'm thinking."

"About what?"

"About what she did to you."

"How touching," he mocked.

"Look, Gordon, I'm not Adrienne," Taylor stated simply. "And, whether or not you believe it, I'm sickened by how she abused and used you."

"Are you?" One dark brow rose. "Sickened enough to understand?"

He was testing her. She knew it. And she wouldn't give in to the urge to lie. Because that's just what he expected.

"No. The crimes you committed turn my stomach. You killed innocent people. One of those people was my cousin and my very best friend. She was all I had. So if you're asking if I forgive you, the answer is no. But if you're asking if I'd deny you the help you need, the answer to that is no as well."

Gordon tipped his empty glass to her in tribute. "I keep forgetting how refreshingly honest you are—most of the time. When you're not involved in some self-serving pretense. Like playing the unspoiled flower who's really rolling around in bed with Reed Weston. Or the frightened victim who shut me down by taking off on a supposed much-needed vacation."

"Neither of those was a pretense." Taylor came right back at him. "I *was* a frightened victim. Your stalking scared the hell out of me. I went to Palm Beach as a last resort. As for the unspoiled-flower image, it was all in your mind, as was your assumption that I was saving myself for you. My relationship with Reed is real, not a charade."

"It's also over," Gordon snapped.

He whipped out a handkerchief, wiping his fingerprints off the bottle of Scotch and the glass, then setting them back on the counter.

"What about Ally?" Taylor blurted out the first thing that came to mind as she tried to stall him. "If you were so obsessed with me, why did you marry her? Or does she even exist?"

Those questions seemed to amuse Gordon, and he paused for a moment, that smug gleam back in his eyes. "You haven't figured out that part yet, have you? Ally very much exists. She's a Berkley. The last remaining one, in fact. As for why I married her, that was a matter of necessity. After Jonathan gets his life sentence or lethal injection, she inherits everything. At which point, so do I."

Of course. Taylor blinked in realization. That's what Gordon had meant in the car, when he'd said he'd become Dennis Kincaid to get everything that was coming to him when Jonathan was convicted of double homicide.

The man was deranged. But he was also brilliant. And if he pulled off this scheme of his, Taylor doubted Ally would be around much past the trial and the disbursement of her inheritance.

"You're impressed," Gordon observed.

"Speechless is more like it."

"What can I say? I'm a genius." He walked over, plucking the empty Poland Spring bottle from her hand and tossing it on the bench. "No need to wipe the prints off that one. I'll recycle it on my way out, like the good citizen I am." He seized Taylor's chin in a cruel grip, forced her gaze up to meet his. "By the way, *now* you're stalling. I know it. And I don't like it."

She winced at the pain, nodding mutely at his accusation. She was treading in uncharted waters now. There were no instructions for what lay ahead. She'd kept Gordon talking as long as she could. But his need to vent and to gloat had been satisfied. Now he had other, more pressing, needs in mind. Sexual gratification. Domination. Vengeance. And finality.

"It's time," he announced, as calmly as if he were telling her dinner was about to be served. "Shall we adjourn to the bedroom?"

Taylor scarcely heard him. Her gaze had darted to the counter, and was now focused on the nearly full bottle of Scotch sitting there. That might be the weapon she needed—if she could break away from him long enough to get her hands on it.

That wasn't in the cards right now, not with him backing her toward the master suite.

"You're shaking," he observed. "Is that fear or passion?"

"Fear," she answered frankly.

"Because you don't want me," he taunted.

"No. Because I don't want to die."

One brow rose. "More candor. Brava." He continued pushing her toward the bedroom, his weight solid and unrelenting.

Taylor gripped the door frame, her breath coming in quick, frightened pants. "Would begging help?" she asked in desperation. "I'm sure that's something Adrienne would never do."

"You're right. It wasn't her style." A muscle worked in Gordon's jaw.

"It's not really yours either. But I'd love to hear you do it. As for whether it would help, I assume you mean, would it convince me to spare your life? The answer is no. This is more complex than just ridding myself of Adrienne. I need to rid myself of you as well. You're in my blood. I can't have that. So I have to have *you*. And then I have to snuff you out, just as I did her."

His hands slid beneath her sweater, gliding up her back to unhook her bra. "Back to the idea of your begging. It's a tempting offer. I think I'd enjoy hearing you do it. In fact, I want to hear it twice. Once, when you're frantic for me to bring you to climax, and once, when I'm ending your life. That might help me wipe out the image of Reed Weston taking what's mine—even after I ordered you to sleep alone. You infuriated and disappointed me, Taylor. I assumed you were different. You're not."

Taylor could barely hear him over the pounding of her heart. She averted her face as he bent to kiss her, flinching in pain as his mouth moved down her throat in hard, bruising motions—her punishment for turning away. She prayed to God she'd find the strength to do what she had to. She couldn't give in to the urge to fight him. Not yet. Retaliation would mean torture for her, and a surge of adrenaline for him as he re-asserted his dominance. She had to go along with this sick delusion of his. Make it seem as close to a mutual sexual encounter as she could. Play into his desire for her until he was really into it.

And when his mind was dulled by his hormones, *then* she'd attack.

Gordon shoved her the rest of the distance toward the bed, toppling her onto it. "Stay there," he ordered, shedding his clothes in a few quick, practiced motions—including the shoes with the lifts. Then he popped out his contact lenses. "See? It's really me."

He held out his arms and pivoted around so she could admire his naked body. Then he came down over her, bracing one arm on either side of her and effectively pinning her to the bed. "Actually, it's an even better me. Maybe not my face. That needs work. It'll get done when all this is over. But my body is harder, more controlled, than you remember it." He slipped his hands under her sweater and bra, cupped her breasts. "Then again, last time you only got a brief taste. This time, you'll get the full effect. Who knows? You might just thank Adrienne after all."

Taylor forced her mind to disconnect from her body. She had to, in order to make this work. "What happens afterward?" she managed.

He paused, propped himself on one elbow. "After what?"

"After I'm dead."

A shrug. "Just what you'd expect. Dennis Kincaid will continue on at WVNY. He'll be assigned to a new show, of course, since Taylor Halstead will have vanished into thin air. He'll feel terrible about it. But he'll survive. After all, he's a newlywed. So he'll pull himself together, and blend in with the woodwork until Jonathan's convicted and Ally's named sole beneficiary. Then Mr. and Mrs. Dennis Kincaid will get wanderlust and bid our good-byes, taking off for parts unknown."

"That much I guessed. I meant, what happens to *me?*" Taylor's voice quavered. "What are you going to do with my . . . with me?"

He looked intrigued. "You want the details?"

"I *want* to live. But, since that's not an option, yes. I want the details."

Another shrug. "Suit yourself. I'll dump your body in shark-infested waters off the coast. Not too close to here, and not too close to Montauk, where my yacht exploded. No pattern that could link my previous crimes to your death, just in case a piece of you surfaces before the sharks finish you off. I doubt it will. They're pretty quick. But things happen. So if any part of you does wash up on shore, it'll be because your mystery stalker is a rank amateur, and did a sloppy job. Enough details for you?"

"More than enough." Taylor forced herself to sound vulnerable rather than repulsed. "I guess I'm not as stoic as I thought."

"Maybe not." He buried his lips in her throat, his hands curving around her breasts. "But you're even more of a turn-on than I remembered." His thumb rasped across one nipple—hard.

Taylor fought the urge to recoil—at the pain, at the very idea of his hands on her. *Detach, Taylor,* she ordered herself. *Be a psychologist, not a victim. Don't let him win. Think.*

Her mind took over.

Gordon wanted her. Not just to violate. And not just to add as another redheaded notch on the side of his bed. What made her different from all the other women he'd had since Adrienne, poor Steph included, was that she was a challenge. And Gordon loved a challenge. It fired his blood and his intellect.

She represented a worthy opponent. A woman who didn't fall at his feet like all his previous Adrienne substitutes. He wanted to win her over, to make her want him as much as he did her. He wanted her so aroused that she'd beg for her climax, beg for him. If he couldn't have her that way, he wanted her fighting. Fueling his rage with her struggles.

Last time, she'd given him that. Big mistake. Steph and the others had bored him. Different kind of mistake.

She could make neither. Nor could she just lie there, placid and unresponsive. That would drive him over the edge.

She needed to offer him something more. A challenge that piqued his mind as well as aroused his body.

So be it.

As if to confirm her thought process, Gordon shifted irritably, his thumb scraping her other nipple, this motion even rougher than the last. "Relax," he ordered. "You're stiff as a board. Stop worrying about afterward. Afterward doesn't matter. You'll be dead. You won't feel anything. So put it out of your mind. Just relish these last wisps of sheer physical pleasure."

Last wisps . . . wisps . . .

Now, *that* triggered a memory. An ugly memory. But a hell of a good start.

"Smoke," Taylor murmured.

"Hmm?"

"That's what you called me the last time. You said I was smoke. Elusive. Intangible. Hard to capture."

His hand paused. "You remembered. I'm flattered."

She felt his touch gentle. Her reward, no doubt.

That was the lead-in she'd been looking for.

She sucked in her breath. "Gordon—wait." She flattened her palms against his shoulders. "Please."

He raised his head slightly. "Why? More stalling?"

"No. More candor." She licked her lips with the tip of her tongue. "Look, I get it. I know what the end result's going to be. But may I at least have some say about what happens in between?"

He looked a little surprised, and a lot wary. "Go on."

"You say you want me. That I'm in your blood. You also keep telling me what an amazing lover you are. Well, if I'm about to die, I'd like to do it with minimum pain preceded by maximum pleasure. Would you consider going that route rather than a brutal one?"

His eyes narrowed. "What kind of game are you playing?"

"No game. Just two last requests."

"I'm listening."

"First, I'm asking if this can be mutual instead of rape. I'd like you to make this good for me. Use your skill rather than your strength."

"And the second request?"

"I'm asking that you kill me as quickly and painlessly as possible. You had an amazing degree of control last September. You used just enough pressure on my windpipe to make me black out, but not die. Since then, you've had advanced martial-arts training. What I'm asking would be a piece of cake for you—if you chose to do it. I'm hoping you will. In fact, I'm begging you. Please."

There was that cutting stare she remembered all too well—a stare that sent prickles of fear up her spine. He was assessing her, deciding what she hoped to gain, and what he stood to lose.

Please, she prayed. *Let it have worked.* She'd pulled out all the stops. Played into his ego. His intellect. His lust. His craving to dominate.

"Let me get this straight," he said at last. "You're planning to respond to me—just like that?"

"No, not just like that." Taylor didn't have to fake the tears that filled her eyes and trickled down her cheeks. "Right now, I can't imagine responding at all. Right now, all I can think about is suffering and dying. So I guess it's up to you."

A subtle gleam. "Throwing down the gauntlet, are we?"

"If that's the way you want to view it, yes."

"How do *you* view it?"

As a last-ditch effort to save my life, she thought silently. "As a plea for leniency and a final indulgence."

"A plea. You're begging me to seduce you?"

"I'm begging you to try."

Gordon smiled, an ugly, triumphant smile that was so him, Taylor could no longer see a shred of Dennis, different face or not. "If I try, I'll succeed. As long as you go with it."

She gave a shaky nod, her eyes sliding shut. She forced her muscles to relax, to sink into the bed. She wanted her body language to convey that she was prepared to be won over.

He bent down, capturing her tears with his tongue. "Now *this* is the way it should be. You. Me. Heaven and hell. Together for one perfect, frozen moment in time. All I dreamed of. The fitting end we both deserve." He covered her mouth with his, coaxing her lips apart.

She kept her mind and body separate. Her mind watched, dictated her movements. And her body complied.

Gradually. She gave in to him gradually. Anything less would set him off. Anything more would arouse his suspicions.

He kept kissing her, deepening the kisses until she could feel him shuddering with desire, his erection throbbing against her belly. But he made no move to tear off her clothes and thrust into her. He was exercising the control he'd gloated about.

Good. Very good. The longer she was dressed, the better.

She didn't give a damn about her modesty.

She gave a damn about her shoes.

He was really into it now, muttering hot phrases against her skin, kissing her neck, her throat, her mouth. She returned his kisses, first tentatively, then with a kind of hopeful desperation, like the survivor of a shipwreck who'd spotted a life preserver.

"Put your arms around me," he commanded, his voice rough with passion.

Taylor wanted to weep with joy. She obeyed, somehow managing to curtail her enthusiasm as her arms glided around his neck.

Her hands were free.

She sighed into his open mouth, her breath eliciting another hard shudder. His lust was definitely running the show here, all his mental faculties going into maintaining his self-restraint and the careful manipulation of his body. His hands slid down her arms, and for one horrifying moment, Taylor was afraid he planned to hold his grip. But his palms drifted down to her shoulders, his fingers threading through her hair.

He was definitely far gone enough.

Now she had to get him to shift positions so she could have the access she needed.

Her hands unlocked from around his neck, gliding down to explore his shoulders, then easing around front and pausing, as if wrestling with the desire to touch him more.

Sure enough, he shifted his weight to his knees, sitting up and leaning back on his haunches. "Go ahead," he urged thickly, grasping her wrists and bringing them around to his chest. "Touch me."

She licked her lips, which were damp and swollen from his kisses, and kept them parted as if she were transfixed. She didn't have to feign the trembling. She was shaking like a leaf, knowing what lay just ahead.

She'd have one chance. *One*. If she screwed it up, the pain he'd inflict on her would make death seem like sanctuary.

No. She couldn't let her mind go there. She had to channel all her mental energies into what she had to accomplish—and how.

She moved her palms over Gordon's chest, down his torso, wishing like hell he'd let go of her wrists instead of holding them and guiding them along.

Time to take a risk.

She wriggled one hand free, tracing a forefinger down his abdomen. Her gaze dropped to his erection, then lifted to meet his, a questioning look on her face.

His eyes were glazed, wild with anticipation. "Everywhere," he assured her. "Touch me everywhere. Especially there."

He released her other wrist on his own, his entire body quivering. He was totally lost in the moment, his penis jutting toward her as he waited . . . waited . . .

Taylor acted in the blink of an eye.

Fingers locked together, knuckles slightly bent, she slashed her fingernails across his eyes in a blinding finger rake that would have made Mitch proud.

Gordon screamed out in pain, squeezing his eyes shut as he instinctively reached for them. Instantly, Taylor cupped each of her palms and clapped them against his ears in a forceful ear slap she could actually feel vibrate through him.

He groaned, weaving from side to side, his equilibrium thrown off by the blow. Taylor followed through with the motion of her hands, shoving at his head and using the force of her legs to roll him off her.

She was on her feet before he recovered, and making a break for the door.

She was across the berth deck and on the first rung of the ladder, when he grabbed her from behind. "You fucking bitch," he snarled, yanking her down and dragging her back toward the bedroom. "You have no idea what that's going to cost you."

Nor did she intend to find out.

With all her might, she jabbed her elbow into his solar plexus, then crashed the heel of her shoe down on his bare instep.

He half grunted, half cried out, loosening his grip on her as he bent forward.

Perfect.

She slammed her elbow up and into his nose, hearing the cracking sound as it made contact.

He roared with pain, grabbing his face and releasing her simultaneously.

She whirled around, slamming a hammer fist into his naked groin.

With a strangled sound, he fell onto his knees, cursing and clutching himself as he rocked back and forth, doubled over in agonizing pain.

The kitchen counter was two strides away. Taylor took them. She seized the Scotch bottle, rushed back, and crashed it down over Gordon's head with every ounce of strength she possessed.

He crumpled silently on the wooden floor.

She didn't wait to see if he was stunned, unconscious, or dead. She just took off.

She made it up the ladder and was scrambling onto the main deck when a pair of hands seized her from above.

"No!" she screamed. Her arms were trapped. Her legs weren't yet firmly planted. She didn't stop to think. She just used the only weapon she had left.

Her head.

Tilting it down, she bent her knees and thrust upward, slamming the top of her head into her assailant's face. She didn't have time to focus on the point of impact, the way Reed had taught her, nor did she have the luxury of grabbing her target's arms to increase the force of her blow. But she connected well enough for him to bark out a protest and release her.

"Jesus Christ." The target, Detective Hadman, clutched his forehead and weaved a bit. "Lady, are you nuts? We're the good guys."

"Detective Hadman?" Taylor squeaked out.

"Where's Mallory?" Detective Olin stepped past his partner, pistol raised.

"Down there." Taylor pointed. "I don't know if he's conscious."

Olin's lips twitched. "I'll check." He glanced at Hadman. "You coming?"

"Yeah." Hadman's pistol was raised, too. With his other hand, he massaged the bridge of his nose. "If this is what she does to cops, I can't wait to see how she pulverized that son of a bitch downstairs."

Taylor was still trying to process the fact that Detectives Hadman and Olin were here, along with a local backup team who'd boarded the yacht behind them. Mitch was there, too, and Reed was shoving cops out of the way so he could leap onto the yacht and get to her.

"Taylor." He grabbed her, assessing her dazed, rumpled state with excruciating torment. He himself looked like he'd aged ten years and hadn't slept one night of them. "God, sweetheart, are you all right?"

"I—I think so."

"Is *she* all right?" Hadman echoed as he hoisted himself back up the ladder. "I had a migraine to begin with. Your girlfriend just turned it into a concussion." The quick wink he shot Taylor belied his disgruntled tone. "Nice work."

Turning, he leaned down, helping Olin drag a half-conscious, fully naked Gordon Mallory up to the main deck.

"Stop bitching," Olin advised his partner. "It could be worse. Take a look at *this* guy."

"I did. Why do you think I'm being so nice to her?"

In between banter, they hauled a handcuffed Gordon to his feet. Scotch was dripping down his body, and pieces of glass were clinging to his hair and shoulders. He struggled to right himself, visibly disoriented by the blow to his head. His eyes, still tearing from Taylor's finger rake, were scratched and bleeding. His nose was bloody, too, and swollen. He was hunched over, limping, and totally out of it.

Reed and Mitch both stared.

"Hey, Taylor," Olin called over his shoulder, shoving Gordon across the deck and toward the waiting squad car. "Forget the family counseling. Join the force. The NYPD needs you."

"I . . ." Taylor's voice was quavering so badly she could barely speak. What was unfolding around her still wasn't sinking in. Not fully.

She blinked at Reed. "How did you find me? How did you get here in time? How did you know that Dennis and Gordon were the same person?

How—" She broke off, burst into tears, and flung herself into Reed's arms. "I can't believe you're really here."

"We're here. *I'm* here." He held her against him, his lips in her hair, cradling her in his arms like a precious treasure. He frowned, feeling the tremors shuddering through her body. "Did that filthy bastard hurt you?"

She shook her head. "I stopped him, thanks to what you and Mitch taught me."

"Yeah, basic self-defense techniques come in very handy," Mitch agreed, coming up to stand beside them. "Martial-arts types never expect them, certainly not from the average person. So they never know what hit them." He stared after Gordon's retreating figure. "Judging from the shape he's in, I see you used my finger rakes and ear slaps."

Taylor responded to his levity, smiling through her tears. "I went for those first."

Reed wasn't smiling. "You had no choice. He trapped you in bed."

"For a little while," Taylor amended. "Till I got away." She wasn't ready to get into details—not yet. The experience was still too raw. "I had to play a few head games to get him off guard. It was like choreographing a repulsive ballet. Anyway, once he got into his part, I raked and slapped, then ran. I got only as far as the ladder before he grabbed me from behind." She flinched at the memory.

"He must have been ripping mad," Reed surmised. "The guy's certifiable. You took a huge risk."

"I had no choice."

"I know." A hard swallow. "How did you get away the second time?"

"That I owe to you." Taylor tilted up her chin to meet Reed's gaze. Her lashes were spiky with tears. "Remember that acronym you taught me during our self-defense lessons? It kept playing in my head, over and over, like a litany. And when Gordon dragged me off that ladder, when I felt the violence rippling through him, I just used it. I didn't let myself think. I just acted. It was that, or die."

"What acronym?" Mitch demanded.

"Reed taught me to sing."

"To sing? Why—are you tone-deaf? Were you hoping to kill him with your voice?"

"No." Taylor laughed. "S-I-N-G." She spelled it out for him, letter by letter, then elaborated on each one. "Solar plexus. Instep. Nose. Groin. It worked wonders. So did a bottle of Scotch over the head."

"Very catchy. I'll have to remember that," Mitch noted.

"You never answered my questions," she reminded them. Shock was setting in, as was the cold, and her teeth started chattering. She folded her arms across her breasts.

"I'll answer them all." Reed yanked off his coat and wrapped it around her. She saw the fury and pain that flashed across his face when he realized her bra was unfastened. He pulled his overcoat tightly around her, then eased her against him. "Later. Right now, I'm getting you to a hotel. You need sleep."

"Good idea," Mitch agreed. "I'm heading back to the city with Hadman and Olin. They're thrilled. I'm springing for a car." He grinned. "Somehow, I don't think you two will be needing me anymore tonight."

"No, we're fine," Reed assured him. "I'm tucking Taylor in bed, then calling all the worried people back home. Kevin was pretty freaked out. And Jonathan's a wreck."

"Poor Jonathan," Taylor murmured. "This must have been such a shock for him."

"He's free now. He'll also be in therapy, thanks to your referral. In time, he'll heal. We all will." Reed turned to Mitch. "Hey. Before you go, are you doing anything for Easter?"

"Nothing special. Why?"

"My whole family's getting together at my parents's place in Vermont. Rob will be there. You can take out that piece of hide you've been waiting to collect."

A chuckle. "Yeah, but then you'll owe him."

"No problem. I'll be paying him back in spades." Reed glanced at Taylor. "Not just him, but my whole family. I've got the perfect gift for them."

"And what would that be?" Mitch inquired. "Or should I say, who?"

"Who *and* what. The 'who' is Taylor. The 'what,' if I have my way, is an announcement."

"Is that announcement what I think it is?"

"You won't know until you leave us alone so I can ask my question and get my answer."

"I'm gone." Mitch gave a quick wave of his hand. "Good night. And good luck. See you in the Big Apple. And count me in for Easter."

Taylor was staring at Reed when he turned back to her. "Reed . . ."

"Hotel first," he interrupted. "Then a hot bath. Then a glass of Merlot and a cozy fire. And then—"

"Yes," she broke in to reply. "The answer to your question is yes."

EPILOGUE

APRIL 20, EASTER SUNDAY

5:15 P.M.

NEWFANE, VERMONT

REED was right.

It was a good thing the Weston farmhouse was made out of stone. Otherwise, it definitely would have burst that weekend.

By the time a full count was taken, there were eighteen adults, nine kids, one baby-in-waiting, two chocolate labs, one beagle, an orange tabby, her six kittens, an albino ferret, three gerbils, two acrobatic turtles, and a bunny.

Taylor had never seen such chaos in her life. The dinner table alone was nearly caving in from the weight of the food and the people leaning over one another to reach for it.

The kids, having grown bored by food and conversation, were now running around, playing a variety of games. The pets were barking, me-owing, racing around wheels in their cages, doing backflips in their water tanks, or dashing along with their respective owners as they burst in and out of the house.

The adults were drinking coffee, talking a mile a minute to catch up with one another's lives—and hissing out whispered bets over who'd be settling down first, Rob or Mitch. Both guys had brought their girlfriends along, and both those girlfriends were now in the powder rooms freshen-ing up.

"The pressure's on, Rob," his sister Meredith teased. "Now that Reed's taken, you're it. The loner in the hot seat."

"Real cute." He patted Meredith's very pregnant belly. "Have an-other doughnut. My newest niece or nephew is starved. Make sure your mouth's full when Jen comes out of the bathroom. She doesn't need en-couragement. She's already giving me hints."

"So take them." With a broad grin, Meredith helped herself to a frosted doughnut.

"What about you, Mitch?" Joy, Reed's sister-in-law, inquired across the table. "Pam seems like a sweetheart."

"She is. But I'm waiting for Rob to go first."

A collective chuckle rumbled through the room.

"Let's get back to the center-stage couple of the weekend," Reed's oldest sister, Lisa, urged, getting up to walk around the table and squat down next to Taylor. "Now that the initial hysteria has died down, may I see your ring up close?"

"Of course." Dutifully, Taylor held out her left hand for the umpteenth time since Reed had made their announcement yesterday.

"It's gorgeous." Lisa admired the glistening square-cut diamond. "Re-ally gorgeous." She turned to Reed. "My compliments. A surprise engage-ment. A beautiful ring. A terrific woman. *And* a brand-new law firm, one that will bring out the best in you. You hit the jackpot across the board." She squeezed Taylor's hand. "Especially with Taylor."

"I think so, too," Reed agreed.

"Have you thought about where you're having the wedding, and when?" his sister Shannon asked Taylor across the table.

Taylor gave a helpless shrug. "I'm open to suggestions. I haven't had a chance to think. It's been crazy."

"Before we open up the floor to suggestions, there are ground rules," Reed announced. "*Where* we have the wedding is up for grabs. *When* isn't." He draped an arm around Taylor's shoulders. "We're getting married as soon as possible."

"I don't blame you." Reed's father's voice was serious, laced with com-passion. "After all Taylor's been through, she deserves some happiness."

"And some family," his mother added gently. "I'm so terribly sorry about your cousin."

"Thank you." Taylor still felt the pain of loss when she discussed Steph, but the horrible gripping emptiness had diminished. "I miss her."

A nostalgic smile. "But I know she's looking down at me and grinning ear to ear. She always said I was destined for a big family."

"And a hottie for a husband," Reed reminded her. "Don't forget that part."

Rob groaned. "God, what an ego."

Everyone laughed.

"I have a suggestion," Reed's mother offered. "Unless the trip is too much for your guests, why not get married here? We've got thirty acres. I'm sure that's larger than any catering hall. As for when, how about June? It's not too hot yet. And Vermont is beautiful in the late spring. The flowers are in bloom. The trees are full and green. Of course I'm biased."

"That's a great idea!" Meredith burst out. "The baby will be here by then, so we can fly up. Derek wasn't too crazy about the four-day drive; the boys spent most of it bickering."

"It *is* a great idea," Lisa agreed. "We can set up a couple of tents on the grounds, in case it rains. But it won't. It'll be beautiful. We'll have the ceremony in the garden, and the reception across the entire backyard, facing northwest, so there's a stunning view of the mountains."

Shannon snapped her fingers. "I just thought of something. I know an amazing photographer. David Lodge. He grew up here. He moved out to Denver for a couple of years, and Roger and I got together with him and his wife. But he missed New England. He moved back to Vermont last year." She started rummaging through her purse. "I have his new card in here somewhere. He takes exquisite outdoor shots. You remember him, don't you Reed."

"Yes," Reed began. "But—"

"Grandma, you'll have to do the centerpieces." Shari—Lisa and Bill's daughter, who was twelve going on twenty—interrupted. Her ears had perked up at the word "wedding," and she'd rushed over to take part in the conversation. "You can sculpt a little vase for each table. We'll fill them with flowers."

"I'd love to." Her grandmother beamed.

"What about the overnight guests?" Reed's father asked with a frown. "That could be a problem. As it is, the farmhouse is overcrowded when the whole family's here."

"Not to worry," Reed's sister-in-law Jill jumped in. "The accommodations are on us. Mark and I have a ski lodge, remember? Right over the border in New Hampshire. It's just a short drive from here. And it's off-season, so we don't have any advance bookings yet. We can reserve the whole place, and put up as many guests as you need us to." A teasing twinkle lit her eyes. "Including the newlyweds. Need I remind you, Reed, that the VIP suite has an incredible view—perfect for honeymooners."

Reed opened his mouth to reply, but was immediately drowned out.

"You've got a built-in wedding party." Kyle gestured from the table to the shrieking kids racing through the house. "Enough bridesmaids, ushers, flower girls, and ring bearers to fill a room. And that's without whatever close friends you'll want to include."

"I'll cater the desserts." Meredith was already scribbling on a napkin. "You let me know how many guests you're inviting and what your favorite desserts are. Leave the rest to me. Including the wedding cake. I can't wait to design that. As for the food, I'll get in touch with Gourmet Caterers. They're the best in Vermont. I know one of the owners, Joan Carmichael. She'll take care of everything from hors d'oeuvres to entrées."

"What about music?" Joy asked. "We could do a combination of classical and funky. A string quartet for the ceremony and a deejay or live band for the reception. Dignity first, dancing the night away second."

"Great idea," Lisa said. "The kids would love a deejay."

"Yeah, but a live band is great," her husband, Bill, countered. "They can play contemporary stuff for the kids, and fifties, sixties, and seventies stuff for us, so I can get up and strut my stuff."

"And forties tunes for Mom and Dad and their friends," his wife added.

"But no disco," Derek interjected. "To quote the late, great Harry Chapin, 'disco sucks.' Not to mention that inevitably, you get a couple of paunchy, middle-aged guys who've had too much to drink and are convinced they can re-create *Saturday Night Fever.*"

Meredith burst out laughing. "That's quite an image, darling."

"Yes, really." Lisa was grinning, too. "Fine. No disco. And Bill, you're right about a band being more versatile. You and I will make some phone calls."

"I have a name for you," Jill said. "We had two sets of honeymooners at the ski lodge—one in January and one in February—both of whom raved about the music at their weddings. It turned out they had the same band."

"Terrific. That means they're local. I'll call them right away. Hopefully, they're not booked."

"You know," Mark added. "Speaking of our guests, we also had that stationery lady. The one who ended up designing our New Year's invitations. Her samples were incredible. So was her work."

"Mark, you're a genius!" Jill gave him a huge hug. "I forgot all about that. She'd be perfect for the invitations. Ours were simple and clean, but she did everything from traditional to wild."

"Wild?" Lisa frowned. "Not for a wedding. Personally, I prefer—"

"Hey!" Reed cupped his hands over his mouth and bellowed. When that only made a small dent in the noise, he put two fingers in his mouth and let out a long whistle.

That got everyone's attention. They all looked up and blinked, as if suddenly noticing he was there.

"Remember me?" he asked in dry amusement. "I'm the groom. And see this beautiful woman next to me? She's the bride. So, before you sign the contracts and finalize all the arrangements, is it okay if we're consulted? I'd especially like to know how Taylor feels about all this—assuming she hasn't gone into shock. Maybe she wants to get married in Manhattan or in a big church. We love you, and your enthusiasm. But this is *our* wedding." He turned to his fiancée. "Are you in one piece?"

"I'm intact," Taylor assured him. Actually, she was glowing.

"Don't feel pressured by the crowd," Reed advised gently. "They have a tendency to get carried away."

"I don't feel pressured." What Taylor felt was choked up and a little teary. For the first time, she understood what it meant to be part of a family.

It was wonderful.

"I don't feel pressured," she repeated. "I feel touched. And honored. I'd love to get married here. My friends will have no problem traveling to New England." She smiled, thinking about the WVNY gang. "They'll probably all pile into a few big minivans and drive up. And my family's small—only my parents, and aunt and uncle. They love traveling, for business and pleasure. In fact, my aunt owns a travel agency and tries out vacation spots all over the world. So Vermont will be a hop, skip, and a jump for them."

"What about the date—is June too soon?" Lisa asked.

"Not for me." Taylor glanced up at Reed, gave him a questioning look. "How about you? Your firm's just taking off. Can Paul handle things on his own? Or is it too soon for you to break away?"

"Not on your life." He shook his head emphatically. "That's *why* I started the firm—so I could have a life and live it the way I wanted. Paul will be fine." Reed rose, seizing Taylor's hand and urging her to her feet. "Will you all excuse us for a minute? I want to talk to Taylor alone."

"Right. *Talk,*" Rob responded dryly. "Just keep it clean. There are kids in and around the house."

"I'll try to restrain myself," Reed shot back. He led Taylor through the hallway and out the backdoor. In the garden, he turned her around to face him. "Is this really what you want? Because a wedding's a once-in-a-lifetime event. At least in our case, it will be. I want this day to be everything you want it to be."

"It will be. It already is," she assured him. "I'm even more excited now than I was before. Your family's enthusiasm is contagious. They're wonderful—all you said and more."

"They're about to become your family, too."

"I know. And I feel incredibly lucky."

"So do I." Reed tilted Taylor's chin up and kissed her gently—in a way that was totally acceptable for the crowd of kids assembling to witness their display. "I love you," he said quietly. "Never forget that."

"How could I, after all you've done?" She gazed up at him, tears still glistening in her eyes. "I love you, too. I also trust you. Totally and without reservation. *And* I rely on you. You've taught me I can do that and still be strong and independent. Thank you for that. So, no more walls. No more self-protection. Not when it comes to us." She smiled through her tears. "It seems you've tackled your hardest case to date and won, Counselor."

Reed's knuckles caressed her cheek, and she could feel the emotion in his touch. "Hey, I told you I was good."

"Oh, you are. Very, very good."

A slow grin curved his lips. "So, do I get a victory celebration?"

"Am I invited?"

"You're my one and only guest."

"I thought I was the hostess."

"You're that, too."

Taylor's eyes glinted with laughter. "Where and when?"

He pursed his lips thoughtfully. "Let's see. We're leaving my parents' place after dinner. It's just over a four-hour drive to Manhattan. It'll probably take us five, given the holiday traffic. That puts us in Manhattan at about one A.M."

"Sounds right."

"How tired will you be?"

"Wide-awake."

"Okay, then," he concluded, his thumb brushing her lips. "It's settled. My bed. Tonight. One-thirty A.M."

"Dress code?"

"Bare skin."

"Can I bring anything?"

"Nope. Just yourself. And no serving required. Not food, anyway. This is going to be a no-frills, go-for-the-gold celebration. Just you, me, a very big bed, and a very long night. You did say that Dellinger was closed tomorrow?"

"I did," she confirmed.

"Good. Then the celebration can run on into tomorrow."

"Wow. It sounds like quite an event."

"Oh, it will be. You have my word."

"Just your word?" she asked with mock innocence. "Is that all I have?"

"No." His eyes darkened. "You, my love, have all of me. And tonight, you can help yourself to any part you like."

"Can I go back for seconds?"

"Seconds, thirds—whatever you crave."

Taylor's smile was pure seduction. "In that case, I'll be there."